Maria Lewis got her start covering crime in a newsroom as a teenager and has been working as a professional journalist for over ten years. Making the switch from writing about murders to movie stars was not a difficult decision. A former reporter at *The Daily Telegraph* and *The Daily Mail*, her writings on the entertainment industry have appeared in the *New York Post*, *Empire* magazine, *Huffington Post*, *Sunday Mail*, *WHO Weekly*, *Junkee*, *Spook Magazine* and *Penthouse*, to name a few.

The co-host of the *Eff Yeah Film And Feminism* podcast and a founding member of Australian film critics collective Graffiti With Punctuation, Maria also regularly appears on radio and television as a pop culture commentator.

Based in Sydney, Australia she lives in a home with too many movie posters and just the right amount of humans. She's most likely Idris Elba's future wife. Most likely.

Visit Maria Lewis online:

www.marialewis.com.au
www.facebook.com/marialewiswriter
www.twitter.com/moviemazz

Who's Afraid?

Maria Lewis

piatkus

PIATKUS

First published in Great Britain in 2016 by Piatkus

1 3 5 7 9 10 8 6 4 2

A CIP catalogue record for this book
is available from the British Library.

TPB ISBN 978-0-349-41114-9

Typeset in Sabon by Hewer Text UK Ltd, Edinburgh
Printed and bound by CPI Group (UK) Ltd, Croydon, CR0 4YY

Papers used by Piatkus are from well-managed forests
and other responsible sources.

MIX
Paper from
responsible sources
FSC® C104740

Piatkus
An imprint of
Little, Brown Book Group
Carmelite House
50 Victoria Embankment
London EC4Y 0DZ

An Hachette UK Company
www.hachette.co.uk

www.piatkus.co.uk

I dedicate this to you: you lovely, lovely creature.

Thank you for finding this book by whatever miracle has led you to it.

Thank you for getting this far in and, hopefully, thank you for continuing a little bit further.

The Black Keys said it best when they said 'baby I'm howlin' for you'.

high fives

PROLOGUE

I wasn't sure how long I'd been running for or how much land I'd covered. When I felt the ground start to rise slowly uphill I knew it was a good sign. I was moving forward and not in circles. It was about the only thing that had gone right for me so far. The second I thought that, a red-hot stabbing pain burned along my spine. I yelled out and fell to my knees. It disappeared just as quickly as it came and I stumbled up, leaning on a tree for support. What was that? I tried to look down my back to make sure I hadn't been stabbed.

I took a few steps forward to start running and was brought crashing to the ground again by the same agonising feeling. Except this time it was worse. It felt like hundreds of small knives gouging through my skin from the inside out. The pain was beyond screams. My mouth opened and closed in silent agony as I lay on the forest floor, arching my back into the earth. It could have gone on for seconds, maybe minutes. All sense of time and reason was lost to me amid the excruciating pain.

And then it was gone. I was shaking, sweating, and I realised the whimpering sound I could hear was coming from my own mouth.

Excruciating. This is what Steven had said it would be like, wasn't it?

I heard a shout somewhere off in the distance, far, but not far enough. Another shout returned it and I recognised Simon's scent on the wind. No, I couldn't smell him. I was clearly still delirious from the after-effects of the pain, yet somehow I knew it was him coming for me. And the others.

If I was going to escape I couldn't lose any more time. I gripped a tree, digging my clawed hand into it and bit down on my lip until I felt blood running down my chin. I pushed forward. Shadows had replaced the light coming through the trees and I could sense darkness was nearly upon us. I stumbled, screamed and sprinted in bursts, as I battled with what was undoubtedly the worst pain I'd experienced in this or any lifetime.

I tore furiously at my shirts, suddenly frustrated by the material restricting my back and arms as I pumped them, urging myself to go faster. The clothing fell in shreds around me and I didn't worry about leaving a trail. They were too close anyway. I sprinted through the thinning trees with branches lashing at my face and body.

'Tommi!' I heard James shout. It sounded like he was practically at my neck.

I smelled something in the air and sniffed. Salt. The ocean was close. I could even hear waves pounding heavily on what had to be rocks. I could swim. I wasn't sure if the Ihis could. I was hoping I was better. I broke through the last of the trees and on to clear land. I was on a grassy cliff top with the drop-off about a hundred metres directly in front of me.

I paused for a second, suddenly transfixed by the glowing orb that appeared from behind the clouds. I saw it for only a moment before I was on the ground, screaming as the pain returned in all its searing glory. I dug my hands into the earth and felt tears as wave after wave of flesh-splitting torture washed over me. I heard a rip and a crack come from within my own body and I let out a brief cry as it happened. Then it happened again, over and over, faster and faster, until I was begging for death.

Death.

Sweet nothingness would be better than this suffering.

Somehow, through the hell, I sensed the Ihis emerge from the trees behind me.

I smelled Steven among them. Impossible. As I heard their footsteps get closer, I used every last fragment of willpower I had left and sprinted towards the edge of the cliff. I caught them unawares and heard shouts of surprise behind me.

I didn't look back. Within a few strides, I realised I was moving faster than I'd ever moved before. I was bounding towards the edge on all four limbs, each stride throwing me powerfully closer to my goal. I didn't know what lay beneath me. I could smell the ocean close by. Whether it was directly below me or hundreds of jagged rocks were, I didn't care. Freedom or death. Either option sounded promising.

'No!' I heard someone shout, but it was too late.

I launched myself far out over the cliff edge and into the air. I had a second of suspension before gravity took hold and I began to plummet. I screamed, and not with fear this time, with pure exhilaration. It took me a second to realise that I wasn't screaming at all. Following me down into the unknown was a piercing howl.

Chapter 1

Four days earlier

'I wanted to find a level of depth that's as admirable as it is hypnotic, while juxtaposing a part of that impenetrability from my last works, you *ken?*'

No. *A dinnae ken.*

In fact, I was less than a minute into an interview with Wil Garman and the only thing I was sure of was how much I wanted to punch him in the throat. I felt rage bubbling up in my stomach and I began casually flicking the elastic band wrapped around my wrist. Whenever I felt anger or irritation, this is what I did. I flicked the band against my skin until the emotions subsided. It was unsurprising that the flesh there was permanently red, as scars had healed over scars during the many years I'd adopted this habit.

Wil was the hottest young artist to emerge from the local scene in, well, ever. I live in Dundee, which is essentially Scotland's most important city if Edinburgh or Glasgow didn't exist. Or Aberdeen. Or Inverness. So to produce a 27-year-old artist with sell-out shows at all the underground art galleries in the UK was significant and probably why Wil thought he was such a big deal.

Personally, I didn't get it. I may be a junior art curator only one year out of university, but I recognise a mildly talentless hack when I see one. Wil was just flavour of the month, only he didn't know it yet. Regardless of his inevitable use-by date, Wil's exhibitions sold paintings. They filled galleries. They attracted attention from all the right kind of waistcoat-wearers under forty. It was no wonder my boss at McManus Galleries wanted his to be the first show in our newest venture: pop-up exhibitions.

As one of the most prestigious and historic galleries in the country, the place carried a lot of weight. It was also old. The pop-up exhibitions were a way to modernise McManus's reputation. Wil's show on body image was to be a triumphant extravaganza when we launched the first of six shows next month. To be held in various locations throughout the city, the show would open for a space of three weeks before moving to a different location with a different artist. It was a very cool idea and one I had been appointed to organise thanks to my 'youth and enthusiasm', as it had been phrased.

But Wil was making it difficult. Sitting there with his chicken legs crossed in faded skinny-leg jeans, a loosely buttoned flannelette shirt, and a black bowler hat tilted on his blond hair, he hadn't seemed to notice my lack of attention.

I hoped he was midway through his monologue.

'I just wanted to, like, use all this pressure I'm seeing being applied to women as a catalyst for pieces that personify their struggle and puncture through the plethora of labels they're made to carry like contemporary Atlases,' he said.

'Drinks?'

Our waiter reminded me of Niles from *The Nanny*, but I would never tell him that at risk of finding arsenic in my coffee one day.

'A chai soy latte for me,' said Wil.

This was going to be an excruciating fifteen, no, thirteen minutes.

'I'll have a coffee, Irish,' I said.

The waiter raised an eyebrow at me but said no more. Smart man.

Wil-with-one-L and I were sitting at the most secluded table in the Poison Art; it was as modern as a café could get in Dundee and situated directly across from McManus. It specialised in the latest prints and art deco knick-knacks, but, most importantly (and unlike our in-house café), it was licensed. The set-up was sparse; purple and green designer tables stood out against the crisp white of the linoleum floor. It would have been clinical if not for the doodles printed underneath our feet.

'Art is a lie that makes us realise truth,' said a speech bubble sprouting from the mouth of a crudely sketched Picasso.

Exposed light bulbs of every colour imaginable hung at various heights, illuminating the venue. Dale Frank abstract paintings lined the walls, making the space feel like the offspring of a kaleidoscope and hospital room. The atmosphere was all hushed business, which was perfect when trying to interview a pretentious artist in the hopes of writing an exhibition booklet worthy of MoMA.

Yet, when you looked at me, 'all business' isn't a phrase that would leap to mind. 'Holy shit' would probably be first, followed by 'that's really blue'. Those were the exact words that had fallen from a colleague's mouth when I started an internship at McManus. I had an androgynous name, Tommi Grayson, was twenty-two, and had bright blue hair. When I walked through the Poison Art doors on my second day to grab a desperately needed latte, double shot, I literally saw a silver-haired woman draped in pearls choke on her biscotti at the sight of me.

At five foot six I'm relatively normal height, with dark brown eyes and dark skin that's a mix of my mother's Caucasian background and my estranged father's Maori heritage. I'd be all curves if it wasn't for a toned physique courtesy of nearly a decade of Muay Thai training. Add to that image electric blue, waist-length hair instead of my natural black and you have someone who'll make you choke on your biscotti. Yup, Tommi Grayson a.k.a. me.

The waiter came with our drinks. My Irish coffee didn't have nearly as much kick as I would have liked. But hey, it *was* eleven in the morning. I'm not an alcoholic, but since my mum passed away eight months earlier, I liked a touch of fuel to my fire. Especially when, for instance, I was only one-third of my way through an interview with a *bampot* artist on my last day before holidays.

Walking through the gallery to our office twelve minutes later, I was decidedly more chipper due to a) sending Wil and his skinny-leg-jeans-wearing-self on his way and b) a smidge of whisky. It didn't matter how long I had been working at McManus, I never got used to the building's ability to take my breath away. My grandparents even used to bring me here when I was kid. The architect had been a big fan of classic Gothic style when construction began in the mid-1800s. More than 150 years later, both the exterior and interior were works of art. A multi-million dollar restoration had seen some of the finer details restored to their former glory as well as a skylight added here and there.

The entrance to our somewhat cramped working area was situated behind a small door at the top of a metal staircase near the local exhibition room. The senior curator, Gerrick, was hunched over his desk when I entered and whispering furiously into the phone. He only adopted that tone when he was speaking to his wife. I rolled out my chair and began setting up headphones to transcribe the interview I'd recorded on my iPhone. The *clip clap* of stiletto heels announced the presence of Alexis Scales, my boss. I swivelled to give her a grin as she walked in carrying the final designs for the exhibition booklet.

'Tommi, good. How did the interview with Wil go?'

'I could barely get a word out of him,' I said, straight-faced.

She gave me a begrudging smile before continuing. 'Do you think you can have the main profile for the booklet completed by this afternoon?'

'No doubt. I've got everything else finished and sent to the graphics team. Once I write up the chat I'll be done.'

'Lovely. And, Tommi?'

'Yep?'

'You will make him sound . . . you know, not like—'

'A dickhead?' I offered.

'Although not the phrasing I'd use, aye.'

'No problem. When I've finished with this puppy he'll be as interesting and hip as everyone thinks he is.'

'Marvellous.'

And with that, she was off.

'What was Alexis after?' asked Gerrick, as he hung up the phone.

'Her horoscope.'

He sighed. 'I'll go see if she needs help with anything.'

I watched his podgy frame head toward Alexis's office before turning back to my computer screen. Only a few more hours and I would be on holidays, my first since the death of my mum, Tilly, which you couldn't really call holidays. I think 'grief leave' is the appropriate term and, boy, was it fitting. My mum and I were close. My father hadn't been on the scene since my birth and I'd been raised single-handedly by her.

Now that she was gone ... every now and then when the reality of the fact hit home I would find myself curling inwards as my stomach spasmed with the recognition of a beyond-physical loss. Other days, I'd just find myself crouched in my room. No tears. I was beyond that now. Today was not one of those days, I told myself. I would get this done and then I would get the heck out of here. I began subconsciously flicking the rubber band at my wrist.

Opening the door to my apartment six hours later, I had proved myself right; I got the work done and then I got gone. Gold star for me. I groaned as I sorted through the mail that had been slipped under the door, all addressed to me. Electricity bill, internet bill and, hooray, water bill. When it rains it pours, I thought, as I quickly wrote down the amounts on a white-board we had in the kitchen for keeping track of incoming and outgoing finances.

All of the bills were in my name, and I split them with the occupants of the small but comfortable three-bedroom unit I rented on the second floor of an old building a few streets away from the city centre. Our last flatmate had just moved out after taking a job in Edinburgh and I added another note to the whiteboard about a potential roomie we were supposed to interview next week while I remembered.

My other flatmate was Mari Bronberg, one of my closest friends. Mari's real name was Mariposa, which is Spanish for 'butterfly'. Since her mother had been in Spanish class before her 49-hour labour, it had obviously seemed like a good idea at the time. Or a good punishment. Either way, a mentally depleted Mrs Bronberg named her first child Mariposa and committed her to a lifetime of ridicule. It was no Apple, but she preferred to go by Mari.

I dumped some grocery bags in the kitchen and made my way down the hall to my room. Mari was walking out of the shower with a towel around her.

'Baby, you should have told me to pick up the cherries and whipped cream on my way home,' I said, trying to lower my voice seductively.

Laughing, Mari replied: 'Let's all just be thankful there were no mass murders today and I was able to shower before your farewell drinks tonight.'

'Hey, even 24-year-old police reporter extraordinaires deserve a night off. Just one.'

Mari worked at the local newspaper and had a crazy schedule completely indicative of what crimes were committed that day. It wasn't unheard of for her to pull a fourteen-hour shift when something especially grisly occurred.

'Well, just the one then.' She smirked.

'Shit, I almost forgot about my completely unnecessary farewell drinks.'

Mari shrugged, the hair of her straight, black bob swinging with the movement. 'It's only an informal thing, a few of us getting rowdy before you leave tomorrow morning. And it's not like we wouldn't be out on a Friday night anyway. This time we just have a reason.'

'True, all true.'

'Kane and Poc are going to be around in twenty minutes so unless you want to look like the L.E.S. artiste that you are . . .'

'Then I should hustle, hustle.'

With a satisfied smile and a nod, Mari shuffled to her room, leaving wet footprints on the carpet as if it were snow. Kane Goode was Mari's long-time boyfriend and, in his own words, a 'righteous dude'. Poc was an all together different story.

Standing in front of the full-length mirror in my room, I took a few seconds to assess what I was going to wear. After slipping out of my stockings, grass-green pencil skirt and black blouse, I pulled on my favourite ripped jeans and a black, strappy bra. There were five novelty straps that shot out from the middle of the bra and spilled over the mounds of each breast in a way that made it look somewhat like a spider web. I threw on a loose, low-cut white top to complete the look and black combat boots. I was going for casual cool; something that wasn't easy to achieve when your hair was the colour of a Smurf. I had barely finished putting on my make-up and earrings when I heard a ruckus from the lounge.

The lads had arrived. After giving myself a quick once-over, I grabbed my leather jacket and ducked into the hallway. I was blessed with amicable hair that usually fell in waves and that's how I left it tonight.

We were all keen to get to our favourite bar: Eggs and Ham. The bar owner had a thing for Dr Seuss, hence the name, but as long as they served alcohol I didn't care if they called it the Dead Seals Club. Kane and I had both been banned from there once for getting into a fight with a group of N.E.Ds (Non

Educated Delinquents) who had tried to get touchy feely with Mari. Thankfully, that was all just lolly water under the bridge now. The bar was only about five blocks away and across from Dundee University, so we were walking in. I was barely out the door before Poc brushed up beside me and whispered in my ear.

'You look dangerous tonight,' he said, looking down at me like a lion would an antelope.

I rolled my eyes. 'While I appreciate the hollow flattery, I got ready in twenty minutes. I know my underwear is probably hanging out of my jeans.'

He made an exaggerated inspection of my arse before continuing. 'Not that I can see.'

'You know, you actually have to look past my thickness to have an honest opinion on that,' I said with a smirk.

'I never look past your thickness,' he replied, walking ahead of me so that I could see the massive tattoo of a Native American eagle on his back peeking out over the top of his green shirt. This is how James Hughes had earned the nickname Poc, short for Pocahontas.

'How was Wil today?' he asked casually. The look on my face was enough to make him chuckle. 'That bad, huh?'

'*Très* bad. The infinite badness. You know, I wish all the artists I interviewed were as easy to deal with as you were.' Poc was part of a relatively successful street art collective that was making a name for itself in Scotland, partly due to an exhibition I had curated for them over a year ago when I was still in university.

'Easy is the word,' muttered Mari with a giggle.

'Ugh, I walked into that,' I groaned. Poc and I had been sleeping together for the past few months, but it was something we didn't really talk about among our group of friends even though everyone knew about it.

'Yes, you did,' Poc said, turning to smirk at me. His family had emigrated from Nigeria and his beautiful chocolate skin, which went so well with his dark hair and dark eyes, glinted as we passed under a streetlight. If it wasn't for my blue hair and slightly lighter shade of skin, we would look like we came from the same island.

'I'll have four Coronas with lime, a Foster's, Irn-Bru, and four tequila shots,' Kane yelled over the bar.

'You're a bad, bad man,' I said.

'I've always been one for the bad boys,' said Mari dreamily and we laughed because we all knew it was a lie. Kane worked for one of the few local computer game companies that was still standing after the recession and was as far from a 'bad boy' as you could get.

We'd been there over two hours and were on our fourth round, a steady but not sloppy pace. I helped Kane back to the table with our drinks. With a customary *clink* of glasses the tequila was burning its way down my throat. My best friend Joss joined us breathlessly at the table, using his tiny frame to negotiate his way through the heaving crowd like a ghost. I had been watching his ginger head appear and disappear amongst the throng of people and handed him his soft drink when he came to a halt.

'Aye, belter! Thanks, Tommi,' he said, as he grabbed it. At twenty, Joss was over the legal drinking age but tended to avoid alcohol due to a bout of cancer he got last year. He'd been in remission for six months now, but was still being cautious about what he put in his body.

'How you handling that Irn-Bru, son?' Poc asked Joss.

'Meh,' my best friend replied. 'I'm enjoying drinking in all the pretty birds here more.'

I made a gagging noise at his comment while Joss grinned, pleased with the desired effect.

'Weren't you supposed to be meeting a dame here tonight?' Poc asked.

'Cindy, from my economics class.'

My face scrunched with disapproval.

'Stop looking at me like that. You look like grumpy cat.'

'It's not that there's anything particularly wrong with Cindy, it's just . . .'

'What?'

'She has the personality of a bathroom tile. A bathroom tile with bleached blonde hair, breast implants, a good four layers of fake tan and what I suspect might be a nose job. If the girl could hold up a conversation then maybe I could overlook the Playboy Bunny shtick. Maybe.'

'Please, don't hold back.'

'She's a Celtic supporter!' I pleaded.

'Speak of the she-devil,' muttered Poc, gesturing to the incoming Cindy. 'Come on.'

He linked his hand in mine and I let him pull me away to the dance floor. I barely had enough time to grab my Corona off the table before our hips were falling into the steady rhythm of the Young Fathers song playing through the speakers. Poc and I were strictly a casual thing. I had been clear from the start I was not a relationship person. I wasn't built that way. What Poc and I had was as perfect as it could be. We were friends and free agents who happened to have no-strings-attached sex when we wanted. We enjoyed each other's company, but it wasn't exclusive.

I had my back to him and we were moving in time from behind. It was kind of cheating because he got all of me and the only part of him I got to feel was his chest muscles against my back. One of his hands was secured to my hip while the other had moved from my thigh to stroking the skin of my midriff under my top. His hands were warm and I could tell from his heavy breathing in my ear that he was getting turned on. Sweaty bodies bumped into and against us and I spun around to face Poc. I lightly grabbed the neck of his shirt, pulling his lips to mine. We were all fire, and his kiss was long and deep. I could feel myself getting carried away as we found each others natural rhythm.

'Stop,' I said, slowly pushing him away.

'What?' he mumbled against my neck, moving lower towards my collarbone.

'Public displays of intercourse on the dance floor are unbecoming.'

'It's dark, it's packed, no one can see us.'

I chuckled, pushing him further off me. 'Take a walk, cool off.'

'I might need to,' he said, letting out a deep breath before kissing me on the cheek.

We parted ways and I weaved my way back to Joss, passing Cindy sitting on the lap of some guy with a Celtic tattoo.

'That was quick,' I said, looking between Joss and Cindy. He shrugged it off, but I could tell the dafty had hurt his feelings.

'What did you do with Poc?' he asked.

One scowl from me was enough to silence him on the subject and he smirked into his Irn-Bru.

'Am I still staying?'

This was very *Dawson's Creek* of us, but Joss and I regularly had sleepovers.

''Course,' I said, making a puzzled face.

'Cool, I just know how you and Poc . . .'

'Screw?' supplied Mari

'I prefer bonk, but I'll give you that,' I replied.

'Yeah, yeah,' said Joss, 'I just thought he might be—'

'Hun, we organised for you to stay. I'm not kicking you out of my bed for some guy.'

'Cool.'

'Bevvies,' I said. 'I'm going for more bevvies. Kane, rum and Coke?'

'Ow, we on to the hard shit now?'

'Hell yes. Irn-Bru on the rocks for you, *My Sister's Keeper*?' I asked, pointing squarely at Joss and he nodded. I left them chatting amongst each other and made for the bar. On my way, I watched Kane and Mari together, hands linked, swaying at the edge of the dance floor. Tonight we would party. Get drunk. Be jolly. Tomorrow, I'd set out for New Zealand to find my father.

'Make it stop,' groaned the person next to me.

I laughed. It was 10 a.m. on Saturday morning and I'd decided to subtly wake Joss by playing Dead Man's Bones. He hated it. I loved it.

'It's too early for zombie music, Tommi, please.' He pushed a pillow over his head.

'It's not too early for sunlight,' I said, pulling up my blind.

A guttural sound was his only response. I crawled to the edge of the bed and sat there in an oversized Wednesday Addams T-shirt for a moment, letting the being-awake sensation roll over me. My room wasn't small, but it wasn't huge, either.

At its centre was my double bed covered in a dark purple blanket and lilac pillows. Multicoloured mini Chinese lanterns were strung up around the walls.

I believed blank walls were meant to be covered and mine were plastered with everything from band and movie posters, to art prints and paintings I'd done myself. The rest of my room was taken up with an overflowing bookshelf, my easel with a canvas-in-progress balanced on it, a vintage orange phone table I'd picked up from a second-hand store, a worn chest of drawers, an aqua stool and my stereo, which I now bent down to and skipped to my favourite track on the album.

'Oh great, the one about flowers growing out of my grave. You know I nearly died right? This is too morbid.'

I smiled and made my way to the shower. An hour later I had my bags at the door and was eating eggs Benedict on the balcony with Mari and Kane.

'You got everything?' she asked.

'Aye,' I said, through a mouthful of eggs.

'Passport? Warm clothes?'

'New Zealand's climate is warmer than ours, babe,' said Kane.

'Right, sorry. I'm just nervous. For you. Do we need to go over the plan again?'

Kane went to get up to leave.

'Kane, no, you can stay,' I said. 'I know you and Mari tell each other everything and I'm cool talking about this with you.'

'Thanks, but this is between you guys. Private stuff. And I don't do . . .'

'Emotionally complex situations?' teased Mari.

'Yeah,' he said, bending down and pecking her on the lips. 'I'll go wake Joss up.'

'I've found jumping on him is most effective,' I said and I heard Kane's laughter echo down the hallway. Mari and I sat there for a moment enjoying the yells coming from my room as Kane woke Joss up in some ungodly manner.

'So,' said Mari, leaning forwards with her business face. 'The plan.'

'The plan is,' I started, 'I go to Rotorua, check in to the motel and suss things out. Casually find out who knows him and, if I can, find out where he works and what he does. I see what he looks like and—'

'Then you come home,' finished Joss, who had slipped out on to the balcony without us noticing. I smiled as he pulled up a chair. Glancing between Mari and Joss, my two favourite people in the world, I felt beyond lucky to have their support with this. I looked out over the balcony at the tops of building upon building shining in the morning light.

'And then I come home.'

Chapter 2

'Peanuts?' the Air New Zealand hostess asked, distracting me from my sketch of the elderly lady sleeping to my right.

I shook my head. She pushed her cart down the aisle and I returned to my drawing. I turned up the volume on my iPod just as 'Needles & Pins' by the Ramones came on. I abandoned the old lady and started a Joey Ramone caricature, something I'd drawn enough times to have his gangly, lollipop frame staring back at me from under his bangs in less than a minute. I sighed. I was trying to distract myself and it wasn't working.

My whole life I'd grown up without a father and it hadn't bothered me until I was about eleven. I started picking men out of a crowd in the street, wondering if they were my father. Maybe that tall guy in the supermarket? Or my English teacher, Mr Kirby, who always stayed back and helped me with my spelling? I even went through a stage where I imagined he was a blue-haired bounty hunter named Spike.

It never occurred to me to just ask my mum until one day when we were driving home from junior Muay Thai class. I can still remember the look on her face. She immediately pulled over to the side of the road and burst into tears.

'I'm sorry, Mum, I'm sorry. I don't care, really, I just wondered,' I said, undoing my seat belt and leaning across to hug her.

She held me to her tightly. My shoulder was getting wet where she cried into it. I wanted nothing more than to un-ask the question. I sat back in my seat and waited. Whether I was waiting for her to restart the car or tell me the answer, I wasn't sure. It felt like the silence dragged on for days with nothing but the sound of her crying and rain hitting the roof of our car. It was probably closer to minutes.

My father, she told me, had been a bad man. She never knew his name, only that he was a Maori guy who played in a cricket team with her cousin back in Rotorua, New Zealand. She'd been twenty-two and walking home from a post-match party when she'd been attacked and raped. By him. A friend had found her curled up, naked, and crying in a park near the cricket clubhouse and called my grandfather. Tilly was humiliated and wanted nothing more than to forget the incident and move on. Despite my grandparents' insistence she report her attack to the police, she never did. And she never told them who her attacker was. When she found out she was pregnant, she left Rotorua immediately, staying at a women's shelter in Auckland. She never intended to keep me. In fact, after giving birth, she left me at the women's shelter to be adopted. A fortnight later she returned. I was still there, unnamed.

'The nuns had called you Mowgli after the boy brought up by wolves in *The Jungle Book*,' Mum had said, giggling through tears.

I knew the Disney movie. The snake freaked me out.

'They said instead of crying you used to howl like a little lost puppy without its mum. Plus you drank like a wild animal.'

When she came back and saw I was still there she decided to keep me. It had been eating away at her, she said. She packed up and moved to Scotland where no one would know her and she could have a fresh start.

'I didn't expect your grandparents to come,' she said. 'They'd been so great after the attack and coming to visit me in the shelter. I thought keeping you might have been too much. They're very traditional people. But Hal said there was no way he would let his granddaughter grow up without her grandparents. He resigned from his job as a rugby coach that day. It meant everything to me to have that support and family there for you when I would be working double shifts. It's been like having three parents for you. They gave you as much love as two would have. More.'

I didn't say anything. This was such a huge story for me to handle. There I was thinking maybe things just hadn't worked out between her and my father and we'd moved away. Yet deep down I knew it was something big, something that made us never talk about it all these years. It also explained why we never went to the North Island when we visited relatives in New Zealand every few years. Sure, my uncle and great aunts all lived on the South Island but I knew they still had friends there.

We'd never talked about it again. I tried to ask her more details once when I was in high school. She started crying in the middle of dinner. I hated to see my mother weep and since then every time I tried to work up the courage to ask her I would chicken out at the last minute. I couldn't handle the crying. And I couldn't ask my grandparents, everything was too perfect with them. I was always terrified I would wreck whatever harmony we'd had all these years if I tried to press them about it like I did Mum.

Then Tilly met Deter Hoy, an owner of one of the local pubs. She'd never really had a proper boyfriend while I was growing up and they started dating when I was fifteen. They were married in a small ceremony two years later. It was his third marriage and Mum's first. I was way too old for a father figure and, although I found Deter pretty boring, he made Mum happy. Really happy. I never wanted to shatter that peace by asking upsetting questions about the past.

Now it was too late. Mum was dead and my grandparents . . .

I didn't want to rub salt in the wound. But I did want to find my father. Not meet him, mind you. I had no illusions about that. The guy was a rapist. I didn't exactly daydream about him taking me out for gelato in the park. I wasn't delusional.

I just wanted to *know* about him. See what he looked like, see what he did, see where he lived. No one in my family had ever been artistic or particularly passionate about the arts. I wanted to see if that came from my father. Then I wanted to fly home and never think about him again.

Joss had been the first person I'd told about my father's true identity (or lack thereof). I'd broken my silence shortly after my sweet sixteenth. It had been unbelievably freeing to speak about something that had remained strictly unspoken. It felt like there had been this dark bird nesting in my chest and, as soon as I spoke the words aloud, it took flight, soaring up into the sky and away from me for ever. I think I would have told someone eventually: it was too big a secret to keep on my own. Thankfully it was Joss. He'd kept his word and never told anyone. After I moved in with Mari, about a year after we'd met, I told her too. It had been like letting another raven go.

My mother had died after her car was swept off the road in a flash flood that hit the country. Following her funeral, I'd explained to Mari that I wanted to find my father. With her Lois Lane skills and my access to Mum's records, we were able to find a likely candidate for my father. Joss didn't really help besides eating popcorn while watching us trawl through pictures and public records. His presence helped. We managed to find someone Mari thought was 98 per cent likely to be my father. His name was Jonah Ihi.

The breakthrough had come when I discovered a team picture of Mum's cousin's cricket team. From what we could tell there were three Maori guys in the team and, after a bit of Google-stalking, Mari had found one of them on a gay dating site. He was older and chubbier, but it was definitely him. We felt it safe to rule 'ChocolateLovin4u' out. Leaving us with potential rapist number two and potential rapist number three. It was liked a twisted version of *Perfect Match*.

The best we could do was try to compare their history from around the time of the attack to now. Potential rapist number two had been, and still was, an electrician. Mari found an article in the social pages of the *Rotorua Daily Times* that showed him getting married three years after my birth. Which didn't mean squat. John Wayne Gacy had been a married and upstanding member of the community. He'd also been a sadistic serial killer who raped, murdered, and mutilated dozens of boys.

Once we started digging into potential rapist number three's background red flags popped up. Around the time of the attack he'd already been arrested four times for breaking and entering and once for punching an ex-girlfriend in a bar. She later dropped the charges. In the past twenty years he had made a career as a mechanic and petty criminal. After serving a three-year stint in jail for armed robbery in 1996, he'd remained relatively clean from what Google, court records and contacts Mari made at the *Dunedin Bulletin* could tell us.

'There's no definite way we can know it's him. Or any of the three really,' she said, a fortnight earlier when the three of us had continued working on 'our project' over beer and roast lamb. Printouts, newspaper clippings and photos were scattered across the floor of our apartment.

'I know,' I said, sitting cross-legged in the middle of it. 'When I see him face to face I'll know.'

She looked at me sceptically from the computer desk and after a pause said, 'I don't want you to get your hopes up.'

'And she won't,' said Joss. He'd somehow managed to spread his skinny frame across our entire couch.

'He's a convicted criminal. It's not like I'm going to go up to him with my arms spread going "Daaaaddy",' I replied.

Joss had started to laugh before Mari's look cut him off.

'Be careful about this. If you pass him in the street and you don't know, then you don't know.'

'And I can come home with the beginnings of an autobiographical weepy and a surrogate father in your dad.'

Mari's dad Walter and her four little sisters were like an extended branch of my own tree. Well, my lineage was more of a stump.

'If you think it *is* him, are you going to go to the police?'

Sweet, naive Joss. Mari and I scoffed.

'And what would I go to them with?' I said. 'Hey, um, pretty sure this dude sexually assaulted my mum twenty-two years ago and after going through her stuff and trawling the oh-so-reliable net I found him. The sole witness is dead, but we have the same birthmark so we must be related.'

'You have a birthmark?'

'No, I was being sarcastic. There's no proof, Joss. I'm not going there to have him arrested. I'm going for closure.'

'Plus,' said Mari, 'Tilly didn't report him to the police. There must have been a reason for that.'

As my flight began to descend into Rotorua International Airport, I was still unsure what that reason was. I was about to find out.

Chapter 3

Two days.

It had been two days since I'd gotten off the plane and I was no closer to bumping into my dad accidentally on purpose than I was if I'd stayed in Dundee. I hit bars, cafés and shops that were roughly around his last known address and nada. Not a thing.

At first I'd been wary to ask anyone if they knew who Jonah Ihi was or where he might work. Who would have guessed locals in a small New Zealand city would have looked at a girl with a Scottish accent and blue hair like someone who just announced they hated the All Blacks? OK, sure, it was an oversight on my behalf. When I did get frustrated enough to ask people – looks of discomfort or not – no one knew him. Maybe I was asking people in the wrong places.

For the second time that day, I left my motel and the fruitless hunt to go for a jog. Usually one long run was enough for me, but the frustration I was feeling could only be vented in physical activity. There was something about the crisp New Zealand air that kept luring me outside. I didn't know the area, so I'd been running along the side of the main road when I found a track that said it led to hot mud pools nearby. Apparently the pools had incredible healing properties and I planned on indulging before I left. I paused, breathing heavily, at the top of a small summit and looked down over the pools and tourists who were submerged in their steamy depths. I'd barely stopped for a few seconds and a flick of my rubber band before I was itching to move again. This was unusual. I ran purely for fitness and the sense of freedom. I preferred to hammer away the hours in a close-spaced gym with boxing pads, roundhouse kicks and upper cuts.

As I pounded the pavement, I realised I was moving faster than I ever had before. And speeding up. When I hit the main road, it felt like I was still going downhill, I had that same momentum. I utilised it right to the door of my motel room where I leaned against the frame, sweat clinging to my face. I'd run roughly fifteen kilometres today, more than I usually ran in a week. The bizarre thing was that I was literally aching for more. My left leg twitched as if it sensed my desire to keep going and I gripped the door handle tightly to get a hold of myself.

'Pull it together,' I whispered.

Before I could hurtle down the road again, I hastily opened my door and made for the shower. I got the water running and pumped out three quick sets of push-ups while I waited for it to warm up. I kicked away my trainers, blue of course, and peeled off my black exercise tights. I unzipped my hoodie and removed the first of my sports bras. One of the hazards of having a D-cup is you have to double up on the supportive attire. I didn't want to be able to tuck my boobs into my belt by the time I was thirty. I was just about to take off my panties and final bra when I sensed something behind me. I spun around quickly, bringing my fists in front of my face.

Nothing.

Nothing but an empty bathroom and a semi-nude girl looking at herself with a puzzled expression in the mirror. What
was up with me? If I hadn't finished my cycle a fortnight ago I
would have said I was going through PMS – Paranoid
Menstrual Symptoms. I relaxed my stance and tried to do the
same to my racing heartbeat. I let the searing hot water do the
rest.

A solid half an hour later, I was out of the shower and
padding towards the clothes in my half-opened suitcase. As I
lifted up a shirt, I noticed a note slipped underneath my door.
I tightened the towel around my body and bent down to pick
it up. There were no words, only a URL that linked to something on the *White Pages* site. I opened my door an inch to see
if whoever had left it was still around. The motel car park was
deserted.

I shrugged and shut the door. I hadn't brought my laptop
with me so I grabbed my phone off the bed and opened the
internet browser. I had a message from Mari. I'd read that
later. I typed in the URL and got dressed while I waited for it
to load. The page was a street address in the map directory
and located in Paengaroa, a town just on the outskirts of the
city.

The address was listed to G. and K. Tianne. Hmmm. I tapped
the note in my hand, wondering what it meant. Turning the
piece of paper over, I gasped.

On the back was one word written in tiny, delicate hand-
writing: 'Ihi'. That was all I needed to see before I was calling
a cab and heading for the door.

The cab must have been in the area because it was pulling into
the car park just as I stepped out of my door. The driver told

me it was a forty-minute trip and I settled into the front seat with nothing but my thoughts. What was I doing? I had no idea who had left me the note or why, but it was the first tangible lead I'd had since I'd been here. If he didn't live there, nothing lost. I could continue asking about town. If he did . . . well, this wasn't exactly bumping into him on the street. I had to think of a decent cover story as to why I was knocking on his front door. Remembering I had a text from Mari, I checked my phone: '*Hey, how's the search going? Any luck yet? I didn't want to bug you in case you were busy trawling the streets of Rotorua but whatever. Kane and I have been having wild sex in your bedroom. We don't miss you at all. You will have to come home to find out if that was a joke or not. Interviewed a roommate replacement and he was awful. And transferred you the bill money. Joss said to call him if you get a chance. He has been hanging out here like your lost little brother and driving me mad. Anywho, we miss you. Good luck and we're here if you need us. Mari xx P.S. Bring me back Legolas.*'

Mari, she never quite got the short message idea of texting. I guess mini-Bibles were to be expected from someone for whom words were their living. It was comforting anyway.

I replied: '*Hey, the hunt has been slow here. I'm on my way to a lead now at 86 Ngati Rd, Paengaroa. I'll let you know how that goes. Tell Joss I know he has a phone too, the lazy stinge. Also, I'm burning my sheets. P.S. I'm bringing you back Gimli.*'

I'm not sure whether Mari would have approved of me going directly to a home address and she definitely wouldn't have approved if she knew where I'd got the information. The least I could do was cover my arse and give her the exact location in case anything went wrong. Not that it would. I hoped.

As if sensing my trepidation, the cab slowed down on what appeared to be a relatively normal, albeit slightly old-fashioned, street.

It looked like the last residential area before the wild green landscape took over. The one-storey houses were spread far apart, each with a large side yard and acres of property behind them. The house the cabbie pulled up in front of had wild grass threatening to envelop the chain link fence that separated number eighty-six from the footpath.

I paid the driver and hopped out, asking him to wait a moment while I saw if anyone was home. After shrugging into my black parka, I rubbed my hands together and watched my breath form thin clouds of steam in front of my face. The house seemed quite large and I guessed there were about six or seven bedrooms to it from the outside. It was a traditional brick home, the kind you see all the time in New Zealand. It even had the customary chimney with grey smoke issuing into the sky.

As I pushed open the waist-high gate, it made a piercing creak and I hesitated, wondering if I should turn around and jump back in the cab before anyone realised I was there. But there was something inside of me, something drawing me closer to that house and the answers it might hold. I pushed forward and made my way up the crumbling cement path.

Dozens of Maori totem poles – *pou whenua* – stood in the front yard, some taller than me and others that barely reached my knees. Wild eyes stared from within the grimacing faces on the wooden poles, tongues and teeth exposed. I was vaguely familiar with Maori art and these were beautiful. And intimidating. They were undoubtedly hand carved by someone with decades of experience and told a story of cultural significance:

a story of travelling here by canoe centuries ago and the land, the iconic mountain and water source that were important to these people. I felt a slight pang at the thought that these were *my* people and this was *my* heritage, yet I was so far disconnected from it. Other totems depicted male and female warriors holding spears and each other as they climbed up the length of the totems. Towards the top, the warriors appeared more and more beast-like until they morphed into ferocious-looking wolves. I wondered if it was common for old Maori tribes to have a particular animal they associated with or used as an identifier for their tribe. I'd never heard of wolves being used before since they weren't native to New Zealand. In fact, I didn't think they had ever existed here. That wasn't the creepy thing though. It was the eyes. Within the face of each snarling wolf was the same style of eyes set in the face of every warrior. I looked away. Maybe the artist had a limited range and could only carve one type of eye for everything: animal or man. I peered around to see what kind of eyes the other animals on the totems had. I could only see wolves. Wolves and people.

I continued up the path, quickly forming a cover story that was somewhat inspired by the sculptures. Looking to my right, there were overgrown trees and a large tin garage that had three cars on blocks out the front of it. A fourth car had the hood up and tools scattered around it as if someone had been working on it only moments ago. I was in the right place. I could feel it my bones. My head was telling me to turn back and forget this whole thing, but every fibre of my being was drawing me closer and closer to the front door. I felt like a measly paper clip helpless to resist the draw of a magnet. I finally stepped on to the landing and lifted my hand to knock on the door when it opened suddenly. A young Maori woman stood in front of me in tracksuit pants, sandals and a knitted jumper. She didn't look much older than eighteen and her face seemed to peek out from under an unruly mess of tangled hair that was cut into some kind of bob formation.

'Who are you?' she asked, with more surprise than hostility in her voice.

Taken aback I spluttered, 'I, uh, my name's Tommi and I'm a tourist from Scotland. I was looking at buying some art to take home and a man in town recommended Jonah Ihi because he's the best carver in the district so—' I paused, as a look of pain crossed her face '—I came here.'

'Who is it?' yelled a voice from the back.

Silence. The girl stared at me hard.

'A Scot with blue hair is here asking about Jonah. Says she wants a *hei-tiki*,' she replied. 'Jonah's dead.'

'Oh,' I said, trying to keep the shock and disappointment out of my voice. 'I'm so sorry, I didn't mean to come and disturb you like this. I'm sorry, thanks for your time and I'm, uh, going.'

I backed away from the front door quickly, wanting to leave this awkward situation and these people as fast as possible. I turned and went to hurry down the path towards what I hoped was a waiting cab.

The young woman yelled out behind me. 'Wait, you l—'

'I'm sorry for your loss and I'm going now,' I shouted over my shoulder with a wave.

I found my path blocked by a Maori man who looked as if he'd just finished work, with his business shirt hanging out of his pants in a distinctly 'off the clock' fashion and a tie loose around his neck. He was standing halfway through the gate and was a touch over six foot, with facial hair that seemed to start at his chin and work its way up into his sideburns. It eventually led to a head of thick, black hair. One of his hands was still on the creaky gate and he was staring at me open-mouthed.

Behind him I heard someone mutter: 'Simon, what i—' and then he stopped dead too.

An equally tall man had pushed past him and was now gawking at me with that same I-just-saw-a-ghost expression. Unlike the first, he was clean-shaven and you could distinctly see his proud jawline. In cargo pants and no shirt, you could also see every detail of the intricate tattoos that started at his ribcage, working their way up his chest, across his biceps and collarbone and down both arms. He seemed oblivious to the season, with just a pair of flip-flops on his feet. I suspected both to be in their late twenties. When I took a good look at the second man's face I heard myself gasp. His eyes. He had my eyes. Those almond-shaped eyes with the dark brown irises looked at me like I was staring into my own reflection. His nose was larger than mine, but he also had my full, wide lips. It couldn't, he couldn't be my . . .

'You're after a carving?' came a strong female voice from behind me. It was the one I had heard earlier from within the house.

I turned to see another woman walking slowly down the path towards me. She walked with authority. As she moved closer, what I thought to be a shadow on her face turned out to be *Tāmoko* – a facial tattoo that was an ancient custom of the Maori people. It used to be carved into the skin with chisels and, as she stepped into the dim sunlight directly in front of me, I could see the black grooves on her chin. They curved up to her top lip, which was coloured completely black. I wasn't afraid of tattoos, even very permanent ones on your face. I had two on my own body and loved them. Yet the look on this woman's face made me gulp. Her mouth parted and the same expression of shock appeared before being replaced with an almost businesslike manner.

'You should come in,' she said. 'You mightn't have known about Jonah, but we do good work here. You can have a look around.'

'Thanks,' I said warily. 'Really, I didn't mean to upset you all. I think I'll just go.'

'Nonsense, no one's upset. Are we?'

She looked around and I noticed for the first time that she was strikingly attractive. Nobody moved or took their gaze off me.

'You weren't to know. He passed recently in a car accident and only close family was invited to the *tangi*.'

There was a pause and she smiled at my confusion. 'Funeral,' she explained. 'We like to keep things quiet and traditional. You should come in, have a look around and, if you don't like anything, you don't buy anything.'

'Your cab's already gone,' came a deep voice from behind me. It belonged to the unshaven man in business attire. 'After you've called another one at least have a look while you wait for it come back.'

His voice sounded like I imagined a black bear's would if it could talk. His face was open and genuine, as if he really wanted me to stay, and his hands were spread in an 'it's-up-to-you' gesture. The man with *my* eyes was staring at me expectantly.

'All right,' I said slowly. 'I'll call the cab first.'

I pulled out my phone and started dialling the cab company right there on the path. I didn't want to go inside until I knew a ride was coming. These people hadn't been rude exactly, but there was something off. They couldn't know who I was, they didn't. Yet the eyes and lips of the shirtless man were so similar to mine . . . I hoped they wouldn't read too much into it. Since they were both in front of and behind me, I turned to the side to tell the operator my address. I sensed movement and turned to see them all walking into the house. Except the businessman. He was leaning against the fence waiting for me.

'And how long do you think that will be?' I asked the operator, trying to sound conversational rather than desperate.

'About twenty minutes.'

'Thanks.' I hung up.

Great, twenty minutes. I could last twenty minutes in the house of my now dead father. I looked up to see the man making his way towards me with a casual smile on his face.

'Everyone has gone in,' he said and motioned to the door.

'Oh.'

We moved back up the path side by side.

'I'm Simon, by the way. Simon Tianne.' He offered me a hand.

I shook it. It was cold and nearly completely enclosed mine.

'Tommi,' I said, supplying no last name.

He raised his eyebrows. 'That's very . . .'

'Masculine.'

He let out a deep chuckle. 'KTK. I was going to say unique.'

'Sure, that too. And KTK?'

'Uh.' He shrugged. 'It's like . . . Think of it as the Maori version of LOL.'

'Oh. I'm KTKing internally right now.'

He smiled. 'Mean Maori, mean.'

We stepped up on to the landing.

'You're not an Ihi?' I said. I couldn't help myself. 'And I apologise if I'm pronouncing it wrong. I'm not very good with the Maori names.'

'No, no. My mother is Tiaki's sister, that's the woman with the tattoo. Jonah's wife, widow now, I guess. We live next door and all grew up together: the Ihis own the whole street and all the land around here. We keep pretty close. Tiaki's eldest son James, you saw him in the yard, is like a brother to me and we're both trying to get used to being the heads of the family now.'

'That must be hard.'

I honestly didn't know what to say. This was a lot of information to be telling a stranger and information I didn't know what to do with. Simon might have been friendly, but he didn't strike me as stupid. I think he and I both knew I was more than a tourist off the street. He was leading me through a wide hallway off the front entrance and deeper into the house. I'd been right about the size and we passed the doorways of half a dozen bedrooms, maybe more. The hallway opened out into a large lounge area with a fireplace at its centre. Plush couches were scattered around the room and a massive TV was showing a rugby union game.

There were a dozen other people in here, mostly male and all Maori. I saw two middle-aged men with *Tāmoko* down the entire right side of their faces sitting at the couch closest to the TV. Both were clutching beers and staring at me with interest. A lean but severely toned young man, about my age, jumped up from where he'd been sitting on the couch

37

closest to my left. Tattoos covered his entire body, right up to his jawline, where they stopped abruptly. His black hair was shaved on both sides, but the middle was long and slicked back into a ponytail. A bone earring looped through his left ear and he looked back at me with . . . my eyes. His mouth curled into a smile I could only describe as a combination of malice and lust. Maybe I was reading too much into it.

As I looked around the room, I was shocked to discover more sets of *my* eyes looking back at me. Even the young girl with the bob seemed to have the same almond shape and colour to her eyes.

'Have a seat,' offered James in a smooth and controlled voice.

He gestured to the couch the tattooed boy had jumped off and I moved to sit down. Simon remained where he was. The tattooed chap leaped down into a sitting position on the opposite side of the couch.

'I'm Steven,' he said, grinning at me while gesturing with one hand to himself.

'Tommi,' I said, offering a fleeting smile. I didn't want to encourage him.

The matriarch of the Ihi family, Tiaki, pulled up a wooden chair so she was sitting in front of Steven and directly in my line of sight.

'Tommi,' she said. 'How about you tell us why you're really here, hmm? Whose pack are you from?'

Right, time to come cl—wait, what?

'I'm sorry, "pack"? What do you mean?'

'Pack, tribe, those you run with,' said a man with a gruff voice from across the room.

I laughed, a quick burst but a thick relief of tension nonetheless.

'Ah, none. I'm a one-woman wolf pack,' I said, knowing only I would get the joke.

I think that last statement took them by surprise because there was a loaded pause as they glanced amongst each other. Tiaki was looking at me intensely. I was beginning to think there was only one way she could look at people.

'What are your iwi affiliations?' asked the bob girl.

'Um . . .' My cheeks felt hot with everyone's attention on me.

'Iwi?' she repeated with a huff. 'What's your *whakapapa*? Who's your *whānau* – your family, where are you from, who's your sub-tribe?'

'These are a lot of new words for me,' I said honestly.

Tiaki frowned. 'You do know what you are, don't you?' She spoke slowly, as if I didn't understand English.

'Yes,' I said, pausing.

This was it. This was my moment to tell them why I'd travelled across the entire freakin' world and to their front door. Take your oil, Tommi, and get on with it.

'I believe I'm Jonah's daughter.'

The room exploded. Whatever they'd been expecting me to say, that wasn't it.

'WHAT!' yelled the gruff man from the back, dropping his beer bottle.

It smashed dramatically on the ground splashing beer over his feet.

'Who's your—' said Simon.

'Where d—' said James.

'Who the f—' said bob girl.

'*Our* iwi no—' said Steven.

They were all talking over the top of each other, throwing questions at me and to the room. Yet it was something Tiaki said that made my head snap in her direction.

'Tilly,' she whispered. She had pushed her chair back and was standing perfectly still, looking down at me with wide, wild eyes. She was muttering something in Maori over and over again. She walked over to an elderly man sitting near the television. I hadn't paid much attention to him when I first came in. Now that she was dragging him towards me I had a moment to take in his surprised but wizened appearance. He was wearing tracksuit pants with a black piece of material wrapped around his top half like a sarong. It only covered half of his body and I could see a Maori tribal band around the baggy skin of his exposed arm. And scars. Dozens of scars. Scars of every size, shape and width adorned his flesh, including one very old and faded centrepiece across his throat. His *Tāmoko* started from his lower lip and spilled down his chin. The once black ink had faded to grey now and was hardly visible from the colour of his skin. He had to be well over ninety.

The man shook her off when he was a few steps away from me. He used a thick, wooden walking stick to limp forward. I stood up, unsure of what to do. The room went silent as he reached out a frail hand towards my face.

I made a move to step away from his grasp when Simon whispered behind me: 'Stay still, stay very still.'

I don't know why I trusted Simon, but I did. The old man's hand cupped my cheek and gently pulled my face to look directly into his. I was surprised to find I wasn't much taller than him. It must have been the other towering men in this family that made him look so tiny. He was still frail, no doubt about it. With his face inches from mine, I had nowhere else to look but into the deep lines of his face and eventually into the hollow of his black eyes.

The moment he touched me I jumped as if he'd been connected to a power point. I felt an inner electric buzz as something outside of the physical ignited. My eyes squinted shut as a stream of images flew before them. It was so quick I could barely get a look at anything except the yellowy gold of a glowing animal eye with a piercing black iris. The power of the image was so strong that when I opened my eyes I saw dozens of the bright eyes dancing around my vision. I shook my head, trying to clear it until only one eye remained.

At least I thought it was an eye. It turned white and started to morph into a near perfect circle. A moon. I could feel my face crinkling in confusion as I watched the moon fade, leaving the face of the old man standing in front of me with his mouth forming a small 'O' shape. I looked down at his walking stick suspiciously, wondering if he'd hit me with it. I could have been experiencing the after-effects of a concussion. Yet now, even more than before he'd touched me, he looked older. Drained. Although he'd removed his hand from my face, he was still staring at me.

'It's true,' he said in a surprisingly strong voice

The room remained frozen, so too everyone in it.

'She is who she says,' he continued. 'She is Jonah's daughter. She is also, most definitely, a werewolf.'

What. The? It was like someone had hit pause on the room. Nobody moved.

The only thing that did was my jaw as it dropped with shock. I was betting my mouth was open so wide the old man could have crawled into it. These people were clearly fucking crazy. I had to get out of here. Now.

I spun around and made a move to the hallway I'd come from. Simon leaped to my side and grabbed my arm, half spinning me back. I used that momentum and threw an elbow up into his face. His nose gave a satisfying crack and he let out a surprised yelp, loosening his grip as one hand tried to stem the blood flow. I made for the hallway again. Bob girl stood directly in my path with her arms and legs spread wide in an almost squat position. She looked as if she wanted to catch me like a housecat springing up into her lap. It was too easy.

I kicked her square in the hoo-hah, something I'd never tried on a girl before and, as she went down, I jumped over her. It was a cheap shot but desperate times call for a jab in the giney.

I'd just cleared her tumbling frame when two hands wrapped around my upper thigh. I grasped my fists together as I turned to bring them down on whoever's head it was. Another strong set of arms blocked the blow. Tiaki was the thigh grabber and she was throwing all of her body weight on to my left leg to try to bring me down. She was a strong woman and it was working. As I dropped to one knee, Steven's hands snaked out to grab me in a headlock. I bit him. Hard.

He screamed and I knew the metallic taste in my mouth was his blood. While trying to pull people off me, I looked up to see my next attacker and was greeted with the sight of that heavy walking stick being brought down on my head. It really was more like a log.

I heard a loud *thunk* from afar as if it was someone else's head being whacked.

The piercing pain that started at my head and flowed down through my body assured me it was not. I opened my mouth to yell with pain, but another whack and I was down. As my cheek pressed into the carpet floor, everything started to go hazy. I felt a warm body scoop me into their lap right there on the ground. My vision was blurring in and out of focus, but I thought I made out James's face staring down at me. I registered the sensation of blood trickling down my forehead while he tried to say something to me, something soothing I couldn't understand. Then everything went black.

Chapter 4

A light rain had started to fall, but it didn't much matter to the residents of New York City at 3 a.m. on a Monday. A few remaining stragglers scuttled to their trains, cabs and buses under the protection of newspapers. Those without shelter jogged hastily to find some. The only entities unaffected by the drizzle were the dozens of yellow cabs. They tooted and weaved amongst each other like angry yellow hornets. One of them swerved to the side of road, braking suddenly to come to an abrupt stop. A gentleman in a dark green trench coat folded out of the car. The rain flattened his chestnut-coloured hair to his face and made it run in slicks to just above his shoulders. He tucked his hands into his pockets and stared up at a sign that said MAO'S 24-HOUR MARKET.

The cab gave an abrupt toot and the man jerked away from the sign, bending down to the window to give the driver his fare. He watched the cab speed off for a moment before stepping over the gutter and on to the path. The fluorescent light spilled from the shopfront and lit his features as he drew closer. Pale skin peeked out the top of his coat and highlighted a chiselled jawline dotted with a layer of hair he had neglected to shave. The man looked tired. Heavy bags under his eyes stood out against the otherwise handsome features of his face.

'HEY! Hey, hottie!'

The man reluctantly paused on the sidewalk, smoothing the hair back off his face with the rain. A woman in a white bondage dress, so tight it looked like another layer of skin, was strutting towards him with purpose. A gaggle of her girlfriends were huddled together under two umbrellas nearby and giggling as they watched her approach the man. He looked bored already.

'Yeah, you. I don't see any other perfect tens on the street, do you?' she said, lowering her voice so the conversation was just between the two of them. The man didn't respond. 'My girls and I are on the way home, but I could be persuaded to stay out a bit longer if you ...' She trailed off suggestively, leaving just the buzz of the city nightlife pinging around them as a silence stretched on. She harrumphed, placing a hand on her hip in an exaggerated gesture. 'Well?'

'Well what?' he asked, his tone flat.

'You're not doing anything, I'm not doing anything, you're structured like a god and you can't deny I'd look good on your arm.'

'I'm busy. Shopping.' He gestured to the tacky convenience store behind him and she gave it a dismissive once-over.

'Come on Annabelle, leave it!' called one of her friends.

'Fine,' the woman agreed, reluctant to relent, but spinning around to meet her posse. The second she reached the safety of her friends she heard her mutter: 'Fucking male models are the worst in this city. Like, I'm trying to *upgrade* you, you know?'

'Uh-huh. Totally.'

'What an asshole.'

'He's basic hun, beneath you.'

A smile played on the man's lips as he stepped over the threshold and into the store. His eyes quickly scanned the aisles, with a shift worker browsing the refrigerated section the only customer. He looked up at the clerk – an overweight Asian man in his forties – who nodded. He nodded back and headed towards a door off to the side of the main counter. He pushed it open and stepped into a narrow hallway with maroon walls and dark carpet. The decor couldn't have been more different to what he'd just left behind. After closing the door behind him, he continued down to the end of the hall.

Two women with shaved heads stood side by side in front of another door. They were identical in appearance and stature. Twins. They smiled in a tight, almost frightening gesture, which one could have been mistaken for a grimace if the man didn't know better. He paused in front of them.

'I suppose he's waiting for me,' he said, more to himself than to them.

The twins nodded in unison and one moved to the side, opening the door. This room, his final destination, was lit only by a lamp leaning over an oak desk. A gangly, white-haired man was sitting at the desk in a leather chair with the ankle of one leg resting on the knee of his other. He was dressed in a classic grey suit and his fingers were laced together in front of his face.

'Ah, Lorcan. Good, come in,' said the man, gesturing to the empty seat on the other side of his desk.

'Anchor,' he said, as a form of greeting.

'I've heard much of your exploits within the Praetorian Guard,' he said, speaking in a clipped British accent. 'Your skill as a warrior is renowned.'

'Thank you, but the honour is mine. What you accomplished during The Crusades . . . it is still taught amongst the Guard,' said Lorcan.

'The Crusades,' said Anchor, with an air of nostalgia in his voice. 'They don't have wars like that any more.'

Lorcan said nothing, leaving the man to his reflections.

'I was just saying to the twins how sorry I was to hear about your friend, the werewolf.'

Lorcan stiffened in his seat, but the rest of him remained blank.

'It's a terrible thing to take one's life. Especially such a promising pack leader. So young, so unexpected,' the man continued.

Silence.

'Yet out of every tragedy comes something good. The Custodians are lucky to have you. Although it pains me to hear you've sheathed your sword. I guess one must find redemption where one can.'

'Thank you.'

'They say you've excelled in your training here, that you're ready. And I have your first assignment.'

Lorcan looked carefully at him and the Anchor nodded, untangling his legs and leaning forward on the desk.

'You leave tonight.'

'Why . . . so soon?' asked Lorcan. 'And no disrespect, but why are my orders coming from you? Assignments are usually dealt out by the Custodians and not the Praetorian Guard.'

'This,' said Anchor, 'is a special case. A case where both of our interests align under the orders of the Treize.'

'This is coming from them?'

'Directly. They informed me of the situation. After speaking to all of the concerned parties we've agreed this is the best course of action.' He gave the information a moment to settle before continuing. 'You've heard of the Ihi clan in New Zealand, yes?'

Lorcan nodded before replying. 'A particularly powerful pack. Respected and deadly. They've been the most dominant were-force in the Southern Hemisphere for over twenty years now. Their alpha Jonah was involved with the Outskirt packs in the nineties before they were defeated by the Guard. Remarkably, he and the pack escaped relatively unscathed. Although not quite as powerful as before.'

Anchor smiled with approval as Lorcan shared his knowledge of the situation.

'There is plenty of unfinished business when it comes to the Ihi pack. And now Jonah Ihi is dead.'

'Jonah's dead?' asked Lorcan. 'How? Who killed him?'

'Who indeed? The Askari on the ground there are keeping a safe distance, much as they always have, but initial reports say it was a car accident.'

'And you believe that?'

'No. Maybe. Jonah's car is said to have gone off the side of a cliff as he was returning to his home in Paengaroa. Certain parts of the New Zealand landscape are particularly unforgiving. Even a werewolf can't heal from a 200-foot drop, let alone survive the inferno when the car exploded at the bottom. Either way, our sources seem confident he is actually dead from the evidence they've found. We're looking at it closely. Ironic though, after all of the battles he's fought, people he's killed, a car accident is his undoing. It would be up there with one of the great ironies of life. Yet it seems to have happened nonetheless. Divine justice, perhaps.'

'What about the Ihis? He had sons.'

'Indeed he did, Lorcan: three sons and a daughter. Plus there's considerable strength in his extended family, particularly the nephews. For the time being a new leader has not stepped up. The grace period for these things in werewolf and Maori custom is usually about . . .'

'A month. Maybe more,' supplied Lorcan.

'Given it's an influential family such as the Ihis, we would expect a new alpha to take over sooner rather than later. Reassert their authority. The shock of losing such a leader in such a human way, despite the irony, has been astonishing and unexpected to them. They're scattered and uncertain. None of his three sons seems to have the power and abilities he had, or his ruthlessness, thankfully.'

'But an heir has emerged?' questioned Lorcan, anticipating where the conversation was heading.

'Yes. An heir we had no idea existed until a few days ago,' said Anchor. He paused for a moment, leaning back into his chair with a scowl. 'It seems he had a fifth child, a secret child. Perhaps one even he didn't know existed. Our records certainly show no proof of it. The mother seems to have gone to great lengths to hide not only the child, but it from its true family. Regardless, this wolf must not take her place at the head of the Ihi clan if we can help it. The Three tell me she has never changed form, never been around others of her kind before, so we can't judge how powerful she is – if at all. There haven't been any indicators she's particularly exceptional, but nothing's certain until after the change.'

'That will happen now,' said Lorcan.

'Being so close to her own blood, so close to a line of warriors as powerful as the Ihis, will almost certainly bring on the change in her come the next full moon phase. Tomorrow night.'

'I will never make it in time before the first transformation,' Lorcan mused.

'There's nothing to be done about that,' said Anchor. 'We need you there for the aftermath, whatever that is. The change, as they say, changes everything. A female alpha is, of course, only a vague possibility. Yet the Maori packs value their women as much as the men and their female warriors can be just as skilled. We need to know who she aligns herself with, what she's capable of.'

'It seems too much of a coincidence that she has popped up and gone to them so soon after his death,' added Lorcan.

'*If* she has gone to them willingly,' said Anchor. 'Perhaps she has always been in contact with them and eluded our notice. Maybe it's just bad luck that she has found them now. Either way, the Ihis aren't likely to let her go and they already have her. We do not need them strengthening their pack, especially when such an opportune moment has brought its downfall. But . . .' He took a long sip from a tumbler full of warm amber liquid before continuing. 'The Custodians have instructed us that if she chooses to be a *kahuatairingi* – a lone wolf – well, then she's entitled to a guide. You understand if that possibility arises why it's so important we have someone there to guide her, instruct her and, if needed, put her down if she begins to follow the path of her father. Think of it as a reconnaissance mission with the possibility of bloodshed.'

'That's why you wanted me.'

'Of course. You're one of the best warriors we've ever had. This is the perfect opportunity to put your new Custodian skills to the test and, if meditating with her doesn't work, the sword is always a reliable fallback option.'

Lorcan chose to ignore the jibe and sat there silently instead. Anchor slid a plain black USB across the desk.

'Your flight's arranged. You leave in two hours and on this is everything we have on her, which isn't much. It's all the Askari could dig up in the brief amount of time she's been on our radar. Tommi, I believe her name is.'

Lorcan raised an eyebrow at the unusual name and took the USB.

'Contacts are also on there, for myself and the Askari at the nearest faction,' he added.

'Thank you,' said Lorcan, standing and shaking hands briefly with him. He was reaching for the doorknob when Anchor called out from behind him.

'Oh and Lorcan? This Tommi ... she might be a cub and have only a fragment of the physical power her brothers possess, but she's still an Ihi. They have a capacity to lead, to unite and to conquer. Much like her father. Be on your guard.'

Chapter 5

There was a bitter taste in my mouth. Its sharp tang brought me out of the darkness. I moved my tongue to find the source of the substance.

Blood. My own blood.

My head was throbbing and drooping uncomfortably on my shoulders. I went to cradle it in my hands but I couldn't move. Something was cutting painfully against them. Ergh. I was going to have to open my eyes.

Rusty, metal cuffs had my hands laced together above my head and secured to a metal pipe. I sagged my shoulders and groaned as I felt an all-new ache towards the left side of my ribs. My legs were bent under me on a dirty, damp floor. In fact, the whole place was dirty and damp. I was being held in what appeared to be an old garage, probably the one I saw walking in. I flinched as a stream of memories came flooding back to me.

What a fucking idiot. Why had I come here on the whim of some anonymous tip?

Why hadn't I run within the first fifteen minutes of meeting these people when my senses clearly told me something was wrong? No, instead I plodded right into their lair and blabbed about how I was their relative. They were probably going to kill me and remove the evidence of Jonah's crime once and for all. Fuck. A deep sense of panic started clawing its way out of my chest and I furiously rattled the cuffs against the pole, searching for any give. It made a hell of a noise, but I didn't care.

'Shit,' I sobbed. I felt tears start streaming down my cheeks. 'Shit, shit, shit.'

I knew this was the moment, this was the feeling that victims of serial killers or abductors must experience. That moment when they realise there's no escape. That although they're here completely by someone else's design, they're also here because of their own mistakes. That inner warning bell they didn't listen to. That one sign they didn't notice. I had barely begun agonising over my stupidity when the garage door started to slide open.

It was James.

As far as I could recall I hadn't broken his nose or bitten him. We should be cool. Ha. I had nowhere to hide the sheer and utter terror I was feeling. I pushed my back as hard as it would go against the pole. James slid the door closed behind him and started to make his way over to me. He had a plastic bag in this hand and knelt about a metre in front of me, leaning against an old car wreck.

He said nothing at first, just stared at me.

'I'm sorry,' he said, breaking the silence. 'I'm sorry it had to be like this.'

I said nothing.

Apologies? What kind of mind game was this? Kidnappers, maybe murderers, didn't apologise to their victims. Did they?

'Maybe if it had just been me and Simon at home ...' He trailed off. 'As soon as everyone saw your eyes, your mouth, your nose even. You look like family.'

He reached out to touch my face and I flinched.

'Sorry,' he said again. 'You must be terrified. But, Tommi, there are some things you have to understand about our family. Especially since you're part of it now.'

'I'm not part of your crazy-ass family,' I spat.

'You're blood,' he said, as if that solved everything. 'Our pack elder confirmed it. The same blood that runs through my veins, through Steven's, through this whole pack, runs through yours. You are Jonah's daughter. My sister.'

He said the last part with a half-smile and I sensed an opportunity.

'Then let me go. Or at least uncuff me. We can all go and make a family tree together in the lounge or something.'

James chuckled. 'I can't do that, you know I can't. Much as I might want to.'

'No, I don't fucking know why you can't,' I shouted. 'All I know is that I should never have come to this stupid house and tried to hunt down some rapist of a father. My life was fine before this anarchy!'

He tutted at me, just once, but it was enough to catch me off guard. 'My father was many things, but a rapist is something he was not.'

'Are you calling my mother a liar?' I asked with indignation.

'Yes,' he replied, not a hint of apology in his tone.

'I grew up with this dark shadow clinging to my soul; why would any mother let her daughter think they were the product of a rape when they weren't?'

'Because the truth was worse.' There was sadness in his eyes, pity.

'I . . . What? I don't know what you're saying, but you don't know my mum. She wouldn't, she *couldn't* fake that kind of—'

Who's Afraid?

The words froze on my lips as James finished rummaging in his back pocket and held up a weathered photo in front of my face. The corners were torn and there were lines where it had been folded over and over throughout the years, but with the image hovering just inches from my own nose there was no mistaking the subjects. It was my mother, young and unmistakably in love. In a daggy halter top and unforgivable Farrah hair, she was smiling with every fibre of her being. Next to her, stoic but content, was Jonah Ihi. He had his arm wrapped around her protectively and she was cuddling into his side. My mouth dropped open and I felt tears prick my eyes.

'This proves nothing,' I murmured, trying to keep my composure. 'This just shows that they knew each other.'

'From your reaction I'm guessing that part of the story is already different from what you've been told.'

'You know nothing,' I spat, repeating a meaningless phrase.

'I know more than you. I know that Tilly Grayson had a two-year affair with my father that nearly ruined this family. I know that it broke my mother in ways that I think she never really got over,' he said, flipping the image over so I could read the writing on the back. In my mother's uniquely messy scroll were the words: '*You said it would be the last time J, but it wasn't. You said you were in control, but you're not. I'm leaving. Respect me enough not to follow. T.*' I gulped.

'I never knew her name of course, none of us did save Mum and, I suspect, my auntie. When Dad died I got a big box of his personal shit. This was in it, tucked deep inside his wallet. He carried this around with for him for over twenty years, Tommi.'

He let that sink in. Jonah was not a good guy by any stretch of the imagination, but my mother ... it sounded liked she loved him. Despite his issues – which were obviously many – and despite his family and his wife, my mother loved him right up until he went one step too far – whatever that was. Despite her disappearance, Jonah was obviously marked by the one that got away – literally.

James continued: 'I asked one of the elders about it and they said she nearly destroyed everything, that she nearly destroyed the pack, and that Jonah was ready to leave it all behind for her. Wehi, our elder, said the best thing Tilly Grayson every did was disappear.'

'What are you trying to say?' I sniffed.

'I think your mother discovered what we were around the same time she found out she was pregnant and she did her best to remove you from this. She wanted you to be normal.'

Who were these people? They kept calling themselves a 'pack' and the more I heard about them the more they sounded exactly like a 'pack' of terrifying individuals. No; werewolves. That's what they had said: I was a werewolf. These people – the Ihis – thought they were werewolves. And my mother believed it. A gasp of terror escaped my mouth before I had a chance to stop it.

'What? What is it?' he asked.

Like it wasn't bloody obvious. He leaned in closer to try to examine my face, but I turned my head to the side so I wouldn't have to look at him.

'Tommi, once you change tonight you'll see that you belong with us. We're weaker now that Dad's gone and I, or Simon, need to take over stronger than before. We can change the pack, make it better under our rule. We can expand the businesses and the properties we're already running into a force to be reckoned with. We could use you.'

I didn't understand any of this. These were the rantings of a crazy person: a crazy person with my life in their hands.

'I don't care how you came into this world or where you've been, but you're our blood. It doesn't matter to me whether you only have half of it. You belong with us.'

James got up to leave. When he reached the light of the doorway he turned and said: 'You can be powerful with us. We need someone powerful with us.'

With that, he slid the roller door shut behind him, leaving me in the gloom.

I spent the next hours trying to work a weak link I'd found in the cuffs and thinking about anything other than my mother and the secrets she may have taken to her grave. The ramifications were too hurtful to ponder and I had to focus on freedom. The skin around my wrists was raw with the effort and thin trails of blood were snaking down my arm. I rotated the cuffs this way and that, trying to catch the link onto screws in the pipe. I'd almost hooked it on one when the garage door opened again.

Simon this time.

His face looked sore. Coming from someone who was chained to a pipe that was saying something. I remained still, watching him walk closer to me. I had definitely broken his nose. It was a mass of blue and black and there was even a purplish tinge beginning to form underneath his eyes. If I wasn't locked in a room alone with him right now I would have been happy with myself.

He stood there looking down at me for a moment. Just looking. I looked back, but this time I'm sure the fear showed on my face. He started rifling through the plastic bag James had left and pulled out a water bottle. He unscrewed the lid and knelt in front of my face, holding the water up for me to drink. I didn't want help from these people. I didn't want any assistance from the monsters who had put me here. I ignored the dry itching in my throat and sealed my lips in a straight line, pushing my head away from the bottle. He sighed and grabbed my head with one of his strong, broad hands.

'Drink,' he said forcefully.

I drank. I'd been so focused on trying to escape and being terrified I hadn't realised how thirsty I was. I guzzled half the bottle before Simon pulled it back.

'Easy,' he said.

He gave me a few moments to catch my breath and then fed me the rest of the water. As soon as the water was gone so too was Simon. He left without another word.

Tiaki and the elder visited next, speaking only to each other and only in Maori. They walked around me, splashing a liquid on me and chanting. I screamed at him, at her, at all of them. It made no difference, it just made me want a cigarette. He left her with me for a moment and she came closer, her eyes poring over my features. I could tell she was searching for what parts of me were Jonah and what parts were Tilly, mentally marking them with invisible Post-it notes.

'Huh,' she said finally. 'You look nothing like her.'

'Tilly Grayson?' I asked, getting confirmation in the twitch of her eye at the very mention of her name.

'Stupid little white girl.' She smirked, crouching down to my level. 'I never thought she'd come back to haunt me two decades later. That shit should be dead and buried. But here you are, showing up on my doorstep with the *gene* no less and looking every bit like an Ihi and nothing like your whore of a mother.'

'How dare you,' I spat.

'Oh, I dare. My husband nearly left his first-born son and his pregnant wife for that waste gash. I very dare.'

Long moments passed as we stared each other out, saying nothing and yet everything.

'She's dead, isn't she?' Tiaki asked after a long while.

'How did you know?' I asked, genuinely surprised.

'What else could push someone to hunt down the father they thought was a rapist? Yeah, James told me your mother's tale. I should be offended on Jonah's behalf but, to be honest, she couldn't exactly tell you the truth,' she said, stretching to her feet.

'And what's that?'

She looked down at me with an amused expression. 'That you're a werewolf, honey.'

She was gone as quickly as she arrived. After she left, I must have dozed off because the next thing I knew I was waking up to the sound of the garage door opening.

Steven.

As soon as he locked the door behind him I knew I was in trouble. Perhaps it was time to try those handcuffs again. I looked above me and started slowly, carefully, positioning the link on the closest screw. Steven had closed half the distance between us in what was an almost feline-like strut. It was definitely predatory. It was obvious in everything about him – from his walk to his demeanour – he wasn't like the other Ihis. I wasn't going to have time to work on the cuffs. I hoped he was going to get monologuing before starting whatever he had in mind.

As if on cue, he said, 'You are somethin'. Look at you, all helpless and chained and completely at my mercy.'

He was standing over me now and he trailed a hand slowly down my arm. I couldn't help but shudder. He laughed, as if my response amused him. He took a few steps back and pulled something out of his back jeans pocket.

'Got your phone here,' he said, waving it in front of him. 'Kinda disappointed you only brought cash and not your wallet. I would've had a lot more fun going through that. Got a text from Mari, she seems pretty worried about you. Doesn't want you coming here, that's for sure. Don't worry, I replied for you. And there's a call from some guy called Joss. That your boyfriend?'

I said nothing, just stared directly at him. Hopefully, the eye contact would keep him focused on my face and not the strain I was trying to put on the cuffs as I moved them back and forth on the screw.

'Nah, like I give a shit,' he said, smashing my phone into tiny pieces on the floor in front of him. 'It's not like they'll find you.'

That last remark caused a sharp intake of breath on my behalf and he heard it.

Laughing, he said: 'Good. Got ya scared, have I? I'm a scary guy. Matter fact, we all are. You will be too, soon. See, 'case you didn't gather from the little magic show in there, we're werewolves, Tommi, all of us. A big, scary pack of the most powerful wolves in the country.' He paused for dramatic effect.

'Well,' I said, 'New Zealand's a pretty small country.'

His face darkened and, in a blur of movement, he was on me. He pushed himself up against me, grinding my back into the pole and grabbing my throat.

'You're making jokes now,' he growled, less than an inch from my face. 'But it's nearly dark. Less than an hour to the first full moon. Then you'll be going through one of the most excruciating experiences of your life. Some don't even survive it, Tommi, you mightn't. But oh, once you go wolf . . .' He let out a blissful sigh. 'There's nothing quite like the power. It's raw, wild energy. And, for us, we're the rock stars of this here species and we got power like none of those other pricks can imagine. We're powerful as, sis.'

He stopped talking and turned his gaze down towards my body. He reached into his back pocket again and came back with a knife. He held it to my throat with one hand while the other slid its way down my neck until it reached my breasts. He grabbed one of them roughly. Oh God. I squirmed, trying to move or shift in some way to escape his probing hand. There was no escape. All I did was cause him to nick my neck with the blade. I let out a little shriek of pain as I started to feel blood ooze down my collarbone.

'See, that's what ya get,' he said. 'There's no disobeying here, Tommi. Fuck you're hot. That hair, that face, those tits.'

He squeezed again and I whimpered.

'You're my brother,' I whispered, pleading to the last defence I had.

'Half.'

With that, he kissed me. He was all tongue and teeth and I did my best to keep my mouth shut and him out. Until I had an idea. I opened my mouth and heard him sigh as he slid his tongue in. I bit down.

He screamed and I didn't let go, biting harder. I tasted his blood in my mouth. He released my breast and punched me in the stomach so hard I was sure I heard a rib crack. He leaped back from me, clutching at his mouth as blood dribbled down the side of his face. I tried not to hunch over from the pain of the punch so I could stay upright and breathe properly.

'Bitch,' he said, spitting out a mouthful of blood.

I started furiously working the cuffs against the screw and I thought I felt it give a little.

'You know, my little bro's coming home from a mate's house. He thought having another sister was choice.'

Jesus, how many psychotic family members did I have? I tried not to panic as Steven inched forward.

'He's gotta theory that pain and anger awaken the wolf. Be grateful I'm helping you with that.'

He punched me in the stomach again. I gasped and went still as I struggled to breathe. It wasn't until he started to undo the zipper of my jeans that I found the energy to move. I kicked and squirmed, trying to throw my body weight and him in different directions. It didn't work and it was only when he had my jeans down at my ankles that it hit me: he was going to rape me.

My own half-brother was going to rape me.

I let out another scream. Not of fear this time, of anger. I threw all of my body into pulling down on the link against the screw. Steven had my legs pinned now and was crawling up my legs, licking them as he went. He reached my underwear and started stroking, rubbing me. It took all of my will not to break down and go into hysterics. Instead, I yanked on the cuffs and felt the most beautiful sensation in the world – they snapped.

Steven jerked his head up at the noise and, in that moment of distraction, I swept one of my hands across his face with a triumphant scream. He went flying off me, landing about a metre away. I leaped up and pressed my back against the opposite wall, looking down at his shrieking form. He raised his head from his blood-covered hands and I saw four huge gashes running diagonally across his face. Confused, I looked down at my own hand and screamed. I was doing a lot of that lately.

My normal hand was gone, replaced instead by a massive brown claw. No, not a claw exactly. My left hand up to my elbow had transformed into what looked like a cross between a wolf's and a man's arm. Muscles jutted out of my forearm and dark brown hair tracked down to my hand. My fingers were replaced with unnaturally long digits that ended in huge, sharp claws. I held my hand up in front of my face and screamed again.

'It's happening,' croaked Steven as he slid closer towards my side of the room. 'But how did you—'

He didn't get a chance to finish his sentence because I picked up a wrench on the ground nearby and brought it down over his head. It made a sickening sound on impact and he collapsed, unmoving. I didn't care about Steven, didn't spare a second thought for him. Instead, I looked at my wrench-less hand, claw, whatever. Adrenaline coursed through my veins and time seemed to stand still as I gawked at it. A dog barking outside snapped me back to attention. Freak-show hand or not, this was my opportunity to get out of here.

I reached down to grab my pants with my clawed hand and, instead of pulling them off the ground like I intended, I tore right through them. This is what I did to Steven's face, I thought. I lifted the wrench to smash out the garage's back window before deciding to use my monster claw instead. I had only a few seconds to feel horrified as I bashed out the glass and half the window frame with it. Amazing. I felt no pain.

The broken glass shards didn't even pierce the leathery surface of the skin.

My skin. It was *my* skin on *my* arm. I leaped through the window, landing on a bed of dried leaves and grass. I turned back to see the garage and the rest of Ihi house behind me. Luckily, I was obscured from view by the structure. Anyone looking out of the house wouldn't have seen me as I took my only escape route and sprinted off into the dense forest. As far as I knew no one had heard the commotion, but Steven had said it was less than an hour until full moon. They would come looking for me then and discover I had escaped. I may have also killed their brother. Nothing I could do about that now and, if I was honest with myself, I didn't care. What I did care about was putting distance between me and the Ihis.

All those years of long-distance running came in handy and I fell into a steady but speedy pace. A few times I nearly ran head first into a tree because I was looking down at my claw-for-a-hand. I was making a conscious effort now to keep my eyes ahead. I wasn't sure how long I'd been running for or how much land I'd covered. When I felt the ground start to rise slowly uphill I knew it was a good sign. I was moving forward and not in circles. It was about the only thing that had gone right for me so far. The second I thought that, a red-hot stabbing pain burned along my spine. I yelled out and fell to my knees. It disappeared just as quickly as it came and I stumbled up, leaning on a tree for support. What was that? I tried to look down my back to make sure I hadn't been stabbed.

I took a few steps forward to start running and was brought crashing to the ground again by the same agonising feeling. Except this time it was worse. It felt like hundreds of small knives gouging through my skin from the inside out. The pain was beyond screams. My mouth opened and closed in silent agony as I lay on the forest floor, arching my back into the earth. It could have gone on for seconds, maybe minutes. All sense of time and reason was lost to me amid the excruciating pain.

And then it was gone. I was shaking, sweating, and I realised the whimpering sound I could hear was coming from my own mouth.

Excruciating. This is what Steven had said it would be like, wasn't it?

I heard a shout somewhere off in the distance, far, but not far enough. Another shout returned it and I recognised Simon's scent on the wind. No, I couldn't smell him. I was clearly still delirious from the after-effects of the pain, yet somehow I knew it was him coming for me. And the others.

I dragged myself up on all fours and stumbled into a light jog again, pushing myself to go faster and harder up the incline. I could hear them snapping back trees and cutting through the bush closer than I would have liked. I would not let them get me again. I would rather die. My vision went white as the pain rocked me. This time I stayed on my feet. They were too close.

If I was going to escape I couldn't lose any more time. I gripped a tree, digging my clawed hand into it and bit down on my lip until I felt blood running down my chin. I pushed forward. Shadows had replaced the light coming through the trees and I could sense darkness was nearly upon us. I stumbled, screamed and sprinted in bursts, as I battled with what was undoubtedly the worst pain I'd experienced in this or any lifetime.

I got a whiff of Simon, definitely Simon, Tiaki, James and most of the other Ihis. They were making incredible time and I could hear their footfalls getting closer as I tried to increase my pace.

I tore furiously at my shirts, suddenly frustrated by the material restricting my back and arms as I pumped them, urging myself to go faster. The clothing fell in shreds around me and I didn't worry about leaving a trail. They were too close anyway. I sprinted through the thinning trees with branches lashing at my face and body.

'Tommi!' I heard James shout. It sounded like he was practically at my neck.

I smelled something in the air and sniffed. Salt. The ocean was close. I could even hear waves pounding heavily on what had to be rocks. I could swim. I wasn't sure if the Ihis could. I was hoping I was better. I broke through the last of the trees and on to clear land. I was on a grassy cliff top with the drop-off about a hundred metres directly in front of me.

I paused for a second, suddenly transfixed by the glowing orb that appeared from behind the clouds. I saw it for only a moment before I was on the ground, screaming as the pain returned in all its searing glory. I dug my hands into the earth and felt tears as wave after wave of flesh-splitting torture washed over me. I heard a rip and a crack come from within my own body and I let out a brief cry as it happened. Then it happened again, over and over, faster and faster, until I was begging for death.

Death.

Sweet nothingness would be better than this suffering.

Somehow, through the hell, I sensed the Ihis emerge from the trees behind me.

I smelled Steven among them. Impossible. As I heard their footsteps get closer, I used every last fragment of willpower I had left and sprinted towards the edge of the cliff. I caught them unawares and heard shouts of surprise behind me.

I didn't look back. Within a few strides, I realised I was moving faster than I'd ever moved before. I was bounding towards the edge on all four limbs, each stride throwing me powerfully closer to my goal. I didn't know what lay beneath me. I could smell the ocean close by. Whether it was directly below me or hundreds of jagged rocks were, I didn't care. Freedom or death. Either option sounded promising.

'No!' I heard someone shout, but it was too late.

I launched myself far out over the cliff edge and into the air. I had a second of suspension before gravity took hold and I began to plummet. I screamed, and not with fear this time, with pure exhilaration. It took me a second to realise that I wasn't screaming at all. Following me down into the unknown was a piercing howl.

Chapter 6

Naked.

That was the first thing I thought when I came to. I was lying face down on a bed of leaves completely naked. I lifted my head to get a better register of my surrounds and had to peel muddy leaves from my face. I picked myself off the forest floor and shakily made it halfway to standing before collapsing back on to the damp ground. My entire body was aching like I'd fought Rocky Balboa and Ronda Rousey in the same day. My strength was non-existent. I lay there for a minute gathering my remaining energy and trying to stop my body from shaking. With a grunt and a heave, I was up and stumbling towards the thinnest part of the treeline.

My leap from the cliff edge last night had turned out to be a fateful one as I had cleared the jagged rocks below and plunged straight into the icy waters off the coastline in the Bay of Plenty. The sea had been calm enough that I was able to swim – correction, doggy-paddle – a few hundred metres to a nearby stretch of beach.

In human form, I'd always been a good swimmer, winning age champion every year back in high school. In wolf form, I was no Ariel, but I was able to get myself quickly and quietly to shore.

Who's Afraid?

None of the Ihis had followed me off the edge and I doubted they would have spotted me slipping through the dark waters below. It was easier for me if they thought I was dead. Yet I wasn't taking chances. I'd barely trotted on to the pebbled shore before I was tearing along the beach, the cool air passing over my fur as I threw myself faster and faster into the night. Fur. Gulp. For a good part of last night I had been covered in fur. A wolf.

No, a were-fucking-wolf.

I'm not sure how long I'd been sprinting away from the beach and through the forest before this hit me. A while, I think, because it brought me to a brake-screeching stop. I padded around, spinning the reality of the situation over and over in my mind. I tried to say my name quietly to myself. A cross between a whine and growl was what came out instead. I nearly slapped a hand over my mouth until I saw that 'hand' was a gigantic paw. I inspected my paws closely, stretching them out in front of me, retracting and extending my claws. Whoa. The things I could do with those claws. I actually lost myself for a moment as I gleefully sliced and snapped trees with them. By digging my claws deep into the wood of the totara trees, I was able to climb them like a panther. What I couldn't climb I could leap. With one burst of energy, I could coil my leg muscles and send myself hurtling incredible distances through the air. The landing part was more difficult, but it didn't matter if I smashed into the side of a tree or stumbled over a few boulders, nothing seemed to hurt me.

I was invincible. I could hear everything. With the heightened wolf senses, I could hear the bubbling of a nearby creek to the shrill call of a kakapo bird miles away.

69

And the smells! Everything had a distinctive scent. Just from sniffing it, I knew instantly what it was, where it had come from and what had been near it recently.

My pulse quickened as the scent of something living and delicious pricked my nostrils. I sniffed deeper and, before I had any grasp of what I was doing, I was following the trail blindly in pursuit of the source. Soundlessly, I picked my way through the forest, careful of where I stepped so as not to alert my prey. Before long, I was low to the ground, cloaking my body instinctively as I watched an adolescent deer drink from a bubbling stream. It was completely unaware of my presence and my stomach growled involuntarily with hunger. I felt my lips curl up over my long fangs as saliva began to drip from my mouth.

I repressed the urge to growl, but the deer must have sensed something was amiss as the forest grew silent in passive warning. Its glossy eyes flicked over the habitat, scanning for danger, and I anticipated flight. We took off at precisely the same time, the deer darting and weaving between trees as it tried to escape my appetite. It was fast, but I was faster. My reflexes were impeccable as I dodged, ducked and leaped in pursuit of my first meal. My body accelerated, as my muscles and legs urged me further and faster, my breath coming out in puffs until I launched myself through the air in one final daring move. I landed on the deer's back, my mouth wrapped around its neck, as my razor-sharp teeth pierced a vital artery. Hot, delicious blood poured into my mouth as I tried to gulp it away and concentrate on holding the deer in my grip.

It fruitlessly tried to kick and pull itself free of me, but it wasn't long before I was resting on all fours with the twitching body secured firmly in my grip. I watched with patience as the last ebbs of life flowed from the animal before I felt confident enough to feast. My body was built for this and, without knowing where, I sensed the location of the best bits and tucked in. My snout was buried deep within the deer's carcass as I devoured the warm, fresh meat. I ate until I felt like I would burst, my belly swollen and sated. My tongue darted out of my mouth and licked the rest of my face clean.

For a moment, I came to my senses, worrying that I had wasted too much time snacking instead of running. I remembered smelling the Ihis when they were in close pursuit and I felt relieved I couldn't smell them now. They weren't close, but for how long? They would at the very least check to see if I was still alive and if they couldn't find a body by morning they would keep looking during the day. Despite being trapped in the form of a beast I still had my brain.

Realistically, what did the Ihis know about me? I hadn't taken my wallet to their house, only my room key and cash. They knew my name was Tommi, but they didn't know where I was staying. Damn, except my room key had been in the back pocket of my jeans when Steven had torn them off. It took me a moment to realise the terrifying growling sound was coming from my own mouth at the thought of Steven and I had to swallow it down. He was still alive, I knew that, but by God if I caught his scent I would hunt him down and tear his throat out. The growling sound started again and I let it; it kept my mind on the task at hand. Worse case scenario the Ihis would find the key, find the motel and eventually find me if I was stupid enough to still be there by tomorrow. What I had to do was get to my motel and get the hell out of there as soon as possible. Only problem was, where in the ever-loving-heck was my motel? In fact, where was I exactly?

I lifted my head to the sky and listened. Far off, I could hear a car fading into the distance with the sound of a truck rumbling along in its wake. It sounded kilometres away, but if I could track back to the main road I could find my way to the motel. A frothing warmth of voices could be heard even further off, humans, and I knew that was the town centre. I started jogging in that direction, stopping to sniff at intervals and see if I could pick up any scents familiar to my motel. I increased my speed and found my tongue drooping out the side of my mouth as I darted in and out of the forest. I threaded through the trees and the night. Animal noises would come to an abrupt silence as I passed.

Soon I smelled gasoline and bitumen. Once I caught sight of headlights through the trees, I stopped again and sniffed, long and deep. Pine. Amongst the cocktail of strange smells and noises pine stood out to me. My memory flagged a struggling cluster of pine trees the motel owner was trying to grow out the front. Tracking the scent, I made it back to the motel in quicker time than I'd thought possible and circled around it, trying to think of a way I could sneak into my room. Sneak. I was a huge, black wolf. There was no way I was sneaking anywhere. From the heavy sounds of their breathing, I could tell all the occupants were asleep, but what was to stop someone driving by and spotting me trying to 'sneak' into the building. And how exactly would I get into my room? Huff and puff until I blew the door in?

No. I would have to wait until I was human again and try. This thought brought on a whole new wave of panic as I contemplated when exactly I would become human again. Is it different for a first-time wolf? What if I stayed like this for a week, a month, sprinting through the New Zealand forests eating wild animals and losing all sense of my humanity? What if I wasn't strong enough to turn back? After all, I was entirely new at this.

No. I had to believe the wolfing-out was reliant on the full moon, which is why the Ihis had kept harping on about it. Turned out I was right. I'm not exactly sure how far away dawn was when I calmed myself enough to lie down with my legs curled up under me. It didn't feel like long. The last thing I remembered was grey on the horizon.

Now, I was awake, human and naked. Good thing I'd moved into the undergrowth closest to the motel's clothing line. I only had to scale a small wooden fence and a few metres of open space to make it to the hanging clothes. I used all my energy to make sure I didn't get a splinter somewhere really uncomfortable and then streaked to the line, snatching a light blue floral dress as I went. Leaning heavily against the rough brick of the motel, panting, I was concerned at how much that small act of physical exertion had cost me. Clumsily, I slid the dress over my head. It isn't easy to get your arms in the right sleeves when they're doing their best to register on the Richter scale. As I adjusted the dress, I looked up at the sky. The sun was far from rising, let alone making it over the horizon, so it still had to be early morning.

I pushed myself lightly from the wall and towards my room. It felt like I had webbed feet as I stumbled along the concrete floor towards door number six. It was locked, like I knew it would be, but I couldn't resist trying my luck anyway and I rattled the doorknob. I only meant to loosely give it a shake when I heard a metallic crunch and felt the door give. I jerked my hand back in shock and looked down at the knob hanging limp from its silver frame. Every fibre of my being was aching,

I felt terrible, and yet some part of my wolf strength must have remained. I pushed the door open in a daze, closed it behind me and drew the blinds.

Suddenly the enormity of the past twenty-four hours came crashing down and I dropped to my knees. Lowering my head into my hands, I let out a sob. I felt my long, damp hair spill over and down my wrists as I sobbed again.

A robotic beeping from across the room made me leap against the wall, pressing my back into the plaster. It was the bedside alarm clock going off at 6.30 a.m. like I'd programmed it to yesterday morning when I got up and went for my first run. Back when everything was normal. If the Ihis shifted back to human form around the same time I did then I estimated I only had an hour minimum before they found my motel key and fanged it over here. I had to be well and truly gone by then. Thankfully, I'd barely unpacked since I got here and I lunged across the room for my wallet. I threw it into my shoulder bag along with my sketchbook and pencils. I grabbed a pair of jeans, fresh underwear and the first jumper I saw before chucking everything else into my suitcase. The cab company said they could be there in twenty minutes and, as I hung up the in-room phone, I resolved to have myself waiting in the car park by then.

Looking in the bathroom mirror was an awakening of sorts. The oversized floral dress covered most of me, but it was my face that told the story. My hair clung to my skull like thick, wet, blue vines that flowed down past my shoulder blades.

My face was pale and for a half-Maori girl that was saying something. Dirt was smeared across my cheek and there was faint bruising on the left side of my mouth. A wound under my hairline stung. Dried blood was caking near a cut on my eyebrow and bags under my eyes told a tale no amount of make-up would cover. I tore myself away from my reflection and into a steaming shower. I could only give myself ten minutes to get clean. I savoured every second as I let shampoo and conditioner wash away some of the physical damage. I scrubbed myself until my skin was raw and then climbed out of the shower. Reaching for a towel, I was overcome with another wave of exhaustion and I had to steady myself on the towel rack.

Deep breaths, I said to myself, in and out, in and out. I wrapped the towel around me and walked out of the bathroom and threw my toiletries into the bag. I sensed something, no, someone, in the room and I whipped my head up in the direction of the presence. A man was standing in the darkest corner, leaning against the closed door. I had nothing to defend myself with and from the look on his face he knew it. I hurled the alarm clock at him and he ducked quicker than I'd seen any human move before. It shattered against the door and I made a move to back into the bathroom before I tripped over my own feet. I landed with a thud against the wall. Thankfully, my towel didn't slip and I clung to it like a lifeline. If I was going to die at least I wasn't going to die naked. I lay there, half-propped against the wall and panting.

I stared at the stranger. He made no move to come closer. He just stared at me with his hands deep within the pockets of a black coat. He wasn't an Ihi. That much was clear. But he was still a strange man in my motel room, uninvited, after the most terrifying night of my life. He was probably six foot two or so, and his light brown hair fell loosely around his face while the rest of it was tied into a small ponytail at the back. He had that kind of chiselled beauty Calvin Klein models are renowned for, but there was an imperfection in his face that numbed the handsomeness. He was the kind of man I would have thought hot under different circumstances. A defined jawline was highlighted by an extremely close shave and thoughtful green eyes stared at me from beneath a heavy brow. He was lean, not overly muscular, but I could tell the frame under his layers of clothing could do serious damage. And that's what I was worried about.

'You're not taking me back there,' I breathed.

Whatever he'd expected me to say, that wasn't it. I saw a look of surprise flash across his face.

'Back where?'

'To them, the Ihis. I don't know if they sent you to drag me back or kill me. The latter would be preferable so you may as well get it over with.' I tried to say this as bravely as I could. My wavering voice betrayed me.

He paused. 'I'm not here to kill you. And I'm not here on their behalf either.'

'Oh,' was all I said.

I waited for him to say something else, but he didn't.

'Well,' I said, slowly getting to my feet and reaching across the bed for my clothes. 'I suggest you get to some kind of point because I'm hankering to get dressed and the hell out of here before those psychos find me.'

'My name is Lorcan. I've been sent here on behalf of the Treize to determine your allegiances and whether you need the Custodians' assistance.'

I blinked. 'I have ... no ... id—'

I couldn't even form a proper sentence and my knees gave out on me. Again. Traitors. He made a move towards me and I held up a hand in protest.

'Don't. No closer.'

He froze mid-motion and stood there looking down at me. His jacket swung forward with the gesture and beneath it I could see something that made my pulse race. Weapons. What looked like a Bowie knife was strapped at his waist along with a gun and . . . was that a small sword?

'You're exhausted,' he started. 'That's to be expected. Considering it was your first change it's remarkable you're even still conscious.'

I snorted. 'Remarkable? You know what's remarkable? How about the fact I turned into a huge sodding werewolf last night? How about the fact I have an entire family I never knew about, a family that makes the Mansons look like the Brady Bunch? How about that the fact my mother *lied* to me for twenty-two years so she could hide her secret affair, letting me think that I was the product of rape because the truth was more horrific? How about the fact that after spending the better part of the past twenty-four hours being beaten, locked up, nearly molested and hunted by those animals, you come through my door talking a bunch of crap I have absolutely no understanding of? And is that a bloody sword?'

I realised my voice had risen and that I was ranting at the man from my crumpled position on the floor.

'Listen,' he said. 'We had no idea about the specifics of your situation. You went to them willingly and that doesn't look good to us. The Askari in this area stay as safely away from the Ihis as they can while remaining close enough to gather in—'

'WHAT THE FUCK IS AN ASKARI?!'

Whatever traces of frustration might have been forming evaporated as soon as I shouted at him. He calmed immediately and I could almost see an icy mask snap into place.

'I can see you're upset.'

A *pfft* sound escaped my lips and he continued. 'You can't expect me to explain everything – your situation and what happened last night – in some cheap motel room when you can barely stay upright.'

'I'm perf—' I started, but he cut me off.

'You need to come back with me, not to the Ihis, but to somewhere you will be safe before tonight's full moon and we can both learn about what happened last night.'

'Dundee?'

'Sure.'

I glared at him. 'I don't know you,' I said.

'I know.'

'I don't understand most of what you've said.'

'You will.'

A loaded silence filled the room. I reached for my clothes and staggered to standing position once more.

'Fine. I'll come with you. I need to get out of this motel quickly.'

'Agreed.'

'Can you . . . give me some space to get dressed and get my shit together?'

He nodded. 'I'll check you out and get your name and details wiped from the register to cover our tracks. Of course they'll still pick up your scent at the room a—'

'OK, OK. I get it. Let's just hurry.'

The second he was out the door I was tugging on my clothes and tying my hair into a loose bun. I zipped up my suitcase, grabbed my handbag and peered out the window. I could see Lorcan striding across the car park to the reception desk with his back to me and I took my opportunity. As quickly and as I quietly as I could, I dashed out of the room, shut the door behind me and darted to the safety of a nearby brick corridor. I was exposed to pretty much every other view of the motel, except the view from the reception desk. The *ding* of the bell on the door as it slid open and he walked inside let me know he hadn't spotted me.

I hurried down the brick corridor until it opened out on to the back lawn of the motel. After jogging along the side of the building, I made it to the driveway entrance. The building shielded me from the reception desk and any rooms looking out on to the motel car park, which was most. From this angle I also had a clear view of the road. I waved madly when I spotted the cab nearing the motel.

As I jumped in and barked at the cabbie to take me to Rotorua International Airport, I had a second to think about the impeccable timing. Twisting around in my seat, I looked back through the windshield to see if Lorcan was sprinting madly after the car. Nothing. I smiled to myself as I thought of how pissed he would be when he came back to my motel room and discovered I was gone. Long gone.

It had been ridiculously stupid and naive of me to go to the Ihis and trust complete strangers. Fool me once and all that. There was no way I was blindly going off with yet another sinister stranger no matter how many official-sounding names he spat at me. This Lorcan and whoever he claimed to represent had an agenda, an agenda I didn't know, yet somehow factored into. He might have information about what was happening, but at the end of the day the only person I could trust was myself. He was also very obviously dangerous. Not in an Ihi way, but in a manner that made me sweat nervously and spin around to check again that he wasn't sprinting after the car like the T-1000. Right now the smartest course of action felt like getting out of New Zealand as soon as possible and back to Dundee before the next full moon which was … tonight. Shit. Steven had said last night was the *first* full moon. Lorcan too had referred to an impending full moon tonight. Whoever spouted that 'night of the full moon' nonsense was a *haver*. Exactly how many nights did I have to go through this? And how in the name of Zeus was I going to get back to Dundee before tonight's full moon?

I did some quick calculations in my head: New Zealand was almost a full twelve hours ahead of Scotland. It was still evening back home. The problem was that I had a good twenty-four hours' flying time ahead of me, not including a connecting flight from Heathrow to Edinburgh then a train back to Dundee. I wasn't going to make it home before my next transformation. My stomach knotted with tension and I felt beads of sweat begin to cling to my clothes. I think in my fear and determination to escape the Ihis I had somehow remained very conscious of who I was during my time as a wolf.

But I hadn't run into any people. I'd heard them, sure, far off in the distance or breathing safely inside their rooms. I feared what would happen if I came across someone when I wasn't motivated by a goal or, worse yet, there wasn't a physical barrier between us. I couldn't deny the way my pulse had quickened and my ears flattened when I heard the sounds of humans around Rotorua last night. It was hunger. I felt hunger and the undeniable building anticipation of a hunt. The recollection of how the deer tasted as I ripped and chewed its flesh was still too present in my mind. I didn't want to be around people when I felt that again, let alone confined inside a plane thousands of miles above the Earth. The reality was I couldn't get on a plane and fly home before I would shift into a ferocious beast.

Trapped. I was trapped on the smaller of New Zealand's two main islands. I was trapped without any friends or allies while two different groups hunted me. I was trapped by the moon, with every second ticking closer and closer to the moment when I would be consumed by pain and become a werewolf again.

Time was against me.

I took the cab to the airport as planned. Pulling the hood of my jumper up over my head, I walked quickly to the front of the taxi line and, ignoring the shouts of protest, jumped straight into the back seat of a waiting car.

'Drive,' I said. 'Quickly, please.'

Without a second word, my driver pulled away from the kerb and into the throng of airport traffic.

'Where to, miss?'

The man was severely overweight and I guessed in his late fifties. He had what looked like a prickly ginger beard and soft, kind eyes that peeked back at me in the rear-view mirror.

'I need . . .'

I ran through what I knew about this area, which wasn't much. I needed a plan and most importantly I needed to be further away than I was now. This wasn't a huge island and these were resourceful people, of that I had no doubt. I ran through everything I had studied about New Zealand and the North Island's geography in the lead-up to my trip. It hit me.

'Lake Taupo,' I said.

'Lake Taupo? Miss, that's over an hour away.'

'That's fine. It's a good fare for you.'

'That's a beaut fare, miss.'

'And I need to stop at a hardware store on the way, preferably somewhere out of town.'

'Yes, miss.'

As soon as we cleared Rotorua, I let out a sigh of relief and rested my head against the smooth leather of the seat. I could relax knowing none of the people after me were getting near for the next few hours. I dropped my head into my hands, letting out one brief but powerful sob of despair and frustration. I mentally slapped myself together with a deep inward breath and adjusted into a sitting position. Getting to Lake Taupo was only one part of the problem. Lorcan wasn't kidding about the unconscious part (not that he struck me as much of a kidder). The cab driver had to wake me up when we pulled into the car park of a hardware store half an hour outside of my destination. Looking at the endless line of aisles stacked to the ceiling of the massive warehouse, I had to fight to stay upright. Thankfully, what I needed wasn't too far from the entrance. I wheeled a trolley over to a wall of chains with dozens of variations in length and strength dangling before me.

'You right there?'

I turned around to see a pimply-faced teenager looking at me with anticipation. Glancing at his name badge, I looked back at my options.

'Taylor, I need six metres of the strongest chain links you've got here and half a dozen padlocks.'

The pubescent kid grinned at me as if I'd just flashed him my female person.

'No worries,' he said, nodding.

I watched his mop of blond hair bounce down the aisle before returning less than a minute later with an armful of impressive-looking padlocks.

'Are they waterproof?'

'The Johnson 3000's are just about everything proof,' he said, dumping them into the trolley. 'I'd feel safe locking up a Lamborghini with one of these, if that was possible.'

'Good.'

Thanks to Taylor's surprising efficiency, in less than fifteen minutes I was back in the cab with my unusual purchases. I just hoped the kid knew his hardware. All I wanted to do was curl up into a ball and fall back to sleep right there in the car. Yet I couldn't. There was too much to do. Aches and shakes had caused me to pick away most of the skin around my fingernails as a way to relieve tension. It wasn't working.

'Once you launch, just head straight towards Motutaiko Island. That's the big one. There's no other islands out there so that makes it pretty simple.'

'I can make it there by sunset?' I asked.

'You most certainly can, especially in calm conditions like these.'

I lifted my head up from the map laid out in front of me and frowned at the horizon. Ominous black clouds were rolling in over the smooth waters at Lake Taupo.

'Argh, don't let them fool you. Nothing but rain in those there greys. Look how calm it is, barely a breath of wind.'

I smiled at the elderly fisherman who manned the run-down Halletts Bay Bait and Tackle store. He returned a toothless grin at me and I did my best not to wince.

'Thanks,' I said. 'Truly, for all your help.'

I bent down to carry my small suitcase around the counter but he rushed to stop me.

'No, no, no. You leave that to Jimmy, that's what you're paying us for.'

'I don't mind, it's n—'

'Nonsense. You be on your way now.'

I thanked him again as I rolled up the map on the counter. Once out of the shop, I headed along a weathered board-walk before stepping off and down on to a bed of small stones that turned to coarse sand the closer I got to the water's edge. Lake Taupo was the largest lake in New Zealand and fed into several smaller rivers. It was created by a super volcanic eruption thousands and thousands of years ago and the result was a jaw-dropping sight: smooth, blue waters as far as the eye could see with mountains barely visible on the horizon as they framed the lake. The only thing that broke up the crystal-clear surface was a large, bulbous shape covered in a canopy of ferns so dark they almost appeared black: Motutaiko Island. It was uninhab-ited and, from the shores of Halletts Bay, where I asked the taxi to drop me, it was barely a few kilometres offshore. It was a calm day and I was grateful as I watched Jimmy, the store hand, offload a small silver dinghy from the back of a trailer. He dragged it to the water's edge and looked up in time to see me arrive.

'She's all set to go,' said the tanned man with tattoos deco-rating the length of his left arm. 'Still-as out there. Should be no trouble.'

I muttered my thanks and threw a small backpack of supplies into the boat. Jimmy added the chains and padlocks to my cargo without a word, which I appreciated. Barefoot, I didn't bother rolling up my jeans as I ploughed into the blue-green water. It was warmer than I was expecting.

'She has plenty of fuel to get you there and back. You sure you can drive this thing OK?'

'Not a problem,' I said, pushing off from the bottom of the lake floor and hopping into the dinghy in one swift movement.

I set the throttle to start position and kicked the outboard motor into gear on the first go. Looking back at Jimmy's surprised face, I gave him a nod and propelled away from the shore. The loud roar of the engine was a small comfort as the cool air whipped across my face. I took a deep breath and tasted the wind at the back of my throat. I felt like death, but my plan was simple: drive to Motutaiko Island and chain myself up there for the night. I'd paid to have my suitcase left at Halletts Bay Bait and Tackle where I had bought supplies and hired the dinghy. The staff hadn't thought it too unusual that someone wanted to go and spend a few nights on the small island. What they had been surprised at was my ability to drive a boat, something Kane had taken the time to teach Mari and I two summers ago. Man, was I grateful for the lessons now. I couldn't drive anything more complicated than your basic motorboat, but that was going to be more than enough to get me there, apparently.

'You could even paddle a kayak if you wanted,' Jimmy had suggested. I had rejected that idea immediately.

An icy water drop landed on my cheek followed by others, which quickly descended in succession. I loved the rain, always had.

I relished the sensation of being covered in it now as I was cloaked from the possibility of other boaties passing by. The poor visibility made it difficult to navigate, but, once I caught sight of the hulking mass of land a few hundred metres out, I started circling offshore until I spotted what I was looking for. Through the blanket of rain and what was now a thin mist forming across the water, I could see a collection of boulders and rocks on the southern side of the island. They were the lowest to the waterline I had seen, with smooth, steep rock faces staring me down on the other sides. I could navigate my way easily enough into the heavy vegetation from that point. Perfect.

My small victory was snatched from me as I lurched forward with a spasm that began in my chest and spread outwards. I screamed as I felt the muscles in my breasts and stomach tear and rip before reforming. Shit, it was starting. I didn't have as much time as I thought. I still had my hand pushed down on the throttle and realised too late that with the pain I had gripped it harder than I intended. Snapping my head up, I saw the rocks rushing to meet me a second before the dinghy hit at full speed. I was catapulted out of the boat and landed in a heap on the stones.

My arms went beyond aching with the impact. They felt more like gaping wounds attached to where my arms used to be. The rainwater running down my face was mixing with tears, of this I had no doubt. I rolled over on to my back for a moment, my chest heaving with the physical and emotional effort of the past series of events. Climbing on to all fours, I pulled myself up using the edge of the boat. The motor was silent and dangling forward at an angle that didn't look healthy. That was something I could worry about later.

I grabbed my bag of supplies and the chains, dragging them behind me and into the thick treeline. I made my way deeper into the bush. Once I was far enough in, I spotted a tree that looked sturdy. Bending down, I untied the bag containing the padlocks and yanked the chains forward to form a pile at my feet. Inside a tacky waterproof backpack, I had stuffed a change of clothes, four towels, a dozen water bottles, my passport, wallet and a collection of junk food. It wasn't much. I figured it was enough to get me through the next two days if I was lucky. I grabbed one of the water bottles and drained its contents before throwing the bag under the palms of a low-lying plant. I was drenched, but I tore off my hoodie and jeans anyway, not wanting to ruin good clothes when I didn't need to. I started unwinding the chain around my body as I made my way over to the tree. I fought exhaustion as I laced the chain around the base of the tree and over me, again and again, until I was satisfied it would hold.

It was a tedious process as I began using the locks to secure myself, via the chain, to the tree. I had barely clicked the last lock in place when the second bone-crunching tremor of transformation ran through me. If possible, I thought it more painful than last night. Or maybe I had no energy left to fight it. I had a scant understanding of what was happening to me. I had no idea what I was capable of, only that I became an inhuman, humongous beast once the full moon rose.

A werewolf. I became a werewolf.

If there was one thing horror films had taught me in my formative years, it was that werewolves killed people like Jason Voorhees did campers. I just prayed the weather stayed bad enough to keep fishermen or anyone else away. My musings were interrupted by another wave of pain. My body contorted and I screamed, the blood-curdling type. I had but a second to wonder if I could ever keep myself safe from myself. It was a fleeting thought, lost quickly to the white noise of relentless agony.

Chapter 7

Numb. I was comfortably and utterly numb in the never-ending darkness of my unconscious. Every now and then this bliss would be punctured by a shard of pain, but it would disappear eventually and I would return to swimming in blackness. I couldn't remember how I'd got here or why it was better than the state I'd come from, I just knew that it was. A sensation, an impulse, an urge: they were all tourists in the vacation of my numbness. There were flashes of a face, a man's face. For a second, I felt coarse fragments running over my body. Sometimes, I heard murmuring getting louder and louder until I was close to the surface. But it all faded away.

Someone was shaking me, no, not someone, something. It was shaking me continuously, back and forth, sliding me this way and that. A scratchy material was covering my body, teasing me awake. And then came the pain. Like a puzzle being put back together piece-by-teeth-grinding-piece the pain brought me to. I barely had the will to open my eyes, but when I did I saw I was lying in the back seat of someone's car. The shadowy figure at the wheel turned around and said something to me before looking back to the road. I couldn't understand what they said but I hoped they could understand me.

'Kill—' my voice was a raspy phantom of its former self and I fought to get the next crucial word out '—me.'

They heard. I'm sure whoever was driving heard because next came the screech of brakes and I was jerked forward into the black once more. Hello numbness, my old friend.

'Tom? Tom, can you hear me?'

'It's Tommi.'

'Right now it's unconscious so I shall call it Tom, Dick or Harry until it's verbally able to refute me,' snapped the female reply.

I heard a deep sigh and murmuring as someone moved further away from me. My mouth was dry and my throat raw as I tried to move my lips to talk.

'Ah, we have a live one,' said the voice.

I swallowed and blinked open my eyes. Shades of tan and cream decorated the interior of an expensive hotel room. It looked classically modern with small, round windows positioned down the length of it. I was lying in a thin bed to the right of the room, propped up on thick white pillows that matched the thick white sheets. It was around this point I realised I was naked. Again.

The sheets were pulled up almost to my neck but I felt self-conscious nonetheless and made a move to pull them higher. My arm snagged on something, a clear cord that was running from a needle in my hand and up to a drip. I reached to yank out the IV line. My hand was smacked back by a stern-looking Asian woman sitting near me on the edge of the bed.

'Oh no you don't,' she said, softly grabbing my arm and placing it on the mattress.

'I'm naked,' I croaked.

'Yanking your IV out isn't going to change that now is it?' Defeated, I agreed.

'Good. Once you get some juice back in you and recover some of your strength then we'll try for clothes. OK?'

I nodded. Even that slight movement of my head hurt and I winced.

'My name's Doctor Sue Kikuchi.'

'Hi.'

'I'm going to get you some water from just over there so you won't have any time to try for that IV line again while my back is turned. OK?'

I silently agreed.

'Good.'

Dr Kikuchi got up from the bed and brought me back a glass of water.

'I'm going to bring it to your lips. Slow sips now.'

I sipped, slowly, and Dr Kikuchi gave me a few moments rest before giving me more. It was an eternity before I finished the glass. A movement in my periphery drew my gaze to the corner of the room where a man had started towards us. Lorcan.

I tensed and tried to jump out of the bed. Dr Kikuchi was on me and, with a surprising show of strength, she forced me back down.

'Settle now, settle! He's not here to hurt you. He brought you to me, settle.'

I stilled, physically at least. He continued towards us and I pushed myself into the pillows, ignoring the sharp pain coming from my back and legs. Dr Kikuchi snapped her attention to him.

'Back up, will you.'

'For God's sake, I'm not going to hurt her,' he said, annoyed.

'I know that. Yet clearly your presence is alarming enough and in case you haven't noticed I've been trying to calm and heal her rather quickly.'

'Fine.'

Dr Kikuchi held his eyes for a moment with a steely gaze.

'Good,' she said, before returning to me. 'I don't think you're ready to eat anything. I have a bit of a concoction you should be able to swallow down. Think of it as soup, except with more purpose.'

She brought a steaming mug of something towards my face. It smelled delicious. I sipped slowly from the straw and tasted a meaty liquid. It was over all too quickly and Dr Kikuchi took to checking my wounds, which required an extensive once-over of my body. Lorcan disappeared out of the end of the rectangular room for this part and returned after Dr Kikuchi yelled I was decent. She'd helped me into an oversized basketball jersey, one of her wife's apparently – 'she loves the stupid sport' – and settled me back into the bed. Lorcan re-entered my line of sight and pulled a chair up to beside the bed.

'I need to speak to her now,' he said, as he folded into the chair.

'Good,' said Dr Kikuchi, turning to him. 'And, if you don't mind, I'd like to sit just over there so Tommi can see me and I can provide some worldly advice when needed.'

He smiled slightly and nodded. As she plopped herself on a caramel reclining chair directly parallel to me, Lorcan came closer.

'Tommi, I have a lot to tell you.'

'Were you driving?' I asked.

He looked at me carefully. 'Yes.'

'Then you should have done it.'

'Done what?' asked Dr Kikuchi from her position.

I was almost ashamed to say it now. Turned out I didn't have to.

In a quiet voice weighted with a sadness I didn't understand, Lorcan replied: 'Killed her.'

The room was silent. I wasn't sure if it was my imagination or whether I could actually hear their heartbeats.

'It's not uncommon,' Lorcan said, interrupting my thoughts. 'Werewolf suicide rates are alarmingly high, especially within the first year of transformation.'

He said this matter-of-factly, making it sound like statistics pulled from a supernatural census.

'Werewolf.' I rolled the word over my tongue.

'Yes,' he said, looking at me with an unflinching gaze. 'This is what you are, Tommi.'

'Now,' I said. 'I wasn't always, though. I'm pretty sure I would have noticed if I started sprouting fur and eating villagers once a month.'

Lorcan chuckled, an act that surprised me almost as much as being repeatedly told I was a werewolf.

'Actually,' he said, 'you were. Always. It's merely that the wolf had never been awoken in you. Your mother took you far away from the Ihis before you were even born. No one on her side of the family has the gene and the werewolf presence isn't what it once was in Scotland, especially in Dundee. Imagine that your werewolf side is highly flammable, like a match in a room full of flames. But if you take the match away from the inferno and place it in the ocean the odds of it igniting are virtually gone.'

'Virtually?'

'Have bad things ever happened when you were angry, Tommi? Have you ever had uncontrollable outbursts of rage or felt a sudden need to run and never stop?'

Yes. I'd been experiencing that my whole life. In fact, those outbursts had somewhat defined me. Those who loved me called me passionate. Others ... let's just say I'd heard the term 'hard-ass bitch' volleyed around. The whole reason I'd got into Muay Thai in the first place was that I kept getting into fights at school. The guidance counsellor had recommended to my mum that she enrol me in karate classes or a 'very physical sport' as an outlet for my aggression. I realised I'd been quiet too long and looked up to find Lorcan studying me closely.

'Those times you're thinking about, that was your wolf trying to surface.'

'So ... the Ihis brought it out?'

'In part,' piped up Dr Kikuchi. I'd forgotten she was even there. 'Being so close to the dominant part of your bloodline brought it out. Extreme anger, fear or pain are also triggers. Those combined with the proximity of the Ihis and the full moon ...' She trailed off.

'With or without them you would have shifted eventually. No matter how isolated you were, you cannot fight the gene. In fact, it's quite extraordinary you haven't transformed before. How are old are you, twenty?'

'I'm twenty-two.'

'Interesting. I've never heard of anyone over eighteen in my lifetime being able to hold off the shift. It would have been due to happen any day for you.'

'They performed a ritual.'

'Ha,' said Dr Kikuchi. 'What did they do? Sprinkle some herbs on you and chant a few incantations?'

'They sprinkled something on me. I couldn't tell what they said because it was in Maori. I only understand a few words. I don't think it was a spell.'

'She's joking,' Lorcan said. 'Tommi, I need you to tell me everything about what happened with you and the Ihis.'

I gulped.

'Would bullet points do? Or do you need excruciating detail?'

His voice softened when he said: 'It's extremely important you tell me everything.'

I looked over at Dr Kikuchi and she nodded solemnly. So I told the whole sordid tale, from Mari and my investigations to my foolish arrival at their house. I gave them the details of my mother's secrets and everything she'd had me believe. Keeping my eyes fixed firmly on the unusually low ceiling, I told them every word said, where I landed every blow and vice versa. I even managed to keep my voice neutral as I spoke about the sexual assault at the hands of my half-brother. By the time I got to the end, I was mildly surprised to find silent tears running down my cheeks. Wiping them away seemed cowardly. I left them. A silence stretched through the room and I wanted desperately to break it. I didn't want to look at either of their faces, these two strange people I had just met. I wanted to look anywhere but at their faces.

'On a scale of one to Hulk, how mad were you when I bailed?' I asked Lorcan as I turned to look out the window. I frowned. It was an incredibly cloudy day outsi—Oh. My God.

'WE'RE IN THE SKY!' I screamed, bolting upright in bed.

Desperately, I glanced around what I had thought to be a room and recognised what it really was. A plane. It was the interior of a plane. In my pain and drug-addled state I'd failed to associate the circular windows with the only place you find them: on commercial aircrafts. They ran down the length of both sides of the plane, which was considerably smaller than anything I had flown in before. There were half a dozen seats gratuitously spread about the aircraft and another bed identical to mine at the front.

'Holy shit,' I said, finally tuning into the steady thrum of the powerful engines.

It was a private plane and those only came in one variety: wealthy.

'Er, yes, I guess we should have mentioned that,' said Dr Kikuchi.

'Where the hell are you taking me?' I couldn't keep the alarm out of my voice.

'Home,' said Lorcan. 'Dundee.'

I gaped at him.

'That's . . . the flight's too long. I'll never make it back before the next transformation and—' The realisation hit me. 'You need to get off the plane! Now! You can't be trapped on here with me when I shift, it—'

Lorcan gently grabbed my shoulder and pushed me back down on to the bed. 'This is a private plane belonging to the Treize. Not only is it fitted out for situations like these, it also flies like a demon. See over there.'

He nodded behind me to a solid metal door I hadn't seen before. I squirmed around in the bed to get a full look at it.

'Aye.'

'That's a cell strong enough to hold any full-grown were-wolf. It's more than enough to hold you if we need it, which we won't. We'll touch down in Dundee exactly one hour before sunset,' he said, glancing at his watch. 'I have measures in place that will see you as far away from harming people as physically possible.'

Lorcan looked at me for a moment before reaching into his pocket and pulling out an iPad. 'Excuse me.' With that he got up and left.

'Jeez,' was all I said.

'It's not you,' said Dr Kikuchi. 'The Ihis are a big priority and there are people who are going to want to know what happened as soon as possible.'

'He's not exactly Mr Smiley. Or Mr In-Depth Explainy.'

'Not for a while,' she said, adjusting the sheets around me.

'Did you find me on the island?'

'Me? No, no, I hate the water. Lorcan tracked you down and found you as you were shifting back this morning. Said you were out of your mind with pain, dehydration and whatnot. He brought you to me straight away because I'm a specialist in this type of thing.'

'A werewolf specialist?'

'Among other things. I'm a Paranormal Practitioner. I operate within the standard hospital system usually, except I have a special set of skills and client base.'

She'd lost me at 'other things'. What other things could there be? How much more didn't I know besides, heck, everything?

'Now, dear, I've given you quite a bit of morphine but your werewolf metabolism is burning it off very quickly. Is it all right if I give you some more? You're conscious now so it seems prudent to ask your permission.'

On schedule, a sudden yet somewhat muted spasm of pain rolled through me almost as if it was saying, Hey, remember me? I've made your life hell for the past few days, kid.

'Doc, whether it's morphine or heroin – hit me with all you got.'

After fiddling with my IV, Dr Kikuchi gave me more water to drink and, by the last sip, I could already feel myself being pulled under.

The tinny sound of rain hitting a metal roof and jazz music playing softly in the background was what I awoke to. I was lying in the back seat of a car and Lorcan was at the wheel. No, not a car, a jet boat. I was sprawled across a long, leather seat inside the enclosed cabin of a high-powered jet boat. We were pounding across the ocean at a rapid rate.

'Hey,' I growled.

'Hey,' he said without turning around.

'For future reference, waking up in the back seat of a boat with you driving me into the abyss is not OK.'

He looked out the window and up at the sky. It was overcast so it was difficult to tell exactly what time of day it was. There were enough shadows to say it was late afternoon.

'Oh.'

'I couldn't wait until you woke up. I needed to move you somewhere safe before the next transformation.'

I slumped against the seat at the thought of the next transformation and having to go through that torture for a third time.

'You haven't got a smoke, have you?'

'No,' he replied with a finality that communicated his thoughts on smoking.

'Christ.'

'There's only one more. Then you have a month to learn and better prepare for the next phase of the moon.'

'Really, a whole month? Gee, that seems like forever between the spates of excruciating physical pain. This will be a breeze.' My voice dripped with sarcasm like honey off a spoon.

He said nothing.

'So there're three nights.'

Lorcan looked back at me with a question on his face.

'I was wondering how many there would be,' I explained. 'It's not like the movies is it, where there's just one night of the full moon?'

'No.'

'Figured. Usually the moon is full for a few nights in a row, not just the one. I guess three is better than four or five.'

'Technically, the moon we see is never full. It's a common misconception. The scientific definition of a full moon lasts for only a second, literally one moment in time when it's exactly opposite the sun. That happened last night.'

I was slightly puzzled by this.

'What we on Earth perceive as a full moon can last anywhere from two to five days a month. That instant when the moon is perfectly full occurred towards three a.m. last night. The pull is strong enough on either side of that to affect werewolf transformation, hence the three days.'

Everything that happened in that past few days had me *feart*. Yet it was this – what I didn't know about the moon and the Ihis and my hairy condition – that had me scared the most. There was too much to process.

'Where are you taking me?'

'Your idea about the island was a good one, albeit poorly executed. I'm stealing it.'

Island? There weren't any islands off the coast of Dundee. There were a few closer within the River Tay, but I could tell we were well out through the seaway now. The nearest islands would be south, past St Andrews way. Unless . . .

I hunched down and peered out through the clear glass at the front of the boat. There, like a lone soldier standing on an open battlefield, sat Bell Rock Lighthouse.

If you had never seen it before it was a bizarre sight. An endless expanse of grey sea spanned on either side of it, while the structure sat abruptly in the centre of it all. It seemed like an impossible feat of engineering, to have a lighthouse this far out – some twelve nautical miles – without a single land structure supporting it. It wasn't until you got closer that you saw black rocks jutting out at the base. At high tide you couldn't see them at all, it merely looked like a pillar of concrete floating off the Scottish coast. However that's what Bell Rock Lighthouse had been built on: a deadly hidden bed of jagged rocks, which had claimed many a ship in their time. Every local knew the tale of Bell Rock. Built in the early 1800s, it was one of the first lighthouses ever constructed and was an integral beacon during both World Wars. It was de-manned in the eighties and since then a handful of locals had claimed it was haunted.

'It's isolated and secure. Perfect for our purposes,' said Lorcan, following my gaze.

'Better than Lake Taupo, I suppose.'

'Yes, but that was quite inventive.'

I grumbled.

Half an hour later, Lorcan and I were negotiating our way over the sharp, wet rocks of Bell Rock Lighthouse. He had got us as close to the building as he could considering the treacherous reef surrounding it. We had moored the boat less than twenty-five metres from our destination and had to take an IRB (inflatable rescue boat) the rest of the way. I had gained some strength from Dr Kikuchi's care and the rest I'd had on the plane, but I was still hurting. My hands wouldn't stop shaking and my limbs weren't as responsive to my commands as they usually were. I was aching all over. The cuts and scrapes and minor broken bones that I had received from my time with the Ihis had mostly healed, miraculously. A werewolf trait, I was told. My right leg spasmed as I was balancing on the last rock before reaching the front stoop of the lighthouse and I lurched downwards.

Lorcan grabbed me just as I was about to land face first.

'Thanks,' I said, pulling myself up with his help. The guy had crazy-fast reflexes.

'We're almost there.'

I nodded. This gave me little comfort as 'almost there' meant my third night of transition was very close. After stumbling the last steps, we came to a stop at a massive black door that marked the only entrance and exit to the lighthouse. A heavy chain, thick with green moss, was linked around the door handle and through a solid latch built into the outer wall of the lighthouse. Lorcan weighed the chain in his hand thoughtfully. With one sudden movement, he yanked it with all his strength. The links broke apart instantly and the chain fell to the wet ground like a discarded snake.

'Old chain,' he muttered, pushing the door with the front of his body.

It took two good heaves before it finally budged and we were inside Bell Rock Lighthouse. Gloomy didn't quite cover it. Everything seemed damp. From the dripping walls to puddles littering the floor, it was clear the old building wasn't doing a very good job of keeping the elements out. Then again, no one had lived here in years. You never had to worry about upkeep if the place was abandoned. The interior was almost pitch black except for pale light coming from the windows at the top of the 35-metre building. I craned my neck to follow the path of an immense spiral staircase that led up, up and into the unknown.

'There are rooms up there?'

'From when it used to be manned,' replied Lorcan.

I was somewhat amazed at the thought of anyone living here. Alone. Isolated.

'There's a dry patch over there,' said Lorcan, handing me a folded-up mattress. 'This is for after the change.'

I took it without a word and walked over to the slightly less miserable spot of ground he had pointed out. I laid it down in the far corner and sat on it. Lorcan disappeared out the doorway and, from the soft splashing, I guessed he was retrieving something from the boat. Looking around the circular base of the lighthouse, I couldn't help but feel an overwhelming sense of despair. Hurriedly, I wiped whatever tears had been forming at the corner of my eyes when Lorcan returned, arms heavy with supplies.

'So . . . I'm going to wolf out in here?'

'Yes,' he said, bluntly.

'And what are you going to do?'

'I'll be right outside.'

'The whole time?'

'The whole time.'

'Will this place be strong enough to hold me?'

Lorcan patted the wall closest to him and looked at it casually. 'These walls are made of granite, two metres thick.

A rhinoceros wouldn't be able to get through them. This may have been built over two centuries ago, but it's impenetrable.'

'I was thinking more about the door.' I nodded at the one weakness.

'The door's strong enough to hold for tonight,' he said. 'I have reinforced steel chains and new anchors to secure to the outside wall. You won't be getting out.'

I took his word for it.

'And,' he continued, 'It's the third night of your first transformation sequence. You will be at your weakest.'

Hmph. I certainly felt it.

'Here,' he said, walking over and handing me a black towel.

I looked at him, confused.

'For you to get changed behind.'

'Oh. Thanks. I'm getting sick of people I don't know seeing me naked.'

'I didn't see . . . much.'

'Much?' I asked, my voice rising unbelievably high.

He met my expression and held it, the corner of his mouth turning up. My mind was racing through all the ways I would prefer for someone who looked like *him* to see me naked for the first time. It's funny, unconscious and chained to a tree was most definitely not one of them. I felt my face burning and, after a long moment, he finally turned away to open up a fold-out chair. He reached into the bag once more, then tossed a bottle of water and a white package at me. I caught them both and, after guzzling some water, I peered at the bundle with curiosity. It was a bread roll.

'You should eat that. It will make you less agitated when you're in wolf form.'

I unfolded the wrapping, bit into it and wrinkled my nose. 'Jeez, is the meat of every animal in existence in this?' I lifted a piece of beef to explore the carnivorous buffet beneath.

Lorcan sighed. 'Just eat the roll and I'll start explaining the rest to you quickly.'

I shrugged and took another bite. 'Explain away.'

'Tommi, you've come into a world you never knew existed.' He paused for dramatic effect.

'Obvious, but continue,' I muttered.

'This world, the supernatural world, has always been here. It moves in and around the everyday life of humans. There never used to be a structure for it until a few decades before the first Crusades.'

I started counting back in my head. 'Like . . . the 1000s? I don't even know the right abbreviation for that. Back in the 1000s? The thousies?'

'I don't think there is an abbreviation for that century but yes.'

I took another bite.

'For over a thousand years, the supernatural community has been governed by the Treize: a body of thirteen elders with different abilities and interests. The supers, ah, supernatural community, has for the most part never wanted to become an accepted part of human society. Most of them are happily integrated into it anyway. Others live on the outskirts or in isolation. Maintaining secrecy or a silent order has never been a concern of the Treize. Their main aim is to maintain peace amongst our own kind. One of the defining elements of our character is infighting: infighting amongst the various sub-species and even infighting within specific species.'

'Like werewolf pack versus werewolf pack?'

'Yes, especially werewolf packs. In fact, with werewolves being the most widespread species amongst the supers, most of the problems stem from them.'

I paused mid-chew at this last piece of information. Magnificent, I thought, I've been born into the animalistic brawlers.

'The Treize are guided in part by the Three – I'll come to them later. There are two main bodies who operate under the Treize: the Praetorian Guard and Custodians.'

He had picked up a stick and was drawing some sort of umbrella formation for me in the grime, pointing to specific parts to explain the supernatural hierarchy as he got to it.

'The "P" one sounds ominous.'

Lorcan gave a half-smile. 'Basically, they're enforcers: an elite legion of warriors selected to carry out the orders of the Treize. The Custodians, on the other hand, are, say, counsellors. Maybe guardians is a better word.'

'Aren't the other ones called P-something guardians?'

'Praetorian Guard,' Lorcan corrected. 'And there's quite a difference between a Guard and guardians.'

'What are you?'

'I'm a Custodian. In fact, I'm your allocated Custodian.'

'You're my guardian-slash-counsellor?'

'As of this morning, yes. When tonight is over and you've returned to human form, I'll work with you on how to control your wolf. I'll teach you werewolf customs, how to defend yourself and the best ways to utilise your abilities. I'll also help you come to terms with . . . this,' he said, gesturing around him.

I'd finished my roll a while ago. Thankfully, there wasn't any food still in my mouth as it hung open with the information-bomb Lorcan had dropped on me.

'How long?' I whispered.

'What?'

'How long do you stay to teach me all of that?'

'As long as it takes.'

I swallowed even though I had no food left to digest. Almost as a way to distract myself, I asked, 'Who are the Askari?'

'You remember,' he said, leaning back on the chair.

'Unfortunately, I've been remembering every single freakin' detail since the whole ordeal started.'

'What about when you're a wolf?'

'Yup, when I'm a wolf, when I'm a woman, when I'm a werewolf woman. Everything's seared right in there.' I tapped my skull for emphasis.

'Interesting . . .' He looked thoughtful.

'What? What part?'

He shook his head slightly. 'Nothing. We'll talk about it later when we have more time. Askari are based all over the world and in larger numbers where there are supernatural hot spots. They're not particularly skilled fighters, although some of them are. Mostly they're researchers and a way for the Treize to keep informed about what's happening in places they can't b—'

I cut him off with a short, piercing scream and curled over myself. It was happening again, the third transformation. The final night. The pain subsided quickly but I knew it would be back. And soon. I dragged myself up from the mattress and tried to pick up the towel, but I couldn't keep my hands steady.

Stuff it, I thought. I glanced at Lorcan and he received my message, stepping outside of the lighthouse's interior. He had lent me a pair of grey tracksuit pants to put on and I slid them down now. Well, basically I undid the knot at my waist and they dropped off. They made MC Hammer pants look tight.

'You don't have to—' he called from outside.

'No, no, it's cool. There's no point ruining good clothes. Plus,' I said, folding the basketball jersey on top and hurling both garments through the open doorway, 'I think Dr Kikuchi's wife would miss ol' Kobe's shirt.'

Lorcan picked the clothes up from their crumpled pile and I pressed my hands against the wall as I was rocked by another wave of pain. I didn't scream this time. Bonus points for me. It's all in the little victories, I said to myself, as I dropped to all fours and heard the unmistakable crack of my bones.

'See you on the other side,' came Lorcan's quiet voice and I heard the door shut behind me.

Surrounded in complete darkness, my high-pitched scream echoed over and over as I contorted in my own private prison and the transformation took hold.

Chapter 8

It was nearly 7 a.m. when I slipped the key into my door and quietly stepped into the apartment. Mari wasn't awake yet. Good. I tiptoed past her room and towards mine at the end of the hall. Soundlessly, I shut the door and pulled the blinds. What I really wanted to do was have a shower but I was afraid the noise would wake her. Also me passing out in the shower would freak her out. I collapsed on the bed, pulling one side of the blanket over me in the process.

My body ached, my head ached, my heart ached. I had barely a few seconds to wallow in self-pity before sleep took me.

Rolling over warm and sleepy several hours later, I tugged a T-shirt off the screen of my alarm clock. Holy shit, it was 4 p.m.! I'd slept the entire day and – not saying I didn't deserve it – but the last time that happened was after a very heavy day and night of drinking. I edged my way to the side of the bed, trying to move slowly and not aggravate the throbbing pain throughout most of my body. The apartment was dead quiet and I let the calming sound of nothingness wash over me for a moment. Mari wouldn't be home for a few hours. Then I'd have to tell her about my trip (the fictional version of events).

I grabbed my De La Soul CD and headed for the bathroom. Turning the volume up to full, I let the throbbing bass lines and steaming hot water work me over. It's amazing how a shower can instantly make you feel better. Wrapped in a towel, I sat on the couch in our lounge and combed through the knots in my hair.

Although the last time it was modern was the seventies, I truly loved this apartment. It wasn't much of a view. Looking out the glass doors, the most you could see were the rooftops of other buildings and activity on the street below. I couldn't count how many afternoons we had all spent on that balcony watching the world go by. Good didn't even begin to cover how it felt to be home.

Grabbing an apple from our fruit bowl, I read a note Mari had left on the kitchen bench saying she had tried my phone and was dying to catch up when she finished work at 8 p.m. Usually seeing Mari would excite me, but the thought of having to tell her such a colossal series of lies was exhausting. Brooding on this, I bit into the apple and went to my room. With my favourite pair of ripped jeans and a navy blue knitted sweater on, I started unpacking my stuff. Thankfully, I hadn't taken many clothes (it always seemed to be the toiletries that took up the most room anyway).

Dr Kikuchi said it had only been a matter of time before my wolf fully manifested. I guess I should be grateful it happened out in the wilds of New Zealand instead of while I was sleeping here in my apartment. I felt like I had control of myself, but did that count as having control of my werewolf? To what extent could I 'lose' control? A shudder ran through me at what could have happened if I'd transformed into a werewolf with Mari and Kane inside. What if Joss had been staying over? Or Poc? But that hadn't happened. I would learn of a way to master this utterly unbelievable side of me so that I could feel confident in keeping those around me safe from, well, me.

I wasn't alone. I had Lorcan and all the frosty wisdom he could impart for as long as I needed it. There was practically a whole supernatural governing body with a millennium of resources and experience at my disposal. And then there were the Ihis. A cold, dark thing dropped in my stomach when I thought of them. How many half-brothers and -sisters did I actually have? How long until they found me? There had been a distinctly cultish vibe to the way they had delighted at the thought of a new family member. It wasn't an emotional response. It was like an army relishing the opportunity to increase their numbers.

Maybe that's what all packs were like. They had wanted me to become one of them. I'd seen the hope in both Simon's and James's eyes. I'd felt Steven's incestuous desire.

Suddenly, I needed a task and I looked at my reflection in the full-length mirror. My hair. The usually vibrant colour had faded to a muted pastel blue and I made for my stash of permanent hair dye in the bathroom. My preferred shade was called Brutal Blue and in light of recent events I tried not to read too much into that. Once it was lathered in, I finished the rest of my unpacking until I felt the faint tingling on my scalp that meant it was time to rinse. I towelled my hair with more force than I should have, trying desperately to think of anything but Steven. Plugging in the hairdryer, I kept trying to think of other topics to keep my mind occupied. I had plenty to choose from, but the harder I tried the less successful I was. I shut off the hairdryer abruptly.

I sighed. Placing my hands on either side of the basin, I stared down into the sinkhole, wondering if that's where I would end up eventually. My ears pricked at a sound on the stairwell outside. I could hear each footstep, each breath, and even the sound of material as it rubbed with the friction of movement. This werewolf-hearing thing had its perks. The movement stopped at the front door and I heard a light knock. I'm not sure if it was because I had just been thinking about the Ihis, about Steven, but my heart was racing. I tiptoed to the door and peered through the eyehole. Lorcan.

I opened the door. 'Hi.'

'You look relieved. Who did you think it was?'

'Uh, no one,' I spluttered. 'Not ready to face Mari yet, I think.'

'Oh.' From the look on his face I wasn't sure he believed me.

In the boat followed by the car trip back from Bell Rock Lighthouse, he had grilled me about the people in my life – friends, family, flatmates, boyfriends, job etcetera. Despite battling the come-down of being locked inside a dank light-house for the night, I had given him a debrief on everything. I realised Lorcan was still standing at my front door looking vaguely uncomfortable and the time to invite him in was a few minutes ago.

'Come in.'

He stepped over the threshold and looked around. It was petty of me, I know, but I enjoyed seeing him a little awkward and in a situation he wasn't completely in control of. I smiled. I shut the door behind me and the noise turned him around.

'This is where you live,' he said, more as a statement to himself than anything else.

I nodded. 'You want anything? Water? Food?'

'Water, please.'

His attention had been drawn to a large canvas hanging on the wall. It was one of mine. I'd wanted to hang a Molly Crabapple print instead, but Mari had demanded my painting. I slid the glass of water across the bench and grabbed another apple for myself.

'Thanks,' said Lorcan, not looking away from the painting and picking up the glass.

I watched him staring at it. Contemporary art was my favourite genre, closely followed by pop and street. The painting was a fiddling amateur's homage to all, mixing graffiti lettering and populist images with big splashes of colour and thick textures of paint. It was a touch of everything, no skill required. Mari said the reason she loved it was because it looked like, and I quote, 'A rainbow cartoon apocalypse.'

'You did this?'

'Guilty.'

He made a *hmmm* sound before turning to me.

'How long until your flatmate comes home?'

'She finishes work at eight so she'll be here around eight-thirtyish. Her boyfriend might come earlier.'

'Good. We need to make plans.'

'I think I'm going to need a bevvy for this,' I said and reached back into the fridge for a beer.

I wiggled the bottle at him. 'You want?'

'No.'

I shrugged and popped the top.

He opened the glass door to the balcony and I followed him out. We had a collection of chairs scattered out there as well as a small table, barbecue, pot plants and a tattered couch we had found on the side of the road. Dusk was still a few hours away yet but it was chilly enough for me to grab a blanket. Lorcan settled into a wooden fold-out chair and I eased on to the couch. I sipped my beer and welcomed the comforting taste as it flowed down my throat. Lorcan, who had been looking towards the street, glanced at me.

'How much do you remember once you transformed?'

'I told you last night, everything.'

'Yes, but are you remembering your time as a wolf – the instincts, the scents, the thrill of the hunt?'

'That's not how I would describe it. It's . . . more. I feel like myself trapped in a wolf's body. I'm still me, I just have those added things.'

'Did you have this level of awareness from the first night?'

'Pretty much. I got distracted playing with my claws and breaking trees, but I was completely aware. Still Tommi. I never forgot the Ihis were on my tail, literally, and once I worked out how to do a few things I traced the scent of the pine trees out the front of my motel back there and hung around the bushes at the rear entrance until I shifted back.'

'You didn't attack anyone? Hunt anyone?'

'No. Well—'

'What?' he asked, seeming alarmed.

'I ate a deer.'

'Huh.'

I took another sip of my beer as I watched Lorcan roll this information over in his mind.

'There are a lot of things I need to explain to you, most of which I think are best incorporated into your training,' he started. 'You're at a disadvantage because you've chosen to live outside your blood pack.'

'Damn straight,' I muttered.

'*Kahuatairingi.*'

'Bless you.'

'That's Maori for lone wolf.'

'Oh.'

'Your histories, the histories of our world, there's too much to even begin to tell you. I'll try to relay the important information, starting with your recall. For most werewolves it takes years to develop a memory of what happens when they shift, to establish their consciousness in wolf form. What might take a decade for some to master others never develop and they lose themselves entirely during the nights of full moon. You have total recall and from your first transformation no less. That's the sign of a powerful werewolf, Tommi.'

I had to make a double grab for my beer as it slipped from my hands. I caught it moments before it hit the ground. I took a big swig and placed it at the foot of the couch. My heart was racing again as I followed the flight of a sparrow into a nearby tree with my eyes. Lorcan was waiting for me, I could tell. He was waiting to see if I could handle more.

'Go on,' I breathed.

'It's not an unheard of skill. The completeness of your recollections on the first transformation is a trait of a powerful werewolf. It's something that's been evident amongst the most powerful werewolves in history like Niciros, St Christoper, the Laignach Faelad. On its own it's endlessly useful because it means you can have definitive control over your actions in wolf form. Your human side can override the instincts of the beast.'

'The Ihis?' I asked, interrupting Lorcan's debrief.

'Yes. It's a skill that has been passed on with every generation of the Ihis. The Ihi bloodline is one of the purest in existence. They're descendants from the dominant Maori tribe of its time. Both men and women were skilled and fierce fighters. Their greatest talent was that they could turn into huge wolves on nights of the full moon, making them impossible to defeat. It's no coincidence the Maori people were one of the only indigenous populations never physically defeated by the British. Already they were extraordinary warriors, but with the added strength of the Ihi tribe they were invincible. For the most part the original Ihis wanted to be left alone. They had no ambition outside of the New Zealand islands. Peace treaties were signed and they folded somewhat into modern society, yet always on the outside of it.'

'One of them, James, he mentioned they had businesses, property . . .'

Lorcan nodded. 'Despite being physically tied to the old world with the lycanthropy, they've become very adept professionals. They have a lot of business on the North and South Islands, most of them legitimate, and they've accumulated a lot of property.'

I let that sink in. 'I'm going to need more beer.'

Lorcan didn't approve, I could tell that much from his face. Hey, I'm not one to ask for permission. Reaching into the top kitchen cabinet I pulled down a half-finished bottle of Jack Daniel's and filled a shot glass. I gulped it down and replaced the bottle. Returning to the balcony with two bottles of Foster's, both for me, I couldn't help but laugh when Lorcan said to me: 'Your drinking's a problem.'

'No shit,' I chuckled. 'I thought we were here to talk about my fang problem, not my substance one.'

'And the smoking.'

'I don't smoke,' I corrected.

'You asked for a cigarette on the boat.'

'OK, I *used* to smoke. I quit when Joss got cancer. He quit too, obviously.'

'It won't help.'

I folded my legs under myself on the couch. 'What?'

'The alcohol.'

'It's been helping OK for the past eight months.'

'When your mother died,' he stated.

I choked on a sip of beer. 'I never told you that.'

'You didn't have to. It was in the casework the Askari prepared for me.'

'Askari . . . the nerds of the outfit, right?'

Lorcan laughed, deep and loud. It was a pleasant, unmistakable sound and one that took me by surprise. 'When you meet them one day you'll realise how accurate that statement is.'

'There's a file on me? KTK,' I said, shaking my head.

'What?'

'Never mind. What does the file say?'

'Not that I would tell you usually, but very little. You'd never been on our radar until you got in contact with the Ihis. Your mother hid you well.'

'She lied very well,' I said, the words sounding like poison on my tongue.

'What would you have done?' he asked, the honest question startling me a little.

'Me?'

'If you'd found out your secret boyfriend was actually the head of a powerful werewolf clan and that you were pregnant with his child, what would you have done?'

I sipped as I thought. 'I would have run, like she did. But I wouldn't have lied like that. I would have found a way for my kid to exist without this toxic chip on her shoulder.'

'She needed a guarantee that you wouldn't go digging,' said Lorcan. 'If you thought he was a rapist, you'd be likely to leave it alone. It was smart.'

'It was hurtful,' I retorted. 'It's a twisted thing to have that kind of perception of yourself. And I keep wondering if my grandparents knew, if they were in on it too.'

'Do you think so?' I sighed.

'Honestly, no. I don't know what story she told them to get them out of the country but it worked. They've never looked at me like I was. . . no. I think they're none the wiser and everything remains sunny and perfect with them. A lie, basically.'

My words hung in the air for seconds that could have passed as minutes.

'There is no past that we can bring back by longing for it,' I said to myself, thinking once more on how different things were a few days ago.

Lorcan was looking at me curiously.

'Johann Wolfgang von Goethe,' I said. 'Interesting dude.'

'You're familiar with his work?'

'More his life than his work. I like reading biographies.'

The sun had started to set on the horizon and it was casting a beautiful light that reminded me of a blood orange.

'How long until you return to work at the . . .'

'Gallery?' I supplied. 'I have two weeks' holiday. Not this coming Monday, the Monday after. There's also—'

'What?'

'I'm supposed to be starting a Masters in August. I was lucky there was an opening for a junior role during my internship, but if I want to keep progressing—'

'You will have to defer.'

'I can't! I already deferred once after mum died and Alexis was really good about it.'

He sighed. 'We'll talk about this later. In the meantime, you need to start your training right away. Tomorrow. All day. When you return to work we can do morning and night sessions up until the full moon.'

'You do realise that I do more than work, yeah?' More than slightly annoyed I added: 'I interact with friends, see the occasional band, perform Jenny Lewis karaoke, play croquet—'

'Drink?' he interrupted.

'What's your problem with my drinking? I'm twenty-two, I've been legally allowed to drink for four years. I'm an adult and I enjoy it.'

'Please, twenty-two is barely an adult and, while you might enjoy it, the main reason you drink is to forget.'

'I can see where the counsellor part comes into your job description. Is "asshole" listed there, too?'

Lorcan shut his eyes for a moment and took a depth breath. 'This isn't a game, Tommi.'

'No shit,' I said bitterly. 'A game would require fun at some point.'

We stared at each other and I could imagine how he saw me: mouth pulled in a tight line and nostrils flaring. His game comment had been insulting. I didn't want to run through the list of awful things that had happened to me again. I was trying really hard not to keep spinning those things over and over in my head. Lorcan's jibe had made me want to remind him. Opening my mouth to do just that, I snapped my attention back to the door as I heard a key rattle.

'I thought you said your flatmate wasn't home until eight-thirty?'

'Her name's Mari and she wasn't supposed to be. This isn't her.'

The visitor had the scent of sweat and . . . caffeine? Kane. My body relaxed.

'It's her boyfriend. Stay here.'

I closed the glass door behind me and met Kane in the doorway.

'Tom,' he said, a lazy smile crossing his face.

'Come here, you.'

Kane grabbed me in a quick hug and I made way for him to get through the door.

'How was your holiday?'

I smiled and, wanting to spare him the agony of this awkward conversation, I said: 'Quick, actually. I found out Jonah died in a car accident a few weeks ago and he had no relatives to speak of, so that's that.'

'Oh, um, good,' he said, shuffling on the spot. 'I mean not good, ah—'

'Kane, I know.'

Lying to Kane was remarkably easy because he was so eager to avoid this conversation. I heard the glass door slide shut and turned around to see Lorcan walking inside.

'Uh, Kane, this is my friend Lorcan,' I said, gesturing to our visitor.

I tried to catch his eye, but Lorcan was deliberately not looking at me.

'Hey man,' said Kane, extending a hand. 'Interesting name.'

Lorcan shook it and replied: 'Irish. It's a tad outdated now. My parents thought it was a good idea at the time.'

Kane nodded. 'Ha, I think my girlfriend would agree with you there.'

'Mari, right?'

'Yeah. Have you g—'

'Lorcan just moved here,' I interrupted.

'Oh yeah? What do you do?'

'I'm a freelance graphic designer. I work from home mostly. I've been keen for a change of scenery for a while and it will give me a chance to see the rest of Scotland in between jobs.'

Lorcan was a good liar. Scary good. He told his story naturally, relaxed, and if I didn't know he wasn't telling the truth I wouldn't have been able to pick it. Looking between Kane and Lorcan, it was suddenly obvious how *different* Lorcan was. Besides his good looks, standing next to Kane in our very normal apartment he seemed . . . otherworldly. Dangerous. It wasn't the first time I had thought that about him, but with his frame towering over Kane and his measured performance being thrown into every answer, I reminded myself that this man was *other*.

'Tommi will love having another artist around,' said Kane, as I rolled my eyes.

'I wouldn't exactly call what I do fine art,' said Lorcan smoothly. 'It's mainly diagrams for magazines, that kind of thing.'

If you drew pictures you were an artist to Kane, simple, but he nodded politely.

Turning to me, he said, 'Mari wanted me to come around and start clearing out the spare room because she said you guys were getting people in to look at it tomorrow.'

'Righto.'

'I'll help,' offered Lorcan.

A graphic designer and a helper, all within the space of a few minutes. *Well, aren't you full of surprises?* I wanted to say to him sarcastically.

'Great,' said Kane. 'I think it's only a few boxes and a couch or something. We can put them down in the shed.'

'Let's get started then,' I said.

Mari's room was the first in the corridor, closest to the door, and we had a shared bathroom midway down the hall. The spare room was located directly opposite mine at the end of the hall. It was getting dark so Kane switched the light on. There was a deconstructed bed frame in the corner, something we'd keep for the new flatmate. The rest of the room was boxes and old paintings I had propped up against the wall.

'Do you know what's in the boxes?' asked Kane.

'Some stuff Rick left behind. I think the rest are full of Mari's books and old notepads.'

I bent down and grabbed the one nearest the door. I let out a sharp intake of breath as I lifted it even though it couldn't be more than a few kilos. Oh, yeah. I forgot last night my body had been ripped apart to turn into a werewolf. I gritted my teeth and made for the front door and the shed that lay beyond. I'd barely cleared the threshold when Lorcan caught up with me. He was carrying a box, the cardboard of which was straining at the weight of books inside.

'Tommi, wait.' He tried to take my box from me.

Always the martyr, I said, 'No, no, I've g—'

'You have not got it. Let me take it, Kane's still inside, he won't see.'

I held the box there for a few more seconds, every one of them bringing on a forgotten ache or pain.

'Tommi.'

Lorcan said my name with such authority I handed it to him.

'Are you sure you can carry both?' I asked meekly, as he threw the other one on top.

He gave me a look that said *puh-lease* and headed down the stairs. I followed.

Our cluster of apartments shared one large tin shed, which had been sectioned off into resident numbers. It sat to the side of a small yard area next to the clothesline. After unlocking the shed door, I turned on the interior light and Lorcan followed me in. He propped the boxes on one of the lower shelves with ease and dusted his hands off on his black jeans.

'So,' I said. 'You're from Ireland?'

'Yes. A long time ago.'

Lorcan's voice was low, not gruff. When he was saying something urgently the words came out perfectly pronounced. Yet his voice was practically accentless, something I'd never thought possible until I met him. It sounded vaguely American, but every now and then there would be a certain pitch to a word that would spike your curiosity. Now I knew that twang was the remnants of an Irish accent.

'How long ago? You couldn't be more than thirty. I guess twenty-eight.'

'Close, twenty-seven.'

His light brown hair blew into his face as a breeze came through the shed door and he used one hand to sweep it away.

'*Argh*,' came a sound from the stairwell and Lorcan ducked out of the shed to help Kane.

A few hours and plenty of swear words later we were done and I whipped around the spare room with the vacuum cleaner. With my back to the door, I stood, hands on my hips, and admired the now empty space. As I made to unplug the vacuum I heard a familiar whistle from behind me and turned to see Mari grinning from the doorway.

'Why oh why haven't you called me back after the eight abusive messages I left you? And who, pray tell, is that rugged romantic hero lurking in our kitchen?'

'Mari.'

'It's good to have you home, Tom,' she mumbled into my hair as we embraced.

'It's good to be back.'

'What's with the lack of phone contact? Only a few messages? I was worried.'

'I'm sorry about the radio silence. Second day in I broke my phone and I was more interested in getting back than getting a new one.'

'OK,' said Mari, batting my answer away with a hand gesture. 'Next: who is he and where do I get one?'

I wrinkled my nose. Mari's comparison wasn't far off. I guess I hadn't associated Lorcan with anything positive because, well, since the moment I'd met him he had brought nothing except bad news. Sure, he might have dragged me off an island so I didn't starve to death in the wilderness, brought me to a doctor *and* found a nice, damp lighthouse for me to spend the night in. He was still a *bawbag*.

'That's Lorcan. He's a freelance graphic designer friend of mine that's moved here. Another Dundonian to join the ranks.'

'Lo-what? He sounds like an elf.'

'It's Irish or something.'

'Or something. How long have you known him? He looks kinda rough.'

'Uh ... a bit. He did some diagram work for the gallery once and we got chatting. We were hanging when Kane came around and we cleared out the spare room.'

'Just hanging? Please follow that up with a "for now".'

'Just *hanging* for always,' I said, placing an emphasis on the hanging part. 'He's like a scary school teacher, Mari, not a play thing.'

'Speaking of play things, Poc has been asking after you.'

'I'll see him when I see him,' I said, picking up the vacuum.

'Oh!' Mari grabbed my shoulders and made me drop the appliance. 'I can't believe it wasn't the first thing I asked! Jonah's dead?'

'Yeah. A few weeks ago in a car crash, apparently.' At least I didn't have to lie about that part. 'No kids left behind, merely a disgruntled wife and sister-in-law.'

Liar, liar.

'Tommi, I'm ... "sorry" isn't the right word.'

'I know. It actually works out better this way, though. I can't get into icky situations and I don't have to spend the rest of my life wondering.'

'And when you went to that address?'

'Dead end.'

'Literally.'

Mari looked guilty almost as soon as she said it and it took a moment before we both burst out laughing. She threw her arm around me and we strolled out of the room.

'We'll talk about it later,' she giggled into my ear.

Walking into the lounge was like walking into another world. Mari had brought home Italian and Kane was digging into the spaghetti Bolognese while explaining the politics of local football while Scream played in the background.

'. . . world record for closest rival stadiums because they're only across the street from each other,' he ended.

Only I could tell Lorcan looked bored, but he was nodding while trying to keep up his 'everyday bloke' shtick.

'Lorcan, is that a beer?' I asked, my voice rising unnaturally high.

Kane's fork froze midway to his mouth as he said, 'What of it?'

'Nothing. I just didn't know he drank.' It was with a second glance that I realised it hadn't actually been touched, and Lorcan made a move to hide it behind his leg.

'Not everyone's a borderline alcoholic like you, Tom,' said Mari affectionately, as she wiggled next to Kane on the edge of the couch.

'You guys met and everything?'

'Uh-huh, we became old pals when I got home,' said Mari, winking at me.

'Kane's giving me a baptism of fire into the soccer teams.'

'Football teams,' I murmured.

'We'll make you an Arab yet,' said Kane, referring to the nickname bestowed on Dundee United supporters.

'I'm more of a rugby union man,' said Lorcan and Kane grunted with approval.

Lorcan caught my eye and gave me a knowing half-smile. I folded into the armchair next to Mari and stayed silent as we watched Ghostface brutalise a teenager. When the game was over, Lorcan made a move to take his plate to the sink. I met him halfway and took it.

'I've got it.'

'Let me help,' he said and he gathered the rest of the dishes.

As Mari began telling Kane about her day, Lorcan and I started rinsing the plates and loading the dishwasher.

'What time does Mari leave for work tomorrow?' he asked quietly.

'Yo, Mari, what time do you start work tomorrow?' I shouted over the bench.

Looking up from the couch she said: 'I'm on the seven a.m. shift.'

'Cool.'

I looked back at Lorcan and had to suppress a chuckle at the horrified expression on his face. 'Not everything has to be so covert,' I said.

'Clearly. I'll pick you up from here tomorrow at nine-thirty for training.'

'Where are we going?'

'I'm not sure yet. I'm staying at the Queen's Hotel so I—'

'That's practically next door!'

'I need to be as close to you as possible over the next few months to make sure there aren't any slip-ups or if there are, that I'm near enough to bring them under control.'

Under control? I gulped.

'What about the Hilton in the city?'

'The Hilton is a lot further away,' he said in a tone that ended the conversation.

Once the dishes were done he declared to the room: 'I'm off. It was nice to meet you both.'

'Yeah, man,' said Kane, getting up from the couch. 'You should come around again sometime. We can go to a Dundee United game. You staying nearby?'

'Yes, down the road until I find something more permanent.'

A nagging warning popped in to my mind.

'Actually, when are you looking at putting that spare room up for rent?' Lorcan asked.

A-ha!

'From tomorrow practically but . . . hey, are you interested?' Mari said.

'Certainly. How much a week?'

'It's sixty pounds plus throwing in for the wireless bill if you want it and other facilities. Tommi takes care of the finances.'

I felt like I was watching this conversation happen from an isolated bubble where I was powerless to stop it.

'Sixty pounds a week is cheap for the location.'

Mari shrugged. 'It's an old apartment and this *is* Dundee. Plus, we only have one bathroom but I stay at Kane's a few nights a week so that's usually not a problem, even with three people.'

Please. Stop. Talking.

'Great. I can move in as soon as it's convenient for you.'

'Fantastic!' squealed Mari. 'Ha, how great is that? I was dreading having to keep going through the whole flatmate interview process and weed out the cat people.' Mari's smile faltered for a moment. 'You don't have a cat do you?'

I almost wanted to shout: *Yes! He has a thousand cats! In fact, he's known as the crazy cat man, Mari, and has a calendar with a different breed in a flower garden for every month of the year!*

'No,' Lorcan said.

'Good, I'm allergic.'

Was I not being consulted at all during this process? Nope. Seemed not.

'Great. I can come by on Saturday. Will you be home?'

'Home and hungover probably. You'll be here won't you, Tommi?'

'Uh-huh,' I croaked.

'Excellent,' chirped Mari.

'I'll see you Saturday,' he said and made for the door.

I followed him out as they issued goodbyes behind us. I was fuming and I pulled the door shut behind me. This had clearly been the goal of the friendly flatmate interactions.

'What,' I said, taking a deep breath, 'was that?'

Lorcan gave what was fast becoming his signature – a half-smile – and said, 'Not everything has to be so covert.'

He gave a deep and gravelly laugh at my expression before disappearing down the steps. I'm not sure how long I stood there, mouth gaping open, but when I came back inside Mari and Kane had already gone to bed.

'Clearly,' I whispered to myself.

Chapter 9

My heart was pounding against the inside of my chest and my breath was coming out in quick pants as I sprinted through the forest. It was almost night and the little light left was lost amongst the canopy of trees. It didn't matter. Since I'd experienced the transformations, my eyesight had improved dramatically. It wasn't perfect by any stretch, but I was able to see where I was placing my feet in the darkness. I dodged between the massive pines as I tried to throw off my pursuer. It wasn't working. I could hear tree branches snapping behind me as he moved closer and closer. My legs were pumping as fast as they could. I pushed them to go faster. I spotted a deep ditch at the last minute and sprang over it, landing on all fours on a bed of dead leaves. There was no time to rest. I was back on my feet and sprinting through the forest again in the blink of an eye. A low-hanging branch whipped across my face and I ignored the sting that meant I'd have a cut there tomorrow. Throwing a quick look behind me, I tried to catch a glimpse of where he was. He was moving too fast. I turned around just in time to sidestep the stump of what had once been a wide conifer tree. I leaped up the side of another, used my feet to push off and flew metres through the air. As my left foot hit the ground, I felt something yank it out from underneath me. I kicked and screamed as this thing pulled me into the air towards the tree-tops. The movement paused for a fraction of a moment then gravity started to pull me back. Fast. Instead of hitting the ground, I bounced upside down for a while with one foot caught in what looked like a bungee rope trap. I felt like a human yo-yo as I dangled above the forest floor. Sensing movement nearby, I tried to turn towards it. I ended up spinning myself in circles instead. I stopped moving and waited for the rope to do the same.

Lorcan was lightly panting as he slowly picked his way through a nearby cluster of trees. 'What did we learn?' he asked, pausing in front of my suspended form.

'That blood rushes to the head very quickly.'

He made a frustrated sound. 'And?'

'Ergh,' was my only response.

'You have fitness already. With your werewolf abilities everything is increased: your speed, your senses, your strength, all of it. When I was chasing you, you didn't use those skills.'

'Speed.'

'You were so focused on trying to get away, Tommi, that you didn't think about how you could do that. Even in human form you should be able to sense obstacles and traps like this one; you should be able to anticipate the moves of your opponents to some degree and think ahead.'

'I was kind of distracted by other problems.'

'Problems are only opportunities with thorns on them.'

'Don't go all Mr Miyagi on me while I'm dangling upside down from a tree and you're standing there looking smug,' I growled.

Lorcan was wearing black running pants and a black hoodie. It was a testament to my improved senses that I could see his outline in the dark. He unfolded his arms and slipped a knife out of his pocket to cut me down. We'd been at this all day. And I literally meant *all* day. Right on 9.30 a.m., he'd knocked on the door and like a good werewolf-in-training I'd been waiting in gym clothes. He said he'd been up early looking at training locations and had found the perfect place: Templeton Woods.

Located across from Camperdown Country Park, the wood was populated by a combination of conifer and oak trees. Their thick, bushy branches blocked out most of the sky when you were on the forest floor. There was your typical selection of Scottish wildlife with squirrels, rabbits, owls and the occasional deer. With only a dozen trails and a single road leading to it, there were dense sections of Templeton Woods where you could be obscured from everything. I also accounted this fact to the unsolved murder of a nurse here back in the eighties, which had seen many locals steering clear ever since. Lorcan said it was ideal for our purposes. At first, we'd just stretched and he asked about my fighting experience. I told him about my years of Muay Thai and hobby of long-distance running. He'd tested the latter straight away with a twelve-kilometre run. I held a good pace throughout most of it even though it was longer than my usual route. I could tell Lorcan was hanging back. He barely got up more than a light sweat by the end of it. I was a river. With hardly any rest we moved on to 'intermediate self-defence' as he called it.

'You've got power and skill,' Lorcan stated after a few hours of sparring drills and combinations.

I soon learned a compliment meant more work as we pushed into the advanced stuff.

'Muay Thai is a combination of boxing and mixed martial arts,' he said.

I nodded and drank greedily from my fourth water bottle of the day.

'What you need to learn isn't a new skill entirely, it's the ability to anticipate opponents and adapt your fighting style.'

A few hours more of that and thankfully he called a timeout for lunch and a much-needed rest. The break wasn't long enough and I could have eaten five more of the beef and salad rolls I'd made for us. I munched on a banana as Lorcan went through various yoga poses and tried to teach me meditation techniques that would come in handy during my next transformation. He seemed to know a lot about everything. After much protesting, he sent me on another run – only six kilometres this time, whoopee – while he constructed an obstacle course in a section of the woods. The fading light gave it added difficulty and I had to appreciate his ingenious set-up.

The task was simple enough: get from one segment of the woods to the other. The catch was Lorcan had laced the woods with booby traps, relatively harmless ones, and that he would be chasing me. The course was meant as a way for me to incorporate everything I'd learned and to improve my werewolf senses. The first time he'd tackled and pinned me in under a minute. Second go I eluded capture a touch longer, but ended up falling into a pit similar to the ones usually filled with sharpened spikes in Indiana Jones movies. We'd been on my fifth try and although I'd become more creative at eluding Lorcan, the end result was still me hanging from a tree by my ankle.

'That was nearly two minutes,' he said, while working on the rope.

I rolled my eyes, forgetting he couldn't see them in the dark. The tension on my leg suddenly loosened and I landed on the ground with an ungraceful *oomph*. Standing up, I started to brush pine needles off my back. It was a relatively cool night for early spring and a light breeze gently rustled the trees together. The sweat dripping down the side of my face had begun to cool as I arched my neck and looked up at the sky through the treetops. The glimpses I could see were dark blue, turning black. A shrill whistle suddenly cut through the night and I jerked in the direction of the noise.

'Owls?'

'Friday night football,' I replied

'We should go,' said Lorcan, bending to collect the remnants of the rope.

They didn't actually play soccer through the woods, in fact, the sporting fields were a fair way from where we were. I wasn't telling him that. We'd been at this for almost nine hours and I was ready to get the heck out of there. I made my way out of the woods with Lorcan pausing to pick up various booby traps on the way. To my surprise he'd managed to find and buy a sturdy-looking black jeep in less than twenty-four hours.

'Keys,' I shouted behind me and I heard something swoosh from the trees.

I turned and ducked to the left, grabbing the silver bundle that Lorcan had thrown. With keys in hand, I thought to myself, Everything's a test with this guy.

The back tray of his jeep was full of practical bits and pieces like ropes, pulleys and cord. Then there was the unusual stuff like wooden poles, metal chains and . . . was that a box of daggers? I grabbed my towel and started wiping off the sweat while leaning into the jeep to get a closer look.

'Scipio daggers,' said Lorcan at my shoulder.

I didn't jump. In my head I'd followed the sound of every step he'd made and kept track of where he was moving. I was learning. 'Hmm,' I said, tilting my head. 'They look pointy. And lethal.'

'They are.'

I moved out of the way so he could load the rest of the equipment into the car.

'They're standard issue in the Praetorian Guard. I'll teach you how to use them once you're more experienced.'

'This is like looking in the boot of a serial killer. How did you get these into the country? I'm assuming they're not the only weapons you brought.'

'Of course they're not the only weapons I brought. The Custodians are part of an international organisation that's over a millennium old. If we didn't know how to get weapons across country borders we'd be a pretty useless entity.'

I furrowed my brow in thought. 'So, what, you have the border control people on your payroll?' The scale and potential reach of this world I'd unintentionally become a part of was starting to dawn on me.

Lorcan sighed and turned around, leaning on the bumper of the jeep. 'Tommi, out of everything you've learned in the past few days, is how we get weapons across oceans something you really want to know about?'

No, when I thought about it, not really. It was just the tail end of a much larger monster. 'The names. What's with those?'

'Ah,' he said, closing the jeep door. He made his way to the driver's side and I climbed into the passenger seat.

'They're all foreign,' I said, as he started the ignition. 'I know "Treize" is "thirteen" in French, but I have no idea what the others mean.'

'They're not French. Obviously "Custodians" is English, "Praetorian Guard" is from Roman origins and "Askari" is a word used in many languages – Arabic, Swahili, Urdu, Somali. It translates to "soldier" or "foot soldier".'

'Why the United Nations-naming?'

'Four of the beings who founded the Treize were French. The others were from various countries around the world. It was decided that the leader of each organisation within the organisation would have the honour of naming it. The founder of the Praetorian Guard had been a member of the original guard, which was a force of elite bodyguards used to protect generals and emperors in ancient Rome, hence the name. A very resourceful soldier from South Africa came up with Askari. The Treize has no one nationality or geographical identity. Its supernatural nature *is* the identity. In a way, the names are not dissimilar to mathematical theories or scientific discoveries often being named after a person.'

'Nash's equilibrium. Pythagoras' theorem.'

'Exactly. Except it was a different time. Naming after your roots had more prestige.'

I glanced out the car window and was shocked to discover we were almost home. It wasn't a long trip from my apartment, but the ride had flown by. Watching the lights and cars and landmarks flash past the window, I felt that drowning feeling I'd experienced a few times since learning I was a werewolf. It was the sensation of knowing you were part of something more gigantic than you ever imagined, something that was almost completely out of your grasp of understanding. Drowning.

I'd been silent too long and I appreciated Lorcan for leaving me to my own thoughts. 'Beings,' I whispered to the window. I felt Lorcan's eyes on me for a moment before he turned back to the road. I shifted in my seat to face him. 'You said there were beings. Are there . . .' I paused, trying to bring myself to say the word. 'Vampires?'

Lorcan's reaction made me jump about an inch off my seat as he burst out laughing. I'd heard snippets of it before, when we'd been sitting on my balcony or I'd said something particularly daft. Watching him full-on laughing was something else. His laugh was loud and throaty, like gravel hugging your ears. I wished he'd do it more often, but right now I was a bit peeved.

'Well?' I raised my voice over his continued laughter.

'I'm s-s-s—' He crouched over the steering wheel as laughter overcame him again. I crossed my arms and watched him pull himself together. 'Sorry, no, Tommi, there are no vampires. Practically none.'

'Wait, so there are?' He nodded through a big smile. 'Then why are you pissing yourself laughing at me?'

He fought to control himself and glanced at me. 'It's the way you said it, Tommi. Your tone was so serious and . . .' He shook his head for a moment. 'At last count there are probably under a hundred left in the world, all living in dark, remote corners of the planet.'

'They're not dangerous? They're not all "*I vant to suck your blood*"?' I asked in my best Count Von Count accent.

Lorcan let out another burst of laughter. 'I didn't say that. I'm sure they are dangerous to small predators like cats or rabbits. Once you've seen one in the flesh they're quite pathetic.'

'Why are there so few?'

'Disease.' He shrugged. 'I don't know. There have never been that many. The reality is very un-Hollywood. Except . . .'

'What?'

'Have you read *Lord of the Rings*?'

'Of course.'

'You've seen the movies?'

'By God, man, yes.'

'They're similar to the Gollum creature.'

Interesting. I leaned back in my seat and imagined the practically extinct species lurking in a cave whispering 'my precioussss'.

'But there are other beings out there, Tommi, much more deadly.'

'Like what?' Now I was curious.

'They're mostly variations of human: a lot of immortals or supernaturally skilled individuals.'

'People who live for ever?'

'Yes. Then there are those who have telekinetic powers, and psychics are on a similar branch. There are ghouls, elem—'

'Werewolves are the most common right?'

'Yes, in varying degrees.'

'Then let's stick with those for now. I don't think I'm ready to grasp all that other . . .' I made a motion with my hand to emphasise the wider supernatural community.

Lorcan got it. 'Sure.'

We pulled into my apartment complex car park and, like a slap to the face, I realised as of tomorrow I'd be calling it 'our' apartment complex. 'Hey!' I said angrily.

'What?' He started looking around the open-air car park quickly and at the walkway above us. His hand had gone for something under the seat and it was at this point I whacked him on the shoulder.

'Not out there. You,' I said, thrusting my finger into his chest.

'What?' He had the cheek to sound offended.

'That was bullshit what you did last night.'

He opened his mouth and I'm sure was about to say 'what' again before it clicked. 'Oh,' he said. 'Moving in.'

'Yes, moving in. Although I'm not sure if you could call it that. You totally blackballed me!'

He sighed and shifted himself to face me properly in the seat. 'Tommi, you're at a very difficult stage. This is the hardest, most difficult, painful, terrifying and confusing time for a werewolf.'

'Go on.'

'Being a new werewolf isn't easy. It's one of the most challenging things you can experience out of . . . anything. Especially for a rogue. You're without a pack and until now you've even been without the knowledge of what you were. I need to be there every step of the way to guide and teach you, and that includes at home. What you're experiencing and what you need to know doesn't end when we leave Templeton Woods.'

'I know that,' I snapped. 'But you can't simply invade my life like this. I already have to spend the next week with you all day, every day. Then when I'm back at work it's every morning and every night. I don't want to have to come home and deal with you and with this batshit insane new aspect of my life, too.'

'I'm sorry, but that's the way it has to be. I need to be with you as often as possible to fulfil my duties as one of the Custodians. I'm also here to protect the people around you. If you suddenly transform or go into a rage, who's going to protect them?'

'What do you mean transform? I can't do that unless it's a full moon, which isn't for a full month now.'

'Maybe, maybe not. The Ihis are a powerful line of were-wolves. Who knows if you can develop the ability to change at will? We haven't even begun to discover what you're capable of.'

'You're going to babysit me for the next ever?'

He sighed again. 'Be an adult about this.'

'Right, like how you were all adult about suggesting you move in, in front of everyone so I couldn't say no? Like how you just made up a whole graphic artist backstory for yourself? Like how you gave an Oscar-worthy performance of an everyday Joe so my flatmates would be tricked into liking you and thinking that you were normal?'

Lorcan didn't even look guilty. 'I didn't go about it in the best way.'

'Fuckin' aye.'

'Tell me, if I'd asked you about moving in would you have said yes?'

'Lorcan, you didn't give me that option. You didn't even explain how tight a leash you'd need to have on me.'

'I'm doing what I have to, to guide you.'

'It's barely been a day and you're doing too much.'

'You need to be watched for your own good.'

I scoffed at that comment and scrunched my face.

'Tommi,' he said, leaning in. 'You've already asked me to kill you once.'

I jerked back and felt tears welling up in my eyes. I stared at him, hurt. That was a hard blow. It's true, at my lowest point, I'd wanted nothing more than for it all to end. I had been through a hell of a lot, through days of the most excruciating pain I'd ever experienced. I went through most of it not knowing what was happening to me. I had been alone and broken.

I'd meant it when I'd asked him to kill me, but I was ashamed of asking in retrospect. I was better than that. Tougher. Or so I thought. It was my weakest, darkest moment. Lorcan bringing it up now felt like a stab in the gut.

'You're on suicide watch,' I stated. I angrily wiped away a tear as it started to spill down my check and I flew out the passenger door with my bag.

'Tommi, that's not wh—' he started.

I slammed the door in his face and ran up the stairs. He didn't get out of the jeep, but he stayed sitting in the driveway while I fiddled with my keys in the doorknob. I pushed myself through the door and used my back to shut it behind me. I leaned against it for a moment, waiting for the sound of his engine starting. As soon as I heard it, I closed my eyes with relief. I let out a shuddered breath and felt a few more tears trickle down my face. My back started to slide down the door and I flopped to the floor. After a day of exercise and rolling around in the dirt, quite literally, I smelled terrible. I ignored the stench and rested my head on my knees for a moment. Shutting my eyes, I sat there. Just breathing. A cough nearby made me jerk upright, but the noise came from outside. Listening carefully, I could hear Kane talking on the other side of the glass doors of our balcony. I sniffed. Mari was with him and ... marijuana. Joss was here too. Weed was something he'd got into on the advice of his doctor when he was going through chemotherapy at a specialist clinic in Berlin. We had both given up smoking when he'd being diagnosed and the weed helped with his cravings and the pain. He'd been in remission for six months. Every now and then he liked to indulge. I could do with a bit of escapism myself tonight and I thought about asking Joss to roll me a joint.

Dragging myself up from the floor, I figured I'd rather a shower and clean clothes before I faced anyone on the balcony. I slipped soundlessly into my room, threw my stuff down, and once I was at the door to the bathroom I shouted, 'Hey,' down the hall before ducking inside. Half an hour later, I was clean and hungry. Naked, I paused in front of my wardrobe and contemplated what to put on. No doubt they'd be going out and it wouldn't be right if I wasn't with them ... I was emotionally and physically shattered. The last thing I wanted was to be surrounded by people, even my friends, and having to pretend that I was the same ol' Tommi. I wasn't Lorcan, I didn't want to pretend to people I was normal. I was having a hard enough time convincing myself of that. Instead, I grabbed my *The Nightmare Before Christmas* jammies and slapped some moisturiser on my face. I was finishing combing through the knots in my hair when there was a light knock on the door.

'Come in.'

It was Mari. 'We're heading to Eggs ...' She paused when she saw my outfit. 'I guess you're staying in?'

Putting the brush down on my drawers, I shrugged. 'Much as I'd like the catch-up with everyone I can't bring myself to do it. I'm exhausted. I want nothing more than to eat a tub of Ben & Jerry's and fall into a sugar coma.'

Ben & Jerry's ice cream was a vice Mari and I shared. We made a conscious effort never to have any in the house because we'd devour it almost straight away.

'Funny you should say that,' she said with a sly smile, 'because I happened to be passing Dodo's Dinner on my way home and—'

'Don't tell me you have some in the freezer?'

She grinned and nodded at me.

'Maple Tree Hugger?'

'Of course. Kane and I already inhaled Chunky Monkey after dinner.'

'Did someone say "monkeys"?' Joss poked his head through the door.

'Come here, chimp,' I said and Mari jumped out of the way so I could give him a hug.

'Ew ew, c'mon, you're all wet and braless,' said Joss, trying to squirm out of my grasp.

'Don't pretend you don't enjoy it,' laughed Mari.

'It's weird, no, To—' With a final evasive manoeuvre, Joss backed into the hallway.

'I'm hurt, Joss, really,' I said, trying to keep a straight face and failing. 'How are you ever going to shag Cindy if you're afraid of boobs? Mine are under a shirt, hers will be all plastic and in your face.'

'Yes, but they're not yours so it won't be weird.'

I batted a hand at him.

'Not coming out? I haven't seen you since you got back and you know Facebook messages don't count,' he said.

'She's being a nana tonight, staying in and eating ice cream,' smirked Mari.

I nodded and pushed my way past them towards the kitchen. Joss trailed behind me.

'You're not going to watch a rom-com are you?'

I heard a whimsical sigh from Mari and rolled my eyes at him. 'Don't confuse me with Mari's fetish for romantic movies. I took you to see your first horror film, kid.' I wiggled my finger at Joss and he gave a mocking bow.

'Of course, my apologies, ma'am.'

'Accepted.' I opened the fridge to grab a steak I'd taken out to defrost that morning. I chatted to Mari while working on my dinner. I'd just finished cooking up potatoes when the party headed out the door.

'Are you sure you don't want to come?' Joss hovered in the doorway and I gave him my best brave smile.

'Positive. You go forth and be merry.' And then I was alone. Surprisingly, it was exactly how I wanted it to be. I didn't want to talk or to think about anything. With the *Kill Bill* soundtrack cranking from the speakers, I ate my hearty meal of steak, potatoes and veggies while flicking through an old magazine. Half a tub of Ben & Jerry's later I was cleaning my teeth in the mirror and trying very hard not to think about having to share this bathroom with Lorcan tomorrow. Come to think of it, he hadn't mentioned if we were training or what time he'd be around to move in. Not my problem. The only thing I was caring about at this second was getting in bed and sleeping for an eternity. Wiggling into my sheets I was about to reach over and turn off my string of Chinese lanterns when I paused. I'd rather not sleep in the dark tonight. Their familiar glow was comforting and I let its visual warmth send me to sleep.

Chapter 10

There was someone in bed with me. I'm not sure how long I'd been asleep. It felt like early morning, around three o'clock. And there was someone in bed with me. I could feel their figure lying beside me and hear their soft breathing. My entire body relaxed with the recognition of my mystery bed partner. Joss.

Rolling on to my back I turned my head to look at him. Still dressed in his clothes from the night before, shoes and all, he was lying on top of my bed with his hands lightly crossed over his chest. I smiled and had only a second to get grossed out at the pool of his drool forming on the pillow before falling back asleep.

'Ergh.'

'Sorry, what was that? You'll need to speak clearer,' came Joss's painfully chirpy voice.

'Not the French man,' I said through my pillow.

'Oh, right, more.' Joss turned up the volume on the thumping dance track.

'ERGH!' With that I sat bolt upright in bed. 'All right, all right, I'm awake, just turn it off,' I mumbled. 'I see the student has become the master.' I threw my pillow at his head and got him square in the jaw.

He laughed. 'It's going off.' After turning the volume down, Joss leaped on to the bed and rested his chin on his hands like an adorable kid.

I squinted. My blinds were up, grey light was streaming into the room and my lanterns had been switched off. Joss was even in different clothes. 'How long have you been trying to wake me?'

'I've been up for ages. I had breakfast with Mari and Kane, showered, started helping the new guy move in – he's a bit weird – and had lunch. I've been actively trying to wake you for the last half an hour.'

That was a lot of information for my sleep-clogged brain to process.

'What time is it?'

Joss shifted his head to get a better view of my robot alarm clock. 'It's 1.32 p.m. precisely.'

'Shit, I've been asleep for—'

'Ever.'

'Even my joints are dusty. When did you get in last night?'

'Um . . .' Joss tried to look vague and failed.

'What?'

'Probably only a few hours after you went to sleep. I actually didn't want to go out. I came by to see you and thought you'd be coming out.'

I smiled at him and reached out to ruffle his hair. Since he'd been in remission his rusty locks were growing out of control. I think he was just so happy he wasn't bald any more that he was going to let it grow to waist length. 'You scared the shit out of me when I woke up in the night,' I said, pushing his hair over his face.

'Stop it,' he said, smacking my hand. 'And I don't believe that. Nothing scares you.'

If only he knew how much had been scaring me lately. I looked away and grabbed a pillow from the floor to prop behind me. Crossing my arms over my chest, I gave Joss my best parental look. 'So.'

'So.'

'Those few hours you were at Eggs and Ham, did you happen to see a certain Playboy Bunny in training?'

'Oh,' he said and his face dropped.

'Oh? What does "oh" mean? What happened?'

'I don't want to tell you.'

'Why not?'

'Because you'll say, "See, I told you."'

'That's because I'm always right. I'll restrain myself if you tell me what happened.' I gave an encouraging smile.

'We ended up going to the Vu and Cindy pashed, like, five guys and went home with some RAF pilot who had a fiancée,' he blurted out.

I didn't laugh. I wanted to: the whole thing sounded so juvenile. But I tried to keep my face straight for my best friend. The RAF had an airbase close by in Leuchars, Fife and we'd regularly get pilots in town looking for a good time. It seemed one of them found it in Cindy.

'She had a nice side to her Tommi.'

'Sounds to me like she was always on her side,' I muttered.

'What?'

'Nothing. She was a lampshade, man, you felt less bright by being around her. I'm sorry if she hurt you. I'm not going to pretend to be sorry you guys didn't end up together.'

'Not everyone can be content with being a spinster like you.'

'A what? I'm twenty-two! I can't believe you just called me a spinster!'

He laughed and ducked a slap. I was poised to attack when I heard a heavy thud from outside the hallway. 'What was that?'

Joss looked behind him. 'Your weirdo friend, what's his name . . . Lorde? Lordy?'

I made a disgusted sound. 'Lorcan, his name is Lorcan.'

Joss shrugged. 'Whatever. I told you, he's here moving in.'

'Goodie.'

'You don't look excited. Isn't he *your* pal? Mari and Kane seem to like him.'

'Yeah, look, he's OK. He's a bit of a knob. And the only reason Mari likes him is because she thinks he's gooorgeous,' I said, dragging out the word in a high-pitched voice. 'Plus you know what Kane's like with dude's dudes.'

'I guess. He seems too pretty to be a dude's dude like Kane, though. I mean—' Joss lowered his voice '—he has a ponytail.'

I burst out laughing and had to bury my face in the pillow to smother the noise. Joss was looking at me warily, like he wasn't quite sure why what he'd said was funny.

'A ponytail, Joss? Seriously? You can't be manly if you have a ponytail? Isn't that the direction you're heading in now?'

'Shut up,' he said, rolling off the bed. 'He's too pretty, that's all.'

'Not you, too.' I headed for my wardrobe.

'If you're getting naked I'm leaving.'

'Righto. Wait – want to come with me to buy a phone?'

'You smashed the other one in New Zealand?'

I nodded. Joss's eyes lit up. If there was one thing he loved more than gadgets it was buying gadgets with other people's money.

'I'll meet you in the lounge,' he said and bounded out the door. I shut it behind him and pulled on one of my favourite T-shirts – it had a punk-rock unicorn on the front. I added a black miniskirt, purple tights and my black Doc Martens. After grabbing my keys, wallet, lip balm, and shoulder bag, I made for the door. Lorcan was just appearing in the doorway of his room and I thought about turning around and going back into mine, but it was too late.

'Hi.'

'Hey,' I replied flatly. I could see a few boxes behind him in the room. I didn't want to take a closer look.

'You going out?' he asked, looking at the black bag on my shoulder.

'Why? Are we supposed to be training?'

'No, I j—'

'Joss and I are going to get a new phone. I believe you've met him already.'

'He stayed the night with you?'

'He's my best friend, it's not like that. Plus, if there's someone in my room with me I'm less likely to kill myself, right?' I savoured the shocked expression on his face before I turned and stormed down the hall. 'Hey, guys,' I said to Mari and Kane who were standing in the lounge with towels in their hands.

'They're going swimming,' said Joss from the couch. 'Like, swimming in a pool. How crazy is that?'

'It's warm, Joss. And indoors,' Mari defended.

'Mari probably won't leave the sauna anyway,' said Kane.

'Joss, you coming to get this phone?' I wanted to leave. The longer I lingered in the flat the less impact my verbal slap to Lorcan would have.

'Yep,' he said, pulling himself up from the couch.

'Try and get her to buy the new iPhone,' Mari whispered to Joss as he passed.

'I heard that,' I said, as I walked out the front door.

Joss probably thought I was out of earshot when he replied: 'Leave it to me.'

I did buy the new iPhone. Joss did a better job selling it than the store clerk and, in the end, I bought it simply so I could stop hearing about the different features. 'There's even this app where you can paint and draw things with tools.'

'I can already do that on my computer,' I said, unimpressed.

'Now you can do it on your phone too.'

I caved. Joss had set it up for me while we waited for fruit smoothies in the food court. The shopping trip had been relatively uneventful. We got the phone then Joss dragged me to HMV to buy *Attack the Block* on Blu-ray. Wasting more time, we browsed a few shops and ducked behind a jewellery stall when Joss spotted a particularly annoying guy he'd gone to high school with. We also bumped into Poc coming out of a sports shop with a friend. Joss and the guy had sparked up a conversation about the outcome of a local boxer's fight the night before when Poc asked me about New Zealand.

'It was good,' I said. 'Very Kiwi.'

'You've been before, yeah?'

'A few times to visit extended family. Never recreationally, though.'

'Cool.'

Our brief conversation came to a lull and I didn't know what else to add.

'I sent you a few messages while you were away.'

'Really?' No wonder he was acting reserved, he probably thought I was barring him. 'I didn't get them. I broke my phone over there on my second day – hence the shopping spree.' I held up my Apple store bag to emphasise the point.

'Right, yeah it di—' He paused mid-sentence. He was looking at something on my face and I was about to check my reflection when he reached his hand to my cheek. He lightly touched the scratch I got yesterday in the forest. I felt my cheeks heat up but I didn't look away. 'What happened?'

I shrugged. 'You know me – got into a fight. The stick won.'

'Always causing trouble,' he said, smiling.

'Always.'

'When are you coming by the studio? You've got next week off, right?' Poc and his crew of street artists had converted a garage into a makeshift art studio that was also an unofficial hangout spot for a lot of people within our circle of friends.

'Uh, yes. I've got some stuff planned with my grandparents. Hopefully, I should get there maybe at the end of the week?' Honestly, in between the intensity of Lorcan's training and Lorcan himself I didn't know when I'd have time to breathe, let alone time to visit graffiti HQ. The grandparental plans were a lie, but that wasn't something Poc would pick up on.

'Cool. We should catch up anyway.' He tried to sound casual.

'Sure.' Poc had a pretty easy time with the ladies. He was rarely in pursuit of anyone and, although he'd already 'caught' me many times, my nonchalance was attractive to him.

'What about tonight? I could come around if you're not doing anything.'

'Tonight's not good. In fact, my place isn't good for the next while,' I said, lowering my voice. 'We have a new roomie. A freelance graphic designer I know. He moved in today.'

'In the spare room next to yours?'

'The one and the same.'

I could almost see the disappointment on Poc's face and I had to suppress a laugh. Men, sheesh.

'Well, you know where I live. If you wanna come by, text me before or something.' Poc was being mighty persistent.

'You'll have to put your number in again. Everything's been wiped.' I handed him my phone.

'Now it's 0800-B-O-O-T-Y-C,' said Joss, suddenly tuning into our conversation. I elbowed him and he shut up.

'Cool,' said Poc, passing me back the phone. 'We're going to get a bridie, you guys wanna come?'

'No, I'm good. I just had a smoothie and I think Joss has had, what? About three lunches now?'

'And it's getting close to afternoon tea time,' he said.

We bid farewell and I put up with Joss's romantic jibes the whole way to the car. It was only when we were about to do a U-turn in the direction of the apartment that I realised I didn't want to go back there.

'Hey, why are you pulling over?' asked Joss, pausing mid-conversation.

'Do you reckon you could drive my car home? I have a craving for air.'

'Seriously? Here? At the side of the A85?'

'I need to go for a walk or something. I don't feel like being inside yet.'

'OK, Tommi the Strange. We're not far so I'll have no chance to crash it.'

'Good,' I said, jumping out of the car. Joss grabbed my keys a little too eagerly and I wondered if my battered Ford Fiesta would survive this act of charity. I turned and headed towards a nearby park as Joss drove away, tooting madly as he went.

I knew exactly where I was going. Magdalene Green wasn't big enough to be a proper park and it was in a bizarre location. The size of two football fields, the park stretched out between one of Dundee's main roads and the railway line. The land rose on a steady slope towards the residential area that ran along behind it. I walked through the finely cut grass of the park and straight towards the band pavilion, which looked like a giant thumb tack. I leaped the sturdy steel barrier and exhaled.

The Tay Rail Bridge extended into the distance like a massive index finger with a train rattling along it to some unknown destination. It wasn't a particularly beautiful bridge, never had been, but there was something reassuring about the familiar structure. A sharp evening breeze was coming in from the east as the hours ticked over into late afternoon. I'm not sure how long I spent there, staring at the towns built into the soft, green mounds across the other side of the river. Couples and power walkers passed by, consumed in their own idyllic daydreams. It was beautiful. There had been no sun today, but the setting sky looked as if someone had bled shades of grey and yellow into it. I was glad I'd picked this spot to avoid my new flatmate.

Who was I kidding? This was always the spot I picked. After my mum died I spent a lot of time here, sometimes with my grandparents, mostly alone. Arched over the railing I was far enough removed that I could just stand there and think, uninterrupted. Or so I thought.

I'd barely sensed his presence when a voice behind me said: 'You've been avoiding me.'

Lorcan. Who else?

'With detective skills like that I should start calling you Bruce Wayne,' I said.

I heard him sigh. That was a response I was very good at getting from him, I thought. Lorcan stood beside me. I remained unresponsive.

'I'm not here to fight, Tommi.' It was true, he sounded rather exhausted.

'I don't *want* to fight,' I replied. 'It feels like all I've done is fight in the last few days and the last thing I want to do is fight with you. But—'

'You can't help it,' he finished.

I smiled. 'You bring out the bitch in me, what can I say? And I've never had a problem with being called a bitch.'

'As long as that's the figurative bitch and not the literal one I can handle it.'

I nearly snorted in shock. 'Did you . . . did you make a joke?' I asked, turning to look at him.

'It's been known to happen.' He was smiling lopsidedly at the sunset and I liked the effect the dying light had on his face. I returned my gaze to the horizon. 'Tommi, I know I'm not doing the best job at guiding you so far, but this is new for me too.'

'You've never had a rogue before?'

'Actually, I've never had a ward before.'

'I'm your first case? Ever? I thought you said you've been doing this for years?' I was more than a little alarmed. Lorcan really knew his stuff, but did I feel comfortable placing my werewolf future in the hands of a first-timer? Realistically, what other option did I have? I was alone in this. Alone with a plus one.

'I should have clarified earlier. Everything has been happening so fast,' he started. I watched his expression, as he struggled internally to explain the situation. 'I do have years of experience, only not with the Custodians. I was a member of the Praetorian Guard.'

I heard myself gasp and couldn't help it. 'You were one of the elite, lethal, sacred warrior people?' I sounded stupid, even to myself. I was in shock.

'I was. For many years.'

'Huh. That kind of explains a few things.'

'Does it?'

'You seem to know a lot about weapons and fighting. I've only been to a normal counsellor a few times and he couldn't kill a man with his bare hands or dangle a girl from a tree.' Having no experience with 'the norm' for Custodians, I'd figured Lorcan was simply one with a particular emphasis on self-defence. That also explained why he wasn't great with the complex emotional side of my werewolfism. Mind you, I was emotionally stunted myself. I couldn't criticise.

'Why did you leave?'

'What?' Lorcan had been fiddling with the banister and was lost in his own thoughts. 'I, oh . . .'

'If it's a personal question you don't have to tell me.'

He looked at me carefully. 'Tommi, if we're going to get through this and I'm going to teach you as much as I can, we need to have an open relationship. We need to have trust. There's nothing you haven't shared with me, which hasn't exactly been your choice. The least I can do is be honest with you.'

I held my tongue and waited for him to continue.

'I had a friend, my best friend actually. Amos. He was a werewolf like you. In the Praetorian Guard you can be called to travel anywhere at any time, but for the most part I was based in Texas. Amos was a few years older than me and he was the head of the dominant pack in the state. We'd met through Guard business years earlier, when he was still a teenager, and we became friends. He was a loyal, brave, kind person, and a better man than I'll ever be. We'd fought side by side dozens of times and I trusted him with my life.'

That feeling of dread had started to form in my stomach. It didn't take a genius to tell this didn't end well.

'He killed himself. Almost two years ago now.'

I didn't know what to say. The only thing that could be heard was the faint rustling of leaves as the wind moved the trees behind us. 'Lorcan, I-I'm . . .'

He shook away my condolences with a movement of his head. 'It was a huge shock. You have to understand this was a man who never showed a sign of damage, who was always happy and trying to find the positive in every situation. He had the respect and control of a renowned pack, he was in the confidence of the Praetorian Guard, he had a fiancée, friends, family. It was unfathomable. I still find it hard to believe. I found him; I found the note. I picked up on how he was the day before at his thirtieth birthday party and I should have realised. I should have helped him. I never thought . . .'

He sighed. The pain was clear in his voice, in the sag of his shoulders, and when he looked up at me his eyes screamed of it. 'He was thirty. He'd been a werewolf for nearly twenty years. It never even occurred to me that he'd still be struggling to handle it. But he was. I think that and some of the things we'd seen ... He sighed again. 'We'll never know. After he died, I lost interest in the Guard. I lost my faith in it and in my friends there. I wanted to be more than merely someone who lived and died by the sword. And I guess I wanted to make amends for Amos, to help others like him. I requested a move to the Custodians and it was granted. You're my first assignment.'

I'm not sure if my eyebrows were visible any more, but I'd bet they were beneath my hairline. 'Whoa.'

I tore my gaze away from Lorcan and once more to the sunset. Well, faintly glowing horizon now. Night had descended and the lights of the occasional boat bobbed on the skyline. 'Does that happen a lot?' I said, asking the first question that came to mind. Worrying that he'd think I meant suicide, I added, 'Transferring, that is.'

'No,' said Lorcan, sounding far away. 'I'm the first.'

'The first? As in, ever?'

'Yes.'

'Ever? In the millennium history of the Treize no one has ever switched from the PG to Custodians?'

He gave a fleeting smile at my abbreviation. 'The PG. I like it. And no, I'm the first. Most within the Praetorian Guard have no desire to learn what Custodians know or the specifics of what they do. It's not only uninteresting to them but it's also ... everything's about battle, about fighting and action. The physical. The Custodians are the ying to their yang. For them it's about the mental. The inner-fight.'

'Are you in trouble because you left? God, that sounds so childish out loud,' I said, frowning.

Lorcan chuckled. 'No. I served the Guard well for many years. They were, uh, not happy to let me go but willing. They understood. And I'm still of use to the Treize with the Custodians, it's just a different kind.'

'Why are you telling me all this? Besides the honest guardian-ward-relationship scenario?'

'Honesty and openness are the primary reasons. Also because I want you to understand where I'm coming from. I want you to understand that although I can guide you flawlessly in some aspects, there're others that I'm learning with you.'

'Flawlessly?'

'I will not fail you, Tommi. Just because I traded the sword for another weapon that doesn't mean I'm any less dedicated to fulfilling my duty. In fact, more so.'

Lorcan was staring at me with an almost inhuman intensity. His green eyes seemed alight with the sincerity of his words. 'You need to be dedicated to this too.'

I would have looked away if I could have. Lorcan's stare and the direction this conversation had taken kept me hooked. 'I am.'

'You have to mean it, Tommi. I know you want to keep your old life and the illusion that things are normal. You're a part of something bigger now. You have to accept that.'

'Lorcan, I need time to do that. Everything has happened so fast and violently, there's no way I can just automatically come to terms with the fact I'm a werewolf. Let alone the fact that I'm a werewolf from an insidious family line and that there's a supernatural community, which I'm a part of now. Just saying all that out loud makes me want to shave my head and storm at people with an umbrella.' I could feel my hands shaking as I spoke and I ran them through my hair to calm myself. 'This is my life now, I get that, but that doesn't mean I accept it. I'm dedicated to learning to control my werewolf side and to learning everything I can from you. This rest is going to take time.'

'OK,' he said.

'OK? You're not going to fight me on this?'

'I told you, I didn't come here to fight.'

I nodded.

'Tommi, you're not an ordinary werewolf. There's more to you. You've picked up things quicker than I've ever known anyone to. In other respects, you're merely a pup alone in the woods. We have a month to make you ready to be a wolf again. Then another month, and another. We'll take it one moon at a time.'

'Phase by phase,' I said.

Tearing my gaze away from Lorcan, I looked out across the water once more. We fell into a comfortable silence as I let his words wash over me. 'See that bridge there?' I tilted my head as I pointed at the very obvious structure in front of us. Lorcan raised an eyebrow at me but didn't dignify my question with a response. I laughed. 'It's a rail bridge, no cars can use it. A few years after it was built in the late 1800s there was a violent storm and the whole thing came crashing down. There was a train passing over at that exact moment and it plummeted into the river.'

Lorcan looked at Tay Rail Bridge with a new-found fascination. 'Any survivors?'

'None. All seventy-five people died.'

'Hmmm.'

'You see those pieces of exposed concrete sitting next to the bridge?'

'Yes.'

'That's what remains of the original one. The replacement was built right next to it.'

I felt like we'd come as far as we were going to that night and I straightened up from my hunched position on the rail.

'Thanks for the history lesson.' Lorcan smirked.

'My gift to you. At least you know the next time you take the train out of town there's a slim chance it could end in catastrophe. *Final Destination* style.'

Lorcan rose with me and we silently made our way up one of the alleys sprouting away from Magdalene Green. It was then a ten-minute walk back to the apartment.

'You all unpacked?' I tried to keep the annoyance out of my voice and the tone neutral.

He looked at me as if he knew exactly what I was thinking. 'Yes. I didn't have much to unpack, a few weapons and clothes.'

I groaned. 'Tell me none of my roomies helped you carry an axe up from the jeep or anything?'

'They were well hidden. Although I'm sure Kane and Joss probably wondered what was making some of the boxes so heavy.'

'No doubt.'

Chapter 11

Physically, I don't think I've worked harder than I did over the next few days. Damn Lorcan and his quasi-tragic story. Our days were broken up much the same way: stretching, running, fight drills, lunch, meditation, running and ending on the obstacle course in the thickest part of the woods. Lorcan slipped in two pool sessions for cross-training and, although my muscles were aching from everything else I'd been doing, laps definitely helped recovery. That is until he threw a five-kilogram medicine ball into the pool and had me run with it underwater.

'What good will this do? I'm not going to be surfing twenty-foot waves off the coast of Australia any time soon,' I'd said.

'Doing rock-running regularly will help increase your lung capacity. Learning to control against your natural desire to get back to the surface and get fresh air will help you become better at controlling your instincts.'

Undoubtedly, I learned the most from fighting him. At first, Lorcan hadn't really invested in any of the fight drills. He seemed to concentrate more on gauging my level of ability and pointing out things here and there. By the fourth day he was an opponent and a formidable one at that. I'd seen professional boxers fight, I'd trained in a gym with some of the country's best mixed martial artists, but no one moved like Lorcan. He said with my werewolf reflexes I would be faster and stronger. Yet still I wasn't faster or stronger than him. He might be one of the Custodians now, but Lorcan's warrior past was definitely not behind him. Maybe you never lost that kind of skill. Maybe you could never unlearn those abilities.

My hands were raised in front of my face and I was bouncing on the balls of my feet. It was late on a Wednesday afternoon and we were in a clearing near the edge of the forest. There was no one around.

'Again,' he said.

I pushed forward at him and he was gone before my elbow even came close to connecting with his chin. I felt a jab on my left side and, instead of turning around, I leaned forward and launched a back kick. That connected. Just. Lorcan was in front of me again and I feinted to the right as he sent a punch my way. I quickly dropped to all fours as I saw him tense for a roundhouse kick and I felt the air swoosh over my head as his foot narrowly missed me. Extending my leg, I went to kick his out from under him but he anticipated my move and jumped lightly. I leaped up and came at Lorcan again, throwing hooks and upper cuts to his body as fast as I could. He blocked most of them with his forearms and elbows. Then it was his turn. He flew at me in a blur of movement and I did my best to block. In my attempt to do so, he found an opening. Dodging one left cross, I went to throw an elbow when I found I was moving towards thin air. Lorcan locked his forearm around my neck from behind and silently I swore at myself.

'You're always so busy trying to attack, Tommi, you forget to defend.'

'Really,' I said, drawing back my elbow before ploughing it into his abdomen. Lorcan let out a guttural sound as the shot connected. I felt his grip loosen slightly and I threw myself forward, taking him with me. He landed on his back on the ground and before I was able to press my knee to his throat he grabbed it in an incredible display of reflexes. He used my own downward motion to throw me sideways and pin himself on top of me. I was pleased to see he was panting and, with his face hovering just above mine, I noticed he'd worked up a sweat too. I knew he was taking it easy on me. I'm sure the blows he'd been delivering were nowhere near as hard as he'd unleash on a real adversary. Still, it felt good to know he had to exert himself.

His hair was tied loosely in a small bun at the back of his neck. Strands had escaped the band during the fight and were dangling over his face. He'd worn a baggy singlet to train in and I could see the muscles on his bare arms bulging as they held me down. I wasn't afraid of Lorcan like I had been initially. I'd been working hard at trying to think of us as a team, but the guy definitely had some scary abilities (says the she-wolf). He was looking at me with an intense expression and not for the first time I noticed how green his eyes were. The pupils were like muddied emeralds and staring into them I was enveloped in a forest.

Lorcan's grip loosened as he rolled himself off me. Propping himself up on an elbow on the grass, he exhaled and looked over. 'Good.' He nodded.

I was still puffing. 'Yes, up until the point you owned me.'

'What?'

I looked at him to see if he was serious. 'It's an expression, like "you just owned me with your mad PG skills".'

I saw him think it over. 'When do we get to try using the daggers?'

'When you pin me,' he said.

My face sagged with disappointment. 'C'mon, you know that's never going to happen. You weren't even going one hundred per cent and look how it ended.'

'Time, Tommi, give it that.'

The next day I didn't pin him, but we did start practising with daggers. Not on each other, mind you. I'd seen how deadly Lorcan was with his hands. I didn't want to add another pointy object to the mix. When I would be meditating or he was instructing me through a particular drill, he'd often be causally leaning against a tree while flicking a knife through his fingers. He had one black-handled switchblade he seemed to favour and I would sometimes be hypnotised by the way it would spin and flip with his movements, so fast that the knife was a blur. The act seemed like a subconscious tic to him, much in the same way I would flick the rubber band at my wrist.

We used the innocent conifer trees for target practice. I wasn't great, I'm not going to lie. Yet after about three hours of trying to hit the width of a tree I'd actually managed to get the blades of two daggers to stick. 'This is the perfect place to do it because you're surrounded by identical targets. It makes aiming for the same one more difficult and also more realistic if you ever tried to throw them at one person in a fight,' he said, twirling his own blade before hurling it into the tree with perfect precision. It landed with a heavy *thud* and the blade vibrated with the force of the action.

I'd come to love the meditation segments of our training where I could slow everything down and concentrate on tiny, seemingly insignificant things like breathing and my heart rate. Especially because afterwards became question and answer sessions between Lorcan and I. While he stretched out and cooled down, I finally had the opportunity to think of things I'd forgotten to ask.

'OK,' I said, keeping my eyes shut and remaining in the plank position I'd been in for the past five minutes, 'are ghouls real?'

'I thought you didn't want to know about all the different beings?' asked Lorcan, who was also in plank position parallel to me.

'You're right. I don't. Not at all.' Silence washed over us for another few minutes and we moved into a comfortable sitting position, folding the top half of our bodies forward and extending our arms on the grass in front of us. 'How about I say the name of a creature and you give me a yes or no answer whether or not they're real?'

'OK,' he said, his voice somewhat muffled from under his body.

'Yes or no.'

'Tommi—'

'Ghouls?'

'Yes.'

I let that sink in for a moment. 'Succubi?'

He chuckled. 'No.'

It went on that way for a while: me trying to pluck names of mythological and supernatural creatures from my mind and Lorcan providing a one-word answer. Ghosts, yes. Centaurs, no. Shape-shifters, yes. Witches, yes. Dragons, no. Elves, no. Demons, yes. Loch Ness Monster, no. Big Foot, possibly.

I was tugging down at the edges of the black beanie I was wearing when my eyes flew open at the thought of another question I hadn't asked. 'Who are the Three?' I was watching Lorcan when he looked at me seriously.

'I'm going to need more than a one-word answer.'

'They're English-speaking, right? Because they called themselves the Three.'

'No one's really sure where they came from . . .' He trailed off for a moment and I didn't push it. 'Have you heard of the saying "See no evil, hear no evil, speak no evil"?'

'Of course.'

'That's them.'

'You mean they came up with the phrase?'

'No, they *are* that phrase.'

Lorcan waited while I tried to run that information through my head. I was confused. 'Explain.'

'We all operate under the Treize, but the Three operate within them. Essentially, they guide the Treize. They're three physic women of unrivalled ability. One is blind, one is deaf and one is mute.'

'A-ha,' I said, as it all clicked together.

'The term was created to describe them. They operate as one entity and have for centuries. They live within the Treize's headquarters and are in many ways their greatest asset because they can alert them to unforeseen dangers, monitor enemies and often see the outcome of various paths we can take in this life.'

'Wow.'

'They saw you coming.'

'That's how you got to me so quickly?'

'Not quickly enough,' he said and I picked up a hint of annoyance in his voice. 'We should have known about you, the fact you existed at the very least. Instead, we knew nothing. They saw nothing until you came in contact with the Ihis.'

The Ihis. I'd been so busy focusing on everything I was doing with Lorcan that I hadn't thought about them for days, which seemed nearly impossible. Now the memories of my bloodline flowed back. Whenever that happened my thoughts always ended on Steven.

Steven groping, Steven touching, Steven punching.

'Tommi?' Lorcan's voice woke me from the uncomfortable memories.

'Huh?'

'I asked if you were all right?'

'Yeah,' I said, standing up. 'Obstacles next?' I poured myself into the remaining hours with more aggression and passion than I'd experienced since transforming. When I walked through the door of the apartment that night I didn't even feel tired. Lorcan and I always drove to Templeton Woods separately now. Sometimes, I might come home later or he would. Mari and Kane never suspected anything, but we wanted to make sure they never thought we were spending a lot of time together. I made it home before Lorcan and jumped in the shower. When I'd finished I stared at myself naked in the mirror.

I'm fit, not thin. Surprised, I looked closer. I wasn't sure if I was imagining it but all relativity was gone. Stretching my limbs in front of my eyes, I was astounded to see I was already leaner and more muscular than I was this time a week ago. My stomach had been tight and flat before. Now, I was seeing the starting outline of a six-pack. It was faint, but it was there. And there were definitely muscle bulges in my back that hadn't been present before.

I had two tattoos. The first I got when I was eighteen and it was a design I'd drawn after being inspired by *Dia de los Muertos*. The tattoo was large and started a few inches under my right armpit and ran down the side of my body, ending above my hip. It was a side-on view of a woman's face who was painted for Day of the Dead and her brown hair snaked around her and down the side of my ribs with five purple and red roses placed strategically along its path. Where the last strand of hair ended was a single grey skull, also on its side but looking in the opposite direction.

My second tattoo was more subtle and on the inside of my left bicep. You'd never know it was there unless I was flexing my arm muscles, which I never did, so that wasn't an issue. It was smallish, only about the length of my hand, and it looked like someone had artfully splashed three different shades of purple paint there. My tattooist Pip had never done something like that before and had appreciated the process. I loved the end result although I knew most people who saw it either hated it or were strangely fascinated by it. It had been a year since I'd got it and Mari was still undecided. 'It looks like a mistake,' she had said. 'A gorgeous arty mistake.'

I glanced once more at the changing shape of my body before pulling myself away from the mirror and walking to my room with a towel wrapped around my person. I opened my underwear drawer and got out a matching bra and panties set in green. My favourite black knit dress was slightly less snug than it had once been as I shrugged it on over a pair of patterned tights and black boots. Since Lorcan and I had been training, I'd had a huge appetite, which made sense considering how much physical activity I was doing. I'd always been a relatively normal eater. Now I was eating almost double at dinner and close to that throughout the rest of the day. Clearly it wasn't enough. I'd have to ask Lorcan if that was a werewolf thing. First, I needed to cook.

It was after nine by the time I finished whipping up some veal and mushroom pasta. Mari wasn't home yet, which was unusual since she was working the day shift, but not completely unheard of.

'Mari here?' said Lorcan, walking into the kitchen. He was wearing grey, loose-fitting cotton pants and a long-sleeved khaki shirt that highlighted the muscles in his chest.

I gulped down my mouthful of pasta. 'Nope. Usually that means there's a big story breaking. If she's not home by ten I'm betting murder.'

Lorcan was drying his hair with a towel and looked at me with mild amusement. The main industries in Dundee were called the Three Js: jute, jam and journalism. In my opinion, Mari worked in the most interesting of the three, despite the sporadic hours sometimes required of her. Nodding at my food, Lorcan asked what I was eating.

'Veal and mushroom pasta. I made enough to feed a small dinosaur so help yourself. Only leave some for me to put in a container for Mari when she gets home.'

'Thanks,' he said and disappeared to get rid of the towel.

I picked my bowl up off the bench and made for one of the stools on the opposite side. We didn't have a dining table; no point when Mari and I were usually around at different times and preferred to eat on the couch or at the bench. We had a mismatched collection of stools we'd picked up from garage sales on the other side of the kitchen so you could eat at the breakfast bench. I plopped myself on a retro vinyl one and grabbed my monthly copy of *Inked* magazine. I had my head buried in the magazine when Lorcan returned and filled a plate with pasta. Feeling his eyes on me, I looked up. He was leaning against the sink on the other side of the bench and his wet hair was hanging stiff and straight to his shoulders. He had that amused expression on his face again as he chewed on a piece of pasta.

'What?'

'I don't get your generation's fascination with tattoos.'

'*Your* generation? You're what, twenty-seven, buddy? Don't get ageist on me.'

He shrugged. 'Having something put on your body perma-nently and usually where people can see it—'

'What about the Picts? They certainly weren't "my genera-tion" and they were all aboard the tattoo express,' I stated.

His fork pierced another morsel of pasta and he plopped it in his mouth.

I continued. 'My theory is this: if you love something, a particular image or a message and you think you're never going to get sick of it, then why the heck not? Who cares what other people think? You're the one who has to have it inked on you for all eternity. If you're happy with it and happy with the art, go wild.'

'Like your tattoos?'

'Sure. Though I'm betting what I have seems stupid to other people, just as I think getting a dolphin on your ankle is stupid. Haven't you ever thought about getting a tattoo?'

Lorcan nodded through a mouthful and swallowed. 'I have . . . had a friend who was covered in tattoos from head to toe, all over his body. When I was younger, I thought about getting my Irish family crest here,' he said and motioned to his pec.

'Why didn't you?'

He opened his mouth to answer when a shrill ringing came from his room. He frowned and put down the bowl. I returned to my magazine as I heard him talking quietly on his mobile. I'd finished my plate of pasta and was grabbing a beer from the fridge when Lorcan returned to the kitchen in jeans and zipping up a black jacket. 'Something has come up,' he said. The look on his face said that 'something' was serious.

'Can I help?'

'No. I need you to stay here, inside tonight.'

'Sure. Can you tell me what's going on? The look on your face is giving me the wiggins, Lo.'

He had been scooping pasta into a clear Tupperware container and looked at me with a half-smirk. 'Lo?'

I'd shortened his name without thinking. I kind of liked the nickname. 'Yeah, Lo. It can be your new nickname. We Scots tend to nickname everyone and/or thing.'

'What was my old nickname?'

I started putting my plate into the dishwasher and said: 'Let's not get into that.' It had been 'bawbag'.

He laughed and headed for the door. 'I don't know if it's serious. I'll explain everything when I get back because, honestly, I don't what's going on.'

I sipped my beer and watched him pause in the doorway. 'Righto,' I said. And with that he was gone.

I locked the door behind him and tried not to feel uncomfortable about whatever supernatural situation he'd been called to. He said he'd be back tonight which meant it was local. And he wanted me to stay inside. I was already feeling energetic when we got home and now knowing I couldn't leave I had to try to keep myself busy. I cleaned my room, cleaned my art supplies cupboard, vacuumed the apartment, tried starting my Helen Duncan biography, finished a painting I was working on and tried watching *Dogma*. Nothing worked. I was on edge. I returned to my room and threw myself on the bed. Looking at the ceiling, I thought about trying to find a distraction and my mind naturally went *there*. Sex. The second I thought about the physical act Lorcan's face swam into my vision. I lurched forward, sitting up on the edge of my bed, breathless. I shook my head slightly, trying to banish him from my thoughts. It's because he would disapprove of me leaving the house to get my rocks off, I reasoned. And we've been spending so much time together lately, it's completely normal to have him at the front of my thoughts, I tried to rationalise. Now I was driven by the need to get out of the house and take action. Poc lived only fifteen minutes down the road and I sent him a text. I heard back almost instantly that he was home and free. I jumped up and paused, looking at myself in the mirror for a second. My blue hair was drying into loose waves and I could have thrown some make-up on, yet I couldn't be bothered.

I grabbed my keys, condoms, phone and headed out the door.

Poc's roommate was a Lebanese guy named Joey, who worked as a bouncer at Fatties and whom I suspected was on steroids. Joey and his bulbous triceps greeted me at the door. He barely had time to give me a knowing smirk before Poc grabbed my hand and led me to his room.

Closing the door behind him, he said: 'Sorry, the quicker I get you away from Joey the better. He's got a thing for you and has been drinking with his dickhead cousins.'

'I wondered why he was a bit leery. And since when has he had a thing for me?'

'It's not so much you as . . .' He gestured to the top half of me. I laughed. 'Real D-cups are rare in his line of work.'

'Tell me about it, stud,' I said in my best Olivia Newton John voice.

Poc's room was huge, like mini-apartment huge. His older brother had bought the house as an investment a few years ago and Poc had been living in it ever since. It was an old building that had been renovated fairly recently with timber floors, new carpets and a state-of-the-art fireplace. Poc's room was considerably different from the rest of the house. He had a framed Dead Prez poster on the wall and a signed poster of Vernon Sollas on another. The rest of the wall space was covered in graffiti that he had done himself in beautiful red, blue and bold lines. His bed was at the centre of the room, pushed up against the wall. There was even enough space for a leather couch and a low-lying coffee table, which had various magazines scattered across it. The door leading to the en suite bathroom had a poster of an Anthony Lister street mural on it, a new addition. I wandered over and peeled off the Post-it note stuck to side of the poster.

'"Blood is just red sweat",' I read. Very macho.

'It's an Enson Inoue quote. He's an Asian mixed martial artist,' he said from behind me.

'Don't you have another one of his somewhere?'

'Over there.' Poc pointed to a piece of paper he'd laminated and stuck at the top of his mirror. It said: 'At least one time in your life, train with the will to die.'

'Merry,' I remarked. I didn't add that that pretty much summed up how I'd been training in the past week. 'What's with all the Fitspo?'

'I've been going to the gym a lot lately.' He shrugged.

'Not with Joey, I hope.'

'No roids,' he laughed. 'One of the guys at the studio has been trying to convert me to your gym, actually. Plus I watched *The Fighter*.'

'Heh. That will do it.'

After chucking my keys and phone on the coffee table, I bent down and grabbed a CD that was lying on Poc's couch. 'Serpent City. Is it good?'

'Judge for yourself.' Poc pressed a button on his stereo and the first song began blaring out of his high-tech speaker system. It was a bit screamo rock for me. Korn were about the heaviest I could handle before my ears started to bleed.

Poc walked over and grabbed my hand softly.

'I don't think you came over here to listen to music, though,' he said, pulling me towards him. His other hand skimmed over my butt and my heart rate accelerated as we moved closer.

'That's for sure,' I whispered, as our lips touched with the first kiss. I felt his tongue in my mouth and a slow burn started in my chest. I pressed my body against his and ran my hands up his muscular arms before moving to his back. He shivered as my fingertips ran over his skin. Poc pulled me tighter against him. We were kissing passionately now and I could feel his hardness against my leg. He leaned back for a moment and pulled his singlet off. My hands slid over his body until they rested above his belt line and he moved in again. We weren't wasting any time here and I didn't mind. Poc pulled my dress over my head and ran his hands over my breasts with a hungry look in his eyes. He buried his head in them, sucking and groping, and I ran my fingers through his hair. He started kissing his way up from my bust to my neck and I heard myself gasp as he reached a particularly sensitive spot near my chin. Moving my hands down from the back of his head, I skimmed his lower back before running one hand up and down his boner.

'Tommi,' he breathed into my ear.

In a particularly magnificent feat of multitasking, I leaned in to kiss him and undid his zipper at the same time. I got the pants undone and started to work them off his hips when his hands found my crotch. Instead of feeling the usual shivers of excitement as he stroked the material in between my legs I felt something else. Terror.

I tried to ignore it. I tried to get lost in the sensation. My lips had stopped moving as Poc kissed me and he began to slide my tights down. I had a sudden flash of Steven, animalistic and brutal, as he tugged down my jeans in the shed. Squeezing my eyes shut, I tried to block it out as Poc undid my bra. My body stiffened as his lips found my bare nipple. When I looked down at the back of his head I saw Steven's slicked ponytail and hair shaven at the sides. Suddenly Poc's hands weren't warm any more. They felt foreign, rough, cold. Like Steven's. His grinning face leered out of the darkness at me and I screamed.

I leaped back from Poc, wheezing. Poc stood there with his arms frozen in the position they had been when they were holding me and not thin air. His pants were barely hanging on to his body and I could see the starting line of his pubic hair.

'What?' he said, shocked.

I was staring at him and trying to focus on his face. It kept shifting back and forth between his and Steven's. I was topless and crossed my arms over my chest as Poc made a move to come closer.

'What the hell, Tommi?'

started within my belly and I took comfort in the wild sound issuing from my mouth. How weak and pathetic was I that I couldn't even let a guy touch me without flashing back to that one horrible moment with Steven? In fact, that whole horrible day with the Ihis was haunting me. Less than twenty-four hours with them and my life had been altered for ever. As much as I wanted to pretend, there was no going back to normal. I was still growling and my lips withdrew over my teeth as I snarled, something that was decidedly inhuman but also felt perfectly right. My fists clenched and unclenched. The skin felt foreign to me and I looked down to see transformation beginning to take hold. I watched as my fingertips shifted, my wrists, my forearms, my entire arms, as it spread along my body and I could do nothing to stop it. I didn't want to. A hot tear start to trickle down my face and instead of wiping it away I hurled my keys across the room. They knocked over my alarm clock and I watched it fall to the ground. Staring at my room, I wanted nothing more than to shatter every part of it. It was a life I would never get back.

I swept my arm across my chest of drawers and the jewellery, perfume and picture frames smashed to the ground. My claws dragged through the wood and it felt sensational. I picked up a perfume bottle that had survived and hurled it at my mirror with a triumphant scream. It shattered into tiny pieces. I grabbed a shard of mirror and tore it through the canvas that was resting on my easel. When the jagged piece got stuck in the wood frame I ripped at the material until there was nothing left. Snatching the easel off the ground I threw it across the room at my lamp and heard a satisfying crunch as it connected. The door to my room burst open and Lorcan came flying in just as I tipped my chest of drawers over.

'Tommi, stop!'

I could barely hear him over the sounds of my own destruction. As I reached for my wrecked mirror frame, Lorcan's arms grabbed me from behind and I fought to shake him off.

'Calm down!' he shouted.

'LET ME GO!' I threw myself from side to side to get free of him but he just grabbed me tighter and linked his arms around the front. 'IT'S RUINED! EVERYTHING'S RUINED!'

'I know!' he yelled back. 'It's OK, Tommi, I know.'

Fighting against him was fruitless; he just gripped me tighter and tighter until I couldn't escape. My screams started to turn to sobs and I sagged against him. The sobs elevated to tears and I began crying hysterically. I leaned forward and my body convulsed with emotion. Hunching over, I watched the wolf disappear from my limbs like a tide ebbing away. Lorcan never loosened his grip as I sank to the ground. I sobbed over and over and it felt like a stream of tears and snot were pouring down my face.

My hair hung over my body and Lorcan brushed it back, telling me it would be OK, that I was safe. He said other things. I couldn't hear them through my crying. I must have cried myself to sleep right there on the floor in his arms because the next thing I remember was being carried to bed. Lorcan had me cradled like a little kid, which would have been easy considering his height. He must have sensed that I had awoken because he looked down at me abruptly.

'I'm sorry,' I whispered. I'm not sure if the words even came out right.

He seemed to understand. He replied. I never heard what he said because my eyes were already closing shut again. It's amazing how exhausting crying can be.

I woke on my bed the next morning lying on top of it in the foetal position. Lorcan had taken off my boots and thrown a blanket over me. I pulled it tighter as I curled into myself. I could hear rain splashing softly on the roof outside. That explained why it was so dark for what must have been mid-morning. The weather was reflecting my mood. Great. I closed my eyes and breathed in the smell of the blanket. I felt empty. I had cried myself out.

My door made a low a creak and I looked up to see Lorcan looking in. His hair was out and it covered one side of his face like a curtain as he leaned forward. 'You're awake.'

'Yes,' I replied, surprised at how Vin Diesel-esque my voice sounded.

He walked into the room and shut the door behind him. Stepping over the remnants of my furniture, he negotiated his way to the bed and sat on the edge. I could feel him looking down at me. I couldn't bring myself to meet his gaze just yet. 'I need you to tell me what happened last night,' he said quietly.

I knew this was coming. I nodded, but kept my eyes firmly fixed on my hand as I played with the blanket. 'I know you said not to go—'

'I don't care about that, Tommi. I just want to know what caused this.' He looked pointedly at the room around him. 'You partially shifted.'

'I went round to Poc's. He's a man I'm seeing . . . casually.' God, this was an awkward conversation. I neglected to mention what had sent me there in the first place and gulped as I digested what Lorcan looked like in the morning. I took a breath and continued. 'We got to fooling around and . . . Then it went bad.'

I could have sworn I saw a flash of hurt in Lorcan's eyes, but it was gone before I could even be sure it was actually there. He was quiet for a time, before he reached out and touched my shoulder. 'Did he hurt you?'

I was taken aback by the anger in his tone and the intensity with which he strangled out those few words. My eyes widened as I looked up at him. 'What? No, Poc didn't hurt me at all. It wasn't like that. Well, I kind of punched him in the mouth but not very badly. There was hardly any blood.'

Lorcan loosened his grip on my shoulder and leaned back. I could see the tension as it released from his shoulders.

'It was me,' I said, turning my face away. 'I couldn't see him. It was fine and then all of a sudden it wasn't. When he touched me I felt Steven's hands, I saw Steven's face. God, I even smelled him.' My voice broke on the last word and I cursed myself.

Lorcan was silent and I shut my eyes to try to prevent any more tears.

'Steven sexually assaulted you,' said Lorcan.

'No, he tried to b—'

'He tried to rape you and was unsuccessful. He did sexually assault you, Tommi. Out of everything that happened, the physical pain you experienced, that has to be the most traumatic incident for you.'

I said nothing. The single tear that raced down my face said enough.

'Feeling this way and feeling the pain associated with that is normal,' he said in a soothing voice. 'Not to mention the cruelty your mother faced at the hands of Steven's father. There's enough pain in that alone. It's not your fault, Tommi. It's not your fault.'

I looked over at him and at the truth in his eyes as he repeated the words again. And I began to believe. It wasn't my fault. I was a victim. Whatever I did or didn't experience was in the past. What I did or didn't feel now was OK. 'I know,' I said, sitting up.

'What happened with you and Poc isn't your fault either.'

'I . . . I guess I wasn't ready for that.'

'You didn't know it. Now you do.' Lorcan looked a little uncomfortable and he shifted on the edge of the bed looking away. 'I didn't know that you were going to be . . . active. Otherwise I would have encouraged you to wait, to put some time between everything that happened.'

Now I felt uncomfortable too. 'I will,' I said, resting my head on my knees. 'Now.'

Lorcan looked back at me suddenly. 'You didn't shift, did you? You didn't lose control or turn in front of him? Even just a part of you?'

I shook my head. 'No. It was only when I got here.'

He looked relieved. 'That's a small triumph. Even with all the fear, the anger, the uncertainty, you were able to keep that side of you in check in front of another human.'

Sounded like a miniscule victory to me. 'Right. I might have turned into Joan Crawford but at least I didn't eat anyone.'

Lorcan smiled and looked around at the aftermath. 'It is a mess. I cleaned up most of the glass but I didn't want to touch anything else in case I woke you.'

'Lo, that's really nice of you,' I said, surprised. I sighed and continued. 'What you did for me last night, this morning, I can't . . .' I sighed again.

He put a hand on my knee and I looked at him as he said: 'It's not even mentionable.'

He gave me a lopsided smile. Standing up, Lorcan ran a hand through his hair and made for the door. He paused just as he was about to leave. 'I was thinking you could do with the day off. You probably need it to clean this place. It might do you good.'

A day off. In my head flashed a list of all the things I would rather be doing than running through a forest. I can't say I wasn't tempted. 'Actually, I think training is the best thing for me right now. After the boot camp you've put me through this past week, I can't believe I'm even saying this – I think physical activity would help. There's nothing I'd rather do than go all *Dog Soldiers* in Templeton Woods.'

Lorcan raised an eyebrow.

'BUT.'

'There's always a but,' he muttered.

'Tonight we're going out. It's Friday.'

Lorcan nodded. 'I think that will be good for you, to have some time with your friends.'

'Oh, you're coming, mister.'

'I don't think that's really my . . . scene.'

'You don't even know where we'll go!'

'No. Odds are I wouldn't like it.'

'Even if it was Eggs and Ham, which is practically next door? It's very grunge. Minimal N.E.Ds.'

'Thanks,' he said, shaking his head. 'I'll let you guys do your thing.'

'Meh.' I shrugged. I had to admit I was more disappointed than I thought I would be. I was getting used to having Lorcan around and I couldn't shake the feeling that he wanted space . . . from me.

He left me to get ready and I navigated my way through the rubble to find workout clothes. I would have to speak to

Poc. Apologise. I would also have to start keeping my hormones in check until I got through whatever it was I was going through. Somehow I knew the latter task would be harder.

Chapter 12

Close to two hundred bodies were packed into Eggs and Ham. It wasn't a particularly large venue, which suited the owner just fine. Even when the crowd was small the place looked busy. Not quite as busy as tonight though. Smokers mingled on the front stairs that led down to the basement venue. Inside, people bumped and moved against each other as the DJ started playing a heavy bass track. Tables were scattered around the venue with small groups gathered at them, laughing and chatting. Against the wall was a long, black bar and punters shouted their orders to the bartenders whose hands moved in a blur, pouring, mixing and grabbing drinks.

At the far end in a shadowy corner sat a tall stranger. He was wearing a snug black T-shirt with a weathered leather jacket over the top. Denim jeans led to a pair of black boots and, as he moved in his seat, a loaded knife sheath strapped to his ankle was visible to anyone looking. They weren't. For those that bothered to glance his way the attention went straight to his face and shoulder-length brown hair, which was tucked behind his ears. He was attractive: the longing looks from surrounding females were testament to that.

He wasn't paying attention to them. His gaze was firmly focused on a young woman at the edge of the dance floor.

'Give me a second,' I said, turning my back to him. I looked up at the ceiling and tried to calm my breathing, which was coming out in shuddered puffs. Get your shit together, I said to myself.

Poc's hand touched my shoulder and, before I could stop myself, I spun around and punched him in the face. He jerked back in surprise and grabbed the side of his mouth. Blood trickled through his fingers and I took a step towards him.

'Oh my God, Poc, I'm so—' Steven's bloodied face came back to me and his look of outrage as I brought the wrench down on his head. I shivered as I remembered his scent following me in the forest.

'Fuck, Tommi,' said Poc in a muffled voice through his hand.

'I-I . . .' I had to get out of here is what I had to do. I grabbed my dress, threw it over my head and picked up my keys and phone. I practically ran for the door and it was only with the movement that I realised I'd left my bra behind. Too late now.

'Wher—' started Poc.

'I'm sorry, I'm so sorry,' I shouted over my shoulder before flying out the doorway.

I nearly drove off the road twice on my way home. I wasn't crying, but I wasn't thinking straight. Soundlessly, I made my way into the apartment. Walking down the hallway, I felt a numb sensation, yet only on the outside. Inside, I felt like a Dante painting. I barely noticed the faint glow coming from Lorcan's room as I shut the door to mine, or the hushed voice as he engaged in a heated conversation. Standing at the edge of my bed, I stared at the crease in my purple blanket. Just stared.

At the end of the day nothing had actually happened. Thousands of women had suffered terrible sex crimes at the hands of men and survived to live another day. A deep growl

She was dancing with a small group of people and her movements seemed to enthral him. Black combat boots were laced up over a pair of acid wash jeans, which hugged her body. She wore a loose-fitting silver top that appeared to be a mesh of some sort and fell in cords to just above her thighs. It wasn't completely see-through but enough so that you could glimpse her blue bra and a tattoo underneath. Electric-blue hair was tied in bun at the top of her head and loose strands curled at the base of her neck and around her face. Tiny black skulls dangled off her earrings and they flew outwards as she spun around on the spot laughing at something a companion said. The man was nursing a whisky, which didn't look like it had been touched, as he sat there, still and staring. The hunger in his eyes was unmistakable to anyone who had experienced the sensation of more than mere desire.

'What's your name?' came the sultry voice of a buxom redhead who had sidled up beside him.

He hadn't noticed her approach and looked at her now. She oozed sex appeal and was the only female game enough to approach him so far. The eyes of other curious women darted over. If she was successful, they would be kicking themselves all night.

'Lorcan,' he replied flatly, before returning his gaze to the blue-haired woman.

'Lorcan. Exotic name. I'm kind of exotic myself. My name's Jada,' she purred.

He took a sip of his drink and ignored her.

Undeterred, she placed a hand on his shoulder and said, 'Buy me a drink?'

'No,' he said in a matter-of-fact tone.

The woman jerked her hand away with a look of disgust and made an outraged sound with her tongue before storming off.

The female eyes, and a few male ones, quickly looked away. Lorcan, unfazed, took another sip. A series of quiet claps came from behind him, but he didn't turn around.

'Well, well, well, the impenetrable Lorcan certainly lives up to his reputation,' said a short Asian man, laughing.

Uninvited, he sat down next to Lorcan and ordered Frangelico on the rocks adding, 'I have a sweet tooth.'

Lorcan nodded and, after looking closely at the man, said, 'Let me see your wrist.'

The Asian man held out his wrist under the bar and Lorcan quickly ran his thumb over the symbol tattooed there. He held out his hand and the men shook.

'It's nice to meet you, Akito.'

'Pleasure's all mine. Getting to confer with a warrior of your calibre.' He let out an impressed whistle.

'I'm not a warrior any more.' Lorcan tried to keep the annoyance out of his voice.

'Details, details.'

Akito took a sip from the drink the bartender had handed him and gave him a wink.

Once he was out of earshot, he turned his attention to Lorcan. 'I have to thank you, though. After I graduated in Japan, I'd been stuck gathering ground truth in Romania with the Askari there. Bo-ring.' He took another excited sip. 'Coming to Scotland to work with you – a Custodian now of all things – I couldn't be happier.' His big smile proved it. 'And this new werewolf too, Tommi, she sounds exciting. All that untapped potential.' His eyes almost glazed over at the thought.

'Where is she? Have you seen her tonight?' Akito shifted in his seat as he tried to spot her.

'She's over there with the bright hair,' said Lorcan, discreetly pointing.

Akito let out another impressed whistle. 'Exciting.'

They were silent for a few minutes as they both watched her.

'What's with the jacket?' asked Lorcan, breaking the silence.

Akito was wearing a bejewelled denim number with a matching pair of dark jeans.

'What, this? I'm trying to fit in,' he said, pinching the material.

'You might be trying too hard.'

'Don't let my enthusiasm fool you, Lorcan, I'm very good at my job. There's a reason they sent me here to monitor this unique situation.'

'Let's get to it then.'

'Certainly,' said Akito, unabashed. 'How's the training going?'

'Good. She already had a solid fitness base but, within the week we've been working, she has dramatically improved the use of her heightened senses and abilities. At this stage, she can almost completely control her wolf side. We're still a touch from the next full moon, so it will get harder.'

Akito nodded with keen interest. 'My supervisor told me you said she has total recollection during the shift?'

'Yes.'

'Really, on her first change? I didn't quite believe it at first.'

'Believe it. Her recall is sharp, completely unflawed. From her progress and the way she has taken to the meditation drills, my assessment of her potential stands.'

'Noted. Any rage outbursts or casualties?'

Lorcan paused for a moment before replying. 'None.'

'Incredible.'

'I still have a lot to teach her and I think she'll continue to improve. However, I would like her to have contact with another werewolf. Not the Ihis, obviously, but there's a small population based in Thurso, another in Glencoe Village or the old pack outside Edinburgh. I'm not a werewolf. There are things she can only be taught from her own kind. There's a lot of uncertainty and she's scared. She rarely shows it but she is. I think speaking with one of her own would fix a lot of that.'

Akito nodded. 'I'll make the request.'

'Thank you.'

Although Lorcan was only halfway through his whisky, Akito ordered them two more drinks.

'Any updates on last night?' asked Lorcan.

'Did you go to the scene?'

'Yes.'

'And what did you think?'

'Definitely a werewolf.'

Akito sculled half his drink and put the glass down on the bench with a noisy *thunk*.

'The results are inconclusive at the moment. I'm still trying to find more evidence and establish exactly what happened. I'm leaning towards a werewolf as well. You sure it wasn't your girl?'

'One hundred per cent positive. I was with her at the apartment when it happened. She was nowhere near the property.'

'That's right. You're keeping a close eye on her, aren't you?'

'That's my job,' said Lorcan, swallowing a sip and continuing. 'And it wasn't an accident.'

'What makes you say that? The dead sheep?'

'Yes. He killed them, didn't eat them. The noise of that was used to draw the man outside where he was killed and eaten.'

'That's all going on the theory that it was preconceived. It could have very well been an accidental killing.'

'Not on a full moon? That's a strong accident.'

'Unless it was an outburst of rage that got out of hand.'

Lorcan finished his drink and leaned towards Akito. 'You saw the body.'

'I did,' replied Akito with a visible shudder. 'Anyway, we have no record of other weres besides your girl in the area, not for over four decades. I let the Praetorian Guard know and they have someone on standby in case. I have another colleague arriving from London tonight, who has been sent to assist the investigation. Like I need the help. I guess it's better to be safe than sorry. It's just a shame the media got on to it so quick.'

'The neighbours heard the man's screams and called the police straight away. As soon as a unit's called and that goes over the police scanner the press hear it. That can't be helped.'

'Still,' said Akito, looking gloomy, 'it's annoying. Today's front page had: MAN TORN APART BY WILD BEAST. It will get people in a panic.'

Lorcan looked thoughtful. 'It might help. Things like that don't happen here. At least this way people might take precautions.'

Akito sighed. 'Sure.' He lifted his glass to his lips and finished the remaining half of his drink. He set the glass down and patted Lorcan on the shoulder.

'I've got everything I came for,' he said, getting off his chair. 'I'll send a report on your progress with Tommi to the Custodians and update you on the feral werewolf situation.'

'I'd appreciate that.'

Akito headed towards the exit and moulded quickly into the crowd. Lorcan watched him leave before returning to his drink. He took a small sip of the second whisky and pushed it aside. A thin woman with ghostly white skin was weaving her way through the entrance towards the bar. She was taller than most of the other women there and wore a pair of orange flats with fitted brown slacks. A busy necklace of orange, brown and black beads hung low over the top of her white blouse. With a frustrated movement of her hand, she pushed her straight black hair out of her eyes and moved into the clear spot next to Lorcan.

'Whoa,' she said. 'That was a nightmare.'

Lorcan looked up, surprised for a moment, before recognition crossed his face. 'Hi, Mari.'

'Hey,' she said, waving the bartender over. 'Vodka Sunrise, please.'

As she waited for her drink, she turned to Lorcan, resting an elbow on the counter. 'I thought I was never going to get here,' she said, sounding exhausted.

'Animal attack keeping you late?'

'You have no idea. I pulled a double shift yesterday to cover it, which is kind of expected when something this crazy happens. But I started early on the death knocks this morning trying to get comments from his family and attending the police pressers etcetera, etcetera.'

She handed the bartender a note and took a deep sip of her tropical coloured drink.

'Mmm,' she said, closing her eyes briefly. 'I hoped I'd be out of there by seven at the latest. Police media said they were going to have an update so the night editor wanted me to stay and then they didn't and here I am, three hours later than I intended and nursing a headache.'

She took another sip, smiling.

'I'll get front page again tomorrow. Kind of worth it.'

'Any developments? Do the police know what attacked him yet?'

Mari leaned in closer to reveal the gory details. 'At this stage, their official line is a wild dog of some sort. A detective buddy of mine told me – off the record, of course – that they got an expert in from a wildlife sanctuary and it's unlike any dog attack she's ever seen. She thinks it might even be a pack, given how messed up the guy was.'

Lorcan nodded, but displayed nothing more than mild curiosity.

'The others here?' asked Mari, looking around. 'Kane sent me a text ages ago saying they would meet me here but . . . ah, found 'em.' She adjusted the enormous handbag on her shoulder and started to make her way to the dance floor. She paused. 'You coming?'

Lorcan shook his head. 'No.'

'Righto. Tommi's made Kane dance with them so as soon as I drag him away we'll grab a table if you want to come and hang.'

He nodded in non-committal way. Mari smiled and disappeared into the crowd. Lorcan watched as she arrived at her group of friends and Tommi drew her in for an embrace. She gave Kane a quick kiss and a wave to Joss and two other people in the group Lorcan didn't know. Something Tommi said made her laugh and they moved closer together, exchanging words between dance moves. Lorcan knew the moment Mari told Tommi he was there because she stopped swaying and jerked her head up in his direction. Her eyes scanned the crowd for less than a few seconds before she spotted him sitting in the corner.

As she smiled at him and ducked away from her friends, Lorcan took a quick sip of his drink and swivelled on his stool to face her. She pushed her way through a group of men who looked like they belonged in an indie band and he smirked at the look on their faces as they watched her pass. Coming to a stop in front of him, she placed a hand on her hip.

'Look what we have here. Mister "I don't want to come out tonight, it's not my scene and all that".'

Lorcan smiled and replied: 'I'm a Dr Seuss fan.'

She laughed. 'I'm glad you came, Lo.'

She tilted her head and looked down at his glass. 'What are you drinking? Whisky?'

She picked up the glass and sniffed it, wrinkling her noise. 'It gets the job done.'

'I'm surprised not to see a drink in your hand,' he said.

'Restricts my break-dancing.'

'Oh,' he said seriously. 'That's what that was?'

'Har-de-har. You've been watching, have you? Sitting over here all Jack Torrance won't do.'

He looked at her cautiously. 'It's safer here. Comfortable even.'

'Come on,' she said, moving forward and leaning on his shoulder. 'Did I or did I not turn down the offer of a day off training today?'

He said nothing.

'One dance, up there with all of us and the apartment initiation ritual is over.'

As he looked at her sceptically, she gave him her best cheesy smile.

He laughed.

'As soon as this Nirvana remix is over,' he said, with a sigh.

She looked upwards with a concerned expression. 'Poor Kurt.'

Almost on cue, the dance track ended and the throbbing pulse of the Chemical Brothers took over. Lorcan got up from his seat and, when Tommi turned her back, he sculled the remainder of his drink.

He shook his head slightly and said: 'I'm going to need that.'

With his height and physique combined, it wasn't long before he parted the crowd and caught up with Tommi's blue hair as it bobbed through the chaos. He had just reached her back when she suddenly turned around, sensing his presence. He glanced at the dance floor with a look of uncertainty before a hand grabbed him and pulled him forward. Looking down at Tommi's hand in his, he met her eyes and she smiled sweetly at him.

'Life shrinks or expands in proportion to one's courage,' she said.

He leaned down. 'Who's the teacher here? Shouldn't I be quoting Anaïs Nin to you?'

A flash of surprise crossed her face and she muttered: 'I love that you know that.'

She looked forward at the mass of moving people and yanked him towards a small circle of familiar faces. As they threaded through the crowd, he linked his fingers in hers and tightened his grip slightly.

'Aaay,' said a man with bronze, almost red hair, 'if it isn't the prettiest man in all the land.'

Lorcan looked confused but replied: 'Joss.'

'And of so many words, too,' he said, holding his hand up for a high-five.

Tommi pulled her hand free of Lorcan's and snatched Joss's extended arm down.

'I hate to break it you, kid, but no one does high-fives except creepy uncles and teenagers from the nineties,' she said.

'I was born in the nineties, does that count?'

She gave him a light shove before moving into the music. Joss dashed off in the opposite direction as he spotted someone he knew. Kane, who was dancing behind Mari and holding on to her waist, nodded at Lorcan before returning his attention to his girlfriend.

Lorcan looked comfortable on the dance floor.

His body shifted in time with the beat and he moved his head as if he were familiar with the song. Tommi was watching him with an amused look on her face. He noticed and moved towards her.

'What?'

She shook her head and moved closer to reply. 'You're a good dancer. The way you were looking out here like it was kryptonite . . . you're good.'

She was blushing and lowered her head to hide it. They danced together, hips and bodies moving in time with the beat but never touching. Subconsciously they moved away from the others until they were merely two figures in a sea of heaving people. Occasionally, his hand would brush her arm or her thigh would touch his. For the most part, it was like two compasses circling around each other. She could never meet his gaze for long, yet he never took his eyes off her. A bachelorette party came racing through the crowd and one of the veiled women knocked Tommi forward into Lorcan. They both grabbed each other, stopping the momentum. Lorcan, who had one hand on her shoulder and the other on her waist, held her out in front of him.

'You OK?'

'Please,' she huffed.

They stood there for a moment, both with their hands resting lightly on the other, eyes meeting. Tommi slowly slid her hands down the leather of his jacket until they rested at his elbows and they began moving with the music again. This time their eyes never disconnected. They were barely touching. Lorcan was resting his hands lightly on her swaying hips and Tommi's were cupping his elbows. Couples and groups danced around them, not noticing what was sparking between two people with a foot in a world very different from their own.

Chapter 13

He had his hand on my hips and his thumbs were rubbing small circles over my skin. Music was playing but I had no idea what song. I was oblivious to what was going on around me. I couldn't look away from his eyes. I felt myself move forward and lightly press against his chest. Running my hands from his elbows and up to his shoulders, I didn't feel self-conscious. The way he was looking at me made me feel extremely confident. This was Lorcan. He was a little scary, sure, but he was my teacher. My counsellor. My guardian. He brought one hand to my face and ran it slowly down the length of my jaw. He lifted my chin, tilting my head upwards. My heart felt like it was turning into a mini-wolf inside my chest as he leaned forward and parted his lips . . .

'Tommi?'

'Huh?'

'What do you think?

'Um . . . uh, lower. I want people to be able to actually see the pieces without having to pull an exorcist neck move.'

'Gotcha,' nodded Travis, our gallery fitter.

When he turned back to examine the blank wall I shook my head slightly. I needed to get in the game and stop daydreaming about something that would never happen.

Shouldn't happen.

I'd been like this all week: lost inside my own head more than I usually was and inventing alternative endings to my dance with Lorcan. My imagination came complete with the DVD special features. I was trying very hard not to be one of those girls who obsessed over every detail. I was failing, but in my defence it was a very intimate and sexy dance drawn out over three songs. It had ended abruptly, with Lorcan pulling away and disappearing into the throng of people. All romance pretty much evaporated then as he left me alone, wondering what the heck had just happened. I had rejoined the group in a daze.

'And you know what?' I said, suddenly back on the job. 'Let's not crowd people. Each piece of Wil's work complements the other beautifully. Let's let it do that. We have the space, we may as well use it.'

Travis, who had been marking the wall with a pencil, pulled out his measuring tape. 'A piece per wall? We don't have enough space for that.'

'No, more like . . . let's group some of the fifteen by fours together, three to a wall. Then anything larger is two at the most. I want a wall for each of the centrepieces. They'll be here by Friday.'

Travis nodded, running a hand over his shiny bald head.

'That will work. We should have everything up by Tuesday afternoon, night at the latest. That leaves you Wednesday to make any changes and the *dobber*—'

'Wil Garman,' I supplied.

'You know they're all the same to me. The *dobber* has Thursday to give it a once-over before the opening that night.'

'You're the man, Travis.'

'Try telling my husband that.'

'I'll leave you to it,' I said, smiling.

The first of the season of pop-up exhibitions was being held in what had once been a bar on the outskirts of Dundee. Yet like so many businesses here the place had gone under in less than a year. It had failed to find someone to take up the lease and so had sat here abandoned and gathering dust. Walking through the empty space, I gave a wistful sigh. This was always my favourite time, the days just before an exhibition opening when you had nothing but bare walls daring you to make something of them.

The building's shape was unusual: a long, rectangle structure with platforms creating levels where you would least expect them. It was an abortion of architecture, which is one of the reasons I had chosen it. That and the owners had offered us the venue for free in the hope that one of the exhibition attendees might see some potential in it that the citizens of Dundee hadn't. I smiled deeper at the thought of how this place was going to look in a week's time. That reminded me, I needed to call the caterers. I picked up my pace as I started making a mental list of all the things I needed to do when I got back to McManus.

Really, it was amazing I was balancing an exhibition opening with four hours of training a day (two before work and two after). It was half of what Lorcan and I had been doing before I returned to work. He said he didn't mind. I believed him; especially when he followed that up with how it was important to have something else to occupy me besides wolfie business. Of course he hadn't actually used the term 'wolfie business'. That was my addition. It's not like I was missing out on anything. In fact, my training was going really well. Not kill-you-with-my-bare-hands well, but close, which was even more impressive considering the potential awkwardness after our sexy dance.

I don't know why I kept calling it that in my head. It wasn't *that* sexy. We were barely touching yet somehow it had been the most stimulating seven minutes of my life.

'And breathe out, letting go of everything else as you hear yourself exhale.'

It's not that I wasn't trying. I was. Lorcan's voice was making my pulse race instead of relaxing me. How did this happen? I found him so terrifying at first. Followed by annoying. When did the attraction pop up?

'And out,' he said.

I had my eyes shut and was sitting cross-legged in the yoga room of my local gym. It had been raining when I finished work so Lorcan sent me a text telling me we'd be coming here. Since he trained me directly before and after work he had taken to dropping me off and picking me up each day. We'd alternate between cars to avoid suspicion. Mari never noticed anyway.

I don't know how he wrangled it but we had the whole yoga room to ourselves.

He seemed buddy-buddy with the police officer who co-owned the place, which was jarring. When I asked him how he knew the guy and when he'd had time to make friends, Lorcan just gave me his token lopsided smile and an evasive answer. It made me think the cop could be involved with the local Askari somehow. Or not. Maybe he and Lorcan went to book club together. Suddenly, I had an image of the two of them discussing *Sense and Sensibility* over a cappuccino. I giggled, completely losing focus.

'Tommi,' he said in a disapproving tone.

'Sorry,' I said, opening my eyes and swallowing another giggle at the look on his face. 'After an hour and a half of hand-to-hand combat I can't wind down tonight.'

Lorcan smiled at me and I did my best to keep my face straight.

'You're developing,' he said.

'Ah, I think puberty's way over for me.'

He blushed and I liked it.

'No, as a wolf. Your energy levels are higher than a normal human's and as you get stronger you'll begin to heal faster.'

Without thinking about it my hand automatically went to my throat where an unattractive cut sat. It was where Steven had pricked me with his knife. Dr Kikuchi had applied butterfly stitches to it and a 'special' healing balm, but I was going to have a scar there. Lorcan followed my movement and looked at me with sad eyes.

'That won't heal,' he said softly.

'Why not?' I couldn't help sound like a petulant child.

'Because it happened before you had shifted, before you were an activated werewolf complete with the healing and abilities. The cut was too deep.'

'It only happened a few seconds before.'

He held my gaze for a long moment. 'I'm sorry, Tommi.'

I sighed. My fingers traced the fading red bands at my wrists where the flesh had been worn away as I tried to free myself from handcuffs at the Ihis. These were the ugliest marks and so far I had managed to cover them with strategically placed clothing and jewellery. I'd taken off my rubber band altogether, no longer finding a need for it, and the scar it gave me seemed tiny and insignificant compared to my new ones. I would permanently have two rings running around my wrists as a constant reminder of what I went through. I didn't want that reminder.

'Will I get hyper?' I asked, trying to change the topic.

'No, the same as you are now, except you won't get tired as easily, excluding after the full moon. And you'll hardly ever get sick.'

'Awe-some.'

Besides the blood-curdling pain of transformation and the fact I could end up humping someone's leg for three days a month, there were definitely perks to this werewolf thing. By the start of the week, I'd mastered full back flips and fly kicks. And I don't mean the acrobatic kind: I mean the *Crouching Tiger, Hidden Werewolf* kind. They were moves I would have to keep in check depending on who was around if I did get in a fight because Lorcan assured me there was nothing 'human-looking' about them. My running speed was Olympic level and I could do a hundred push-ups before I even started to feel a burn.

Lorcan was holding back less and less every time we fought. He was still vastly superior but at least I didn't feel like he was humouring me any more. We'd moved on from daggers and bamboo poles to machetes and crossbows, which was insanely fun. Tomorrow, Lorcan wanted to teach me how to make everything into a weapon – starting with household appliances to, pardon the pun, sticks and stones. They can, as it turns out, break your bones.

We'd also been working on tracking. That was a lot harder to master than the physical side for me as it was trying to harness one of my most wolf-like aspects days out from the full moon. I had to compartmentalise the two separate sides of me to find the scent (wolf side) and analyse what it meant (Tommi side). Even though we had less time it seemed like we'd been cramming a lot more into the sessions, ever since . . . well, Friday night now that I thought about it. Maybe I was reading too much into it, like every stupid rom-com heroine I'd made gagging noises at Mari to over the years. Or maybe Lorcan was trying to keep my mind occupied. Maybe he was trying to keep his off other things, too.

We hadn't talked about 'the dance' since it happened. As soon as we'd rejoined the group everything went back to normal. He didn't bring it up and I didn't want to.

My mind might be playing daily screenings of it, complete with deleted scenes, but I knew the reality. It wouldn't work. For starters, I didn't know enough about Lorcan. Besides mentioning the thought of getting his family crest tattooed he never spoke about his family. He never spoke about friends back in America or Ireland – excluding that one conversation about Amos – and he had no social life that I knew of. But we weren't bickering like we used to. We didn't fight at all now during training and home life, which was probably the biggest change since 'the dance'. And that worked for me. I was focusing on keeping my hormones under control and trying to stay nonchalant about the whole thing. It wasn't easy. A few times I'd caught Lorcan looking at me strangely. Every time he shook it off almost the second I noticed.

'I want to try something else.'

'OK,' I said, pretending I'd been lost in Zen-land instead of Tommi-land.

'The most powerful werewolves aren't controlled by the full moon.'

'Wait, what? Teach me that!'

'It's not really something you can teach. You're either born with the ability or you're not. Even then a lot of wolves never learn how to harness it.'

'You're saying some of us don't have to turn on a full moon?'

'Yes. They usually do anyway because the pull is so strong. They can resist if they want to but it's exhausting. Most would rather not be in such a weakened state for three days and nights in a row, as well as recovery time.'

'Whoa,' was my only response.

'They can also shift at will, whenever they want.'

'You want me to try and shift right now?'

'No, that would be impossible for such a young wolf between moons. What I want you to try and do is shift a part of you. I don't expect you to get it on the first go. Realistically it will probably take months and most werewolves can never do it. Your father could. I don't know how many of the other Ihis can. I'd hazard a guess that most can. With how quickly you've taken to everything I've taught you, I think you could do it in a few weeks if we start work now.'

Shift just a part of me. Sure.

Accidentally, doing it when I was emotional was one thing. Trying to go from zero to fifth gear with only a few instructions, that was something else entirely.

'Sounds like controlling water as it's slipping through my fingers, Lo.'

He looked thoughtful for a moment. 'We'll start slow. Try stirring the wolf within you tonight. In a few days, we'll try directing the energy to a specific part of your body.'

'Anywhere but the ears,' I whispered, closing my eyes.

'Try to block everything out, like we've been doing,' he said in a soothing voice.

I exhaled and did what he said.

I let everything go, every emotion, every task, every scar, every memory and every pain. I tried to just *be*. There was nothing else, only me. And my wolf.

It was strange to explain. The wolf wasn't separate to me: it was as much a part of me as my blue hair. Yet I was able to identify it, recognise it and mould it. I didn't know what to do at first. I slowly got comfortable with this small thundercloud inside of me. What did Lorcan say to do next? He didn't. He said I wouldn't be able to channel it for weeks. He said eventually I'd try directing it to a specific part of my body. He didn't explain how. As I was thinking this over, I felt it slowly begin to slip away from my core. I tried to chase after it but chasing something with your mind is unbelievably hard. It was gone. I sighed, disappointed. I'd been closer than I expected.

'I lost it, I lost the connection,' I said flatly, still keeping my eyes shut.

'Tommi, I want you to remain calm.'

There was a strange note in his voice, wary almost.

'Calm? Of course I'm calm. We're meditat—' I opened my eyes to reply properly and came to a stop mid-sentence.

Resting with my palm facing upwards on my knee was a monstrous claw where my left hand used to be.

'Fuck me gently with a chainsaw.'

My mouth was hanging open and I couldn't tear my gaze away from it. It was almost an identical effect to what had happened when I escaped the Ihis.

I hadn't felt the form change, like then, but this time I wasn't under emotional or physical duress.

'Stay calm,' said Lorcan.

'Claw. I have a wolf claw. Or paw. Oh God. What do I do?'

'I don't know,' said Lorcan, staring at it. 'I didn't think you would get this far.'

'What do you mean you don't know? How the fuck do I get rid of it?'

'Stay calm, Tommi. It's important you stay calm. You can't shift here. Not that you could . . .'

He trailed off and I took a deep breath, swallowing my pulse. My heart was thudding against my chest and I could feel a cold sweat starting to form around my forehead. I shut my eyes and breathed in and breathed out. In and out. The room was completely silent.

'How,' I said, slowly and calmly, 'do I . . . get . . . rid of it?'

I couldn't exactly go walking out of the gym waving goodbye to everyone with a hand like *Teen Wolf*.

'Try and think it away,' said Lorcan.

'Are you trying to make me mad? "Think it away"?'

'Relax, Tommi, relax.'

I did what he said and tried not to dwell on the impossibility of thinking anything away. Instead, I visualised using my left hand. I was right-handed, but I imagined using my left to hold a paintbrush. I tried to invoke the sensation of digging my hand into the sand and grasping the grains. I imagined putting my hand in a stream and pushing it against the current.

'Open your eyes,' said Lorcan.

It was gone. I don't think I've ever been so happy to see my very ordinary and hair-free left hand. I let out a shuddered breath of relief and stretched my fingers. Lorcan was looking between me and my hand with amazement.

'Let's not try that again,' I said.

'I can't believe you were able to do it on your first attempt, basically master it.'

'I wouldn't exactly say I mastered it. I thought I failed until I saw it all—' I curled my hand into what I thought looked like a menacing posture and made a growling sound.

Lorcan laughed, slamming the door to his jeep and walking around to the passenger side.

'Still, the fact you were even able to manifest something on the first go. It's incredible, Tommi. I'm not even sure what this means yet, but it's incredible.'

He had been like this the whole way home. I'd never seen the guy so excited. It felt like this was as close as Lorcan got to punching the air and whooping. I was less impressed and more alarmed at the thought that I had the ability to shift a part of me at will. Sure, I had to think about it, hard, but this presented a whole new set of problems.

'Lo, did you have any idea how to get me to return to normal?'

'None. Only theories. I actually hadn't done that much research into it. I thought it was something we could start working on and, by the time it became a reality, I'd have a plan.'

I laughed. I couldn't help be amused at seeing a more carefree, less prepared side to Lorcan. The physical side of my training definitely played more to his strengths than the deeply Custodian stuff.

'And what if it was my leg that transformed? Or I grew a tail? What kind of mentor would you be if the whole gym saw me wagging like Old Yeller?' I teased.

'You're enjoying this.'

He fished his house keys out of his pocket.

'Yes,' I said, leaning on the door. 'I love having my normally beautiful specimen of a hand turned into a mutant paw.'

'No, but you love getting high and mighty with me about this.'

'That might be true.'

He laughed and I laughed with him as we stumbled through the door of the apartment.

'Oh good, you're home just in time. There's a guy here to see you, Tommi,' said Mari from the kitchen. 'What did you say your name was again?'

'Steven.'

My blood ran cold. That voice. I would recognise the malice and slime in that voice anywhere. I'd been facing away from the kitchen when we walked in and I slowly turned to face Mari and my visitor.

Steven.

He was wearing a dark jacket over a black shirt and leaning casually on the breakfast bar. Mari was on the other side of the bench, resting her hand on the sink and smiling politely. I barely saw her. All I could see was Steven, in my home, smirking while those black eyes pierced me like laser beams. I froze. I couldn't move. Everything I'd learned, all the skills I'd mastered, they were useless now. I was paralysed with fear as the feature of my nightmares licked his lips at me. Something big flashed in front of my eyes and the loose strands of my ponytail brushed against my face with the force of the movement. I blinked and the scene had changed entirely. Lorcan had Steven by the throat and pressed up against a wall. I hadn't even seen him move. He had Steven's arms pinned behind his back with one hand, while the other was clenched tightly around his trachea.

'Lorcan, what are you doing?' screamed Mari, making a move to go around the kitchen and help Steven.

I grabbed her by the hand before she passed and gently pulled her behind me.

'Tommi, he's going to kill him!'

It certainly looked that way.

Steven's face was going purple and bits of spittle were coming out of his clenched lips as he struggled to get oxygen. His feet were off the ground and flailing madly in the air like a floating tap dancer. He tried to say something and Lorcan lifted him off the wall slightly before slamming him back into it with enough force to send a nearby picture frame crashing off the mantelpiece.

'Tommi,' Mari pleaded, sounding less sure of herself due to my inaction.

'Leave it,' I said.

Lorcan pushed his face right up to Steven's with just centimetres separating them. During the scuffle, Lorcan had got his switchblade and he had the sharpest point pressed against Steven's throat for emphasis.

'You don't get to talk,' he said in a voice unlike his own. 'You don't get to do anything here.'

As he said the last word, he drew Steven off the wall again and threw him across the room into the lounge. He landed on our coffee table and it turned into a fountain of splinters as Steven connected with it. He lay propped on his elbows and knees, coughing and spluttering. He looked up at Lorcan and a thick trickle of blood ran down his face. Hate poured from his eyes and I could almost see him trying to plot a way to attack. He glanced at me, but as Lorcan took a step towards him that hate was replaced with pure fear.

'You don't get to look at her, you don't *ever* get to look at her. You don't even say her name, you hear me?'

He was menacing. Terrifying. Lethal. Steven coughed some more and took a shuddered breath.

'Fuck you,' he spat.

Lorcan was on him in a flash and delivering a rib-cracking kick to the stomach. It might have broken more than one rib because I was sure I heard multiple cracks.

Mari squealed and I winced at the sound of impact. Steven let out a yell of pain before rolling on to his back and cradling his stomach. Lorcan leaned down and pressed his forearm to Steven's throat.

'I don't think you understand the gift I'm giving you,' he growled. 'I'm handing you over to the Treize, but I'm letting you keep your life.'

'Yes-s-s,' Steven strangled out.

Lorcan pressed down on his throat once more before removing his elbow and standing up. He looked enormous bearing down over Steven's pathetic, whimpering form.

'Tommi, in my room there's a chest. Inside it you'll find some restraints,' said Lorcan, not taking his eyes off Steven.

'Got it,' I mumbled, turning towards the hall.

I had just passed Mari when she let out a shriek. Spinning around, I managed to see Lorcan hit the ground with a *thud* as Steven sprinted for our balcony. Pausing for a split second, he hunched over the balcony railing. The wind lightly rustled the end of his ponytail, which was slicked back in its usual style. He turned and took one last look at me. It said he'd return. Lorcan was back on his feet and moving towards him. Before he could get any closer, Steven launched himself over the balcony. Mari gasped and clapped a hand over her mouth. Lorcan stepped out on to the balcony and I saw the back of his head move as he followed Steven's movement with his eyes.

The apartment block was a low rise and only three storeys. We were on the second and even if a normal person fell from the balcony the fall wouldn't kill them. You could almost safely jump to the ground. Joss had certainly threatened to a few times. I shivered. It was a warm night for August but the whole incident had left me chilled, inside and out. The remnants of our coffee table crunched beneath my feet as I walked to the middle of the lounge and stared into the darkness, wondering where he went. The noise of my approach must have alerted Lorcan because he spun around. I barely had a chance to meet his eyes before he strode forward and pulled me to him. He wrapped his arms protectively around me and drew me towards him. I was shocked at first. Then comforted. I closed my eyes and rested my head against the expanse of his broad chest as he held me tighter. I unfurled my arms, linked them around his back and gripped him.

The person I feared most in the world had strolled out of my nightmares and into real life. He'd sat here, in my kitchen, comfortable and patiently waiting for me to get home. What if we hadn't come home when we did? What if he'd done to Mari what he tried to do to me? I squinted my eyes shut at the thought of what could have happened and tried to block those images from my mind. I was safe here in Lorcan's arms. I felt like nothing could hurt me. Still holding on to me, Lorcan pulled back and looked down at my face. He brushed a loose strand of hair away from my eyes and cupped my face in both his hands.

'Are you OK?'

His voice was soft but strong at the same time. It couldn't have been further away from the fearful tone he'd used minutes before. I looked into his eyes and, like my daydreams, I nearly found myself lost in the forest. I couldn't bring myself to say anything so I tried to nod, which was difficult with him holding me the way he was.

'Aye,' I said in the bravest voice I could muster. 'Are you?'

'A tiny knock.'

He lightly ran his thumb under one of my eyes and I was surprised to feel wetness there. I hadn't remembered shedding a single tear. My body, always betraying me.

'I would never let him hurt you,' he said with so much emotion I couldn't help smile.

'I know,' I whispered back, as the breeze blew his hair around his face.

'Can someone please tell me what the hell just happened?'

Mari's weak voice came from behind us and I was thrust back into the moment. She was resting against the door and looked equal parts terrified and confused. Lorcan looked at her over my shoulder and I could tell he wasn't quite sure what to do.

'Mari, I'm so sorry you had to see that,' I said, walking towards her.

'You j-just smashed him,' she said, pointing a shaking finger at Lorcan. 'You were so fast and threw him around the room like a rag doll.'

She was looking at Lorcan with a frightened expression. That was the last thing I wanted. I placed a hand on her shoulder and turned on my best calming voice.

'Mari.'

'And you did nothing!'

'Because Lorcan was protecting me,' I said forcefully. 'That guy, Steven, he tried to rape me in New Zealand. Got pretty close, too. I was lucky to escape with my life.'

Mari's focus was only on me now. 'W-what? You never said anything?'

'I know and it was stupid of me. I told Lorcan, but besides him I just wanted to forget about it and deal with it in my own way. I never for a second thought that he would come here or that you would be put in danger.'

'You think he would have tried to attack me if you two hadn't come home?' she asked, her voice going higher than I thought possible.

'I doubt it,' said Lorcan, who had taken a few steps closer but was remaining a distance away from Mari. 'I think he was here to mess with Tommi.'

Mari didn't look relieved. 'Did you report him to the police in New Zealand?'

'Yes. By the time they went to press charges he'd fled Rotorua,' I said, thinking on the spot.

'We have to tell them now!'

'I will, Lorcan and I will. I think the most important thing for you to do right now is rest. I'm so sorry I put you through this, Mari.'

Her mouth formed a small 'O' before she leaned forwards and hugged me.

'It's not your fault. I let him in! I'm so sorry this happened at all,' she said into my shoulder.

I held her for a moment longer before pulling back. 'Do you want me to call Kane?'

She sniffed and nodded. I dialled his number and explained what had happened. Despite my cover story, Mari was standing as far away from Lorcan as she could and they weren't talking to each other. The second Kane arrived Mari burst into tears and fell into his arms. They went to her room shortly after and I could hear him comforting her through the closed door. Lorcan was speaking very quietly and fast to someone on the phone. I watched him pace up and down the lounge room. He was speaking to the local Askari and explaining what had happened. He thought Steven was the feral werewolf responsible for killing the man last week. He suggested they should start hunting him, now. They agreed.

'It was my fault. I underestimated him and didn't restrain him quick enough. No. No, I'm staying here,' he said. 'He originally came for Tommi. He's smart enough to know that you will start hunting him tonight and he'll expect me to join in. He might even be watching the apartment now to see what I do.'

I shivered at that thought.

'I'll stay here with her to make sure he doesn't come back.'

'You really are one of the Custodians now,' said the voice on the other end.

'Keep me posted,' replied Lorcan and he hung up. He looked up at me watching him. 'Did you hear all that?'

'Most of it.'

'Good. You need to know what's going on.'

'Are you sure you don't want to be out there with them?'

He walked around the bench and ran his hand over my shoulder. 'I let him get away. I'm not leaving you unprotected.'

'Pfft,' I said. 'I'll be fine. Leave me some daggers and a machete and I swear I won't freeze up again.'

He stilled for a moment with his hand on my shoulder. He withdrew it slowly and let it hang at his side.

'Of course if you'd rather be alone I can arrange f—'

'No,' I said, interrupting him.

He was already beginning to turn away and I pulled him back to face me.

'The last thing in the world I want is to be alone,' I said, staring fiercely at him.

The disappointment that faded from his eyes made me feel powerful and I linked my hand in his. I had just seen those fingers crush a man's throat. At that moment they were soft and gentle as they intertwined with my own.

Chapter 14

We switched up training for the next few days. Toning our usual session down somewhat, we trained at the gym the day after Steven's visit and again on Saturday.

'Until he's caught or we at least have a better sense of where he is I want to take precautions,' said Lorcan.

We were training inside for the time being. I was a harder target if I wasn't dangling upside down from a tree in dark woods. In a testament to how cautious we were being, our usual Friday night outing was replaced with a nice, quiet movie night. We filled Joss in on the situation (the werewolf-free version) and he was more than willing to stay in with Kane, Mari, Lorcan and me. Lorcan fell asleep halfway through *The Fifth Element*, which I thought was adorable. He'd stayed up the entire night after Steven showed himself. I'd somehow fallen asleep after a shower, but I imagined Lorcan had spent the evening pacing the lounge room and glaring into the night.

We were two-thirds of the way through a day session on Saturday when the Askari called Lorcan to tell him they'd lost Steven's trail.

'They followed it to Manchester before it went cold,' he said, looking frustrated. 'They think I might have scared him off for good.'

Lorcan, who was clenching his mobile phone extremely tight, glanced over at me.

I raised an eyebrow.

'No,' he said. 'I don't believe that either.'

'You messed him up royally,' I said. 'You threw down and it's going to be a while before he can get the courage to come back again. Especially knowing you'll kill him next time.'

Lorcan looked at me, hard, as if searching for something in my eyes.

'I will kill him.'

'I know. I wish I could be forgiving and believe people are redeemable and all that good stuff. The truth is I want him to die. I'm just ashamed I wasn't able to do it myself. I turned into a mannequin.'

'Hey,' said Lorcan, placing his fingers under my chin and tilting my head up towards his. 'You have nothing to be ashamed of. Nothing.'

'I froze up. You had to step in to defend me. I'm a traitor to the feminist movement.'

Lorcan smiled briefly. 'You'll be ready next time. You shouldn't be embarrassed by what happened, Tommi. It isn't your natural instinct to fight yet, especially when it's someone you never expected to see again. And what I did was as much for me as it was for you. I've spent a long time fighting and killing and it isn't easy to turn that off. The old me still slips out sometimes.'

He let go of me and I could see him physically withdraw into himself. He turned and walked away until he was staring in the mirror that ran the entire third side of yoga room. Lorcan was wearing black three-quarter cargo shorts with a baggy, black singlet that had a faded motorcycle club logo on it. He had his hair pulled back off his face with a black bandana and the rest of it was out and hanging loosely behind his head. I walked up to him, slowly. He was staring hard at himself and, although he didn't react to my approach, I knew he noticed it.

I stood still at Lorcan's side when he said: 'I'm glad you're not afraid of me. I thought that after the Steven incident you might have been. Like Mari.'

'I could never be afraid of you. You saved my life that night and Mari's. She was only afraid at first because she didn't understand what was going on.'

Lorcan said nothing. He kept staring at his own reflection. What he was looking for I didn't know.

'You saved my life, Lo. And not just then. OK, you were pretty scary and hostile when I first met you, hence the running away, but you saved my life the very next day. And the one after, and after, and after. Every day that you're here, teaching me and supporting me, you're saving my life. You brought me back from the brink. You must know that.'

Looking at my reflection in the mirror, Lorcan said: 'I've done terrible things, Tommi.'

I didn't know what to say to that. I felt if I replied 'everyone has' that would be belittling. The truth was I didn't know what Lorcan had seen or done. I'd never seen him plagued by past acts like he was now. I never knew the Lorcan that was with the Praetorian Guard.

'I don't know what you've done with the PG. I think you know that whatever you did it was for the greater good, otherwise you wouldn't have done it.' I lifted my elbow and rested it on his shoulder. 'Plus,' I said, smirking at the reflection of the two of us, 'I can only go off the Lo that I've come to know in the past few short weeks.'

I hadn't felt self-conscious until that moment when I came dangerously close to saying all the things I felt for Lorcan. He did the most unexpected thing then and turned his head to the side, like he was about to give my elbow a quick kiss. He jerked backwards, as if he had internally scolded himself for even thinking about such an affectionate gesture. I couldn't help feel my mouth open in surprise. The room suddenly filled with the sounds of The Heavy as my mobile rang in my bag. I seized the distraction and made a move for it.

Lorcan had a strict 'no calls during training' policy and I sensed he was about to remind me of that when I shouted over my shoulder: 'You took a call.'

Not looking at the caller ID, I grabbed the phone and hit the answer button while trying not to smile too big at the look on his face.

'Yellow,' I said.

'Tommi, thank heavens, it's Alexis.'

'Hi, boss. What's wrong?' Alexis never called me on a weekend. It was safe to say something was up.

'I have a very strange message that Wil Garman left on my voicemail last night. It says he doesn't want to do the exhibition and he's through with trying to establish himself as an artist in the UK. Also, he's moving to New York.'

'Did he sound *blootered*?'

'Yes. That's not the point. We've invested too much in this exhibition to have it go pear-shaped now. You know where he lives, don't you?'

'He works and lives in a studio at Broughty Ferry.'

'Can you go over there and make sure he's not having any last-minute jitters? I need to know that everything is fine heading into next week.'

'Sure,' I said, 'I can pop around this afternoon.'

'Now, if you can, Tommi. As soon as possible. I know it's a Saturday and you probably have plans but the opening is important.'

'I'll head over straight away.'

'And call me when you're done? Let me know what happened?'

'Sure.'

'Thanks, Tommi.'

I hung up and looked over at Lorcan, who didn't look happy about cutting training short.

'We weren't done.'

'I know, I know. Can you add it on another day? This is my job, Lorcan. I can't blow it off and I wouldn't want to.'

'What does your boss want you to do?'

'The artist, Wil, left a message on her phone last night freaking out about the exhibition and the opening. He lives about fifteen minutes away. I need to go and check he hasn't gone van Gogh on us.'

Lorcan gave me a confused look.

'Never mind,' I said, waving away the comment. 'I'll have a shower, get changed and we'll go, aye?'

Frustrated as he was, he agreed.

We were making our way up the stairs to Wil's studio when I used my werewolf hearing to find out if he was home.

'He's here. And alive. I can hear him talking to someone.'

Lorcan was ahead of me and turned to give a quick nod of approval at the use of my extended senses. There was enough room for Lorcan and me to stand side by side on the doorstep. Before raising my hand to knock, I paused.

'To warn you,' I started, 'this guy's a bit pretentious.'

'Aren't all artists?'

He brushed a finger over a Turkish evil eye that was hanging in the middle of the door. The bells dangling from it jingled. Classy.

'No, not all artists are pretentious. Some are depressed.'

He laughed as I knocked three times. It was a surprisingly stuffy day and I'd thrown on a pair of denim cut-off shorts over leggings and a vintage *Jem and the Holograms* T-shirt I'd found on eBay. I had a pair of grey and silver Converse All Stars on as well and my hair was pulled back in a braid. A bright-eyed looking Wil answered the door in navy blue skinny-leg jeans, of course, bare feet and a woollen cardigan thrown over his exposed chest. He had necklaces with various symbols on them draped around his neck (one I noticed was a mini-harmonica).

'Tommi,' he said, mildly shocked. 'It's good to see you here. And who's your friend?'

His eyes had moved to Lorcan and the way he was looking at him made me grateful he'd changed from his arm-bearing gym singlet to a baggy T-shirt. Wil dated women, I knew that for a fact, but there was something very bohemian about the way he was looking at Lo.

'Aren't you quite the male specimen?' Wil said as his eyes ran over Loran. 'That jawline ... I'd love to get you to model for me some time.'

Lorcan looked like he'd swallowed a lemon doused in Listerine.

'I've already asked Tommi dozens of times.'

Lorcan looked at me sideways, curious.

'I said no,' I muttered, watching relief turn to amusement on Lorcan's face.

'No,' replied Lorcan, turning to Wil, 'I don't, er, model.'

He looked so uncomfortable saying those words I had to bite my lip to hold back an outburst of laughter.

'Wil, this is my pal Lorcan. I dragged him here with me because we were hanging out when I got a very distressed call from Alexis, telling me you were having second thoughts about the exhibition. Say it isn't so?'

Wil had the grace to look embarrassed. He opened his mouth to say something when a voice came from behind him.

'Who is it, babe?'

A leggy brunette wearing nothing more than an oversized polo shirt appeared behind him and draped herself over his shoulders.

'Hey,' she said lazily at me before turning her attention to Lorcan.

I felt my cheeks burn as she gave him a sultry smile. Seriously? This chick had just crawled out of Wil's bed and sure, plenty of people dig the anaemic thing, but she was deathly thin.

'Yeah,' said Wil, ruffling his hair. 'That was my fault.'

Well, duh, I wanted to reply. I held my tongue.

'Cassie and I partied a little too hard last night. You know what it's like when you're coming down and you hit those low lows.'

'I don't, but continue.'

'All those insecurities and outside pressures come bearing down on you when you're living in the hyperreality of a creative mind.'

Ah, that sounded like the Wil I knew. Lorcan looked like he wanted to punch him in the face. The way Cassie was looking at Lo made me want to punch *her* in the face.

'So you're not having any second thoughts? You can talk to me about this stuff, you know. Any concerns that you're having or tweaks you want to make, we can still work those in up until the show.'

Wil stopped ruffling his hair and looked at me. 'You mean that, don't you, Tommi?'

'Of course. I'm not here to hijack your art and turn it into a completely foreign beast. This is a smaller, quirkier project. We can play around.'

'That means a lot,' he said.

I nodded. 'Why don't you bring a few of the pieces around yourself and I can show you where I'm going with everything? I know I've already explained the basic premise to you. Physically seeing it might reassure you.'

'I'm reassured,' purred Cassie, looking at Lorcan as she said it.

Lorcan had a neutral expression on his face and was ignoring her by staring at a coat rack to his right.

'I might come by then, that would be good,' Wil said.

'I'm there all day from nine to five-thirty, probably a bit later closer to the exhibition.'

'Thanks, Tommi.'

'Don't worry about it. You can pay me back with no more chemical-induced phone calls to my boss.'

'Yeah, I'm really sorry about that. Demons, you know?'

'Sure. I'll see you.'

'Later.'

'Bye now,' I heard Cassie whisper as he closed the door.

I looked at Lorcan and sighed with relief.

'Demons?' he said.

I smiled and put a finger to my lips, pointing at the door.

He leaned down and whispered in my ear: 'Not everyone can hear like you can.'

As his lips brushed my ear it gave me goosebumps. I started down the stairs and he followed behind me.

'I'd like to show that guy real demons,' he said.

'I'd like to show that girl a real meal,' I replied.

Lorcan snorted.

'Seriously,' I continued, 'did you see the box gap between her legs? You could fit the width of the Bible between there.' I paused. 'Actually, don't respond to that, I'm being sizeist.'

Lorcan turned to look at my uneasy expression as I hit the pavement of the street below.

'I don't find starvation sexy, Tommi,' he said with a smirk.

He looked towards his jeep almost directly after he said it and I was glad he wasn't paying attention to notice my breath catch. The way his gaze had run over me . . .

'Besides, I'm not the one modelling for the artiste,' he said in a mock French accent.

'Hey, I never modelled for him. And he wanted you to model for him too, Mr Manly Specimen, you.'

Lorcan groaned. 'Has he really asked you to model for him a dozen times?'

'It was eight at last count. I thought it rude to correct him.'

'Why didn't you say yes? For the sake of "art" I thought you might consider it.'

'You're not wrong and maybe if it was someone else I might. Might. But I have a feeling that as soon as I got into the studio he'd offer me fava beans and a nice Chianti and I'd be all creeped out.'

Lorcan laughed, long and loud. A passing couple were walking their dog and looked over in our direction at the sound.

'Or you might end up wearing a fedora,' he gasped.

'That too,' I conceded.

I wasn't sure what had awoken me as I lay there in the dark, staring at my ceiling. I'd left the heater on for too long and my room was toasty by the time I went to bed. In just a singlet and panties I was shivering now. I wriggled under my covers and settled in. It wasn't my phone. I'd already called Alexis and smoothed over the Wil situation. Mari was staying at Kane's. Lorcan had gone to bed before me.

I was about to close my eyes when I heard a muted bang from across the hall. My whole body went stiff as I tried to slow my heart rate, which had already leaped to erratic levels with one unusual sound. What if it was Steven coming back to finish what he'd started?

The noise had come from Lorcan's room. If Steven was coming to get me it would make sense that he would try to take out Lorcan first. I strained my ears for another sound and heard Lorcan groan. I leaped out of bed and soundlessly raced to the outside of his closed door. I didn't have time to put anything else on but if Lorcan was being killed I didn't think he'd mind if I tried to save him in underpants or a snuggie. I hadn't grabbed a weapon, didn't have time. I also didn't need one. Shutting my eyes, I took a deep breath and focused, trying to draw my wolf to me and channelling it into my right hand as quickly as possible. My clawed wolf paw had just formed when I heard another bang and I burst through the door. I scanned the room as I rushed towards Lorcan. Sweat was glistening on his bare back. I couldn't see any sign of an attacker or injury.

'Lorcan,' I said, reaching out to touch his shoulder.

He yelled, spinning around. He was half poised on the bed and had his switchblade hovering centimetres away from my throat. His face was in a grimace and his eyes were darting quickly over me.

'Lorcan,' I whispered, 'It's me, Tommi.'

I didn't want to make any sudden movements and alarm him so I morphed my claw back to human and slowly raised my hands in front of his eyes. Realisation was beginning to take over as his face faded from the fierce expression.

'Tommi, I . . . Where?' He sounded as confused as he looked.

'You're here at the apartment. In Scotland.'

'W-what . . .'

'I think you just had a nightmare, Freddy Krueger level.'

Whoa. Too soon to be making pop culture references.

'My God.' He dropped the knife and looked at his own hands, disgusted. 'I'm so sorry, I nearly cut . . . I could never . . .'

He dropped back from his crouched position and leaned against the wall his double bed was pushed against. He put his head in his hands and his face was shielded behind the curtain of his brown hair as it fell down in front of him. I saw his shoulders shake and I moved forward, placing a knee on the edge of the bed.

'Lo,' I said, reaching out a hand and resting it on his forearm.

He jumped at the contact. 'Tommi.'

His voice sounded broken and I couldn't bear it. I'm not sure where he'd been or what horrors had been so awful that this seemingly indestructible man had been crushed.

'It's OK,' I said, shuffling forward to him on my knees.

I rubbed my hand along his arm in a comforting gesture and tried to find his fingers through the mass of hair. When I found them, I slowly pulled them away from his head, trying not to spook him. I moved in closer, lifting his slouched head to mine. Damp strings of hair fell down in front of his face. Behind them I could see his eyes staring back at me in pain. I used my other hand to brush the hair out of his face like he had done to me.

He gently tried to turn his head away from me, but it felt half-hearted. 'You can't see me like this.'

'It's OK,' I said, whispering. 'You're a thousand miles away from whatever it was.'

I had both of my hands grasping his face and I barely had time to notice he hadn't shaved when he moved forwards and buried himself in my neck.

'Tommi,' he said, somewhat muffled.

His arms wrapped around me, pulling me downwards as much as he pulled himself forwards into me. I felt his body shake and I pulled him tighter. I wrapped one hand around his back and rested it on his head while the other snaked around his lower back. Pushing his face further into the crook of my neck, I felt like he was trying to keep some part of himself escaping by moulding himself to me. I rested my head on his shoulder and told him everything was going to be all right, that he was safe, warm and home. I told him all the things he told me when I'd been tearing up my room, lost in my own despair.

We must have fallen asleep like that because when I woke up the next morning I was resting on Lorcan's bare chest. He was lying on his back and my head was moving up and down slowly with the movement of his breathing. One of his arms was tucked around me, resting on my hip, while the other was linked in my hand and placed on his abdomen. I was on my side and one of my legs was intertwined with his. He must have loosely pulled the duvet up to cover us as it was resting just above my waist. I could see the top of Lorcan's jocks and I was both relived and disappointed to discover he didn't sleep in the nude. It was nice here. Warm. Safe. Those things I'd promised. This would no doubt create a whole new set of problems and further blur our counsellor–ward relationship. To be honest, I didn't care. That line had been hazy for a while and, in this moment, I was going to enjoy it without worrying about the repercussions. I shut my eyes and lightly exhaled.

Lorcan's hand moved on my hip and slowly ran its way up my back and to my head. He tucked a strand of hair behind my ear and I lifted my eyes upwards to look at him. He was smiling at me lazily. I smiled back. I couldn't help it. I felt ridiculous, smiling at him smiling at me, and I laughed, pressing my head against his chest to hide my blush. His chest jerked with a deep rumble of laughter and I looked up at him, removing my hand from his and resting it on his chest.

'Come here,' he said, tilting to the side and half rolling me off him towards the wall.

His other arm caught me, trapping me between his body while he leaned forward and kissed me. It was soft, as if testing my reaction. My body leaped forward without me and I pressed myself against him as my lips returned the favour. He kissed me sweetly, moving his free hand to keep brushing the hair off my face. The little advertised problem with long hair is it can be a pain in the arse when trying to kiss someone in bed. I ran one of my hands over his back and felt scars among the ripple of his muscles. I traced my fingers along them as my other hand ran its way through his hair. It was still soft but our kisses were deeper now as we pressed ourselves harder and harder against each other. With the passion he was pouring into the movements of his mouth, I felt like he'd been waiting to kiss me since we met. One of his hands found my hip and lightly trailed the bare skin above my panty line before it moved up under my singlet and along my lower back. I drew my hand around to the front and ran it over his slightly hairy chest. Taking a break from kissing, I watched my hand run over his defined abs and slowly up to his pecs.

He shuddered as I reached his nipples and ran my index finger over them in circles. I leaned forward and kissed one, lightly sucking, and he moaned. I kissed my way up to his neck and pecked his Adam's apple before kissing his chin and eventually returning to his lips. He was hungrier on my return and met my lips with a flurry of heat and tongue. He tried to pull me closer towards him. There was nowhere closer to move.

I felt that deep unmistakable burn deep within my body as I ached for him. Every inch of skin he touched felt as thin as rice paper as the sensation penetrated into my very being. Running his hand down my body and over my thigh, he locked his fingers under my knee and wrapped my leg around his waist. Turned out he could get closer. My body wiggled against his for a second to get into the new position and he pulled away from my mouth, kissing down my jawline. Like he knew exactly where to go, he found the sensitive spot on my neck and I gasped.

It felt like a dream, a haze of emotions and sensations and touches as we fought to feel more. Gliding his hand up from my thigh, he ran it over my lower stomach before making his way to my breasts. He lightly brushed over one first to see if it was OK. I leaned in and kissed him passionately. He squeezed my breast, hard this time, and I nearly bit his tongue with the sensation. I felt his erection pressing against my leg through the cloth of his jocks and I ran my hand to the top of his waistband. Pulling away, I sucked on his lower lip before he moved for my whole mouth again. As I led my hand further down into his underwear, he was moving his under my singlet and towards my bare breasts.

'Wait,' he said, through kisses. 'Tommi, wait.'

He paused his hand and I paused mine, slowly drawing it out of his jocks and resting it lightly on his lower stomach. His hand slid down to the beginning of my tattoo and traced the outline of the lone skull there.

'What is it?' I asked, breathless.

He was lightly panting too and, looking into his eyes, I could tell it was taking every morsel of self-control to resist taking the plunge.

'What's wrong?' I said, running a hand along his chiselled jawline.

He really was the perfect manly specimen, I thought.

'There's something I have to tell you before we go any further.'

Our faces were nearly pressed against each other. We barely had to talk louder than a whisper.

'It can't wait?'

I tried to keep the desire out of my voice. He saw right through me and smiled, then leaned forward to kiss me on the lips.

My heart picked up a beat again and, as my eyelids fluttered open, I said, 'Tell me anything.'

'I care about you more than . . . I want us to be as honest and upfront as possible.'

'Lo, just say it, you're scaring me,' I said, running my fingers lightly over the creases in his forehead as he frowned.

I had no irrational fear of him suddenly finding me physically unattractive: the hardness pressed against my body was testament to the fact he found me very appealing. But he was looking at me with such caution I couldn't help but take this seriously. I stared at him, inches away from his green eyes and still intertwined with his body.

'Tommi,' he said, 'I'm immortal.'

Chapter 15

'You're what?'

'I'm . . . immortal,' said Lorcan quietly.

My mouth was hanging open and I felt it curve into a smirk. 'OK,' I said, chuckling over the word. 'Now will you get back to kissing me?'

I leaned forward to meet his mouth, but his hand gently grabbed my shoulder, holding me back.

'Tommi, I'm serious.'

Our faces were nearly touching and I rolled away to get a better look at him. I examined his face carefully, the lines and curves of which I'd come to know so well. As was always the case, I ended with his eyes. There was no lie there. I could see him willing me to believe the truth.

'You're immortal?'

I wasn't quite sure I believed him. He nodded before exhaling heavily and looking up at the ceiling. We were still intertwined and I slowly began untangling myself. Turning on to my back, I ran this revelation through my mind. I couldn't say anything. Lorcan was still propped on his side and staring down at me.

'You're going to have to explain this.'

'I know,' he replied, barely audible.

'You mentioned there were immortal beings . . . you never said you were one. What does that make you? Are you human?'

'Yes, I'm human.'

'Humans don't live forever.'

'It's the Treize's gift,' he said.

I held my tongue and waited for him to give the full story.

'They seek out warriors of all ages from different countries and with different skill sets. The Three guide them somewhat to potential candidates and an offer is made to the individual. The reward for service is immortality. Of course you can be killed in battle and it's an honourable death for any member of the Praetorian Guard. But if you don't meet your end at the blade, you go on living. Indefinitely.'

There was a heaviness to his words as he flopped down on to his back beside me.

'The Treize's identity hasn't always been a secret,' he continued. 'There are plenty of references to them as a shadow agency throughout history. Certainly where I lived we had heard of them. It wasn't taken as fact, more as a myth told from village to village, father to son and mother to daughter.'

'And where exactly were you?' I asked.

'I was fighting the English invasion in Ulster, Ireland. Hugh O'Neil was the most powerful chieftain in the northern provinces of Ireland and I was a valuable fighter under his command. I'd risen through the ranks quickly during the Nine Year War. I was seventeen when I first joined the fight, late considering the time. News about me spread and I was flagged by the Guard. I was a month shy of my twenty-seventh birthday when I retired to my tent for the night and found two strangers waiting for me. I identified them instantly as warriors, but they looked strange. One had a Scottish accent and although much of him was hidden under a cloak, when he took off the hood he was covered in blue tattoos. They were the markings of the Picts, the fierce and wild warrior clan that had died out centuries earlier. Or so I thought. The other man was Indian.'

He took a moment to form the next words.

'Being offered a place in the Praetorian Guard is the greatest honour that can be given to a fighter. They literally scour the world for candidates and they come prepared. I was a black-smith's son. I came from two steps above poverty and was one of eight children. My mother died giving birth to my youngest sister. My oldest brother died in a rebellion when he was sixteen, the second oldest when he was fifteen. I never married like most of the soldiers. I didn't want a family I wouldn't be there for. All I cared about was the fight and defeating the English forever.'

He was fighting the English. When was the last time the Irish fought the English? When was the first time? Weren't we Scots and Irish always fighting the Brits? I had a bad taste in my mouth as I tried to draw on what little ancient history I knew.

'We weren't fighting for exuberant kings and queens like they were,' he said, interrupting my thoughts. 'We received no grand wages. It was the honour and the principle we were standing for. I didn't have much to live off and what I received in gold and land went mostly back to my surviving siblings. My father was maintaining another Irish stronghold on the opposite side of the country. My fellow soldiers were my friends, Hugh O'Neil my fearless leader and family. What I was offered by those men that night was enough to make me abandon it all. They were scouts and high-ranked members of the Praetorian Guard. And they wanted me, Lorcan MacCarthy. They offered financial support to my family and they offered to train me to become a thousand times better than I was, to go down in history as one of the greatest warriors. It was a history that would be invisible to most. Only I would know the gravity of my accomplishments and the achievements of the Guard. I would be fighting for a noble, powerful, and historic force that I thought to be myth. I would see the world and I would see the future.'

My heart pounded slowly against my chest as Lorcan spoke.

'Immortality was something only the Treize had the power to give and only members of the Guard would receive. I couldn't resist. I left that night without so much as a farewell note. I disappeared into the dark.'

Lorcan paused, taking a few seconds to let me swallow the information. I was watching him carefully and, with every word, I felt like I was losing my grip on something I hadn't realised I was holding on to. He shifted his head on the pillow to face me.

'That was 1602, Tommi.'

I was breathless. My heart pounded through my skull and my brain told me to take a breath. After nearly half a minute I did take a shuddered gulp of air.

'Sixteen hundred and two,' I whispered. 'That makes you . . . how old?'

I was never any good with numbers.

'Tommi,' he started, reaching for my hand.

'How old?' I repeated.

His arm hovered over my own until eventually he pulled it away.

'Four hundred and twelve,' he said.

I shut my eyes. His fingers lightly brushed my face and I jumped. He looked at me uncertainly and I moved away from him, sitting up and pushing my back against the wall.

'I'm sorry, I need a moment.'

'This doesn't change anything, Tommi,' he said, staying still and keeping his hands to himself. 'It doesn't change how I feel about you.'

I had been hugging my knees and I threw my hands up in exasperation. 'This changes everything! You've had two bicentennials, Lorcan!'

Running my fingers through my hair, I felt my face flushing with heat.

'And how could you never tell me? I mean, really, this is my own fault. I never knew that much about you and I didn't want to push ... you must have seen so much. You must know so much. How can you even stand to have a conversation with everyday people when you're literally from another time? Times, even. Do you feel like an old man even hanging out with me?'

'It's not—'

'Do you have super powers? Is there other stuff you can do that I don't know about? Retractable steel claws? The ability to project pyrotechnic energy plasmoids?'

He'd done the smart thing and was lying on the bed quietly waiting for me to finish my rant. But I couldn't. I couldn't stay and play pretend. I leaped off the bed and over Lorcan.

'Where are you going?'

Sitting up, he reached out and softly grabbed my hand. I jerked it away from him and felt sorry for the look of genuine hurt that flashed across his face.

'I don't know you,' I said, choking back tears. 'I don't know what I'm doing, but most importantly I don't know you.'

I turned and fled from the room. I blindly threw on some clothes and dashed out the door. Lorcan called after me, but I didn't stop. I needed space and I needed air. It was early morning outside and I walked quickly along the cool pavement of our street. I hit the main road and kept going. Cutting across a deserted park, icy dew from the grass wet the bottom of my jeans. I barely noticed. A cluster of teenagers smoking on a bench shouted something at me. I didn't hear what it was.

Lorcan was immortal. Lo – my Lo – was 412 years old.

It was almost inconceivable. Less than ten minutes ago I'd been in his bed and kissing him like I'd never kissed anyone before. How many women had he kissed prior to me? How many women had he slept with? When you've lived four centuries, I'm sure the tally gets pretty high. You would have done and seen everything. What could I ever possibly say to him that would be original, witty, insightful, when surely he's heard everything before? How many people had he killed? I scrunched up my eyes at the thought. Did Lorcan think like an old man? He didn't exactly have an 'oh, kids these days' air about him, but he never quite fitted. He always seemed to be hovering on the edge of blending in and standing out. Now I knew why.

I ran my hands through my hair and stared out at the smooth stretch of flat land before me. I wondered what Lorcan was doing now. I'm sure he could have caught me if he wanted to. It was pretty clear I desired space. I hadn't handled it well. How exactly did you handle something like this? My mind ran back to the feeling of waking up in his arms. I hadn't ever thought of myself as someone who would fall in love. I guess I had hoped it would happen, I just didn't think that was on the cards for me. My initial plan to not get carried away with my feelings for Lorcan when I didn't know that much about him had flown out the window.

Look where not thinking with my head had got me.

God, I really wished my mum was still here to talk to. It was with that thought I glanced up and realised I was halfway to my grandparents' house. I didn't remember leaving the park and hitting the footpath, but I continued up a small hill and in the direction of their place. I had visited them once briefly last weekend and didn't know if they would be home now. I needed to be somewhere familiar. My grandma Judy was sitting on their chaise longue reading the paper when I let myself in through the front door half an hour later.

'Tommi,' she said, surprised.

After placing her cup of tea on the coffee table, she got up and met me with a hug. My grandparents lived in a small yet cheerful two-bedroom house in a gated community. Their neighbours consisted mostly of other retirees. In their mid-eighties, Judy and Hal Grayson were still in incredibly good shape despite my granddad having a minor heart scare last year. I was taller than Judy, which wasn't hard considering her shrinking height, and I leaned down into her for the hug.

'What are you doing here, dear? Did you walk?'

'Yeah,' I said. 'It was such a beautiful morning I felt like the fresh air.'

She shuffled over to the kitchen to make me a cup of tea. There was no point refusing. If you were a guest in Judy's house then you were having a cup of tea.

'I thought I'd pop around and see how you guys were doing,' I said, seating myself on one of the wooden stools at the break-fast bar.

'Oh, well, it's lovely to see you anyway,' she said over the high-pitched whistle of the boiling jug. 'Hal's not here, he's helping the Mattersons clear their backyard before it gets icy.'

Sliding the cup of tea across the bench, Judy said: 'Can I make you a sandwich, Tommi? You look like you've lost weight.' She gently pinched my arm. 'And be careful you're not spending too much time Muay Thailanding. Boys don't like muscly girls.'

'It's called Muay Thai, Gran,' I said with a quiet laugh, 'and I don't do things to impress boys, you know that.'

'Hmm.'

I loved my grandmother, but there's something so frustrating about maternal figures' drive to see you settled down with a 'nice boy'. My mind went back to Lorcan and the hurt expression on his face when I said I didn't know him. Had I overreacted? Maybe. Deep down, I knew there was a reason Lorcan hadn't told me he was immortal. Maybe he wasn't ever supposed to tell me. Plus he hadn't lied to me, he just hadn't told the whole truth.

'Gran,' I started, 'did you ever find out something about Pop that made you question how you felt about him?'

'Your grandfather? When?'

'Whenever.' I shrugged. 'Like when you guys first started dating.'

My grandma was a curvy woman even in her old age and she had wavy white hair that was cut into a stylish bob. She flattened a non-existent crease on her blue cotton pants with her hands as she thought.

'Oh, yes,' she said, almost excitedly. 'When we first met he told me he was a male model.'

I snorted and giggled at the same time into my tea. 'What? I've never heard this story.'

'Haven't you? It used to be one of Tilly's favourites.'

We both fell silent at the mention of my mum, yet for different reasons. For me, it was the pain of her secrets. Even though I had come to understand why, it was taking me longer to forgive her. For my grandmother, the pain was different: it had been almost nine months since Mum was swept away when floodwaters washed her car off a road outside of Edinburgh. She had moved down there to open a bed and breakfast with Deter and it had been running well when the floods hit. Deter was still trying to get the place back on its feet. Judy's voice chased those memories away as she returned to her story.

'Yes, he told me he was a male model for this big department store in New Zealand and a few other men's labels.'

'And you believed him?'

'He was very good-looking.'

I'd seen photos of my grandfather when he was in his early twenties and he was no Robert Redford, but he was attractive.

'When did you find out he was a rugby coach?'

'It was the day after our fifth date and I went to watch a game out of town with my girlfriends. One of their boyfriends was playing. Sure enough, there on the sidelines swearing and chewing gum was Hal. I didn't say anything at first. I waited until the end of the game and went up and tapped him on the shoulder.'

'And then what happened?' I asked, like a little kid at Christmas.

'I slapped him.'

'Right there in front of his team?'

'Yes. I didn't say a word, just marched on home with my girlfriends who were all sticking their tongues out at him or something silly. He tried calling and calling. I wouldn't answer and my father wouldn't let him through the front door. Do you know what he did?'

I shook my head.

'He left a brand-new rugby ball on our doorstep with the words "I'm sorry, Love Hal" written on it every day for a week.'

I laughed. That was definitely something my grandfather would do.

'After seven days, my mother was so sick of finding them at her doorstep she threw them in my room and said: "If you don't forgive that boy I'm going to have to go out with him just so he stops leaving footballs at our house."' She took a sip of her tea and smiled. 'And so I did.'

'Basically the moral to this story is if the gesture is big enough, forgive him?' I said, half laughing.

'Except if he gives you diamonds. Once you get diamonds you know they're really trying to dig themselves out of a hole that's too big.'

Somehow I thought diamonds were the least of my worries. I spent the rest of the day at my grandparents' house. Judy made me lunch and we argued about authors. I had lived in Scotland my whole life and my own voice was a slightly watered-down version of the strong Scottish accent I was immersed in. It was amazing how spending a few hours in the company of Judy's Kiwi twang could remind me of home even though I was already there. It was late afternoon when I decided I should face the music and head back. Hal still hadn't returned from the Mattersons'. I told Gran to give him a football for me.

I rode home on one of the old bikes I had left at their place and felt considerably better with the dusk breeze flowing through my hair. With one hand loosely on the handlebars, I leaned back and closed my eyes for a moment as I let the air rush over me. I knew what I had to do, it was just that it wasn't easy, especially when my heart was telling me one thing and my head was telling me another. Lorcan was waiting when I slipped into the apartment. I was pretty sure he had been pacing the lounge room, but when I entered he was sitting nonchalant on the couch.

'Hi,' I said.

'Are you OK? I wanted to go after you but I thought you might need—'

'Yeah, I did. Thanks.'

I stood there awkwardly for a moment and wished I could duck into my room and throw a bra on. Somehow you always feel more dignified when you have breast support. I needed to get this over with.

'Mari and Kane have gone to a party at Snowball's or something,' he said.

I smiled. 'Snowy's. We call him Snowy because his hair is white, like snow.'

The smile didn't last as I moved to press my back against the wall directly opposite Lorcan. We both stared at each other, our eyes full of things neither of us had the courage to say.

'Why didn't you tell me earlier?' I started.

'I don't know. You were dealing with a lot of other information and you were already apprehensive about me being here. I didn't want to—'

'Freak me out?' I supplied.

He nodded. 'I guess that backfired.'

'No, I don't think it would have mattered when you told me. I would have still freaked out.'

'Where did you go?'

'To my grandparents' house. I needed time to think and digest.'

'And what do you think?'

I sighed and looked at the carpet. 'So many things, Lo. Is that why you don't have an accent? I mean, I pick up a pitch on some words but for the most part it's indistinguishable.'

'Yes. Living in different parts of the world and away from Ireland for most of my lifetime now, it has faded on its own.'

'And to be immortal, it's purely a gift from the Treize? You don't have to throw virgins into a volcano or anything?'

He chuckled. 'No. It's hard to explain the specifics without you ever having been to their headquarters. After months of training and tests there's a ceremony and you're inducted into the Praetorian Guard. I turned twenty-seven during the mortal stages of my training. I'll always remain twenty-seven until I'm killed or I ask to be relieved.'

'Relieved?'

'Some who have lived many long lives ask to be relieved. It's a respectable request and one the Treize rarely deny. Basically, it means the immortality is lifted and you go on ageing at the normal rate from whatever age you were when they recruited you. You live a mortal life again and die a natural death.'

'What about Custodians? Are they immortal too?'

'Some are, some aren't. Custodians are given a choice as to whether they want to serve for ever or only until the end of their mortal years. Immortal Custodians are recognisable because they wear a necklace with the infinity symbol on it. Like this.'

Lorcan traced the symbol in the air with his fingers. I'd never seen a necklace on Lorcan.

'Where's yours?'

'It's different. Because I was immortal before I joined the Custodians . . . I think they're still working that out.'

'The Askari?'

'No, mortals. All of them.'

'Do you keep track of your descendants?'

Any sadness I expected to see was absent when he said 'no'.

'When I agreed to join, I chose to leave my relatives behind. There's no point digging that up now when all of the family I knew are dead. I've never had any interest in it.'

'In all this time . . .' I paused before saying '. . . four hundred and twelve years, did you ever get married? Have children? Even accidentally?'

'No,' he said. 'Marriage has never been something that appealed to me. Most members of the Guard don't get married. That's not to say they're chaste. They prefer not to have something of value that could be harmed and you would rarely see a loved one. The members of the Guard become your family. The supernatural communities in the cities you're based in become the closest you get to regular, familiar faces. Even then, you usually only stay for a decade or less. Everyday people would get suspicious if you stayed for their lifetime and never aged.'

His hair was tied half up and half down. The rays of the setting sun through the glass doors made the chestnut strands that escaped the band glow. Damn it. I was supposed to be trying to make a conscious effort not to be attracted to him.

He had noticed my silence. Looking at his almost perfect face staring up at me with his hands clasped in front of him, I couldn't believe what I was about to say next.

'What happened with us this morning—' he opened his mouth to say something but I ploughed on '—it can't happen

241

again. At least not for a while. Not until I can get my head around this immortality thing.'

He looked down at his hands as I spoke. I saw the hurt in his eyes. It was breaking me to keep going.

'It's not that you didn't tell me, it's more selfish than that. I've got so much on my plate I'm scared to take another bite. I'm trying so hard to learn this werewolf thing, to understand this world that I'm a part of now and trying to control my place within it. I don't know how I could keep doing that if we were together. Lo, you've seen everything. You've done everything. What could I possibly have to offer you?'

He leaned back on the couch with a blank expression. 'You're right,' he said.

I heard my own sharp intake of breath and I tried not to let myself sink down on the wall.

'You and I, it wouldn't work. It's not the best thing for either of us and I shouldn't have lost control like I did.'

'Hey, you weren't the only one,' I said quietly.

He shook his head. 'Custodian–ward relationships rarely happen and when they do they're frowned upon. The Custodian usually gets moved on quickly.'

'What? I don't want that,' I said, pushing myself off the wall. 'I just . . . I'm not sure if I can handle us. If there was an "us".'

He smiled, the warmth in his eyes making me want to melt into them, in spite of everything.

'I don't want that to happen either,' he said.

'I don't want to learn from anyone else but you.'

The thought of losing Lorcan altogether was a thousand times worse than not being able to have him romantically. I still wanted him in my life even if we weren't together like that. Getting off the couch, he stood tall and then took a step towards me.

'And you won't,' he said.

I believed him.

'I'll keep myself in check,' I said.

Another smile was creeping over his face when his phone began ringing in his pocket. He frowned as he lifted it to his ear. 'Hello?'

I didn't try to use my werewolf senses to hear what the person on the other end was saying. At that moment I was using all my self-control to keep myself together. This wasn't what I wanted. Yet if I was honest myself I knew it was the right thing to do. Lorcan pulled the phone away and looked at me with a sombre expression.

'What?' I said. 'What is it?'

'They found another body.'

Chapter 16

Blood soaked the front of my sneakers as I leaned forward to get a proper look.

Her eyes were frozen wide in the last terrifying moments of her life, unblinking and staring at nothing. The woman's mouth was half open as she tried to give her final scream. She had been pretty. I could see that. Her short blonde hair was spread around her in a muted halo and sprinkles of blood decorated her cheeks like blush. Moving my eyes down from her face, I tried not to turn away when I reached the bloody gash that had once been her throat. There was nothing there now, just tissue and flesh. You could even see the grass on the other side. When Steven had torn her throat out he'd nearly torn her head right off. At least it might have been quicker that way, I thought. She was lying on her back and her limbs were spread out like a starfish as blood tried to pool around her on the grass.

There was so much blood. You always hear about the large quantity of blood there is in the human body. Seeing it was something entirely different. Below her chest there wasn't much left. Her abdomen was a mess. Completely torn open, vital organs were strewn across her corpse as Steven had dug deeper to get at the meat. I made a move to step backwards and I felt something squish underneath my heel. Turning, I looked down and saw I had stepped on a piece of intestine.

'Oh God,' I said, leaping over it and dashing for a nearby bush.

I hadn't eaten much that day, but everything I had came flying up as I vomited into the shrubbery. I had one hand resting on the trunk of a tree and the other holding my hair back. I shut my eyes and breathed for a moment, wiping my mouth and leaning against the trunk.

'Are you OK?'

I opened my eyes and saw Lorcan looking at me concerned. I nodded.

'Yeah, I've just never seen so much . . . gore,' I strangled out.

Lorcan glanced in the direction of the body with an indifferent expression. I'm sure this was his version of an open casket considering everything he had seen and killed in four-hundred-plus years.

'Steven was making a point,' he said.

I'd figured that too. Pulling my hair back into a loose ponytail, I stepped into the open.

I had only seen two dead bodies in my life. My first was at a car accident I tagged along to with Mari a few years ago. We'd been out when Mari had got the call and I drove since she had had been drinking and I hadn't (surprisingly). I stayed in the car, but it wasn't hard to miss the bloodied teenager they carried out of the wreck. It was jarring at first, yet I couldn't look away.

The second body was my Mum's. I offered to identify it because I didn't want my grandparents to see Tilly like that.

The two experiences couldn't have been more different. I drove to Edinburgh, as they wanted to identify the dead as soon as possible. Staring at my Mum on that cold, silver slab was a memory I worked hard to forget. Her skin had turned a bluish purple and she was bloated almost beyond recognition. Yet it was my Mum.

'Tommi?' Lorcan was looking at me, concerned again.

'I'm here,' I said, lightly shaking my head and making my way back towards the body. 'I was thinking about my Mum. She was the last dead body I saw.'

Lorcan went to move his arm towards me but stopped himself. 'I'm sorry this brings up those memories for you, but you need to see this. You need to see what a werewolf can do, what Steven can do. I hate to say this isn't even the worst of it.'

'No doubt,' I muttered.

Stepping towards the mutilated corpse, I wondered what else could be done to a body at the hands of a werewolf? Sorry, claws of a werewolf. Since I was living here the Treize had appointed a single Askari to relocate and be stationed in the area too. He had met us in the car park of Kinbrae Park – where the body had been found – and introduced himself as Akito. He looked like he could be a cheery sort of man. Tonight, however, he was completely focused on the body. On his knees and leaning over it, he examined every inch of skin with tiny metal tools.

'See the tattoo on his wrist?' Lorcan whispered.

The plastic glove was covering half of it, but with his shirt-sleeves rolled up I could make out a symbol on his left wrist. I nodded.

'That's how you know someone is truly a member of the Askari. They must have that symbol tattooed on them. It's an ancient symbol for wood: the foundation of a solid structure.'

'Without a solid foundation the house falls down,' added Akito. The tattoo was a line that ended when three small circles formed at its head, right where the wrist ended and the hand began.

'Without solid information, without solid relationships and monitoring so does the Treize,' added Lorcan.

I looked away from Akito and up at the sky as he lifted a flap of skin.

'The last guy was quick, right? A pretty clean kill?' I said, trying to keep my voice steady.

'What's your point?' Akito asked, looking up from the abdomen war zone.

'It's like Lorcan said: Steven was trying to make a point. This is gruesome. Horrific. He wants to show what he can do to fuck with us.'

I looked at Lorcan to see if I was on the right track and he nodded.

'And this time the victim was a woman,' he said. 'Do we have a name yet?'

'Thomasina Edwick, twenty-two, university student,' came a voice from behind us. A man with the blackest skin I had ever seen was walking out from the trees. Lorcan met him in a handshake.

'Ennis, I had no idea you were part of the Guard team they sent here.'

Ennis was actually quite short, a fair few inches below my height. Yet there was a certain lethality that oozed from him as he walked. He gave Lorcan a toothy grin that was supposed to be friendly. It looked absolutely terrifying to me.

'I was going to get in touch and then we were on the trail. You know how it is. I knew we'd knock into each other sooner or later,' he said.

I left them to their reunion and turned back to the body of poor Thomasina Edwick.

'Subtle,' I scoffed. 'Same age, practically the same name. The only thing missing is blood letters on a wall saying, "I'm going to redrum you, Tommi."'

Ennis crouched on his heels and began examining the body with Akito.

'This message is intended for you. He really wanted to make sure you got it,' he said.

'Received loud and clear. Him wanting to kill me isn't exactly news.'

'Actually,' said Lorcan, 'it might be. Before, he wanted to rape you, claim you as one of the Ihis, breed with you.'

I shuddered. 'He's my half-brother.'

'Yes; to him you only carry half of his genes. Those are odds he'd be willing to work with,' supplied Ennis.

'*Now* I think he wants to kill you,' said Lorcan.

'Well,' said Akito, who was examining Thomasina's bottom half, 'I think he still might "want" you. There are a lot of pseudo sexual wounds around the groin area here that suggest a crime of passion.'

'She's covered in wounds. How can you tell which ones are sexual?' I asked.

Akito stood up, removing his plastic gloves. 'Please,' he said, 'I'm a professional.'

I looked at Lorcan and he shrugged.

'We know Steven is behind this,' started Ennis.

'There are no facts, only interpretations,' Akito piped up.

We all fell silent and stared at him.

'Friedrich Nietzsche,' he said, by way of explanation.

'It's Steven,' said Lorcan and I simultaneously.

Ennis stood and dusted off his hands. 'It's Steven. The body isn't more than an hour old. We need to start tracking him.'

He examined me for a second before turning to Lorcan. 'Can she track yet?'

I opened my mouth to answer, but Lorcan said, 'We've worked on it. She's too young to pick it up yet.'

'At least let me try.'

Lorcan gave me a dangerous look. He was trying very hard to say something without actually having to say it. Ennis nodded.

'Start here. If you can pick up a scent we'll follow you. If not, we've got other methods.'

I exhaled and tried not to look at Lorcan, who I could tell was furious with me.

Shutting my eyes, I stood there silently and listened to the leaves rustling in the breeze around us. I started to identify the individual scents: Lorcan, Akito, Ennis, myself and the disturbingly delicious smell of Thomasina's corpse. Moving closer towards her body, I sniffed, trying to pick up a foreign smell. And there it was: an almost bitter scent that lightly stung my nostrils. Steven. I hadn't identified it at the time, but my mind flashed back to the scene at the apartment. It had been there too. I was recognising it. My eyes flew open and I looked off in the direction of the scent.

'That way,' I said, pointing towards an exposed area of bush where the trees were spaced out. 'He headed in that direction.'

'Can you follow it?' asked Ennis.

I nodded, trying not to lose focus. 'If we hurry.'

'Akito, you stay here and clear the scene of our presence. Grant's on alert and expecting you to call in as soon as we're done.'

I heard Akito shuffle off at Lorcan's command.

'Wait, Grant the cop from the gym?'

'Yes.'

'Ha! I knew it!'

'Not now, Tommi,' he said, unsheathing a sword he had been carrying in a cylinder case on his back.

Holy shit. He had an actual sword. Ennis drew a smaller, thicker sword from a hip sheath and tossed Lorcan a gun. With one hand, they balanced the guns under their swords while the other hand positioned the medieval weapons.

'I thought you said the silver thing was a myth?' I asked.

'These are normal bullets,' replied Ennis. 'Unless you get a good shot in the head or the heart it won't kill, but it will slow a werewolf down.'

'Good to know.'

I had a machete – which had become my weapon of choice – strapped to my calf on the outside of my jeans. I eased it out and moved after Steven's trail. Ennis and Lorcan flanked me on either side with one slightly in front of the other. I was glad I had both of them with me because my concentration was dedicated to tracking Steven. A bat could have flown out at me and I wouldn't have noticed until it was spitting Hendra virus in my face.

We moved fast and quietly through the trees for what felt like miles. The ground began to curve upwards and I directed us across the slight incline instead of over it in accordance with Steven's path. Ahead of us there was a clump of darkness and I recognised it as thick bush. My pulse quickened as we edged closer. If you wanted to pick somewhere to leap out and attack someone this would be the spot. Yet when we were a metre away the trail swerved sharply left and over the hill. Without saying a word, we all crouched low to the ground and moved forward as a unit.

'Sausage,' I cursed, straightening up.

'Get down and stay quiet,' said Ennis, roughly grabbing my leg and pulling me into a crouch.

'No,' Lorcan said. 'Listen.'

The faint sound of moving water could be heard on the other side of the hill. We stood and came over the top, staring down at the black body of water as it wound its way towards the River Tay. Steven had jumped into the water to cloak his scent. It had worked and it made me think he had specifically chosen this location to kill. It provided a clean getaway.

'Like I said, sausage.'

'Where does it lead?' asked Ennis, the disappointment audible in his voice.

'It links up to the River Tay. Ultimately, it goes to the sea, but before that it could take you any number of places. There's an abundance of river and creek systems that branch off it. Depending on how fast he can swim he could be anywhere from Tayport to Perth.'

'He didn't swim,' came Lorcan's voice. He was crouched at the riverbed and examining markings in the mud. 'He had a boat waiting here.'

'That rules out the possibility of him getting eaten by a porbeagle then,' I said, kicking the dirt at my feet.

For the next week we did all morning sessions. I was working overtime at the gallery and Lorcan was working with Akito and Ennis to find Steven, so nights were pretty much out. The bad thing was it meant I had to get up at 5 a.m. to fit in four hours.

'I hate you,' I said one morning as I stumbled into Lorcan's jeep bleary-eyed.

'Your training is more important than ever at the moment,' he said.

'I know.'

He was right. I didn't want what happened to Thomasina happening to me, or anyone else for that matter. When it came to this werewolf thing Steven had years on me. Yet Lorcan kept insisting I had other skills and that I was learning faster than anyone he had ever heard of. I could now morph my hand into a wolf claw in a matter of seconds. All it took was a touch of concentration and I could control the change. Even shifting both hands while keeping the rest of myself human didn't work up much of a sweat.

'That's why I didn't want you to track Steven,' said Lorcan, after I grilled him about it over our Wednesday session.

'You were afraid I'd accidentally part-shift?'

'Yes. Mainly, I was afraid the others would see you do it.'

'Why is that such a big deal? Don't you have to report every little advancement I make to them anyway? They'd already know.'

Lorcan was silent.

'You haven't told them? Why haven't you told them?'

'Because it's unprecedented, Tommi. To be able to do that and be in control within your virgin year . . . it's unheard of. I don't want the Treize paying closer to attention to you than they should.'

I was taken aback. Even though Lorcan and I pressed pause on whatever romantic feelings we had for each other, he was still protecting me.

'Why? What do you think they'd do?' I asked quietly.

'I don't know. Maybe nothing. I want to be cautious. I'll tell them in a few months when it won't be as big a deal. Don't get me wrong, it would still spark a lot of interest. You're an Ihi after all. I think consequences down the track would be better if we told them later.'

'What would happen to you if they found out you'd kept this from them?' I was suddenly alarmed.

'They won't. The only two people who know are you and I. Neither of us are going to say anything.'

'Word.'

Mari had been covering the latest attack all week at work and was pulling mad hours. It turned out Thomasina also went to the same university as us and Mari was able to work her contacts there. Wildlife hunters from around the country were on the news offering their two cents about the attacks and the local police had even employed one of them to front their hunt for the 'wild dog'. Old stories about a tiger that had escaped from the circus and was living in the wilds of Scotland were ignited. There were reported sightings of the big cat almost every day now, which was ridiculous because tigers eat the heart and liver. Those parts of the body were intact. Mostly. Times like these though, people weren't concerned with the facts.

On top of that Wil's exhibition was about to open. He'd brought his pieces to the abandoned bar at the start of the week and made small talk with Alexis and Gerrick. He loved what I had done.

'The themed flow of it and the layout, the space – I dig it,' he said, embracing me in a hug I tried not to pull away from too quickly.

When I came home from work on Thursday I practically collapsed on the couch. Joss was flicking through a *GQ* magazine and talking to Kane as he cooked dinner. I sighed with relief as I stretched my body out on the couch and kicked off my shoes.

'Exhibition opening going well then?' Joss commented.

I groaned by way of response. 'It will be *bravura* tomorrow night, I just need to get to tomorrow night.'

'Mari showed me your dress.'

'She what?' I sat up, horrified.

'Sorry,' apologised Mari, appearing in the kitchen in pyjamas. 'I had to show somebody and Kane doesn't care. Lorcan wasn't home, so—'

'Do *not* show, Lo,' I said quickly.

'He's going to see it tomorrow night, isn't he?'

'Yes, but I'd rather people got the looking over and done with in one go.'

'Why are you embarrassed by it, Tommi? It's so pretty,' said Joss, trying to put on a soft voice.

'Shut up,' said Mari, lightly whacking him on the shoulder. 'She's going to look gorgeous in it.'

Mari and I had bought the dress a few weeks before I went to New Zealand. Since I refused to dye my hair a normal colour, I tried to make myself look as professional as possible at these big events.

'Hey,' said Joss, almost sounding outraged, 'I know she'll look hot in it. All I'm saying is it's very girly for Tommi.'

'Oh, come on,' said Mari, 'It's a neutral skin colour. How can that be girly?'

'Can we please stop talking about the dress? You guys can take a public poll on it tomorrow night. Y'all are still coming, right?'

'Wouldn't miss it,' said Mari. 'Kane's even wearing a suit.'

'A borrowed suit,' he said. 'No way am I buying one.'

'Your brother's wedding one?'

He nodded.

'I have a suit too,' said Joss.

I raised my eyebrow at him.

'OK, a suit jacket.'

I laughed. 'That will be completely fine.'

Lorcan came through the front door looking as exhausted as I felt.

'Hey,' he said, nodding at the room.

'And what are you wearing tomorrow night?' Joss asked as a form of greeting.

'I've got a tux.'

My mind went to a pleasant place where I imagined him in formal wear. Eat your heart out Daniel Craig.

'What are you going to do with your hair? Pull it back with a ribbon?' teased Joss.

Lorcan laughed and ran his fingers through his hair, which was out and hanging around his face.

'Actually, I was going to see if Tommi would cut it.'

'What?' said Mari and I in unison.

We smiled at each other and she returned to helping Kane with dinner.

'Why would you want to cut it?' I said. 'It's so . . . beautiful.' I felt myself blush and hoped the others didn't notice.

Mari spun around and backed me up. 'It's gorgeous, Lorcan. Few guys can pull off the long hair thing without looking like hobos. You rock it.'

'*Rock it?*' I cringed.

'Is "gorgeous" your word of the day or something? First Tommi's dress was "gorgeous" and now Lorcan's hair is "gorgeous",' said Joss.

'At least everything's not "quality",' said Mari, trying to imitate Joss.

'Or "awesome",' supplied Kane.

Lorcan had been looking at me with an affectionate expression and tore his gaze away. 'Or "mint",' he said, joining in.

'"Awesome" I can let slide,' I said, lying back down on the couch.

The combination of early mornings, demanding physical training, long hours at the gallery and stress of Steven were taking their toll on me. I was becoming *crabbit*. Shutting my eyes, I enjoyed the sounds of my friends talking and moving around me. I desperately needed a kip.

'Dinner's ready, kids,' said Kane.

'What are we having, Dad?' Joss chirped as he made a grab for a plate.

'Stir-fry.'

He would never admit it but Kane was a really good cook. Now that I thought about it, he probably did most of the cooking for Mari and me.

'Here.'

I opened my eyes and looked up at Lorcan who was holding out a plate with a knife and fork for me. I squirmed into a sitting position, grabbed the steaming plate and made room for him on the couch.

'Thanks,' I said.

He sat down casually next to me. 'Everything ready for the opening?' he asked through a mouthful.

I nodded as I bit into a piece of beef and eggplant.

'Thank fuck,' I said. 'It's all good. I don't have to start until late tomorrow because everything's done and dusted. It's largely pleasantries until people arrive.'

'I was thinking we should have a rest day tomorrow.'

'Really?' The thought of a sleep-in was more attractive than sex to me. 'That would be *so* good.'

'You've earned it. You can be fresh for the opening and to converse with Wil about the difficulties of living with a creative mind.'

I laughed, burning my throat as I swallowed another mouthful.

'Here, boozehound,' said Joss, handing me a beer.

'I love you,' I said, pouting my bottom lip.

'You'll say anything for alcohol.'

'It's true,' I said, lifting the bottle to my mouth.

'You want one, Lorcan?' Kane asked from the fridge.

'Yeah, actually, thanks,'

I looked at him, surprised.

'It has been a long week.'

'Let your hair down I say,' said Mari, wiggling into a beanbag.

'You really going to cut your hair? No one – and I do mean no one – is going to care if it's long at the opening,' I said.

'It's not for the opening. I feel like a change.'

'You could dye it blue instead,' I suggested.

Laughter from the room was my response.

'Nah, I say cut it,' said Joss. 'Tommi does mine and Kane's. She does a quality job too.'

We all groaned.

A few hours later I was left alone to cut Lorcan's hair. Joss said he was tired and had gone home. I suspected Mari and Kane were not sleepy and had retired to her room for an altogether different purpose.

'You know, if you actually supplied a few CDs I could put on music you liked instead of Tommi FM,' I said.

Placing the now empty Nina Simone CD case back in the pile, I turned up the volume. Lorcan was standing at the edge of the kitchen watching me. I lay newspaper down on the floor around one of our stools and grabbed a comb and scissors.

'What kind of music do you even like?'

I'd never heard Lorcan talk about music.

'This,' he said.

'Nina?'

He nodded.

'Nina, Otis, Aretha, Miles, Jimmy, Frank, Louis, Eartha, Billie, Ray, all the greats.'

He was into old school Motown, blues and soul. Interesting.

'Sit down there,' I said, motioning to the stool.

He had just jumped out of the shower and his hair was damp and clean. In a white singlet and loose grey cotton pants I tried not to notice his pert derrière too much.

'Relax and I won't accidentally cut your ear off.'

He laughed and I tried not to be distracted by his toned back as it rippled with the movement. I started brushing through his hair, which was almost evenly at his shoulders now. He did need a cut. As I worked through the knots with the comb and my fingers, my mind ran over what nearly was that morning in his bed.

I didn't want to be thinking about the texture of the hair on his chest. I couldn't help it. I'm not sure where his mind was. He was silent for a long while, too.

'How short do you want it?'

'Not shaved. Short.'

I sighed. 'You really want your long hair gone?'

'You really think it's beautiful?'

'No comment.'

He chuckled and turned to face me. 'Yes, I really want it all gone. Hair grows back, Tommi.'

'I know, I know,' I said, fingering the first strand to go.

Here goes . . . *snip*.

'Now that wasn't so hard, was it?' came Lorcan's smug voice.

Ignoring him, I kept working on the hair. Cutting hair was something I enjoyed. It was mindless, easy work. Lorcan's hair took a surprisingly long time to cut, mainly because I was so paranoid about stuffing it up. We maintained a comfortable silence as I worked and I enjoyed being able to just *be* in his company.

Why had I decided to call quits on us before anything started? Oh yeah, I didn't think I could handle going out with an immortal. If I ever took the relationship plunge, it would be nice to make sure that was the one normal thing in my crazy life. Standing in front of Lorcan and looking at his expectant expression, I couldn't help but feel I had made a mistake. Not for the first time lately I wished my Mum had been here to give me advice.

I brushed the trimmed hair off Lorcan's face and shoulders and then held a mirror out in front of him. 'What do you think?'

He looked at his reflection and ran a hand over his new do. 'It's great,' he said. 'Thank you.'

I loved his long hair, but with it shorter you really noticed his facial features. Not that I didn't already.

'What are you thinking?' he asked, watching my face closely.

'That you look way too good to be four hundred and twelve.'

My eyes suddenly caught on a tuft of hair I'd missed at the back. 'One more bit, hang on.' I moved behind him and clipped it away. 'There. Done,' I said, sweeping my hands over his head to dislodge any loose strands.

There were a few at the base of his neck and I traced my fingers over the area until they were gone. It was only then that I noticed his goosebumps. I ran my hands to his shoulder and watched the goosebumps follow as I rested them there. Leaning forward, I shut my eyes and lightly pressed my forehead against the back of his head.

Lorcan had come into my life unexpectedly and changed so much about it. Was I wasting an opportunity by not acting on the feelings I had for him, immortality and all? Lorcan's fingers found mine and he slowly pulled my hands down and around him. I smiled and rested my chin on his shoulder as I hugged him from behind. His eyes were shut too and he gave a heavy sigh. I slipped one of my hands free and cupped it around his jaw, turning his face to me. He opened his eyes and met mine, barely centimetres apart.

The sound of Lorcan's phone suddenly rang out and made me jump. It was vibrating on the counter, adding to the noise. I placed my hand over my heart and felt it racing.

'Hello,' he said into the receiver.

'We've picked up the scent again. He's in Ayr somewhere,' said Ennis's voice from the other end.

'Good,' said Lorcan. I was pleased to hear he sounded a touch breathless.

'You all right? Were you training?'

'No, I'm fine,' he said and I smirked at him. 'You startled me, that's all.'

'Don't turn into a Custodian too quickly. We're heading out in the morning. We want to surprise him during the day.'

'That's smart.'

'You're fine to stay with the girl? We want to know there's a backup measure in place in case he escapes. He won't.'

'Yes, I'll stay here with Tommi.'

'We'll let you know what happens as soon as we can. Best case scenario you won't hear from me until tomorrow night, maybe later.'

'I know how it works.'

'Bye.'

'Bye.'

Lorcan hung up and looked at me. 'They'll get him,' he said.

'Will they kill him?'

'They would have preferred to interrogate him initially. But with his body count I'd say this is a kill not capture mission.'

'Good. Steven's not the type to go quietly. It's better to kill him than waste time negotiating.'

'I agree.'

I tried to stifle a yawn but it slipped out and I hated my body clock. Lorcan and I had been close to . . . something. I don't know what. Something.

'You should rest,' he said, 'you have a huge day tomorrow.'

I nodded. 'Yeah, night.'

'Good night,' he said.

I was almost at my bedroom door when Lorcan said from behind me, 'Tommi?'

'Hmm?'

'Thanks for the hair.'

I smiled. 'It looks good.'

Chapter 17

'Keep still, I'm almost done.'

I shifted in my seat eager for Mari to be finished with my hair.

'If you keep moving you're going to have a dorsal fin instead of a braid,' she said.

'Yes, ma'am,' I replied, like a sulky infant.

We were in the staff bathroom at the derelict bar and Mari had come to the exhibition opening early to do my hair. I was grateful, I was. I was also nervous about everything turning out perfectly tonight. Gerrick and I had gone over the final details a thousand times. Alexis was rapt. The place looked amazing. The caterers were popping the bottles of champagne.

'Why are you so anxious, anyway? It's not like this is the first exhibition you've curated,' she said, pulling at a strand of hair.

My blue locks were parted to the side and swept back into a low bun. Mari had pulled some of the wavy strands out so they curled around my face and down my neck. She was now doing a braid across the side part that would be tucked into the bun.

'It's my third exhibition opening,' I said, 'You know what they say about threes.'

'Hmph,' was her reply as she held a hair clip between her teeth.

After adding the finishing touch, she leaned back and examined her handiwork. 'Done. *Très* lovely if I do say so myself. Very soft and understated.'

I stood and looked in the mirror, turning this way and that. I may be good at cutting hair, but Mari was a master at braiding.

'You're a wizard,' I said, my hand hovering over the do. 'I'm too afraid to touch it.'

She laughed. 'I hardly used any hairspray, mainly hairpins, but it will hold. Don't forget mascara.'

After twisting open the lid, I leaned closer to the mirror and began applying a thick coat. My eyelashes were long anyway, but this made them look dramatic, especially complemented by inky winged eyeliner. I'd gone for natural make-up with flawless foundation, a bronze shade of blush and gold shimmer on my eyelids.

'Are you sure it's not because of a certain flatmate of ours?'

'Huh?' I said, looking at Mari in the reflection.

I spotted a gap in my eyeliner and reached for the pen to fix it.

'Lorcan, Tommi. I can see what's going on between you two.'

I nearly coloured in my eyeball as I lost grip of the pen. 'I'm sorry, what?' I turned around to face her and leaned on the bathroom counter.

'Don't act all coy with me. You're falling for him.'

My mouth opened in shock. I didn't even have a good reply. Heck, I didn't even have a reply. I looked down at my bare feet.

'Is it that obvious?' I muttered.

Mari laughed and the sound was amplified by the echo in the small bathroom. 'Good Lord, no,' she said through giggles. 'It would be easier to solve a Sudoku puzzle than read your emotions sometimes. Especially when it comes to guys.'

I smiled at her as she tried to contain herself.

'And he's just as guarded as you are. I thought I was imagining it at first, but the way you two look at each other . . .

I felt my cheeks heating up. I tried to hide a smile and finish my eyeliner.

'The way he defended you that night at the apartment, I think Lorcan would do anything for you, Tommi.'

'I don't know about that.'

'It's the little things, too. At dinner, he's always making sure you have a plate first and if you sit on the sofa he's adjusting to be near where you are. You guys have private jokes and you're affectionate to each other without even realising.'

I took one last look at myself in the mirror and added a coat of matte red lipstick then started packing up the make-up.

'He's mad about you, Tommi. In all the years I've known you, this is the first time I can honestly say I think you're mad about someone too. Despite your best efforts to hide it, of course.'

'Bloody journalists. They pick up everything.'

Mari smiled. 'Only the good stuff. I think you should be careful though.'

'Hmmm? What do you mean?'

'Well, he's a nice guy and everything and not to say you haven't dated rough men in the past but . . . he's dangerous. Physically.'

'And here I was thinking it was my emotions in peril.'

'I'm just saying, you saw the state of our apartment after he beat up Steven. I've never seen anybody move like that, even the guys at your gym.'

'I know, I know.' For a second I admired how good Mari looked tonight.

She was wearing a plain, fitted strapless dress that fell to below her knees in a midnight blue satin. It looked positively regal against her ivory skin.

'So?' she asked.

I looked at her blankly.

'I know you're going to ignore my warning anyway. What are you going to do about it?'

I sighed and began fumbling my way into my pale gold patent pumps.

'I don't know what I can do about it. He's so much older than me,' I said before I could stop myself.

'He's twenty-seven for heaven's sake. You're nearly twenty-three. That's nothing.'

Inside, I breathed a sigh of relief and continued. 'I guess that is nothing. It's not like he's four hundred or anything,' I chuckled.

'Exactly.'

'But there's stuff I'm learning about him I'm not sure I can handle. Before he moved in I didn't know him that well, Mari.'

'That's something only time is going to fix. And I'm serious in what I said about him, *but* what you can't fix is that connection you two have. The spark.'

'Is this the part where you say if you're a bird, I'm a bird?'

Mari rolled her eyes and bent down in front of me. Placing her hands on my knees for balance, she looked at me deeply.

'Tommi, if I thought being in a relationship would make you happy I would have been setting you up with Kane's single friends. You've always been content with the whole—'

'Get mine and get gone approach?' I offered.

'Exactly. You and Lorcan, it's something different. He makes you happy. I can see it in you whenever he's around. You've been through so much. Don't you think you owe it to yourself to give someone who makes you feel like that a chance?'

I stared into her wide eyes, full of sincerity and pleading. 'I could fall in love with him, Mari.'

It took all her self-control not to jump up and down clapping her hands with glee.

Pressing her lips together, she said: 'Good.'

I felt myself blush again and let out a breathy laugh.

'And let's not forget,' said Mari, standing up, 'he is one insanely good-looking man. Even without the pretty hair.'

I gave her a cheeky smile. 'He is very spankable.'

Laughing, we headed out of the bathroom.

'Have you ever noticed how lush and foresty his eyes are? Fuck, I can't believe I just said his eyes were "lush".' I shook my head.

'He has nice eyes, yeah, but it's not his eyes I'm looking at. Tommi, he's cut.'

I almost felt like telling her precisely how cut he was underneath his clothes but I stopped myself.

'And those lips. They're very kissable lips.'

'Should I be telling Kane to worry?' I teased.

'Bugger, I left him out the front. He'll be dying out there with the cultured. See you later?'

'Of course,' I said, giving her a quick hug. 'And thank you for the hair.'

She winked at me and rushed off to rescue Kane.

'Tommi, there you are.'

Alexis was walking towards me with a dangerous wiggle in her step.

'You look lovely,' she said, pausing for a moment.

I looked down at my dress and smiled. To the casual eye, it looked a neutral skin colour, but, once you stood under the light, the layers of fine material sparkled. Mari and I had unearthed it in a vintage shop during a day trip to Edinburgh. It had been perfect from the moment I tried it on. Thin sleeves starting at my wrist led up to a round neckline that wasn't too low, but still showed off a touch of cleavage. The dress ran leotard-tight to my waist where a thin gold band laced around my middle and, from there, the material fell down in layers. Behind, it was scooped low and exposed all of the flesh from the arch of my back upwards. Thankfully, it wasn't low enough to expose my tattoo.

Joss was right: it was very different for me. I was in full-on princess drag and I could handle it for one evening to open this show.

I followed Alexis to the main entrance and started greeting guests as they arrived. I had kept the grungy grey colour of the walls, but I'd had a strip of skin-coloured paint added to run across the perimeter of the entire exhibition. The shape was wavy in spots, angular in others. It was pale in parts, then fading to dark ebony. I had wanted it to vaguely resemble the curves of the human body and the variations of human skin tone. Wil's paintings were placed around the space and three installations in the collection were situated in the middle of the room. I'd chosen a warm light setting and tried to make the entire room feel like an extension of Wil's work without being too overwhelming. The sliding doors at the side of the makeshift gallery opened out on to a courtyard where steps led down to a small dance floor and bar area. Outdoor heaters sat in each corner and a fence of hedges cordoned off the space. I'd smothered the bushes in layers of white fairy lights. When it came to fairy lights, more was more. Another four strings of lights were laced across the courtyard creating a magical effect on this clear, starless night.

The first half of my evening was spent running through the motions, greeting councillors, art buyers, the media and other local artists. There was even a small contingent from the Edinburgh and Glasgow galleries, which I was glad to see.

To my relief, Wil actually wore proper trousers, not skinny-legged jeans. He did team it with a black fedora, though. Lorcan would be pleased.

'It's this woman right here,' I heard Wil say and I turned to see who he was talking about.

He grabbed my hand and pulled me to his side.

'Tommi Grayson is responsible for this mind-blowing set-up. It's more than I could have ever dreamed,' he said, resting a hand on my shoulder.

'Tommi Grayson? You're the junior curator it says here in the exhibition booklet,' said the journalist.

'I am.'

'And how old are you?'

'Twenty-two and one foot in the grave,' I joked.

'Young,' he said, making a mark on his notepad.

'Tell me: every gallery in the country was vying for Wil's next series. What did you do to convince him to exhibit here?'

I was tempted to rework that blow-job line from *Erin Brockovich* but thought better of it.

'I think that was the point. Every gallery wanted him and wanted to do a bigger, better and more expensive exhibition than the next. They'd forgotten the most important thing: the work. We offered Wil a creative way to make people focus on that again. Wil was involved in the curating and I tried to coordinate closely with him to make sure the space nurtured his message about the female body.'

'You've certainly made the whole building feel like part of his pieces. Was that a conscious choice?'

And on it went. The journalist asked me a few more questions before returning his attention to Wil. That was exactly where I wanted the focus and I slipped away into the crowd. I spotted Joss with Mari and Kane and I spoke to them briefly over a glass of champagne. Alexis pulled me away for the opening speeches, which she and our general manager made. The mayor also got up and made an obligatory statement about culture in the community and whatnot.

I had tuned out by that point and was scanning the crowd for Lorcan. Among the three hundred guests I hadn't seen him yet. Once the official duties were over I could relax. After discreetly sculling another glass of champagne, I made small talk with Gerrick and his wife (who was particularly enjoying the hors d'oeuvres). I was surprised to see my model friend Aisha there, and as Wil's date no less.

'I thought you guys were just a casual thang,' I said to her, as we topped up our glasses of red wine.

I wasn't much of a wine drinker, but the champagne waiters had abandoned me in my time of need. If only they served beer in elegant glasses, I thought.

'You see,' said Aisha in a secretive manner, 'that was always the plan. He had been spending a lot of time with this basic Cassie anyway. Apparently, she dumped him for a jeans designer in Dublin.'

'His luck,' I muttered into my glass.

'He called me up and asked if I wanted to come.'

'Booty grazing?'

'He probably was. I'm honestly a bit over him, but these events are always a good place to be seen at.'

You had to admire her sales ethic.

'Especially in that,' I said, nodding at her plunging green dress.

'Hey,' she said, 'I don't deny myself carbs for nothing.'

She did look good. In fact, I'd say every male in the place would agree with me while every female would want to rip the slinky number off her back.

'I'll drink to that,' I said, clinking glasses.

'And I know this is supposed to be classy and all, but would it kill you to have some shots going around?'

'Ah yes, no one would forget the *classy* exhibition opening with the shots of vodka and lines of coke now, would they?'

'Depends on the vodka.'

Wil was beginning to wander over to us and since there was only so much more of his gibberish I could take, I finished my drink and made an exit. Everything seemed to be going well as I made my way to the courtyard bar. Nothing had caught on fire and none of the politicians had been found with their pants down. Yet.

'I was wondering how long it would be until I saw you at the bar.'

'Javier, if it isn't my favourite sarcastic bartender,' I said, genuinely delighted to recognise my usual go-to guy from The Poison Art.

'Good gracious,' he replied, sounding surprised through his familiar drawl, 'you've been here two hours and you're not even drunk!'

Leaning on the bar counter, I smiled at him and blinked my eyes innocently. 'I'll still have to get a cab home, but I'm a professional, sir.'

'Let me guess: you want to make up for the lost time with a double shot of something.'

'Actually, a glass of champagne will do.'

'Really?' he said, with a tone of disbelief.

'Really.'

'What happened to the girl who had whisky in her coffee?'

'A lot can change in a few months.'

'Not quite, but I'll gladly give you a glass of champagne. I have no idea what I'm going to do with the two litres of petrol I put aside for you, though.'

I laughed and took the glass. Javier paused in the middle of drying a tray and looked over my shoulder at someone.

'Ungh. Yes. Please.'

I turned to see who he was looking at. Lorcan was making his way down the stairs and into the courtyard. My breath caught at the sight of him. He was in a black tuxedo that was halfway buttoned, exposing a crisp white shirt underneath. His hands were adjusting a black pencil tie as he made his descent. I didn't call out to him or wave, I just enjoyed the view. I had only seen Lorcan in workout clothes, jeans and T-shirts mostly (and almost naked). The man did rock the formal wear. It looked expensive and made specifically for him, with every cut and curve of the black material fitting perfectly to his frame. He was on the last step when he spotted me. He had been scanning the crowd and paused when our eyes met. He smiled at me, tender, and began making his way through the slowly swaying couples on the dance floor.

'Tommi, please tell me you know that divine hunk of divineness?' came Javier's rushed voice from behind me.

'Mmm-hmm,' I said, taking a sip from my glass.

'Tell me he's gay.'

'Definitely not, you ass bandit.'

Lorcan arrived in front of me and I smiled up at him. I gave up trying not to look as elated as I felt because, honestly? I had spent the whole night counting down until I saw him. Lorcan was no longer looking at my face as his eyes pored over my gown, taking in all the details.

With a deep breath, he said, 'You look beautiful, Tommi. Like you fell from the sky.'

The enamoured look on his face proved he meant it and I felt myself grin like an idiot.

'This coming from the man who just outdid Idris Elba and Kevin McKidd in a tux-off,' I said, shaking my head.

His closely trimmed hair looked like it had always been that way and, although I missed his ponytail, the short hair was ideal tonight.

'Sorry I'm late,' he said, 'I was tossing up between this and a piano tie but I thought that might show my age.'

I laughed.

'I'll show you my age,' I heard Javier whisper behind me.

'It's fine. Fashionably late entrances are very now.'

Lorcan lifted his head to the side slightly, as if listening to something. The band was changing songs.

'Dance with me,' he said, more of a statement than a question.

I placed my glass on the bar and took his hand. 'Of course,' I said, following him to the dance floor.

A jazz band was playing and they must have picked a well-known song because the dance floor was filling up. Lorcan found a spot and turned to face me. I could tell he was hesitant to make any sudden moves. He stood there for a moment as if he was unsure about what would and wouldn't freak me out.

I wanted to tell him that nothing would, not now. I stepped closer to him and slowly moved my hands up the collar of his shirt until they were wrapped around his neck. Peering up at him, gradually I saw surprise in his eyes. His hands found my waist and pulled me closer against him until there was no space between us. We said nothing for a while, just stared at each other and swayed with the music.

'It's Frank,' he said.

'Who?'

He chuckled. 'This song, it's Frank Sinatra.'

'Oh,' I said, trying to recognise the tune and conceding defeat. 'I can't lie, I'm only familiar with Nina, Eartha, Otis and Billie.'

'I'll have to teach you.'

'You already are.'

He linked his fingers a little more firmly around my waist and we moved through a cluster of couples.

'Lorcan,' I said, taking a deep breath and hoping I wouldn't regret what I was about to say. 'I want to do it.'

'Do what?'

'Us. I want to do us, try us . . . together.'

He was silent for a moment.

'Balls, I'm not saying this right.'

'When did you decide this?'

'I don't know. Tonight, maybe.'

He was silent again.

'I know I didn't take the immortality thing well and I said I wanted to put whatever we were feeling aside, but I can't. You're the best thing that has come out of this lunatic were-wolf mess and I feel like a fool for not acting on it. I know you've probably had a million girlfriends and Christ knows I'm terrible at this whole couple scenario but—'

'Tommi.'

'—I want to at least tr—'

'Tommi,' he said again, this time placing two fingers over my lips to stop me talking.

I stopped and he looked at me intensely. He traced the curve of my lips with his fingers before resting his hand on my neck.

'There is no one like you, Tommi. In all my considerable years, I've never met a woman that could hold a candle to you.'

I had stopped swaying with the music.

'You drove me crazy at first,' he said. 'You were so stubborn and so strange. Then I got to know you. I got to know how brave you are, how strong, how unique, how beautiful, how funny, how caring and how smart.'

'Funny girls never get the guy,' I mumbled.

He laughed. The band suddenly changed songs and my body began to move again as I recognised the unmistakable horn intro of a Billie Holiday classic.

'Lo.'

'You know only you call me that.'

'Really? Do you like it?'

'Yes.'

I smiled, turning my head to rest on his chest. I felt like I had said everything I needed to say. Everything except one thing, the one thing I feared would be too soon to say. Screw it, I thought, I've never been one to hold back before. May as well put my cards on the table.

'I can't imagine my life without you in it.'

I didn't move my face, but I knew he heard me as he wrapped one arm further around my waist and moved the other to the bare skin on my shoulder.

'I'm not sure how this is going to work, but I would feel like I'm spitting in the face of some cosmic gift if I didn't tell you I think I'm falling in like with you.'

I felt his chest rumble and I pulled pack to look at his amused face.

'Tommi,' he said, cupping my face with his hand, 'I'm falling in love with you too.'

I was afraid he could see the fireworks exploding inside my chest as he did what I couldn't do and ditched the safety net with those words. He leaned forward, his lips brushing my ear.

I turned my face towards his and he pulled back until our noses were almost touching. He leaned in slowly and kissed me as the thick sound of jazz soared in the background. I moved my hands to his freshly shaven jawline as he held me close. Kissing him back, I lost all sense of where we were. They were slow kisses. Powerful.

We still swayed with the music, but, by the time we pulled apart, the band were playing a completely different song. I had never felt this way kissing anyone except Lorcan. When we touched, it felt like there was a part of me clicking into place. I could tell he felt it too as he slid both of his trembling hands down to my waist again. Grinning, I linked my hands behind his neck as he gently pressed his lips to my forehead. My lips were still tingling from where Lorcan's had just been and it felt magnificent to have him kiss me somewhere else. I wanted him to kiss me everywhere. I wanted to finish what we started in his bed. I wanted to have sex and sincerely mean it.

'How long until we can get out of here?' I whispered.

He laughed and I could sense the excitement in it.

'It is your event.'

'Gah, it is, isn't it? Do you think it would be unprofessional if the curator left before all the other guests?'

'Not if that curator was feeling unwell. All the stress and long hours taking their toll.'

I saw a mischievous glint in his eye and something else. Hunger.

'If that were the case then said curator should definitely go home.'

'Yes, she should,' he said, leaning in and kissing me again.

It was easy to get lost in those kisses. The prospect of getting lost in something much better snapped me out of it.

'OK,' I said, fumbling for self-control. 'Let me get my bag from the side office and we'll go.'

'Which way's the office?'

'That way,' I said, nodding with my head. Taking my hand, he pulled me through the now packed dance floor. He went to take a left at the top of the stairs and I tugged him to the right, towards the fire exit. Next to the red emergency door was the white handle that marked the entrance to the side office and what had once been staff toilets.

'Nice camouflage.'

'Wait until you see the descending staircase on the other side,' I said, as he helped me with the door.

I didn't need it, but I appreciated the gesture. With the door shut behind us, I was suddenly aware of how alone we were in this now dimly lit space. My bag was on the desk and I was reaching out to get it when I felt Lorcan's hands moving around my stomach. I shut my eyes as he pressed against me, hugging me from behind. Brushing the strands of hair away from my neck, he kissed me, working his way to the sensitive spot he'd found last time. I let out a small cry when he found it and heard the sound echo through the empty room. He moved his hands up from my stomach until they were over my breasts, massaging slowly. I reached a hand behind his head, gripped the back of his neck and turned my head to find his face. I'd been right about the hunger and he kissed me passionately.

I flipped myself around to face him. He pushed me on to the desk and lifted me up until I was sitting atop it. He wrapped my legs around him and pulled my dress up around my thighs. I was reaching for the zipper of his pants when a loud bang made us both jump. We paused, looking towards the door where the noise had come from.

'Probably someone banging into it from the outside,' I said, flustered.

He nodded, mouth open and breathing heavily.

Turning back to me, he said: 'We should do this at home.'

I loved the way he always brought a hand to cradle one side of my face and he did that now as he moved his forehead to touch mine.

'I know,' I said, tilting my head to kiss him.

We kept it slow, no fondling. He leaped back suddenly, laughing at himself.

'I need to meet you outside, I think.'

I laughed too, pulling the dress back down over my thighs.

'I'll meet you out the front in five.'

He came forward and gave me a quick peck before striding to the door. As I watched him sliding it shut, I exhaled and lightly shook my head. Jumping off the desk, I realised I was smiling to myself in an empty office. I went to the loo to do a quick touch-up before meeting Lorcan again. My mind was racing at all the possibilities of what could happen tonight.

'And the night after that,' I murmured to no one in particular.

I started to fix my make-up when I heard my message tone. I dug into my bag with one hand and wiped a smudge of mascara with the other. An unknown number had sent me a text. I frowned and clicked on the icon. It was a picture of Mari and Kane, bloodied and tied to a pole in what looked like a warehouse. Mari's mouth was duct-taped shut but her eyes were wide with fear and staring at the camera. Kane had his eyes closed and was bleeding heavily from a gash on his forehead. He had put up a fight. With shaking hands, I scrolled down to read the words below the picture.

'Happy grand opening, sis. Now come and save your friends before I do to them what I did to Thomasina. Come alone. If that Custodian of yours is with you I'll know it, and they'll die slow. Steven.'

An address near the docks was attached to the end of the message and I dropped my phone to the ground, backing up until I was pressed against the door. He said he'd know if I wasn't alone and, with senses that were no doubt better than mine, I didn't doubt it. I ached for Lorcan, outside the gallery and waiting for me. He would know what to do. Yet bringing him would also get Mari and Kane killed. I had to do this by myself. I couldn't risk it. That psychopathic prick had my friends at his mercy, something I knew he had none of.

I had to do this alone. Just Steven and me.

Chapter 18

I had driven through three sets of red lights when I gunned it through my fourth. I was also over the legal alcohol limit, but abiding traffic rules wasn't a priority when two of my best friends were kidnapped and at the whim of a homicidal werewolf.

There was a metallic crash from my back seat as I took the corner twenty kilometres faster than I should have. I skidded on to the straight stretch of road and floored it again. Chancing a quick glance behind me, I saw the weapons had spilled on to the floor. I was less than a few minutes away now and the neighbourhood was already changing from schools and houses to factories and businesses. Slipping out of the gallery had been easy. I had the address memorised so I ditched my phone, heels and everything else I had with me in the staff bathroom. There was a small window in the office and I navigated my way out of that without much difficulty. I wouldn't have been able to squeeze through there not so long ago. Now I was fitter, more flexible and more skilled. I kept telling myself that, as I sped closer and closer to a situation I didn't think I was going to get out of.

In the car park I had broken into the back of Lorcan's jeep and grabbed a supply of weapons. I had taken to keeping a small stash in my boot since Steven had first showed up: a few machetes, chains and a small sword. I wasn't great with the sword, but it could still poke the shit out of something if I wanted it to. I'd taken what I was competent with: daggers, crossbow, more chains and sheaths to house an assortment of different knives. I also grabbed two Hunga Mungas. Although I'd only had a few practice sessions using them with Lorcan, the African fighting tool was the deadliest-looking weapon I'd ever seen. With Steven, I thought it couldn't hurt to put on a good show.

My mind raced over what would happen at the gallery when Lorcan discovered I was missing. He might think I'd been held up with official duties when I didn't show five, ten, fifteen minutes after I was meant to. I imagined him becoming more and more alarmed, retracing my footsteps in the office and finding the pile of my things in the bathroom. As soon as he saw his diluted weapons supply, he'd make the connection. I regretted leaving him behind, but more than anything I regretted getting so caught up with him at the exhibition opening. If I hadn't been having a moment with him on the dance floor I would have been around my friends. I would have been talking to Mari and Kane and they would never have been abducted. Hindsight was a bitch of a thing.

As I pulled into the parking lot of the address I'd been given, I desperately wanted company. I didn't want to be going into this alone. Yet Steven's instructions had been clear. I wouldn't risk my friends' lives for the added comfort of having Lorcan here. If I died and they made it, I would consider it a worthwhile sacrifice. Plus Lorcan, Akito, Ennis and whoever else was on the hunt would be coming after us sooner rather than later. There was a reason I hadn't deleted the text on my phone, which I purposefully left behind. I just needed to buy enough time for Steven to realise I was entirely alone and to spare Mari and Kane's lives.

As I turned off the ignition, I wondered what had happened to capturing him in Ayr. It must have been a set-up to lure the Askari and the Guard away. This was all supposed to have been over and done with by the afternoon, miles away from here.

Yet it wasn't. I was here and I needed to focus on the task at hand. A hundred years ago one of the main industries in Dundee had been whaling and shipbuilding before the bottom fell out of the industry, so there was no shortage of abandoned warehouses in the depressing area that had once been the docks. There was a lone black van parked at the far end of the car park I pulled into. I took the spot furthest away from it and closest to the road. It looked deserted. It was almost completely dark except for the light from one street lamp. I could see the glass on the ground beneath the others where they had been smashed out. My doors were locked and I wound down the driver's window an inch so I could smell the air outside the car. My sense of smell and hearing usually worked better when I shut my eyes, but I wasn't game to block off that extra sense tonight. Every shadow housed an adversary as far as I was concerned. Nothing. There was nothing in the car park. No one. I pricked my ears and sniffed again to be sure. I didn't want to be ambushed before I even got inside. Still nothing. I guess I was going into the warehouse. Slowly, I got out of the car and opened my back passenger door. There was no time to get changed and I had nothing to change into. I would go into this warehouse armed to the teeth and in a formal dress.

Nothing could be done about it. There was nowhere to hide weapons. Except . . .

I pulled my dress up to my waist and resized one of the calf sheaths for my thigh.

It was literally the only spot you could disguise something in this outfit and I strapped a sole dagger there. I cursed myself for not wearing a burqa tonight. I could have hidden Chuck Norris under there. I strapped the two daggers into sheaths on my wrists and a long knife into a belt around my waist. It pained me to leave the Hunga Mungas and crossbow in the car, but I couldn't carry everything. With a machete in one hand and chains linked in the other, I made my way towards the only entry I could see. A small wooden door at the front of the warehouse was illuminated by a security light. The rest of the building loomed around it, grey and sinister in the silent night. Standing to the side of the door and pressing my back against the warehouse, I slowly unfurled the chain. I couldn't take it in with me. I wanted at least one hand free, one hand that I could shift at a moment's notice.

Straining my ears, I tried to hear what was happening inside. The thick concrete walls blocked out most of the sound. I could hear murmuring, somebody moving, and then a whimper. My skin prickled as I recognised the owner of the whimper.

I couldn't delay any longer. The door was unlocked – I'd expected it to be – and the inside of the vast, empty warehouse was dark. The only light was coming from the very centre of the space where an industrial lamp had been set up. It was casting a pool of yellow on two unconscious figures tied to one of the pillars holding up the roof. My pulse quickened. They were slumped and seemingly unresponsive, with both of their heads resting on their chests.

Mari. Kane.

Anger pulsed through me as I moved, step by step, towards them. Steven was there too. I couldn't see him, but my other senses told me he was just out of sight and he wasn't alone. He'd made sure my vision would be tested by having no outside light sources. Yet I could see a rough outline of shadows moving around me, encircling me as I pushed closer towards my friends. I was trapped. I knew from the second I received his text that I would be walking into a trap. I intended to inflict as much damage on this cunt before the snare clasped shut. Breathing heavily, I tried to repeat some of Lorcan's meditation exercises in my head to control my fear. It was working. Barely.

Stopping outside the circle of light spilling from the lamp, I tried to determine if Mari and Kane were alive. I didn't want to expose myself for attack by rushing forward to their aid. I stood still and tried to pinpoint their breaths amongst the other bodies breathing around me. Mari's head moved slightly and I felt a morsel of relief.

'It's good to see ya again, Tommi.' Steven stepped out from behind the pillar.

'And might I say how beautiful ya look tonight. That dress . . .' He shook his head and licked his lips.

I tried not to shudder.

'The weapons ruin the look. We'll get rid of those in a minute,' he continued.

Shirtless, he was wearing only a pair of black jeans and exposing as much of his tattooed skin as he could. My eyes caught on a black face tattooed on his left pec. Done in the Polynesian style like all his tattoos, the face was grimacing in a ferocious declaration of war with the tongue exposed and sticking out. The eyes were wide and black. A cold chill ran through me as I tried to tear my gaze away from the two coal-like spheres. Steven's bare feet brushed over the dust of the warehouse floor as he moved closer.

'I'm glad to see you came alone.'

'Like you asked,' I said, through gritted teeth.

It was taking every bit of self-control I had not to become paralysed by fear. I wanted to utilise that other instinct I had, the one where I wanted to leap forward and rip this monster apart.

'I did, didn't I? Of course that doesn't mean I came solo.'

With that a whirring sound kicked into gear behind me. Lights high at the top of the warehouse ceiling began clicking on, one after the other. I squinted as my eyes tried to adjust. Finally, I got to see my acquaintances. I counted nine, no, eleven other people here with us in the warehouse. They had loosely formed a circle around Steven and me. Including their leader, I was up against twelve. Most of them looked like bikies. One of them had a long, blond ponytail that was loosely plaited and fell to his waist (with a disgusting thick moustache on his face to match). A few looked older, in their early forties, and there was one boy who barely looked fourteen. I thought they were all men until a flash of recognition crossed my face. Bob girl was standing amongst them. Dressed in jeans and a tight black jacket, she had her arms crossed and was glaring at me. I was already out-wolfed, no harm going down with a last-minute jibe.

'Did I break your pie?' I asked.

She looked shocked that I had spoken directly to her and she flinched at the memory of my kick to her privates in the Ihis house. The bikie closest to me stepped forward.

'You don't talk till we tell ya to talk, bitch.'

He was holding a finger up at me in a threatening fashion. I was surprised he didn't punch me. I assumed Steven had given them orders not to harm me until he could first. I tried to keep the knowledge of my impending doom off my face as I replied to the bikie coolly: 'I'm so glad you put "bitch" at the end of that sentence, otherwise I would've had no idea who you were talking to.'

That tipped him over the edge and he made a move to grab me when Steven yelled, 'Enough!'

Like a game of 'What's the Time, Mr Wolf?' they all froze in their various positions.

Steven strode forward and slapped me. The impact sent me reeling on to all fours as stars danced in front of my eyes. I moved my jaw and tried to return to my feet, stumbling slightly. He was still standing exactly where he had been before I went down and the anger in his eyes made me feel it was worth the slap.

'No more from your smart mouth or your friends will be making it out of this warehouse in pieces,' he spat.

I heard a muffled cry and looked behind Steven to where Mari and Kane were.

Mari was awake and staring at me. I'd never seen a look of fear so potent as the one that was on her face. I'm sure it mirrored my own.

'Mari,' I whispered.

'That's right,' Steven said, smirking.

'I'm here now,' I said, turning my attention back to him, 'you can let them go.'

Steven chuckled and began walking back towards them. 'I'm afraid,' he said over his shoulder, 'they won't be going anywhere. They were just bait, Tommi. You're here now. They fulfilled their purpose.'

Mari was quietly crying and I could see the tears spilling over the duct tape on her mouth. He walked past her until he was standing over Kane.

'Hey,' he said, suddenly looking back at me. 'Do they know what you are? Do they know you're a werewolf?'

Mari's whimpers suddenly stopped as she swivelled her head between Steven and me.

'No,' he said, looking at her face. 'They didn't.'

Tearing myself away from Mari's pleading eyes, I said, 'They don't have anything to do with this.'

'Do they also know your flatmate isn't quite human either?'

Placing a hand on either side of Kane's face and lifting his drooping head towards the ceiling, Steven continued, 'Hmm. It will make it even worse for you then, knowing your friends died because of your lie.'

I tried to ignore him. Mari and Kane weren't here because I hadn't told them I was a werewolf. They weren't here because I hadn't told them Lorcan was an immortal. They were here because Steven was insane. Still, there was no denying the look in Mari's bloodshot eyes.

Betrayal. Disbelief. Fear.

'Sha—'

Steven was cut off as the door to the warehouse was flung open with a metallic *thud*. Lorcan came flying into the space at a sprint, sword and gun in his hands. My half-brother glanced from me to him and back again, rage bubbling up under his skin. I returned my gaze to his face just as he made a sharp movement with his arms and broke Kane's neck. The snap echoed through the warehouse.

'NO!' I screamed.

'You lied,' he hissed.

Mari began wiggling furiously in her restraints as the gang around us laughed and howled. Steven grinned, cold and evil, as he stepped back. Kane's head slumped to the side with sickening freedom. My mouth was hanging open and I felt tears prick my eyes as I stared at Kane's lifeless form. Dead. His dead form.

I looked at the people around me, grinning, laughing, whooping.

I wanted to kill them all.

Chapter 19

Slowly, I felt my grief begin to subside as searing hot anger took over. The rage built deep within my chest, stroking and teasing out my wolf. The bikie who had threatened me earlier was standing closest to me and had his eyes shut as he laughed. His friend behind him was paying more attention and saw what I was about to do.

'Jake,' he said warily, but it was too late.

Gripping the machete tightly with both hands, I leaped forward and slashed it across his throat. His eyes jerked open in surprise as arterial blood spurted outwards like a macabre sprinkler system. He took two unsteady steps backwards and made a move to bring his hands up over the wound. By the time they made it there, all that was left was a bloody stump as I hacked his head off with two more swings of the blade.

'GAR!' his friend strangled out the sound as he was shot squarely in the head. Lorcan was still running towards me as he made the shot and he quickly fired off two more, one of which struck a man in his upper shoulder and sent blood spraying across my face. Instantly, I dropped on to my knees and swiped the man's feet out from under him. Landing flat on his back in a pool of Jake's blood, his head made an unforgiving *thwack* on the concrete. Pouncing up, I drove the machete blade straight into his heart. I saw death cross his eyes almost instantly. One of the other men tackled me from the side and I went down. They were all faceless to me now as I hacked, clawed and bit my way free of them. Scrambling from the pile of men, I caught sight of Lorcan doing what he had spent multiple lifetimes doing: killing.

He engaged three people at once, his brow furrowed in concentration as he ducked and weaved his way free of their hits. One had his own sword and a sharp *clang* echoed through the warehouse as Lorcan struck it with his. The gun had been knocked away, but it didn't seem to impact him. He pushed the man back with sheer strength and ferocity, as he delivered sword blow after sword blow until the final hit was so hard the man's weapon flew from his hand. Without skipping a beat, he sliced right down the assailant's middle, killing him instantly.

A thick, cube of a man jumped on Lorcan's back and attempted to strangle him from behind while the other moved around to stab him in the front. Dropping low, Lorcan flipped the man over his shoulders, which pinned the other guy beneath him. Before either man could get a breath, Lorcan locked him between his thighs in what looked like an inescap-able manoeuvre. He used his switchblade and, in a blurry stab-bing motion, delivered three deadly hits. The man stopped wriggling slowly and his legs twitched as the last bit of life left him.

I had been distracted watching him move with lethal effi-ciency and it cost me. A knife was sunk into my calf muscle and I screamed with pain, rolling on my back to see the culprit. The completely bald man glared up at me, snarling, as blood poured from what had been his left ear. He still had his hand on the blade and he withdrew it from my leg preparing to strike again. I kicked him in the face with my good leg and screamed with the pain of the wound.

Arching my back, I could see that Steven had untied Mari and was attempting to drag her away with him. Letting go of the machete, I rolled on to my stomach and propped myself up with one hand and a knee. Quickly drawing one of the daggers from my wrist sheath, I took a second to aim before throwing it at him. It whistled through the air and landed between his shoulder and neck. Damn. I'd missed the artery. He leaped back from Mari, clutching madly at the wound. Bob girl and the teenage boy went to his aid, leaving Lorcan and I with the rest of the pack. I tried biting my lip to avoid screaming again, but the pain from my leg was excruciating. I rolled over and looked down at the wound. Thick blood was oozing from my calf and it looked as if the knife had gone right through to the other side.

Sensing movement to my left, I caught a glimpse of another man edging closer. I wasn't going to be able to stand quick enough so I had to time this perfectly. Sliding my way over to my machete, I tried to make myself look as helpless as possible, like they had finally injured me beyond something I could come back from. I let out another pain-filled cry, which wasn't hard considering the actual pain I was in, and the bald one was on me. In a completely non-human gesture, he crouched before launching himself through the air. When he was mere centimetres away, I swiped my werewolf claw across his face sending him screaming into a bloody pile at my feet. I quickly rolled on to my stomach and used my hands and one good leg to get myself upright. Grabbing the machete in the process, I barely had time to steady myself before two others ran at me.

One held out a gun, which surprised me because guns didn't seem to be a weapon of choice with these people. If they'd had one I figured they would have shot me earlier. With the Glock held out in front of him, he seemed to hesitate shooting me.

His mistake. Clenching my teeth I used my stabbed leg to pivot. I spun around in a flash and sliced his hand clean off below the wrist. Howling, he leaped back and grabbed his stump, trying to quash the flow of blood. The machete was knocked out of my arm by one of the other men who brought me down on my back. He pinned my human hand, trying to make sure I couldn't get hold of the machete. I grabbed his throat with my werewolf claw, clenching tightly and trying to use its strength to pull him off me. His eyes started to roll back into his head as his face went purple.

'Pl . . . ee—' he tried to say.

My rage had no time for sympathy, no need for it. Without a second thought, I crushed his windpipe between my gnarled, clawed fingers. I felt a satisfying crunch and a release of tension as he collapsed on top of me, dead. A shot fired above and I barely had a second to register the sound before a hot fire spread from my shoulder.

'ARGH!' I screamed.

Somehow being shot was worse than getting stabbed. As the heat of the bullet passed through my flesh, it felt like I was being impaled with lava. I looked up at the shooter. He had prised the gun out of the fingers of his buddy's severed hand and shot me through the corpse of another friend. I think he had been aiming for my head but the body on top of me had messed with the target.

That and his hands were shaking uncontrollably. He inched closer, step by step.

'Don't you move now!' he screamed, panicked.

Spit flew from his mouth as he tried to regain control of the situation. Standing over me, he lined up a clear shot of my head. Even at point blank range, it was difficult to do with the sweaty, muscular body of a thug on top of his target.

'Don't you fucking move!'

Like I could move with this guy on me. As he started to wedge the body off with his foot, I willed my werewolf hand back into human form. I couldn't move my right hand without aggravating my shot shoulder, plus my left hand was closer to the long knife still sheathed at my waist. Both of my daggers were gone and the machete was out of sight. I had one, make that two, seemingly minor weapons left. They needed to count. As he made another heave with his foot and the body rolled off me, I sat up and used the movement to thrust the knife into the man's abdomen. I couldn't get any higher from where I was sitting but it did the job. He made a gurgling cry and staggered backwards, lifting the gun above his head as he fell and firing two shots into the roof. The gun was still in his hand as he hit the floor, knife wedged in his gut. The barrel had been turning as he fell and, as a reflex action, he pulled the trigger, blowing his own head off in the process.

My head snapped in the direction of a roar and I had a mere second to register that a half-man, half-wolf was galloping towards me. He couldn't shift himself completely but as his mouth arched open and I caught sight of his drooling fangs I realised that was more than enough to finish me. As if out of thin air, Lorcan appeared at his rear, leaping on to his back and spearing the man with his sword. The blade penetrated the man's skull just behind his eyes and I gaped as he came to a shuddering halt centimetres from my own face. I could even see the silver of Lorcan's sword glinting inside the guy's open mouth, blood trickling down it.

Lorcan thrust the weapon out of the man's carcass, kicking his body to the side as he crouched down next to me. Assessing my wounds, his eyes ran over my body in a flurry.

'I got here as fast as I could,' he started. 'Are you—'

'Later,' I said, placing a hand on his chest. He nodded with understanding and we both froze as the warehouse was suddenly plunged into darkness. An argument had broken out at the exit as the bob girl attempted to plead with her brother.

'Steven, please this has gone too far! I thought you were just going to sc—'

Steven slammed her up against the wall, pressing his hand to her throat as she struggled to get air.

'Now is not the time to back out on me, *wahine*,' he said.

'P-p-please,' she choked. 'Qu—Quaid?'

The teenage boy simply shook his head, meeting her desperate stare with unsympathetic eyes. It was then that I realised *this* must be my other brother, the younger one Steven had mentioned while I was chained up in New Zealand. Wordlessly, Lorcan and I established a plan, and we had to make the most of the opportunity this family bickering had afforded us. Silent and deadly, Lorcan was nearly on top of the Ihi siblings while I was limping as quickly as I could towards Mari. She was lying motionless to the side of the group and I pleaded to any gods that might be listening for her to still be alive.

With relief, I noticed her chest was rising up and down with quick breaths. There were flecks of blood on her face from where Steven's had spilled on her as the dagger hit. I placed a hand over her mouth to quiet any noise she might make. With a jolt, I noticed the scariest thing about her condition was the way she was looking at me.

Terrified. Horrified. She moved her eyes from mine and glanced in the direction of the massacre behind us. I could deal with consequences later. Right now, I had to get her out of here. I used my good hand to retrieve the dagger strapped to my thigh. I held my finger up to my mouth in a 'ssshhh' gesture and Mari nodded. Removing my other hand from her mouth, I began rapidly cutting the rope that had her two wrists pressed together. The movement of freeing her from the restraints was excruciating with my gun wound but time was of the essence. A cry came from behind me and I glanced back quickly to see Lorcan was attacking all three of them. The perfect distraction.

'Tommi, oh God,' she whispered.

'I know,' I said, through clenched teeth. 'Tell me if they're coming.'

'Kane, is he . . .' I felt her move as she tried to see her boyfriend. I could tell the moment she caught sight of his limp body because she started shaking with the effort of weeping silently.

'They were coming for Joss, too,' she said, quietly sobbing.

'What?'

I stopped cutting as she mentioned his name. I hadn't even thought of him in my mad dash to get here. Why hadn't they taken him from the exhibition too? Unless he was . . .

'He's not dead,' she said. 'He was feeling tired so he went home a good hour before they got us. Steven was furious and wanted to go and get him but the others wanted to start.'

Inwardly, I breathed a sigh of relief.

'Listen, as soon as I cut you free, I want you to take this dagger and run out the exit so fucking fast it makes you dizzy.'

She nodded.

'My car is in the car park with the keys in the ignition. Get in, lock the doors and drive as fast you can to the nearest hospital. You can call the police from there.'

She was about to nod again when I was smacked from the side as bob girl leaped on top of me. With a final flick of the blade I freed her as I went down.

'RUN!' I screamed.

To her credit, she was up and out of my line of sight in a flash. I delivered an elbow to side of the girl's head and an *oomph* escaped her lips. I had hit her as hard as I could and I repeated the movement, watching as a momentary dizziness seemed to overcome her. Taking advantage, I rolled to the side and took her with me until I had her pinned under my own weight. My clawed hand was pressed against her throat. I snarled and she whimpered, with the sound slowly turning into a sob. I jerked back, shocked at the outburst of emotion.

'Please don't kill me,' she said. 'I'm sorry, I'm so sorry. I didn't want to come but Steven made me. I'm sorry about your friends, I'm s-s-sorry.'

Her pleas were lost in a fit of sobbing. I rolled off, sitting on the cold concrete next to her. I hung my head between my legs and breathed deeply, in and out. She stopped sniffling next to me and sat up.

'Go,' I growled.

'What?' she asked meekly.

'Go, get out of here before I change my mind.'

She dashed away from me, scrambled to her feet and sprinted for the door. I was just about to look for Lorcan when I heard Steven's cold, calculating voice.

'Hey, Tommi.'

He was standing behind Mari, holding her by the throat, as she shook and tried to stay upright. Lorcan had been knocked off his feet and was bleeding severely from an arm wound. He tried to move towards the pair of them as fast as he could, but it wasn't fast enough. Mari's eyes scanned the area in my general direction and she opened her mouth to say something. Whatever she had intended was cut short as Steven buried his muzzle into her neck and ripped out her throat. He had shifted almost instantly and without a sound right behind her. He tore his mouth away from her and spat flesh and blood on to the concrete in front of him.

I screamed.

I screamed and I screamed and I yelled, as I sprinted towards Mari's falling form, ignoring the pain in my body. She dropped to her knees as blood squirted from her open throat wound. I grabbed her as she collapsed, and her eyes focused on me. Bubbles of blood were forming at the sides of her mouth as she tried to speak. I stared down at her, horrified. I had nothing to say.

My mouth opened and closed as the tears flowed down my face. Her blood soaked my arms, my torso and what felt like every inch of my body, as her eyes stopped moving. They stared, wide and dead, at the nothingness above them. Just like Thomasina's.

'Mari,' I sobbed, pressing my face into her chest.

I felt the warm blood flow around my face. I didn't care. Suddenly, I was knocked to the side by a bone-crunching force. Steven had me pinned to the ground with the hulking, black mass that was his wolf form. The gloss of Steven's usual hair colour made his fur shine now as he lowered his muzzle to just above my nose. He was snarling and hot drool dripped on to my face as I stared at the mouth of razor-sharp canines. Each tooth was about two inches long and I screamed when I saw Mari's blood on them. His glowing yellow eyes crinkled in what I bet would have been a laugh if he was human. With my arms pinned by his two front paws, he dug his claws deep into my flesh. I screamed again, wriggling with the pain and only making it worse as the claws tore through more skin.

A shot fired overhead and Steven jerked half off me. I rolled my eyes back and saw Lorcan advancing towards us. The bullet had skimmed Steven's shoulder. He hurled himself at Lorcan as if it hadn't affected him in the slightest. Lorcan implemented a perfect forward roll under Steven as he was airborne and came up on the other side of him. I closed my eyes for a second as I heard the two of them engage. Lorcan had been a warrior for 395 years, but I couldn't imagine a human ever being able to outlast a werewolf for long. Steven would kill Lorcan, just like he killed Kane, just like he killed Mari. I let the grief of my friends' deaths wash over me and tried to turn it into anger. If Steven could shift without a full moon I was betting I could as well.

I was right. It was like my wolf had been there all along during the fight, waiting for me to tap its hand and step into the ring. Rage filled up my body like the blood coursing through my veins and I arched my back and screamed as the first shudder of pain ran through me. A crack came from within and I spasmed, willing the transformation to work faster. My body shook as if I was having an epileptic fit. The material of my dress ripped into shreds around me, no longer able to contain the expanding body within it. I felt my muscles tear as they stretched beyond their limit, my bones breaking and reforming as they adjusted to my new shape. My grunts of pain died off as my mouth elongated into a snout and my teeth lengthened into fangs. I poured all my hate and fear and aggression into the wolf. I twisted over, stretched out my body and screamed one last time, the echo of my voice turning into a howl.

Lorcan was facing Steven with his back to me, the gun now lying across the other side of the warehouse. He turned to face me and I saw he had three claw marks across the front of his chest that were bleeding lightly. He was wielding his weapon of choice – a thick iron sword – and he stared at me in dismay. Briefly, I thought about his situation: wedged between two ferocious werewolves with nothing but a pointy stick. He seemed to realise the same thing and slowly began stepping out of range. Steven was shocked, I could tell. He hadn't expected to face werewolf Tommi tonight, probably ever. His snapping and snarling had come to a lull as I saw him take me in. I was still injured but considerably less so than in human form. If I wanted to survive this I need to make it a quick fight. Steven began sprinting towards Lorcan, the last person alive and dear to me in the warehouse.

I was faster. Lorcan flattened to the ground as I leaped over him and met Steven in mid-air. We crashed to the ground with a force that shook the warehouse. I had landed on top of Steven and he struggled to regain control as we bit and snapped at each other. His claws grazed me as we rolled around in a snarling ball of teeth and hair and blood. He was erratic, trying to inflict damage wherever he could without a clear aim in mind. I'd been trained better. Defending myself, I kept going for the damaging blows. I'd never thought about where the arteries were on a wolf but I administered deep bites to where I assumed they would be like it was instinct. After ducking a swipe of his paw, I saw an opportunity at Steven's exposed throat and I went in for the kill. Using every bit of energy and anger I had left, I sunk my teeth deep into his neck. He let out a high-pitched whine and tried to claw me off. I ignored the slashes and bit harder until I felt bone. Clamping down on it, I shook my head from side to side to open the wound up wider.

I lost all sense of time as I focused on destroying this man who had set out to obliterate my life. In that moment my half-brother was nothing but flesh to me. It's what he had always been. I didn't let go until he stopped moving entirely. I backed off and stepped over his corpse, which was now shifting back into human form. His head had nearly been torn clean off. His evil face was attached to his body by only a few strands of muscle. I took in what I'd done and backed away further.

Mari. Kane. Dead.

I felt tears prick my eyes again and the sensation of them running down fur was surreal.

'Tommi,' came a cautious voice from behind me.

I spun around, snarling. It was Lorcan. He had his hands in front of him in a truce gesture. It took a while for me to stop snarling. I whimpered and he dropped the sword. He moved forward, slowly, and I could tell it was going against his better judgement to come closer. He reached out a steady hand and rested it on my head.

Rubbing my ears, he moved closer and I brought my face to him. I whimpered again and felt myself shrinking. As a were-wolf I'd been about three-quarters of his height on all fours and I was descending quickly as I slumped into human shape. Naked, I collapsed on the ground in front of me. Lorcan came down with me, grabbing my head before it hit the ground. The severity of my human wounds came screaming back to reality and I screamed with them.

'Tommi,' he said, cradling me to him.

I let out another small cry and tried not to think of my friends. I watched him look over me and noticed the terror on his face. What is there to be afraid of? I thought. Steven's dead. Then I realised he was looking at my body. I tried to move my head to judge the damage. I didn't get very far. All I saw was blood. How much of it was mine, Mari's or any one of the people I'd killed tonight I had no idea.

'Don't move,' he said. 'Ssshh, I've got you. I'm here. Help's coming.'

I was losing consciousness as I struggled to say the words, 'I'm sorry.'

Lorcan looked surprised and lowered his head to mine, pressing our foreheads together.

'Hush,' he said, wiping blood off my face. 'It's all right.'

He didn't get it and I tried to speak again, but he was distracted as people burst through the door.

'Jesus,' I heard someone say.

'What happened?' came another voice.

Other voices spoke, Lorcan's among them. I didn't hear what they said. The pain was pulling me under as the voices turned to indistinguishable murmurs. Lorcan's face danced in front of me as he tried to say something. I couldn't understand him, didn't want to. The darkness was so much more inviting and I let it drag me into nothingness once more.

Ah darkness, my familiar acquaintance.

Chapter 20

There was a steady rhythmic beeping coming from somewhere as I struggled to open my eyes. I couldn't manage it quite yet, so I lay there trying to remember where I was. The beeping seemed to run in time with a heartbeat. That was the only noise I could hear, even with my werewolf senses.

Silence.

The place smelled clean and I realised I was in a hospital. Why was I in the hospital? I fought to open my eyes and immediately felt drained by the effort. It was night and the room was plunged into shadows of blue and black. Lorcan was asleep, sitting in a chair at the side of the hospital bed. A muscle inside my chest relaxed at the sight of him, oblivious and at peace.

He was hunched over and his head was resting on the edge of the bed near my waist. One arm was reaching upwards and I was surprised to find his hand linked with my own. Not quite as surprised as I was to see the IV running from the veins in my hand. I tried wriggling my fingers to let him know I was awake, but the activity made me feel even more exhausted. As unconsciousness tugged at my mind I struggled to remember why I was here. Why did I feel empty? Why did I feel like I had lost something irreplaceable when I could see Lorcan right in front of me? His head started to move as black crept into the corner of my vision and I was gone again.

'How much longer?'

'She has been unconscious for two days and we've started easing off the medication. She'll come to when she's ready.'

'Right.'

'Don't give me that look, Lorcan. She's coming back from some terrible injuries. She was shot, stabbed, had a severe concussion, broken ribs and was covered in deep lacerations. A normal human would have died. Even a werewolf is going to take time to recover. I've done the best I can to speed that process up.'

'I know, Sue. I'm just . . . impatient.'

'Snap out of it. Look, you can even see some of her stitches are going to need to be taken out soon. That's quick. You know how werewolves heal.'

There was a pause.

'And call me Dr Kikuchi when we're in the hospital. I don't want people to think I have friends.'

I opened my eyes and watched the two of them discussing me at the foot of the bed.

As if Dr Kikuchi could sense it, she suddenly looked at me. 'Speak of the werewolf,' she said.

They were still swimming into focus and I waited for a moment until they became perfectly clear. Lorcan didn't wait. He rushed around the bed and directly to my side, face full of concern. I moved my hand slightly to try to grab his but he had already found it and cradled my fingers.

'Tommi,' he breathed.

Anything we should have been hiding from others clearly didn't matter around Dr Kikuchi, who sighed and said 'Give the girl some space, will you?'

Lorcan took a step back, smiling at me. I saw a hand whack his shoulder and he moved out of the way. Dr Kikuchi barged into my line of sight and took to examining me.

'Good to see you, Tommi, good to see you,' she muttered, as she worked. 'Shame it's not under better circumstances but I doubt I'd see you for a regular check-up anyway.'

She lifted my eyelids and shone a torch beam in each one.

'How are you feeling?' she said, placing her hands on her hips and staring at me with an expression of hard concentration.

'Sor—' I tried to talk but a few days out of practice and I wasn't so good at it any more.

'Yes, talking's going to be hard at first,' she said, watching me try to clear my throat.

'Sore,' I managed to say. I sounded like a fifty-year-old smoker.

'That's to be expected. Now, I'm going to run through your injuries so you know what's going on and then I'll tell you what I've done.'

The blinds were open and soft afternoon light was pouring into the room, as I watched the sun setting in the background. Each wound Dr Kikuchi went through brought back a different awful memory from the warehouse. The warehouse where Mari and Kane had been killed in front of me. The warehouse where I had killed a lot of people. I clenched my eyes shut as the memories came flooding back in a river of blood.

'I have a lot of stitches then?' I asked, doing anything to interrupt her.

'Ah, yes,' she said, somewhat taken aback. 'Around a hundred or so. Most of those can come out by the end of the week. Also, given the quantities of blood you were exposed to we ran blood work and the results came back clear this morning.'

'Oh . . . yay. No AIDS.'

'We're keeping you until Friday. The full moon is on Sunday so obviously you need to be gone by then. I think you could walk out of here by Friday afternoon.'

'What day is it today?'

'Monday. Monday night.'

I'd been out for a while. Lorcan, who was leaning with his back against the wall, unfolded his arms and stepped forward.

'I think that's enough for now, Sue.' She glared at him and he shrugged apologetically. 'Dr Kikuchi.'

She nodded and made to leave the room, pausing at the doorway.

'You'll fill her in on—'

'Everything,' finished Lorcan.

She disappeared out the door. I wanted to say thank you but she left so quickly I barely had time to open my mouth. Lorcan pulled a chair to the edge of my bed and sat, grabbing my hand as he went down. It was almost the exact same position I'd found him sleeping in when I came to the first time. I didn't know where to begin. He didn't want to push me and I took some time to formulate my thoughts. I knew Mari and Kane were dead, I'd seen it happen. I'd been covered in Mari's blood. Still, I needed to hear it out loud. Tears formed at the corner of my eyes and he knew what I was about to ask.

'Mari and Kane?' I tried to keep my voice steady.

He shook his head slowly. Hot tears ran down my face as I silently cried.

'Fuck, it's my fault,' I said through ragged breaths.

'It is not your fault. It is *not*. Steven killed them completely independently and regardless of you. He would have been just as happy killing your grandparents or Joss or a busload of children if he could have. He was a psychopath and your friends are not dead because of you. You went to their rescue.'

'And look at what a good job I did. Give that woman a hero cookie.'

Lorcan got up and grabbed some tissues from the nightstand. He wiped the tears from my face until they were all gone. He traced their path with his fingers.

'Lorcan, I killed people.'

'I know.'

'I showed no mercy. I slaughtered them.' I clasped a hand over my mouth as this realisation hit me. 'How many did I kill?' I asked, horrified.

'Six. The rest are on me.'

'Bob girl?'

He raised an eyebrow at me.

'The girl with the bob, Steven's sister. I let her go.'

'She hasn't been found yet. She fled the country and the consensus is that she's returned to the family.'

'The body.'

Realising I needed to clarify which body from my wrath of destruction, I added: 'Steven's.'

'What about it?'

'Can it be returned to the family? There are Maori rituals . . . funeral rites.'

'He doesn't deserve any of those.'

'I know. Still.'

'I'll find out,' he said, brushing a loose strand of my hair into place. 'Representatives from the Guard and the local Askari are going to debrief the Ihis about what happened. They might be able to take it then. It seems they kicked Steven out months ago after they learned what happened between you two when you were in their captivity. '

I nodded. We were silent for a long moment.

'There's a lot of blood on my hands.'

'Innocent blood?' he asked.

'Well, no. Does that make it any better? Those men I killed, *we* killed ... they were still somebody's sons. One of them even started to beg for his life.'

I felt like I was soaking in their blood as I recounted the memories. I wanted to shower in searing hot water for a lifetime and rid myself of this feeling. Lorcan sighed.

'I'm not the best when it comes to mercy,' he said. 'I've been doing this too long.'

I examined his face as he fiddled with the top of my blanket.

'Those men would have killed you if you didn't kill them, you know that as well as I do. It's difficult when their deaths are still fresh in your mind. You did what you had to, Tommi. I don't know how to help you cope with taking a human life because it has always come so naturally to me. It was a different time: kill or be killed. You were in that situation at the warehouse and you survived. You fought better and more bravely than I could have ever dreamed. I saw you and you were a *warrior* in there. Frankly, I can't help you feel sorry for killing those men because if you hadn't, you wouldn't be here right now.'

He leaned forward and placed a soft kiss on each of my cheeks. I closed my eyes.

'I'm sorry I didn't tell you I was leaving,' I whispered.

He looked out the window. I could see a trace of anger on his face. It disappeared so quickly I wasn't one hundred per cent sure it had been there to begin with.

'In future,' he said, returning his gaze to me, 'I don't care if it's the pope handcuffed to a guillotine, you take me with you. I know what Steven's text said but he only wanted to get you there alone. We will always have a better chance if we fight together like we did. The two of us.'

I hadn't felt self-conscious of my appearance until then and I tried not to imagine how I would look to him a hospital gown, blue hair oily and faded. He looked impeccable as always in a plain black button-up shirt and jeans. I couldn't begrudge him that. I sniffed and suddenly smelled a floral aroma coming from within the room. I turned my head in the direction of the smell and was overwhelmed by a mini botanical garden sprouting from the shelves near the door. A dozen or more bouquets in all different sizes and colours were placed there with the ones too big to fit on the shelf sitting on the floor.

'Are they . . . mine?'

Lorcan turned and smiled at the flowers. 'You're loved.'

'What do they think happened?'

'Car accident. Mari, Kane and you left the exhibition early and a deer ran out on to the road causing the car to crash.'

'That's officially how Mari and Kane died?'

'Yes. You barely survived. We had you taken to this hospital because Dr Kikuchi has started working in the region with a few other supernaturals. We could keep the specifics of your wounds under wraps.'

'The gunshot.'

He nodded. 'And the rate at which you're healing. No one knows exactly how severe your injuries were. We played that down. When you're out of hospital at the end of the week it won't seem unusual.'

'What hospital am I at?'

'Saint Theresa's.'

This was where Joss had received the bulk of his cancer treatment. I was here a lot during those months.

'I know people here.'

'So do we,' replied Lorcan with a lopsided grin.

'Mari's family must be shattered, Kane's as well. But Mari's . . .'

I thought of Mari's four younger sisters and her parents. She was their golden girl, mine too, and now she was gone. And Kane's brother. They were as close as brothers could be. He was going to be devastated.

'Joss,' I said, suddenly thinking about my no doubt heart-broken best friend.

Lorcan frowned. 'He sent those flowers, the blue ones, but I haven't seen him.'

'That's strange.' I worried about how he was coping.

'Simon Tianne sent the hydrangeas.'

'That's stranger.'

'Your grandparents have been by three or four times. They seem like nice people.'

'Did they like you?'

'I think they wondered why I was here every time they came by, but they didn't say anything. Actually, Judy pinched my cheek and said, "No diamonds."'

I nearly smiled at the confused look on his face and imme-diately wished I hadn't as every ache in my face flared to life.

'Ow.'

Lorcan adjusted the pillows behind my head before getting me a glass of water.

I drank it slowly, trying to get used to the sensation.

'I'm not hungry,' I said, mildly surprised at the fact.

'No, they've been feeding you by tube. Dr Kikuchi said they'll take it out tonight and you can start eating normally by morning. You'll be hungry then.'

As if sensing how sleepy I was beginning to feel, Lorcan took the empty glass from my hand and drew the blinds.

'Sleep,' he said.

My eyes were already closing as I slipped into the fog.

Eight coffins were laid out in the corridor of the hospital.

I was in my hospital gown and standing a little way back from them. They were all black and identical in size and style. I looked around for one of the nurses, Lorcan, anyone. The corridors were empty. I could see a reception desk in the distance and it too was deserted. It was night and the only light came from the dial above a silver elevator to my left. Maybe this was my time to make peace, I thought.

I took a step closer to the coffins, knowing whom I would see inside each of them. Like clockwork the lid of each swung open revealing the bodies inside. I glanced over the mangled forms of the first lot and, with a shock, realised I didn't know any of their names. Shouldn't that be a rule? The prerequisite for killing someone is you at least know their name? The blood was still spilling from Steven's body and staining the white satin lining on the inside of the coffin. I felt nothing but mild satisfaction when I looked at his mutilated corpse. Peace was never an option when it came to him. But Mari and Kane . . .

A dry, rasping sound escaped my throat as I looked down at them. Had I really just seen them at the exhibition opening a few days ago, happy and alive? They shouldn't be here. My knees nearly gave out at the thought of never seeing them in the apartment again. They would never go to Eggs and Ham. I would never see Mari's byline on another story. I would never find Kane sitting reflectively on our balcony drinking a beer. I grabbed the edge of Mari's coffin for support. The wood was wet and I looked up, horrified to see blood spilling over the edge of it. I gasped, letting go and pushing myself up against the corridor wall as blood spilled over the edge of each coffin like too much milk escaping a glass. It splashed on to the white linoleum floor and pooled towards me as if it knew the person responsible for it.

My mouth opened and shut as I tried to scream. All I could manage was a noise that sounded like a wounded animal. The blood touched my toes and spread around my feet, slowly creeping up my legs. I looked up at the ceiling and gritted my teeth as the blood rose higher and higher. A *ping* sounded through the corridor and the light from the elevator showed it had arrived on my floor. Thank God, I thought. I told my muscles to prepare for flight. But I wasn't going anywhere. As the elevator doors parted a frothy red wave surged out and down the corridor towards me. It knocked me over and I tumbled through a sea of blood that drowned my screams.

I jerked upright, screaming. I was no longer submerged in a sea of blood. But I was wet. Still screaming, I tried wiping the remaining bloody residue off my body. I was soaked in it and the sheets around me were damp with it too. Somebody grabbed my arms and I tried to fight them off until I recognised the voice.

'Tommi, it was a nightmare, it was a nightmare,' said Lorcan as he leaped on to the bed and pressed me against him.

'The blood!'

'It's gone, it's not real.'

'It's wet, I can feel it on me, Lorcan!'

'It's sweat, Tommi. You're drenched in sweat.'

My movements were restricted in the hold he had me in and I stopped struggling.

He gripped me tighter and I relaxed against his chest, trying to let my breathing and heart rate come back down to normal. I was shaking and I moved my arms around him to steady myself.

'It was a nightmare,' he whispered against my forehead.

I nodded, coming to the same realisation myself. The nurses had stopped coming in when this happened now. Since the first evening after I regained consciousness, I was waking up in hysterical fits of panic at least two, sometimes three times, a night. The nightmares were never the same but they usually involved blood and corpses. Figured.

I had managed to convince Lorcan to sleep at the apartment on Monday night. The next day – after the nurses told him what happened overnight – he hadn't returned home. They left it to him now to calm me down after the nightmares, which was just as well after I accidentally threw a nurse across the room on the first night. At least Lorcan could take me. I was out of the hospital gowns, preferring one of my baggy band T-shirts Lorcan had brought back with him from the apartment. The Fairchild shirt I'd been wearing was saturated and sticking to my skin as the sweat cooled.

'I need to shower,' I said, sniffing.

Lorcan held me back from him and examined my face.

'I'm OK,' I said. Thanks and . . . sorry.'

I steadied myself on his shoulders and grabbed a handful of clothes as I padded to the tiny bathroom. Five minutes later, I was clean, refreshed and considerably less shaken. Lorcan had changed the sheets while I was showering and he was slowly making himself a cup of tea when I walked out of the bathroom. My throat was still too raw to take extremes in temperature, but it didn't stop me from looking longingly at the beverage as I pulled a blanket over myself and climbed back into bed.

'Do you want to talk about the nightmare?' he asked.

'What's to say? It was same same but different. Blood, bodies, terror.'

I shuddered and Lorcan took a step closer, extending his hand as if he was about to hold me. For the first time in a long time, I realised that I didn't want him to. I couldn't. I turned my head downwards to sweep my wet hair off the pillow. He sensed my diversionary tactics and paused. We were both quiet for some time.

'There's something I need to talk to you about,' he said finally. The serious tone is his voice made me look up.

'What?'

'I'm here for you, wholeheartedly.'

'I know that.'

'But there are things you're going through I can't help you with.'

'My wolf?'

He nodded. 'Post-traumatic stress disorder is one thing and these dreams could go away on their own. I think being around others of your kind might help, at least for a while.'

I was the only werewolf in Dundee. I knew that. 'Who?'

'I know some people, rogues like you, who live in Berlin. I think they might be able to assist.'

'They're not in a pack?'

'No. There are other packs we could go and visit if you wanted, but you would learn the most from these people.'

I was silent as I thought about it. Mari and Kane's funerals were next week and I was on leave from work. I could probably get that extended if I wanted to. My Masters course was due to start this year, but the notion of study seemed almost an indulgent one compared to my current situation. And I would have to relinquish the rest of the pop-up exhibitions.

'How long would we go for?'

'A few weeks, minimum, or as long as you wanted.'

'It's hard to learn a lot in the space of a few weeks.'

He was silent as I lay there, using my werewolf hearing to listen to his heartbeat across the other side of the room and the sounds of the hospital beginning to wake up around us.

I felt my eyes start to get heavy and I muttered, 'Let me think about it.'

'And that was the first time you've shifted without a full moon?'

'Yes. Besides my first three days of transformation, that was the second time I had shifted. Period.'

'And you had never tried before?'

'No. I had no idea how to.'

Akito looked thoughtful as he scrawled down something on his notepad. He was also recording the interview on a Handycam that blinked at me from a tripod at the foot of my bed.

'And why do you think you did that night?'

'Heightened emotions.'

'Can you explain?'

'For example, seeing my friend get her throat ripped out by the half-brother who tried to rape me was pretty traumatic.'

Ennis made a poor attempt to disguise a laugh with a quick outburst of coughing and Akito frowned at him.

'Sorry,' he said, covering his smile with a hand. 'Frog in my throat. Continue.'

While Ennis could barely hide his amusement, Lorcan looked annoyed. We'd been at this for two hours. Akito was interviewing me for his official report and recording it for the Treize if they asked for a copy. Although I could walk around quite easily now, Lorcan thought it was better to do the interview from bed. I looked more helpless that way. It wasn't as if I was mad at Akito exactly, he was doing his job. I just found this entire process so tedious and unnecessary. They had examined the scene, examined the bodies, heck, they had even been there at the end of it. Ennis said the interview was standard procedure: they needed to go over all the facts and hear exactly what happened from me. The fate of the teenage kid, Quaid, was unknown. When I asked Akito about it he said he 'wasn't at liberty to discuss' and Lorcan had shook his head when I tried to push further.

'We have established that Mari Bronberg and Kane Goode were abducted from the car park at the exhibition,' he said, pushing on.

'I . . . I didn't know that,' I said. My memory tripped on the vaguest recollection of a thought. The night of the attack I had scolded myself for getting lost with Lorcan on the dance floor, whereas if I had been with my friends they would never have been thrown into that awful situation.

'My question is, do you think Steven brought them there specifically to kill them or just to lure you there?'

'Uh ... well, I heard the girl with the bob say how she thought he was just going to scare me. She was telling him he had gone too far.'

'You don't bring eleven weres as backup just to scare someone,' said Lorcan, cutting in.

'Lorcan, please,' snapped Akito, making a gesture towards me. 'We want to hear from Tommi. Now, continue. If you don't think it was his original motivation to kill them, why do you think he did? Why did he kill Kane first?'

'It was when Lorcan arrived,' I said, realising for the first time that this was the case. 'When he saw him, he called me a liar. He thought that I had lied about coming alone and that ... triggered him.'

'Hmmm. So that was the catalyst. And what about Mari?'

I was looking at Lorcan, who was avoiding my stare and concentrating on Akito. I felt a strange disturbance in my stomach and I quelled the unease there.

'Tommi?'

'Huh?' I had missed the question. 'Oh, uh. That. I think Mari was him demonstrating the power he had. You know, that the people I loved were expendable. He was in full-on monster mode.'

With that we seemed to be done, as Akito leaned forward and switched off the camera. He bought my story about never having shifted before, as the alternative was too much for his unconventional mind. As he folded up the tripod, Akito informed me Steven's body had been sent to the Ihis in New Zealand and they had been debriefed on what had happened.

'The eldest, James I believe his name is, requested phone time with you.'

'No,' I said, firmly.

'Are y—'

'No,' I repeated.

He nodded and made for the doorway. 'Very well then, I'll leave you to it. I should hear back from my superiors before the full moon. Given the remarkable nature of your shift I can hazard a guess they're going to suggest you seek the guidance of a mature pack. At least for a short period of a month or so.'

I said nothing. I hadn't given much thought to the future. I was too busy wallowing in the past to have thoughts about seeking anything from other werewolves.

'Any news on bob girl?' I asked.

'No,' said Akito, frowning. 'She hasn't returned to the Ihis yet. We have scouts ready to inform us as soon as she does.'

'I won't hold my breath.'

It was the first dig I had made at Steven eluding their capture and it felt good to say it.

'She's AWOL. For now,' said Akito, before disappearing down the hall.

'Until we meet again,' said Ennis, nodding at Lorcan and giving me his terrifying smile. He had taken a liking to me since I had killed half a dozen people and this change of attitude hadn't gone unnoticed by Lorcan. The second the men had left, Lorcan quietly closed the door behind them. I was staring blankly at my toes, thinking about the interview that had stretched over the past few hours. The questions asked and my answers to them had dredged everything up again, which isn't to say it was very far from the surface of my mind anyway. I sat there quietly pondering for what felt like a long,

long while. Lorcan was staring at something out the window, arms folded across his chest.

'It was us,' I whispered, more to myself than to him.

'What?' he asked, turning to face me.

'If we hadn't been together dancing, then Mari and Kane would have still been in the party. They wouldn't have been abducted.'

'You mean me. You think it was *me* that got them killed.'

'No, I didn't say that Lor—'

'You didn't have to.'

'Hey! I was there too, OK? I had opportunities to save them and change the course of events and I failed to. Their blood is on my hands. I just . . .'

'You just?'

'I wish things had ended differently.'

'You can't change what has happened, Tommi. You can only grow from it.'

'Don't give me that Instagram philosophy bullshit,' I hissed. I was angry: I'd been straight with him about how I felt and in return he was dispatching generic motivational taglines.

'What do you want me to say? You were rash and you acted without thinking? That you flew into action without working the problem through and put more at risk than you had to?'

'Is . . . Is that what you think?' I asked, my voice sounding like a croak rather than my own.

He sighed, running a frustrated hand through his hair. He said nothing. My tongue paused, unsure about asking the next question and the damage it could do. But I had to know.

'Why did you burst into the warehouse?' I asked. He was silent for a long while and I ploughed on, eager to explain myself and fill the void. 'I left my phone there so you knew what he said, that he expected me to come alone or he would hurt them. I wanted you to know the address, but—'

'Because I didn't care, Tommi!'

'You didn't *care?*' I asked, shocked.

'I didn't care if the Guard backup was five seconds away or five minutes. I didn't care if Ennis was bringing the cavalry or just himself.'

'You didn't care if Mari or Kane got hurt? If they got killed?' I was incredulous.

'Yes, because I only cared about you! I assessed the situation and realised that your time was running out. I could have waited, been more covert and hoped the support arrived in time. But I made a judgement call and that was to put you first.'

'I cared about those people, Lo, they mattered to me! They were my best friends. Heck, you lived with them! How can you say they meant nothing?'

'I'm not saying they meant *nothing*, what I'm saying is that it came to a choice between risking your life or risking theirs. You're my ward. I was not willing to put you any further into the line of fire.'

'*You're my ward,*' I repeated. Is that all I was to him? His ward? No, I didn't believe that – especially after everything we had been through. The way he kissed me told a story in and of itself. The way he touched my hair, sweeping it off my face. The way he held me and . . . . No. I needed to stop. I was getting lost in the feelings *again* and disregarding that facts. I needed to think about this, about us, more carefully. Our relationship had already had consequences, was I ready for others?

'Maybe you were right,' I started. 'Maybe this isn't the best idea. Your values and mine . . . there's more than age distancing us, isn't there?'

He didn't say anything. He didn't even look at me. His complete and utter lack of emotion is what hurt the most. He nodded, before looking back out the window. 'I understand. I can sleep at home until you're released.'

'Huh. Just like that,' I muttered.

Several more minutes stretched out between us before he finally made a move to exit the room.

'I'll leave you to it,' he said, sharply. He walked straight towards the door and his abrupt action stalled me for a moment. Just as he was about to leave, he halted.

'For the record, if we could go back in time and do the whole thing over, I wouldn't do anything differently. I'd still put you above everyone else. I'd still make that call.'

And with that, he left.

In a bid to stop the bad dreams, I was taking what I called the *Nightmare On Elm Street* approach. In short, not sleeping. I was going to be discharged tomorrow, Friday, so I was spending my last night in hospital walking the empty corridors. These empty, dark halls had featured so many times in my nightmares lately you would have thought I'd find them terrifying now. Yet there was something oddly soothing about strolling through the hospital and having no waves of blood chase me down, no corpses of friends appear at a doorway or wolves rip me apart.

It was just quiet. Empty. Night.

Of course things were never exactly quiet in a hospital. There was always that background hum of ringing phones, machines whirring, nurses talking. I was perched on the armrest of an ordinary couch in a deserted common room and watching the few cars driving by on the road below. Sensing a presence behind me, I looked at the appearance of my visitor in the reflection of the window. Podgy and with a white man's afro, Doctor Gareth Duzleski looked like a mad scientist plucked straight out of the eighties. Quite a feat considering he was barely over forty. Turning slowly, I placed my legs on to the cushions of the couch in what was a decidedly more human posture to be found in.

'Hello, Tommi. It's been a while,' he said politely.

'I was wondering if I'd see you around here Doctor D.'

'When I heard you were admitted I've been trying to stop by, but it's not easy. Different departments and all.'

'I'm sure you had real lives to save.'

Dr D. was an oncologist at Saint Theresa's who specialised in juvenile and young adult cases. He was a nice guy. Quiet and well spoken, I'd come to know him well when he was treating Joss here. Dr D. was the nickname I had given him after gargling over his Russian surname one too many times. It had stuck.

'The night nurse said I might find you here. I didn't know she meant wandering the entire fourth floor, but I guess I need the exercise.'

'Sorry,' I said, not really meaning it. 'I couldn't sleep.'

'No, I've heard as much.'

There was an awkward silence between us for a moment as I watched him work himself up to what he had to say next.

'I'm so sorry about Mari and Kane. It's truly devastating.'

Dr D. dealt with death every day. I wondered how he ever got used to it. I had nothing to say. I'd been lucky. I hadn't seen too many people outside of the hospital yet so I hadn't had to deal with the barrage of well-wishers and grief hounds. Dr D. wasn't one of them, but I still didn't have a response for him.

'Thanks' was wrong and 'I know' didn't fit right either. Instead, I returned my gaze to the cars below and watched them buzz on, uninterrupted.

'I actually came to speak to you about something else,' he said, clearing his throat.

His tone sparked something in me, a memory of when he would deliver the latest updates on Joss's condition. It was his official voice and I looked at him curiously.

'There's someone you need to see.'

'Someone?'

'I know Joss hasn't been to see you.'

'How do you know that?'

'Because I've been with him, Tommi. He's here, back in oncology. He was admitted to emergency the night of your accident.'

I leaned my back against the glass of the window and wished for an instant that it would disappear, leaving the night to take me whole. If Joss was here, back in oncology, and Dr D. was delivering this news . . . I knew exactly what it meant.

'Take me to him.'

The strange thing about tears is when you're a werewolf you not only taste the salt in them, you can smell it. A small English Channel was running down my wrists as I rested my head on my hands at the corner of Joss's bed. He was fast asleep with deep bags under his eyes. The tubes and machines around him carried on, awake and alert. He had been here less than a week and already the pallor of his skin was shifting from healthy pale pink to the translucent shade only cancer patients and onions seemed to have.

'We got the results a few days ago and it confirmed what I feared. The cancer's back,' said Dr D. from behind me.

He was standing there quietly, letting me have my moment.
'What stage?'
'Three.'
'Already?'
'It's come back more aggressive than before and spread from his throat to his liver and intestines. We're trying to isolate the cells and determine when we can operate.'

I dropped my head into my hands and squeezed my eyes shut as tight as they would go. 'And he didn't want to tell anyone?'

'His parents obviously know, but he wouldn't let them tell anyone else. Especially you. He was going to tell you after the funerals, I believe. He didn't want you to have to deal with too much at once.'

I laughed. 'The little shit.'
'You called?'

Dr D. and I both jumped and looked over at Joss, who was watching us quietly. I stared at him, not able to wipe the tears off my face. He looked past me and over at Dr D. 'I can't believe you told her,' he said in a voice that sounded so weak it did me more damage than a thousand full moons. Dr D. shrugged.

'Shut it,' I said, getting up from the chair to hug him.

I leaned off his arm and he slung it around my shoulder. We stayed like that for a while: me half lying on top of him, attempting an embrace, while Joss patted my shoulder. Finally, sitting back down in the chair, I wiped my face.

'No more, Joss. You keep me clued in every bit of the way,' I said, waving a finger at him.

He sniffed and I leaped up to wipe a few loose tears from his face.

'Thanks. I didn't mean to hurt you, I just didn't want to . . . hurt you.'

'I'm a big girl. Joss, you're one of the only things I have left. Let me be here.'

He gripped my hand with surprising strength. 'I will, BFF.'

I couldn't bring myself to laugh, so I smiled.

'Mari and Kane,' he said, his voice sad and struggling to steady itself. 'Did you see them before they . . .'

He was looking at me hard, searching for answers in my eyes. I felt like Judas. Me, begging the truth out of Joss about his illness, when I was the Queen Secret Keeper. Heavy is the head.

'Kane, no. Mari and I only had moments,' I said, trying to keep it vague.

'Did she say anything?'

'No, her throat . . . it was quick.'

'Let's speak together at the funerals. We were always a foursome. I don't think I can get up there without you.'

I honestly hadn't thought about the specifics of the funerals yet, only the awful reality of having to attend them. I nodded and leaned back in my chair.

'So,' I said, voice solid and resolute. 'How do we fight the C-bomb this time?'

Dr D., who had been busying himself with a chart while Joss and I spoke, looked up with a smile.

'Always in the ring, Tommi,' said Joss.

'Always,' I replied, unapologetic.

'We're starting the first dose of radiation tomorrow, which will knock you around for a few days. By then we should have a definite course of action for surgery.'

'Tell her the other bit.'

Joss had heard this before.

'After the funerals I want him moved to Mechtilde General for the surgery.'

I looked over at Joss, who was expressionless.

'You'd be willing to go back to the clinic? You hated Germany.'

'Berlin specifically,' muttered Joss.

'We could certainly do the first two or three surgeries here and continue the chemo, but this is going to be a prolonged stay for Joss,' added Dr D. 'They're already familiar with your case and the treatments that worked best for you in the past.'

'You could do it here, couldn't you, Doc?' asked Joss.

'Yes, of course.'

'What?' I sensed his hesitation.

'I'm one doctor, incredible as I may be.' He added a self-depreciating laugh. 'Mechtilde General's clinic has a first-rate team, as you know, from surgeons right down to the ward nurses, who would be able to give you a better chance. It's a question of whether you would you prefer Paul McCartney or the Beatles?'

'They have bugs in their hospital?' asked Joss, feigning disgust.

I rolled my eyes at him and addressed Dr. D. 'The Beatles, because it had John Lennon and all the other cats.'

'There are cats too? You're not sending me to this hellhole.'

I glared at Joss and he shushed.

'It's one of the top five cancer treatment facilities in the world,' added Dr D.

'Then we go back there,' I said, looking at Joss for approval.

'But it's expensive.'

I gave a look that communicated I would slap him. His parents were wealthy and had paid for his treatment at Mechtilde General the last time he had been really sick. They'd even relocated there for three months proper while I came and visited every fortnight or so.

'OK, so they can afford it but I won't know anyone there.'

'Clutching straws, hun. You'll know me.' I gave him my best cheesy grin.

'There's still the semi-permanent accommodation facilities for your parents and visitors like, Tommi,' said Dr D.

'I won't need that.'

'Why not? You'll be visiting, won't you?' asked Joss.

'Of course, I'm moving there.'

'What? Since when?'

'Since now.'

'Tommi, you can't just move to Berlin because of me. You have a job here and—'

'And what? I'll have an empty apartment with the ghosts of two dead friends haunting me in it. I'll have memories that cut at every turn. I can get another job, no drama.'

I wasn't sure if the last part was true, but I had enough saved to keep me going for a while. Actually, I had more than enough. The gallery paid poorly, but I loved what I did. That made up for whatever the paycheque couldn't. What I hadn't let anyone except Mari and my grandparents know about was the £120,000 my mum had left me. She had been a successful estate agent before she threw it all in and went to start the B and B. She had invested a lot in that, but there was still a hefty sum she had saved. All of it went to me when she died, along with her possessions. I paid off the remainder of my grandparents' mortgage, which wasn't much, and they wanted to keep her possessions. I hadn't decided what to with the remaining money yet.

Currently, it was sitting in a high interest account with £5,000 put aside for easy access in case of emergencies. The good thing about having been a student is you get used to learning how to be poor and make every penny count. Over one hundred grand was infeasible to me at the moment. It could sit pretty until I grew up or bought a masterpiece. Kane's family would have no trouble paying for the funeral, Mari's might need a little help. I could step in there, anonymously if I had to. A sabbatical in Berlin might soak up a touch more.

'Where did you go just now?'

Joss's voice brought me out of my mental account managing.

'Sorry,' I said, 'thinking.'

'She always does this,' he said to Dr D.

'If Mechtilde General is the best, we go there.'

'And you're coming?' asked Joss in a voice that made me want to wrap him in cotton wool and defend him from the world.

'Fuck yes.'

'And what about Lorcan?'

'What about Lorcan?' His question had taken me by surprise.

'Oh come on, Tommi, how long is it before you two are properly dating? Like, not a Poc thing.'

'Is that an adjective now?'

'Tommi.'

'We're not . . . together. At least not like that. I dunno, Joss, it's difficult to explain. I'm not sure if being with someone right now is healthy.'

'Whatever you say, but just know that I'm the master of what is and isn't healthy,' he said, pointing at his many beeping monitors. I laughed, it was the only thing left to do.

'That's the last stitch, done,' said Dr Kikuchi. She wheeled back from the edge of the bed and grabbed my shirt.

I was sitting in the hospital room in jeans, black combat boots and a purple bra. I stretched my arms and tried to get used to the new stitches-free feeling.

'All gone,' I said, as Dr Kikuchi handed me my black T-shirt.

'That's right, who's a big girl now? I left the lollipops in the children's ward, I'm afraid.'

The door to the room opened and Lorcan came through it, causing me to hurriedly throw my T-shirt on. His eyes lingered on my form a little longer than was kosher before he quickly turned his back to give me some privacy.

'You've been alive for how many centuries, Lorcan, and you still don't know how to knock?' growled Dr Kikuchi. I kind of loved her a little bit.

'Sorry,' he mumbled.

Slipping the shirt on over my head, I tried to avoid Lorcan's gaze but couldn't help it. In the end I met his expression. Looking between the two of us, Dr Kikuchi said: 'What are you going to do about this?' She made a flippant gesture with her wrist. 'You keep looking at each other like that and even the blind member of the Three's going to be able to see what's going on.'

Dr Kikuchi's buzzer went off, causing her to jump off the stool and grab her equipment. She was about to head out the door without saying goodbye again when I stopped her.

'Hey, not so fast,' I said, blocking her path. 'You've escaped every time before I could say thank you. Thank you. Thank you for saving my life, both times.'

She looked flattered for all of a second. 'I'm not sure whether it's my skill or your stubborn desire to live, but thank you accepted.' She held up a hand warily. 'No hugs.'

'Sure,' I said, stepping aside and leaving her a free exit.

'Lorcan.' She nodded and disappeared from the doorway.

We were silent as I quickly looked around the room, which was lit by the mid-morning sun.

'You ready?' he asked.

'So ready.'

We walked down the long, white hospital corridor in silence. He'd honoured my desire for space, and time. The only problem was that I wasn't sure where that left us. I knew I'd made the right call, but I couldn't deny the way I felt about him. To make matters worse, I knew how he felt about me. We were remaining civil, keeping things businesslike and to the point. We had never been friends. We had gone from a Custodian and ward relationship, to briefly being lovers. Now everything just felt too painful.

I pressed the button of the lift and watched the numbers become illuminated as it inched its way to our floor. As the doors pinged open, I felt a sense of relief to be leaving the hospital. It lasted only a precious second before the reality of what was coming erased it.

'Now all we have to do is move to Germany and get through two funerals,' I huffed.

He cast a sideward glance at me before replying. 'Let's worry about the full moon first.'

Chapter 21

The mask was pressing down on the bottom half of my face and I could feel a sweaty top lip beneath. Better than inhaling chemicals, I thought. I leaned back from the wall and examined my work. Almost done. I shook the spray paint can hard as I moved in to finish the border on Poc's lettering. When I told him I was leaving town for a while he wanted to make this our last hoorah. We had gone over sketches the night before and the actual mural had taken most of the morning, even with a dozen of us working on it. It was a dedication to Mari and Kane, something that would stay permanent and visible long after I left. A mix of Liz Phair, Electric Youth, Garbage and Outkast had scored our combined efforts on the street art.

'Sick, I think we're good,' said Poc from behind me.

We were working in an alleyway off one of the main commercial districts in Dundee, next to an abandoned shopfront. Being a Sunday there was minimal foot traffic and Poc had us wearing fluoro visibility vests so we looked 'legitimate'.

'No one graffs here and I doubt anyone will be curious. If they are, these will make us look like we're from the city council or something,' he had said.

I wasn't sure about his logic but we'd been painting for six hours straight and hadn't been tear-gassed yet. Turning my back on the brick wall, I joined the other members of Poc's makeshift crew walking away to get a better look at the finished product.

Strands of hair were falling out of my loose piggy tails and I swept them back as I pulled my mask up to rest on the top of my head. The unmistakable smell of spray-paint stung my nostrils. The mural stretched the entire length of a fifteen-metre wall with every inch now covered in fresh, bold colours. Overlapping characters and block shapes led to the centrepiece: a lifelike portrait of Mari and Kane. Painted from the chest up, they were turned slightly towards each other and faintly smiling as they looked down at the path below. A cartoonish brick pattern in blue was their backdrop before the busy interactions of the remainder of the art took over. Underneath their portraits was a quote from the ANZAC oath, something I had picked up in New Zealand when I visited a war memorial.

It said: 'They will not grow old as we grow old.'

'Mari and Kane RIP' was added directly below in identical sharp lettering.

'Fucking ace, lads,' said Poc's friend Snowy. I cleared my throat.

'And ladies,' he said, attempting to tip his beanie in a mock gesture. 'The portraits are mint, Tommi.'

'Thanks. That lettering though . . .'

I shook my head, impressed. Snowy and his sister Bek were, in my opinion, some of the best freehand street writers in the country. They were able to adjust their style and shading seamlessly to fit whatever they were working on. Here they had done a perfect job of maintaining the graffiti style and adapting it to the memorial tone. We all took a few minutes to stare at it. Joss walked into the alley with a shopping bag in his hand and staggered back at the sight of the completed wall. When he had left we were practically done, yet now it was entirely finished.

'Wow,' he said.

He joined our impressed silence as our eyes returned to the wall.

'Hey, is that champagne?' asked Clint, one of the painters responsible for the some of my favourite impact effects on the wall.

'Uh, yeah,' said Joss, looking down at the bag. 'I brought celebratory champagne.'

'I've got Scotch!' yelled Clint as he ran to his ute.

'I'm trusting Snowy here brought the plastic cups,' I said, elbowing the scrawny guy next to me.

'Only a bong,' he said, 'but I wouldn't say that's safe to drink out of.'

I scrunched up my nose. 'Ew. Definitely not.'

'From the bottle it is!' said Poc.

We were standing in front of the Mari and Kane portraits and we looked up at them. I watched sadness pass over Joss's face fleetingly. He had been deeply affected by their deaths; not like me, but I knew he felt it. Two days ago, I had found him standing in front of our fridge, staring at its contents with a solemn expression. It was only when I went to stand behind him that I saw he was looking at the last three bottles of beer in the fridge. They were all Kane's.

'This is incredible, Tommi,' he said. 'What you guys have done—'

'I know. You bawbags got skills with a "Z",' I shouted over my shoulder.

Various cheers acknowledged my response and someone grabbed the bag with the champagne bottles out of Joss's hand.

'You did this part?' he said, gesturing to the images of our dead friends.

'Aye. I wanted to do them cartoonish but Poc thought the more realistic the better. They were right when you see it like this.'

I started to drag Joss over to the section of the wall Snowy had worked on when Poc spoke up. 'Yo everyone get your asses in here.'

Our small group gathered around him.

'Not real good at this formal shit so I'll get to it. All of y'all knew Mari and Kane and what happened. Good people taken too soon. Props to everyone for putting this amazing thing together.' He gestured to the wall.

'Props to you for coming up with the idea,' I said.

Appreciative yells came from the group.

'Yeah, yeah. This is ours. Now it's everyone else's as well. Whether they paint over it in a month or leave it for, shit, twenty years, this is for them. Mari and Kane. Rest in peace, champs.'

The sentiment was mumbled through the group.

'Let's drink!' shouted Clint.

The bottles of champagne were popped and we took swigs as they were passed around. I'm not ashamed to admit I had some of Clint's Scotch as well. Laughter and talk bubbled up as I slipped away to look at the mural once more. I felt Poc come up behind me and place an arm over my shoulder.

'I've never done something like this,' I said. 'I've graff'd with you lads before, but nothing of this scale.'

'It's remarkable. I don't think anyone's going to have the heart to "clean" it up.'

'Thank you for including me in this,' I said, turning to him.

'Of course,' he replied, nonchalant. 'I wouldn't have done it without you.'

I gave him a sideways glance to see if he meant it.

'You know,' he said, shuffling his feet. 'It doesn't have to be like this.'

'Like what?' I smiled. 'Surrounded by chemicals and illegal?'

He laughed. 'No, I mean you and I.'

'Oh,' I said, my heart sinking just a little.

'It might seem like terrible timing, but you were never just some girl to me, Tommi. We get on well, don't we? Even outside the bedroom.'

Now it was my chance to chuckle. 'Poc pursuing a girlfriend, I never thought I'd see the day.'

His grin met my own, yet there was more than amusement behind his eyes. He said the timing was terrible and, boy, if he only knew.

'Poc,' I started, trying to find the right words to let him down. 'I'm the last person in the world you should be with, *especially* right now.'

'Because of what you're going through?' he asked.

His statement took me by surprise and at first I thought he was talking about me being a werewolf. Poc, sweet but macho, was looking at me the way every woman wants to be looked at. He was out of my league, I realised. I was a murderer and that was the hard truth. I wasn't sure if Poc and I were even the same species any more. Without even bringing Lorcan into the picture, I knew I had to leave Poc behind.

'Partially because of what I'm going through,' I said. 'Also, I'm not sure if I'm good for people right now.'

His eyes flicked downwards only for a second as he nodded. I could tell he had been expecting me to say no. I'm not sure that made it any less painful.

'So we go back to being just friends?' he asked.

'Did we ever stop?'

'HEY!' shouted Bek, wiping champagne from her lips as she jogged over to us. 'We haven't tagged it yet.'

I dried my hands on my paint-covered overalls, grabbed a nearby can of white and took Joss's hand.

'Come on.'

We crouched at the bottom of the mural as everyone started working on their tags around us.

After lightly shaking the can, I quickly scrawled, 'Tommi'.

'Perfect,' he said.

'Not quite.'

Next to it I painted Joss's name and the year.

'Now it is.'

I always enjoyed the sound of the tattoo needle as it buzzed and hummed along human skin. Most people found the noise unsettling. It made them uncomfortable as they associated it with the pain of getting a tattoo. I loved it, both the sound and sensation of being tattooed. Shutting my eyes, I leaned my head back on the neck rest as Pip worked on my wrist. The past week had been one painful event after the other, physically and mentally. The transformation was particularly painful this full moon due to the fact I was still recovering. Lorcan said the pain would get easier to manage over the years, but I doubted that. It was still the worst thing I had ever felt, only I had more to compare it to now.

There was a day between the last night of the full moon and the funerals and I had used every minute of that to recover. Mari's family had come to pack up her things, most of which I'd already arranged into boxes and piles of hers and Kane's stuff. They were grateful, which added to the black pit of guilt I felt for her death. I convinced Joss to let people know about his cancer relapse. He had deferred from university and was going to be flown to Mechtilde General tomorrow. I had deferred too, indefinitely this time. Mari's and Kane's families held their funerals back to back so Joss could attend them both. In a way I was glad they were straight after each other and at the same funeral home. Everything was over in one big, sad ordeal.

Joss and I had spoken together at both of the funerals, splitting a continuous anecdote into two parts, which the procession found amusing considering it was pretty much the same crowd at each. I wish I could say the funerals were a blur, but I remembered every single detail with perfect clarity. I remembered how Mari's mother broke down during her speech and had to be helped off the stage by one of her daughters. I remembered how Kane's brother announced he was naming his unborn son after his best mate and little bro. I remembered and felt everything.

I wasn't sleeping much any more. There was no solace there for me like there once had been. The apartment was empty now. All of the non-essentials were in storage. It was weird to think of other people moving into *our* apartment. It had been Mari's and mine for so long that that sense of ownership wasn't going to go away overnight. Dundee would.

Alexis had tried to talk me out of resigning, but she understood. We were going to stay in touch via email and she was reaching out to her contacts within the Berlin galleries to see if there were any positions opening. If there was work, I would work. But there were two main reasons I was relocating to Berlin and I wanted those to be my primary focus. At the very least Dr D. said Joss would need six months at Mechtilde General to fight this thing properly. In my mind I was living day by day; a year was as far as I was willing to loosely plan. Lorcan had let the group of Berlin rogues know we were coming. He called them a pack, although he said they didn't like to call themselves that. There were five regular members who operated a small but successful nightclub in the city centre. He said I would learn the most from their unofficial leader, Zillia. She had already found us an apartment in a block next to the nightclub. Lorcan said they had cells built underground for the full moon. Peachy.

Both of us were packed for Berlin, each of us carefully dancing around the other in the very empty apartment, making polite small talk while at the same time not really saying anything at all. It was torture and although I knew things couldn't go back to the way they were – with all of those dazzling possibilities – this was somehow worse. With a long train ride and a flight scheduled in two days we were only set to spend more time together, painfully close. Where I went, he had to follow. Two days felt like a lifetime to me right now and I was itching to leave Dundee, to have a fresh start and leave old Tommi behind. I liked old Tommi, don't get me wrong, but she had died with her friends that night in the warehouse. I had to learn to become someone else, someone tougher, someone better.

'Voila,' said Pip's husky voice from the end of my arm.

Opening my eyes, I glanced down at my wrist as she wiped away the blood with a damp towel. The leather of the seat screeched as I moved in to examine the new tattoo. It was a perfect sphere on the inside of my wrist that ran over my hand-cuff scar. As large as the shape you could make by touching the tip of your thumb with the tip of your index finger, two-thirds of the circle was coloured-in black with just a C-shape remaining uncoloured.

The crescent moon. It would always serve as a reminder to myself that I was not controlled by the moon. It was an integral part of me, a part that I wouldn't lose myself to. I wasn't a beast. I was just a slightly more ferocious woman. I was not controlled by the moon.

'It's flawless,' I said, dragging my eyes away from the fresh ink to look at Pip.

'It's a lot simpler than your others. I froth it,' she replied. She wrapped my skin in cling wrap and handed me a tube of Bepanthen. 'Clean it with w—'

'Warm soap and water,' I finished. 'I know the drill.'

'Pip, your three o'clock is here,' came a voice from the counter.

Standing up, I made to give her the cash but she batted it away.

'Don't you dare. This one's on me, Tommi. Think of it as a going away present.'

'This is your livelihood,' I said, trying to tuck the money into the pocket of her rockabilly-style sailor dress.

'Save it and buy me a beer when I'm in Germany next for an expo.'

I sighed. 'Fine.'

'Fine. Now come here, honey.'

She pulled me in for a hug against her enormous F-cups. Pip was a complete pin-up queen. A larger girl, she made full advantage of her curves by permanently looking like she just stepped out of the fifties. As I walked out of the tattoo parlour and into the overcast afternoon, I peeked at my wrist. It was a simple and powerful message.

'I will not be controlled by the moon,' I said under my breath.

When I got home, the apartment was empty. Lorcan wasn't there. My room was just a mattress and two packed bags. As I glanced over the blank walls – posters and art now gone – I thought of everything that had happened here. The memories, the parties, the laughter, the pain, the sex, the everything. I was fighting the undeniable urge to burn the place to the ground and keep the ashes in an ornamental urn, treasuring them but leaving them behind. The past was dead. I was alive.

Before I could even comprehend what I was doing, my keys were in my hand and I was carrying my bags out the door. I paused for a brief moment to write Lorcan a note, then I was down the steps and in my car. I drove out of Dundee so fast speed limits were annihilated. Turning up Operator Please loud on the stereo, I could barely hear my own thoughts over the blaring music. As I prepared to descend the last hill out of town, I gave Dundee a final fleeting look in the rear-view mirror. When Lorcan would get home he'd read my note: 'Lo, I have to get gone. I'll be at Heathrow for our flight to Berlin in a few days as promised. For now though, I need to disappear. I don't expect you to understand this or rationalise running away from my problems, just trust that I'll be there. See you soon, Tommi.'

I needed to get gone.

ACKNOWLEDGMENTS

To my grandfather and Tommi's namesake, Tom Lewis, who told me stories about serial killers and monsters at an impressionable age instead of fairytales. To my mother Tania Lewis and grandmother Teresa Lewis, who didn't protest (too much) about us discussing murderers over many a Christmas dinner.

To Alex Adsett, a woman who I'm convinced is less of a literary agent and more of a S.H.I.E.L.D agent. Girlfriend has some Melinda May-level skillz. Thank you for the unicorn beanie and everything since. And Paul! With the hats!

To the She-Pack at Piatkus and Little, Brown, specifically Anna Boatman and Gemma Conley-Smith. You're both Alpha Females to me. Also, the whole gosh dang team: from the translators to tweeters, thank you for taking a risk on some purple-haired weirdo from Down Under and for being so passionate from day one. Bonus points to Dominic Wakeford for making me look smarter than I am and Ceara Elliot for creating a cover that would make Tommi howl at the moon. To the Aussie Wolf Pack at Hachette who won me over with cake and wooed ME with their incredible hard work.

Samuel Spettigue, for using the word 'proud' so many times I cringed and supporting my dream without question. You're my only Jaeger co-pilot.

To my OG readers and sisters from other misters, Bridie and Anna Jabour – the biggest and longest standing fans of *Who's Afraid?* Bridie offered to be my manager 'pro bono' after reading four chapters, which gave me the first sparkle of hope that there was something in *this*. Y'all read every draft, analysed every sketch and answered every panicked phone call.

To the immensely creative and experienced people who helped me at various stages: Michael Adams, Matthew Reilly, Duncan Lay, Alan Baxter, Tom Taylor, Ineke Prochazka, Abigail Nathan and the super sweet Robin and Ron Cobb.

Kia ora to my generous and knowledgeable Maori experts Marcia Rohario Murray from The University Of Auckland and The Pebble himself, Kristian 'Krit' Schmidt. Thank you for breathing life into aspects of the book in a way I never could and I hope I haven't done you any disservice.

To the many and important: my Pod Save Our Screen co-host and BFF Blake Howard and his wife Sam, Catherine Webber, Rachel Junge, Tuyen Cocks, Dr. Nicholas Cocks, Keegan Buzza, Gordana Willesie, Dr. Stephen Hughes, Cam Williams, Ryan Huff, Hayley and Kieran Sultanie, the Dundonians; Grieg, Gary and Jenny Heubeck, the amazing Caffrey family for welcoming me into their home, the McKeating family, Glasgow geek peeps Pip, Laura and Richard, Dennis at Killstar Clothing, J.Mo, Brad Wagner, Courtney, Bonnie, India and the whole Hancock gaggle, Sophie and Mitch from 2SER, the Dakin family, Lauren 'LOL' Jones, Tahlei 'T-Bag' Watson, Scotty 'Don't' Gearin, Alice 'The Rat' Jabour, Chris and the Jabour family, my Eff Yeah Film & Feminist podcast co-host Caris Bizzaca, my favourite lesbians Candice and Kylie, the Greek chorus of first readers in Tricky Hickson, Kate Czerny, Jessica Huxley, Leah Hallett, Rick

Morton, Deensey, Robyn (Were)Wuth, the Sydney Babe Collective, 'That Movie Guy' Marc Fennell, Sydney Shadows and Anthony Calvert, specifically for being a longtime comrade and artist extraordinaire.

To the artists who reimagined my tale in breathtaking fashion for The Art Of *Who's Afraid?* exhibition: Nicola 'Wonder Woman' Scott, Charles Dowd, Mel Stringer, Fiona Altoft, Ben Brown, Zane Donellan aka Gooney Toons, Rebecca Brown, John Tiedemann, Jak Skallywag, Lucas Brown, Bernadette Wallace, James Stein, Emma Bertoldi, BossLogic, Allison Tyree, Ken Leung, Martin Abel and Amy Blue.

To Gail Simone – the bar setter – and Joss Whedon – at your altar I worship.

Finally, to Tommi Grayson, who walked into my head and decided she wouldn't get the fuck out. Words and werewolves will never be enough to say thank you for being an enabler.